Quinine

Kelly Ana Morey

First published in 2010 by Huia Publishers
39 Pipitea Street, PO Box 17–335
Wellington, Aotearoa New Zealand
www.huia.co.nz

ISBN 978-1-86969-431-9

National Library of New Zealand Cataloguing-in-Publication Data
Morey, Kelly Ana, 1968-
Quinine / Kelly Ana Morey.
ISBN 978-1-86969-431-9
NZ823.3—dc 22

Published with the assistance of

Shirley Ann Morey 1944–2008

Author's Note

Although *Quinine* is a work of fiction, its narrative is populated with people who lived in German Neuguinea at the time and have become part of the country's history. I have endeavoured to imagine the lives of individuals such as Ettie Kaumann, the Parkinsons, Queen Emma, Captain Macco and the improbably named Miss Sommerhoff based on little more than a few facts and faded photographs, and I hope my portrayal has done them no injustice. As is the way of all things fiction, a few things are fudged here and there, for example, I have no idea whether the Neumecklenberg Germans were taken to Kavieng Hospital at the beginning of the war, though it seems likely, and the location of Gethsemane is improbable given the terrain on the island's east coast.

The non-fiction texts that played a huge part in the writing of *Quinine*, were *Queen Emma* by R W Robson, *Pictorial History of New Guinea* by Noel Gash and June Whittaker, *Voyages of Discovery* by Tony Rice, *Out of Africa* by Karen Blixen, *On History and Stories* by A S Byatt, and *Illuminations: A Bestiary* by Rosamund Wolff Purcell and Stephen Jay Gould from which I created the storeroom of the Naturhistorisches Museum, Vienna and stole the line: 'After death the eyes decay first'.

A number of history novels offered solutions and ideas and include, in no particular order, *The Secret River* by Kate Grenville, *Angel* by Elizabeth Taylor, *An Ice Cream War* by William Boyd, *Gould's Book of Fish* by Richard Flanagan, *Possession* by A S Byatt, and lots of Peter Carey's novels.

Marta's collected writings and personal papers are entirely fiction.

Acknowledgements

Throughout much of the writing of *Quinine*, I was lucky enough to be accompanied by Anna Rogers. More than an editor, Anna steered me through numerous cuts and rewrites; it was both a pleasure and an education to work with her. In addition, a shout of thanks to my readers who are an integral part of the process: Catherine (astute as ever), Anne and Sarah, who read the final proof because I couldn't. Then there's Brian and Robyn at Huia Publishers – how patient they were, and demanding too. They paid for Anna, and for that I will always be grateful. Thanks also to my father for his occasional riveting fact about New Guinea; Nurse Melissa for the skinny on trepanation; friends, both Face Book and three-dimensional, who got excited for me every time I 'finished'; Ross for his lovely map and Cousin Emily simply because she's blood.

And, of course, thank you Creative New Zealand for providing me with a grant towards the writing of *Quinine*.

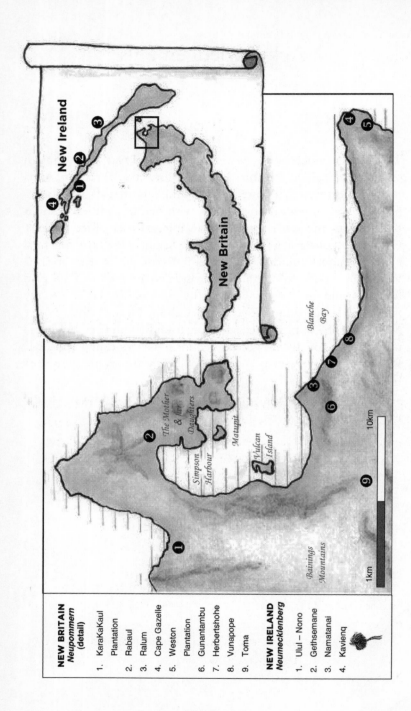

NEW BRITAIN
Neupommern
(detail)

1. KaraKaKaul Plantation
2. Rabaul
3. Ralum
4. Cape Gazelle
5. Weston Plantation
6. Gunantambu
7. Herbertshöhe
8. Vunapope
9. Toma

NEW IRELAND
Neumecklenberg

1. Ulul – Nono
2. Gethsemane
3. Namatanai
4. Kavienq

New Ireland

New Britain

Blanche Bay

The Mother & her Daughters

Simpson Harbour

Matupit

Vulcan Island

Bainings Mountains

10km

1km

One

✳ 1 January – Now that the excitement of Christmas has passed how dull it is to be home once more after my travels with Lady Marmott in Scotland, not that my employer's pursuits were adventurous by any stretch of the imagination. I have come to the conclusion, however, that Lady M. and I suited each other perfectly. I am very amused at how, in spite of all that blue blood running in her veins, she likes to allude to her family's humble beginnings. She has no time for pretension, or art, and for that I *was* truly grateful.

Marta, journal, 1903

In the parlour of a handsome house on Wipplinger Strasse one Sunday afternoon in the early spring of 1903 a grisly narrative about cannibalism was derailed by the approaching sound of footsteps and bright female chatter.

'Did not.'

'Did too.'

'Oh, you're such a filthy liar, Marta.'

'I am not.'

'You are too. Gretchen agrees, don't you? That Marta is a filthy liar.'

'Ouch!' cried the voice that had accused Marta of lying. 'You pinched me. You're so mean, Marta. I shall tell Mama on you, see if I don't.'

'Don't be silly, Gustie. Mama said you must behave. Or you'll be sent to bed without supper and not hear all about the cannibals in Neuguinea,' replied Marta.

'I still say you're a liar,' said Gustie emphatically, resolute in the way only a child can be.

Exactly what Marta was lying about was never ascertained for the three adored daughters of Klara and Doktor Egon Mueller had by now arrived at the door of the parlour and halted their conversation in order to prepare for polite company.

On the other side of the door Doktor Mueller was pouring another aperitif, the Hungarian schnapps of which he was so fond, for their guest.

Bernard Schmidt, a rather tall, faintly corpulent German gentleman in his early forties, had appeared that afternoon, without an appointment, at the door of Egon Mueller's office at the Naturhistorisches Museum. Originally from Berlin, Bernard had been domiciled in the savage isles of East Neuguinea since shortly after its annexation by Germany in 1884, and on this, his first leave home in over a decade, he'd thought to include in his baggage a number of artefacts from the islands of Neupommern and Neumecklenberg. An acquaintance of his in Neuguinea, a keen natural historian, had suggested that such objects might be of interest to a museum, and that there could be a small sum of money involved in their procurement by an institution. When he'd mentioned this to his aunt, Frau Liesl Baumgarten, she'd immediately instructed him to facilitate an introduction with her dear friend Klara's husband, who was in the employ of the Naturhistorisches Museum.

Although Herr Schmidt's artefacts, which included human remains, were not quite Egon's area – insects were his thing – he'd most definitely wanted to hear more about Neuguinea, so had invited the colonist to his bright, noisy household for a little supper and to continue their discussion of the cultural practices and flora and fauna of that distant place. Also in the parlour, seated in front of the fire in a dress of forest-green velvet that accentuated her magnificent bosom, and drinking a glass of Gewürztraminer, was Klara Mueller, the mistress of the house, who had joined the men only a few moments before.

As the door swung open Bernard turned in expectation. The three sisters, standing together with not altogether genuine smiles painted on their faces, were so unalike that it was hard to imagine they were related at all. The eldest Mueller daughter was *not*, Bernard decided in an instant, the slightest bit beautiful. She was considerably older than the other two sisters – later he would find out that she was thirty-three. Strikingly tall, Marta was thin and angular and had inherited her father's strong Slavic features, refigured with a minimal acknowledgement to femininity. There was something distinctly capable about her: the set of her shoulders, the unabashed way she returned his scrutiny and the sardonic smile that tugged at one corner of her mouth. And if Bernard's attention hadn't an instant later been wholly taken up with the middle sister, Gretchen, perhaps he would have felt slightly mocked by Marta Mueller's speculative gaze. To Gretchen, however, his eye was inevitably drawn.

This Mueller daughter, aged seventeen, was an etiolated version of her mother, who was a rosy complexioned blonde Amazon, amply padded with lush, dimpled flesh. In contrast Gretchen was so impossibly thin that it almost hurt to look at her. Her thick, pale blonde hair was tied carelessly back off her face with a ribbon, as if she was still in the nursery, and was so long that it almost reached her knees. Perhaps if Gretchen had been more substantial, her mass of hair might have been attractive, but there was so much of it and so little of her that it appeared as if she was an extension of her hair rather than the other way round. The effect teetered dangerously close to the repulsive. Yet Gretchen's pale ethereal beauty was in such marked contrast to the women Bernard had met in the South Pacific that he was instantly intrigued. Finally he tore his eyes from Gretchen and turned his attention to the youngest Mueller daughter, who crossed her eyes and pulled a silly face.

'Augusta, do behave,' said her mother reprovingly.

But Bernard smiled. The others, even the doctor, who seemed a splendid chap and had proved a convivial host thus far, unnerved him a little. And groups of women, especially those locked into a solid phalanx of family solidarity, he'd always found a frightening prospect.

Augusta, though born sickly, was now a robust young miss and something of an anomaly in the Mueller family. At thirteen she was starting to take on her adult form and it was already clear that she was never going to achieve anything near the height of her parents or siblings. If it hadn't been for the fact that Augusta looked just like a much smaller and plumper version of Marta, Bernard might have assumed her to be a changeling, a cuckoo left in a stork's nest.

The moment of assessment was broken by the arrival of a wire-haired grey schnauzer bitch, which unceremoniously pushed the girls aside and trotted into the parlour, making a bee-line for the flickering hearth where she flopped down and stretched out with a sigh of utter contentment that made them all laugh. The conversation began, light as new snow, politely drifting over such topics as the reason for Herr Schmidt's visit to Vienna, which was an irreparably ailing Mama. From there it progressed to mutual acquaintanceships like the Baumgartens, through whom Bernard had found the Muellers, followed by a lengthy dissertation from Augusta on her current aspirations to join the circus, which Bernard found charming. In fact a great deal of the bright inconsequential chatter that filled the room was generated by Augusta. Marta and Gretchen, by contrast, were much more reserved, content to ask sensible questions whenever there was a lull in the conversation and making various interested noises in response to Bernard's stumbling answers.

Bernard Schmidt had never been particularly good with his fellow man, and twenty years of marching around a plantation in the middle of nowhere shouting at natives had left him graceless, especially with the fairer sex. This lack of skill in society and in the art of conversation hadn't gone unnoticed by the few family friends and relatives he'd called upon since his arrival in Vienna the month before. Liesl Baumgarten in particular had been saddened by her nephew's unease in company. He was, she thought, a little odd, and finding him a wife, which he'd confided was what he hoped to do while home, was not going to be a simple task. In fact among her wide circle of family and friends, she could think of only one family who would perhaps not even see her nephew's deficiencies *and* had a daughter with extremely diminished marriage prospects. The Muellers were a lovely family, make no mistake, but definitely a little eccentric, thought Liesl, after Bernard's first visit. And the eldest one … what was her name? Ah yes, Marta! Well, she'd been sitting on the shelf for long enough now to consider any offer that might come her way. And her friend Klara's eldest was also quite the adventurer, a woman who worked, and that had to be an advantage, bearing in mind her nephew's intention to take his bride halfway across the world to live in a grass hut on a copra farm in Neuguinea. So perhaps there *was* something of a match to be made there. Not an attractive girl by any definition, mused Liesl, and minus a finger, poor thing. But sensible, and really, she concluded, and beggars like her nephew couldn't be choosers.

Liesl's instincts were, as always, infallible. The Mueller family was proving to be quite different from the other families Bernard had been introduced to since his arrival. 'We're not squeamish,' they said encouragingly, once the small talk was done and they'd moved back onto the topic that Bernard had been discussing with Klara and Egon before the girls arrived.

'Are you sure?' protested Bernard. 'Perhaps they are not stories for young ladies' ears.'

'No, no, no,' replied Egon. 'We are free thinkers, and wish our girls to know all they can of the world.' He stopped and laughed. 'There are many cannibals in the insect world, so even Augusta here is not a stranger to the notion. Please, Herr Schmidt, I urge you, speak freely of the things that you have seen.'

So what choice did Bernard have but to sing for his supper? Rather than resuming the cannibalism conversation, he started anew. He spoke mistily of how, armed only with a theodolite and a labour line consisting of imported Asiatics and a gang of the large black Bukas from the Solomons who served as a bodyguard against cannibal attacks, he'd planted the dried hard coconuts into the rich volcanic soil of his land on the east coast of Neumecklenberg. A quarter of an hour later he was still talking, surprisingly lyrically, about the humble *Cocos nucifera* when the maid appeared at the parlour door to announce, with much more formality than was usual, that supper was served.

'I must apologise,' explained Klara to Bernard as they all walked to the dining room, 'for the meagreness of our table. On Sundays we generally just make do as it's Cook's night off.'

'May I be excused?' asked Gretchen, who'd been largely silent apart from the few lacklustre questions she'd asked Bernard and some fiercely whispered asides to her elder sister. 'I don't feel very well.'

'You probably need to eat something,' her father said in firm, practical tones. He fell back and took his middle daughter by the hand. 'Look at you, you're all skin and bones.'

The Mueller family doctor had prescribed food, exercise and a firm parental hand for Gretchen's melancholy, which had manifested itself four winters before. But she'd shown little enthusiasm for any of these cures, despite everyone's encouragement. In truth she wished they would just leave her alone. The mere thought of food made her feel nauseous, and now, drifting down the hall, was the aroma of the hated stuff. The stench of meat, the marrow, the fat and viscous juices that Cook used to thicken and flavour all manner of dishes, all of it repulsed her.

Marta, perhaps sensing that her sister was about to break ranks and make a run for it, dropped back too, taking Gretchen's other arm and whispering into her ear: 'Just eat a little. Some fruit, some bread and perhaps a little cheese.' Outnumbered and lacking the strength to protest, Gretchen allowed herself to be steered into the dining room.

What would the natives make of such a creature? thought Bernard, watching Gretchen as he masticated enthusiastically on a very good veal pudding. He allowed himself to imagine her at Gethsemane surrounded by a host of golden-haired children, the eldest of whom was a strapping son to carry on his legacy. Bernard sighed. The dream was all very well, but he didn't really have the faintest idea of where to start. If only women were as obliging as the prostitute he'd availed himself of the evening before. Still, he thought, swallowing his mouthful and cutting another chunk of the pudding, things seemed to be progressing rather well here with the Muellers. Perhaps things really might work out as he'd imagined they would on the long journey from Neuguinea.

Over the course of the meal, between mouthfuls, Bernard continued to talk of the colony and the expatriate society that had established itself out there. He described, as if they were everyday occurrences, the dancing and lavish parties, particularly those instigated by his great friend, Queen Emma – who wasn't his friend, great or otherwise, nor a queen, but a half-caste Samoan princess who had fled Apia and settled in East Neuguinea shortly before the German annexation, twenty years before.

'Emma's bungalow at Gunantambu is one of the most magnificent in the colony,' explained Bernard. 'With hot and cold running water and a bar made from the unconsecrated altar that was intended for a cathedral at one of the failed settlements in the south of Neumecklenberg.'

'Why a failure, Herr Schmidt?' asked Egon, taking advantage of Augusta's momentary absorption in her food to ask a question of his own.

'The Frenchman de Rays, who instigated the whole idea of settling French and English Cove, was in fact a fraudster who'd never been there, but was happy to take people's money for the right to settle what he called La Nouvelle France.'

Egon laughed. 'How like the French.'

'The promised land was in fact a malaria-infected swamp on a cannibal-infested island and a great many of the four hundred colonists died there.'

'How dreadful,' said Marta, with a shiver. But then history, she thought, was *full* of tragedies of this nature.

'Emma and her …' Bernard had been about to say lover, but thought much more quickly that he was used to and continued, '… business partner Captain Farrell rescued the survivors in the end. They gave them some money for the chattels abandoned at the settlement and passage to New South Wales. The altar was one of the many things that Emma salvaged. She always says she turned it into a bar entirely to annoy the missionaries.'

'Do they really have cannibals in the South Seas?' Marta asked. 'One reads of these things and wonders how true they really are.'

'Most definitely,' Bernard replied. 'The Melanesians are famous for it.'

'Have you ever tasted human flesh?' asked Augusta, who'd eaten her fill and was ready to participate in the conversation once more. Really, Papa had bought home the most interesting guest ever.

'Every Friday,' said Bernard, a twinkle in his eye. 'I can't let a week go by without a hearty meal of roast human flesh. Little dark-haired girls with freckles who can tell jokes are my favourite. They're always the tenderest. Everyone in the South Pacific knows that.'

Augusta hooted with laughter, envisaging herself in a cooking pot with Bernard standing by, knife and fork at the ready. 'Do you have a wife, Herr Schmidt?' Augusta suddenly asked. It was clear that the thought had only just occurred to her.

At this frankly rather rude line of questioning on precisely the subject she herself was interested in, Klara Mueller was suddenly all ears.

'No,' replied Bernard. 'No, I don't.'

'Why not?' asked Augusta.

'Because I haven't met a woman who is brave enough to be my wife.' It was one of his better answers, Bernard thought, witty and self-deprecating. The look of approval on the faces of the assembled company told him he'd said the right thing.

Augusta considered this for a minute. 'I'm awfully brave,' she said with a great deal of conviction, because of course she was. Extraordinarily so: she did everything her boy cousins did, and more.

'Then I'll just have to wait for you to grow up and take you away with me to the South Pacific, won't I?' replied Bernard.

'Do you promise? For ever and ever amen?' demanded Augusta, who was canny enough already to realise the importance of extracting a firm promise from anyone she was negotiating with, adult or otherwise.

'I promise,' replied Bernard with the utmost sincerity. For Augusta would make a wonderful lady copra planter. She was exactly the type who could conquer natives, fight off malaria and various feminine malaises and ultimately triumph. Emma would adore this child.

'It's settled then,' replied Augusta, smiling happily at Bernard, and secretly relieved that she could abandon her plan to join the circus, because in truth her acrobatics, in spite of endless practice, were not looking very promising. Now she could marry Bernard and plant coconuts and tame the natives of the South Pacific, armed only with a heart that was good and true. She would be kind but firm, Augusta decided, and Bernard's natives, *her* natives, would love her unconditionally.

'I suppose,' Augusta continued thoughtfully, 'that if you hadn't met me you could make a native lady your wife, couldn't you? If you wanted to, that is. If she was brave like me.' Augusta stopped, took a sip of her cordial and carried on, oblivious to the shocked silence that had descended upon the room. 'Could you have had a native lady for a wife, Herr Schmidt?'

At this point Marta, who'd completely run out of patience – surely it was past Augusta's bedtime? – intervened. 'Enough!' she said. 'Enough! Truly, Gustie, you are impossibly rude. Who Herr Schmidt marries is his own business.'

'But I want to know if he could marry a native lady,' protested Augusta, turning to where her father sat smiling at her benevolently. 'And Papa always says that if you want to know something you should ask. And why, why shouldn't Herr Schmidt have a native wife if he wants to? If I couldn't marry Herr Schmidt my next best choice would be a black man with a bone though his nose and skin as black as midnight or a gypsy who could tame any horse and charm the birds from the trees or, or … a tattooed strong man from the circus … or, or …' At this point Marta was starting to seriously regret having taken Augusta to the circus last summer.

Bernard laughed a little too heartily. Augusta's outburst had reopened the old wound to his heart that had almost healed into imperviousness. He'd seen its cause, a half-caste woman with whom he'd had a torrid affair in the early days of his arrival in the colony, in Herbertshohe while awaiting passage to Australia on the first leg of his journey back to Germany. She'd been walking in front of the Herbertshohe Hotel, where he'd been staying, with her twisted accident of a husband in attendance. As they'd crossed paths, she'd smiled at him knowingly and though it had been almost ten years since their last carnal encounter, and Gloria hadn't aged well, Bernard's cock had hardened involuntarily and he'd been as besotted as when he'd first met her in the company of her aunt, Queen Emma.

'Isn't that so, Herr Schmidt?' demanded Augusta loudly, having taken not a jot of notice of her sister's reprimand. 'You *can* have a native lady wife.'

Bernard twitched as Augusta's insistent voice broke into his memory of Gloria and the things she'd sometimes allowed him to do to her. Though the movement was small, his claret glass was close enough to be caught by the tips of his fingers and toppled over. 'So sorry,' he said, jumping up and dabbing furiously and ineffectively at the spilt wine with his table napkin.

'Just a spill,' said Klara reassuringly.

'I'll get Johanna,' Gretchen said, seizing the chance to escape.

'Thank you, Gretchen,' replied Klara vaguely.

'So, Herr Schmidt, tell me …' began Egon, finally taking charge of the conversation. 'No Gustie, you mustn't interrupt,' he continued firmly, as his youngest immediately opened her mouth in an attempt to take centre stage once more. 'You've had your turn.'

'But I wanted to ask Herr Schmidt another question,' wailed the girl.

'Perhaps another time, if Herr Schmidt comes back,' said her father. 'You can save it up and ask him then.'

Klara sighed. The tantrum that was about to erupt was inevitable. Although it was less obvious, Augusta was just as highly-strung and difficult as Gretchen and Marta, too, when she'd been younger. As Augusta began to work herself up into a frenzy of petulance, Klara wondered what she'd done to deserve three such trying girls.

'Why, why, why? Why must I wait? What if Herr Schmidt never comes back,' sobbed Augusta, once more the centre of attention.

'Because sometimes you don't get to have it all your own way,' said Marta. Her voice, rather hoarse like Augusta's, but with a deeper adult timbre, smokier somehow and less nasal, was impossible to ignore.

The other three adults turned as one and looked at Marta, shocked as much by her succinct observation as her drawling, matter-of-fact tone. Marta gazed back dispassionately. She was bored with Augusta's histrionics and her parents' not so subtle cultivation of this extremely self-indulgent behaviour. What must Herr Schmidt think? Gustie was, in her opinion, thoroughly spoilt.

'Really,' murmured Klara in gentle reprimand. 'There's no need to be so cruel, Marta. None at all. You know how sensitive our little Gustie is.' Marta resisted the temptation to roll her eyes in exasperation and merely clenched her already determined jaw. Under the table she stroked the stump of her ring finger with the ball of her thumb, soothed by the sensation of skin on skin. When Johanna entered the room to clear up, Marta pushed back her chair and stood. Egon took his youngest daughter's hand as if she was still a very small child, and helped her up. 'A post-prandial drink in the study, Herr Schmidt?'

'Indeed,' replied Bernard.

At that the family and their guest moved out into the hallway and went their separate ways, women in one direction, men in the other, leaving behind the plundered remains of what, in time, would become a historic communal moment in all their lives: the warm spring evening, a week after Easter, when the Muellers of Wipplinger Strasse met Bernard Schmidt from East Neuguinea.

It was almost an hour later that Klara heard the rhythmic, ringing staccato of iron-shod hooves coming down the street, then halting, followed by the unmistakable sound of their front door opening and the murmur of hushed conversation. Klara put down her book, got out of bed and went to her bedroom window. A hansom cab waited below, two distinct silhouettes, horse and carriage, joined together by the thin-shadowed tracery of the harness strapping. The horse pawed impatiently, sending up sparks as its hoof struck the cobblestones, which shone in the gaslight, slicked wet and shiny by a recent shower of rain. The last of the fallen chestnut blossom looked like snow against the darkness of the wet ground. The door closed and Bernard walked down the front stairs, his hat concealing his golden hair. Klara stayed at the window watching until the horse and carriage disappeared down the gas-lit avenue and turned the corner. Only then did she let the curtain drop and return to her bed.

'He might do for Marta,' suggested Klara conspiratorially to her husband later, just as her friend Liesl Baumgarten had predicted she would. Husband and wife had come together, as was their habit, in Klara's bedroom, in order to discuss the events of the day before retiring. Klara had settled herself back under the covers and Egon, in his shirtsleeves and wearing carpet slippers, sat on top of the bedclothes facing her.

'But then she would go away,' Egon replied, suddenly worried, even though Klara had said this before about other gentlemen who'd come and gone. 'I find it hard enough when she's away for only a few months on her travels,' he added. 'I don't think I could bear a lifetime of absence.'

Klara, who'd been finding motherhood rather hard work lately, could imagine all too well what such a lengthy absence would feel like and wondered if all three girls could be sent off to the South Pacific, though she said nothing of this to her husband. 'Hush Egon,' she cooed, as she touched his face. Her fingers were sticky and perfumed with recently applied emollient. 'She'll still be your daughter wherever she goes. Nothing can change that. But this conversation is ridiculously presumptive even for a match-making mama. Here we have her packed and ready to go and live among the natives and the gentleman hasn't so much as looked at her. Though I think Marta herself is interested.'

'How do you know this?' asked Egon.

'A mother knows,' replied Klara, forgetting that, in the past, she had three times been spectacularly wrong about her oldest daughter's feelings regarding gentlemen. Klara laughed and withdrew her hand from her husband's face. Its disappearance was almost more than Egon could bear. 'It was a lovely evening, though, and he seems like a very nice man,' she continued sleepily, wriggling further down into the bed, her eyes closed, oblivious to her husband's sudden moment of distress. 'I wonder if he noticed,' she said with a big yawn.

'Noticed what?' Egon asked.

'Her finger, of course,' Klara replied.

'Of course,' he replied. 'She hides the absence so well that even I forget that it is there … or not, as the case may be.'

'So sad,' Klara said softly, almost to herself, 'for a young girl to be disfigured so tragically. Poor Marta.'

Upstairs in her tiny room under the eaves, next door to the nursery, which she couldn't be persuaded to leave, Augusta slept. Rolled up in her narrow iron-framed bed like a little bear with her snout pressed between her paws, she snuffled and grunted, dreaming not of honey and Bavarian forests, but of heat and colour and dancing. Around and around and around in her dream she spun until she simply ceased to exist except as a blur of light suffused with the burnt-orange colour of her dress.

As one sister's dreams were suffused with colour and heat, another was under ice, in a place where all colour was leached from existence. Her hands scratched at the frozen ceiling above her as she drowned, her sweet pink mouth forming silent pleas for help from a shadow whose face she could never see. A shadow that watched her dying beneath the frozen barrier between herself and the world. *The world. Imagine it.* A place denied to her, where the sun shone and people laughed simply because they were happy. Except this wasn't a dream, this was how Gretchen felt every day. Klara had prepared her a draught of laudanum when the women of the house had gone upstairs to find their beds and Gretchen had drunk it down gratefully. It made the ice above seem not a prison but a blanket covering her. *Warm, so warm.* Just as the Ice Queen had promised. In the darkness Gretchen allowed her hands to creep down the length of her body, up under the hem of her flannel nightgown. Then she touched herself there, in the place where her legs joined and her body began, her fingers working gently until her body sighed and turned hot and molten as it quivered in climax. She fell asleep almost instantly, her hands captured, pressed tightly between her thin white thighs.

Marta, for her part, was awake and writing in her journal in a slow and considered manner:

Herr Schmidt is a most interesting gentleman who speaks of his adventures in Neuguinea as a copra farmer with great conviction and verve. What an extraordinary place it must be, still largely undiscovered too, if the gentleman's information is to be relied upon. This knowledge fills me with some joy as the number of unexplored territories are shrinking by the minute and I fear soon there will be nothing left for the intrepid explorer to discover and stories of this nature will end. But back to H.S. I daresay women would consider him to be rather a handsome gentleman with a fine pair of golden moustaches and I suspect a tremendous intellect.

The pen halted as Marta considered whether such an observation was entirely sensible or even true. At best, she thought with a sigh, it was wishful thinking. But she had recently come to the conclusion that great love had passed her by, and perhaps it was now time to settle if an opportunity of marriage came her way again. Not one of the three gentlemen who *had* looked twice at her over the years had excited even a modicum of passion in her. Not a flicker. And inevitably these perfectly acceptable gentlemen had grown dispirited and gone away to marry warmer, kinder women. Marta caressed the silky flesh that had been dragged over the exposed joint of her amputated finger and sewn down to form a cushion of flesh. It was ridiculous, she knew, to think that there might still be a chance for her, yet now, when she'd least expected it, Bernard Schmidt had been invited into her life. It was a sign, she was sure of it.

Reading back over what she'd written a few moments before, Marta snorted with mirth more than once. Because in truth Bernard Schmidt actually wasn't that handsome. His pale blue eyes were disconcertingly close together and he had a very weak chin and rather poor teeth, but his lack of classical good looks was greatly tempered by his thick hair and tremendous physique. It wasn't often that a man was tall or burly enough to make Marta feel as dainty as Herr Schmidt had in that brief moment when he'd followed her out into the hall after supper. Not that he'd even noticed her. Men never did at first and she really didn't mind. She'd seen the way Bernard had looked at Gretchen – and it hadn't surprised her. Men always looked at Gretchen with hungry eyes, as if they wanted to eat her beauty alive. Marta had spent enough time gazing at herself in a mirror to know that she wasn't pretty, but she was comfortable with this. Besides, it had become her excuse – the reason why everyone thought she remained unmarried. Poor Frau

Mueller, stuck with such an unattractive daughter, and the poor thing missing a finger and well past her prime.

But Marta knew that her unattractiveness and the missing finger weren't the reasons why she was alone. Ugly people found love or something closely resembling it every day; where did ugly children come from if not from such unions? Sometimes Marta wished that she could genuinely desire companionship like other women, and retreat into the invisibility of marriage and motherhood. But it wasn't in her nature.

As she sat in her room, gazing at the pages of the open journal, logic and science told Marta that the heart has no ability to feel, that its sole function was to pump blood around the body. She sighed. This isn't who I am, she thought, as she carefully tore the page out of her journal and fed it to the coals in the bedroom fireplace. How much easier would my life be if I were like other women? And yet if I were a man, none of it, this desire for movement and solitude, would matter.

Pulling a wrap over her nightdress, she went downstairs to the library. She turned up the gaslight closest to the large papier-mâché globe that dominated the darkest corner of the room. From force of habit she sent the globe spinning, allowing her fingers to trace the equatorial line just as they had when she was a child. As she stood and watched countries come and go under her fingers it occurred to Marta that the only constants were the two poles. The lands of snow and ice. 'Where the Ice Queen lives,' she murmured. Enough! With a shudder, Marta brought the spinning world to a standstill, her fingers floating in the Indian Ocean, just off the coast of Western Australia. She walked the globe on a fraction, and there, just below the equator, were the territories of Neuguinea and Papua. And as Marta gazed at these three islands, small and inconsequential, moored between the two great oceans, the Indian and the Pacific, she suddenly knew with absolute certainty that she would go to this place and see it with her own eyes.

Although Bernard had been back in the city for a number of weeks, the artificial gloaming of the gaslit streets still took him by surprise. He missed the impenetrable darkness that fell upon the islands of Neuguinea when the sun went down. Even when the moon was full, rising above the hills behind the house he had built on his plantation, the night was absolute. He felt like a foreigner in this country he had always thought of, until his return, as his true home. But he knew already that once his duty as a son was done, he would journey back to the South Pacific and that's where he would stay. Neuguinea … Gethsemane was his home now. It was strange how far he'd had to travel to learn this, but he was glad he had. But Gethsemane was a home without a wife. Emma Kolbe had harped on about this at length when he'd visited her at Gunantambu before Christmas the previous year.

'Forget her,' advised the Queen, all too aware of Bernard's long-held attachment to Gloria. 'Find a wife in Germany. Someone who will make you happy and give you children.'

Emma always made everything sound so easy, thought Bernard, leaning back against the seat of the cab. As if all he had to do was apply himself to the task and it would happen. 'But pick one who will stay,' the chatelaine of Gunantambu had continued. 'A strong woman. Don't be led astray by beauty. In the end it's not enough. It fades, then withers on the vine and then what? You're left with nothing.' Bernard had laughed at the time, but Emma's logic was, as always, irrefutable. More than anyone, Frau Kolbe knew what it took to survive as a woman in East Neuguinea, among the cannibals and coconuts, volcanoes and earth tremors, in the time of quinine. The islands were no place for the weak. They simply didn't survive. If the malaria and its cure, the bitter quinine powder, disease or childbirth didn't get them, the loneliness and boredom always did. The emptiness of the land bore down on them, slowly crushing from them the will to live. Only a woman already inured to disappointment and possessing a sound constitution could survive such obstacles. Learn, if not to push back, then at least to stand her own ground.

Bernard paid the driver and let himself into his mother's house. The hall was dim, the lamps turned down low, and it smelled of lavender, beeswax and good housekeeping. All was quiet but for the rhythmic tick of the grandfather clock, which began to strike as Bernard hung up his coat and hat. By its fourth strike, a second clock with a more feminine tone joined in. Both struck eleven times before fading, leaving only the memory of their brief duet. Bernard ventured upstairs.

The night nurse sitting outside his mother's door was knitting, as usual. As he approached, she put down her woolly construction, which never seemed to get any bigger, and stood expectantly. Frau Schmidt had had a good day. She had eaten a little of her dinner. The smell of the boiled cod was a pervasive and definite presence in the hallway, fighting a battle of wills with the sickly odour of a long illness. Bernard's sister, the nurse added, had been earlier in the evening and had read to their mother for some time, before the patient had succumbed to exhaustion. Frau Schmidt was now sleeping. Yes, she seemed peaceful, though her breathing was shallow and faint.

Bernard longed to ask how long the nurse thought it would be before his mother simply stopped breathing all together and he would be free to return to his life. But he couldn't. So instead he stifled the immense wave of homesickness that had welled up unbidden in his chest, thanked the nurse and retired to his room at the end of the hall. He undressed quickly and put on the cumbersome night attire that decorum dictated he should wear here in the civilised world. In Neuguinea he always slept naked: it was too hot so near the equator to contemplate anything else. His last thought, before he fell into the deep sleep of the consummately untroubled, was of Marta, not Gretchen, as he would have assumed. I wonder, he thought, a little surprised, as Morpheus drew the curtains shut and pulled up the covers. *I wonder.*

Two

✳ Although I was regarded as well travelled, at the various scientific and botanical societies in Vienna of which I was an associate member, it was always the territories that had never presented themselves as opportunities, which attracted me most. It was the lands of Africa and South America that I always wanted to discover, like the botanical artist Maria Sybilla Merian and her journey to Dutch Guiana, or Surinam as it was known in 1699. But try as I might, in those years after I went out into the world and earned a little of my own living, I failed to secure a position on either dark continent.

Marta, *Neuguinea Memoirs*, Heyward & Barge,
London, 1949, p. 9

'Where do you live exactly?' asked Augusta the following Sunday. Bernard had been invited to tea with the Muellers, though both Klara and Egon were conspicuous by their absence. 'I've found Neuguinea on our globe,' Augusta continued, 'but there seems to be no sign of a place called Gethsemane.'

'Really, Gustie,' protested Marta, 'Herr Schmidt has only just arrived. Allow him at least to catch his breath.'

'Oh no, please, the pleasure is all mine,' demurred Bernard. 'Have you an atlas?' He was talking a little too loudly, showing off for an oblivious Gretchen, who was sitting at a table beneath the window, absorbed in a hand of solitaire.

'Certainly,' replied Marta assertively. It was only when she was poking around library shelves or actively seeking knowledge that she ever felt truly comfortable and in her element. 'My father has maps of every country, Herr Schmidt. Let me see if I can find you something that will serve your narrative's purpose. We're looking for the islands of the South Pacific, I believe.' Marta took possession of a small triangular stepladder, which she carried along the shelves until she found the place she wanted and climbed to reach the uppermost shelves. 'Perhaps this would be appropriate,' she continued casually, pulling out a large loose-bound folio that she had looked at many times in the preceding week. The title, *The Islands of the South Pacific*, was embossed upon the forest-green linen cover in gold, though the gilding itself appeared to be its only extravagance as the typography was plain and small. This was a working collection of maps rather than a rich man's extravagance. As Marta handed the folio to Bernard, he noticed her missing finger for the first time and blenched noticeably, his distaste, just for a moment, clearly evident on his face. Marta pretended not to notice; she was rather good at this, having done it so often.

'The maps, Herr Schmidt?' said Marta once she stood again on solid ground.

'Yes, the maps,' Bernard said, regaining his aplomb. He laid the folio on a nearby table and carefully untied its strings. Marta and Augusta gathered around eagerly, but Gretchen refused to be enticed from her card game in spite of some encouragement from her sisters. Bernard leafed through the very beautiful and intricately detailed maps, past Hawaii, Fiji and the islands of the Samoas, the Solomons and the Kermadecs, until he found the map he was looking for, the one that depicted his own little piece of the world: the islands of the Duke of York, Neupommern and Neumecklenberg, German East Neuguinea, which Marta had hidden right at the very back of the album.

'Aha!' he exclaimed, extracting it with a gentle tug. 'This is the one we want. Now,' he said putting the map to one side and walking to the globe, 'let us find Neuguinea so as to affix our overall location.' Marta and Augusta obediently trotted over to the globe, which Bernard was turning slowly with his index finger. 'There,' he said, pointing at a thin sliver of an island no more than a degree or two below the equator. 'That's where I live. That's Neumecklenberg. Now if we now look once more at the map, I can show you where Gethsemane is on the island.' Bernard pulled the map towards them. 'Now see here, this is Kavieng, the main port on the island. One of two – the other is down the east coast here, in that indentation. A place called Namatanai. Now right here, that little harbour there,' he continued, running a finger north back up the coastline, 'is Gethsemane or thereabouts.'

'But what's it like?' asked Augusta impatiently. She wanted to know how it looked – Bernard's house, his coconut trees and natives – so that she could imagine him there in a white suit and solar topee, which she knew all explorers wore to keep the sun from scrambling their brains.

'Ahh ...,' said Bernard, 'it's the most marvellous place in the whole world. A thousand hectares of *Cocos nucifera*, which I planted myself. And although the plantation has been producing fruit for the last decade, the first block of palms that I planted are soon going to be reaching the peak of their productive life and will produce a veritable mountain of raw copra. Six thousand nuts are equal to one ton of copra. Each palm produces approximately sixty nuts per year, and each hectare yields in the vicinity of a ton of copra per year. Which means,' Bernard said, addressing Augusta, 'that there are how many palms to a hectare?'

'One hundred,' said Augusta promptly. *Sums were easy!*

'Excellent,' replied Bernard. 'It's good that you know your numbers. Do you want to know how copra is made, Fräulein Mueller?' Augusta wasn't at all interested in copra but she loved a story and Bernard's undivided attention, so nodded vigorously. 'Well,' he continued, warming to his recitation. 'We wait until the coconuts have ripened ... '

'How do you know when they're ripe?' interrupted Augusta.

'The husk, the outer layer turns from green to brown.'

'Is there a specific season?' interpolated Marta, beating her sister to the gap in the conversation and pleased to have asked such a sensible question.

'No,' replied Bernard. 'Because of the proximity to the equator there are no real seasons, not like here. It's summer all the time, though from December to May it's wetter. Because of this the harvest is year round and the palms are in constant fruit. Some we collect from the ground where they have fallen, been shaken free by the wind or by gurias, which are a frequent occurrence in East Neuguinea. Most, though, are collected by natives who can climb a coconut tree, which has no branches, with nothing but a rope in double-quick time.'

'I wager I could climb a coconut tree,' said Augusta confidently. She was easily a better tree climber than her boy cousins, even the ones who were older and stronger than her.

Bernard smiled at her. 'I'd wager you could too.'

'Gurias?' queried Marta, determined not to let her little sister get the upper hand on the conversation.

'Earth tremors,' clarified Bernard. 'The place is plagued with them, especially Neupommern.'

'How extraordinary,' said Marta. 'Are they frightening?'

'No, no,' Bernard said breezily. 'One becomes very used to them. They are mostly mild. My great friend Royal Weston thinks that they're somehow connected to the many volcanoes in the territory, and I'm certain he's correct. He's a clever chap.'

'Interesting,' said Marta encouragingly. Volcanoes were infinitely more fascinating than coconuts.

But Bernard wasn't to be enticed away from his dissertation on the manufacture of copra. 'Now, as I was saying, my natives collect the coconut fruit and take it back to the drying sheds. Once it's there they remove the fibrous skin around the actual coconut so all that's left is that hard round shell you would be familiar with, then the nut is cracked open and the flesh inside is scooped out for drying. We dry it on woven coconut frond mats in the sun but I've been experimenting with a contraption to dry it quicker. To smoke it almost. Like bacon.' Marta nodded enthusiastically, surprised that she was genuinely interested. 'Then it's packed into sacks and transported to the wharf below my house, right there.'

He pointed once more at the map. 'And then when a trading ship comes into my area, it stops by and picks up what I have for sale and takes it to the port where the copra barges are anchored at either Kavieng or Namatanai.'

'And the sun curing stops any spoilage?' asked Marta.

'Yes,' replied Bernard. 'Extraordinarily effectively too, I might add. Even in the wetter months we have barely any wastage. The insects and parrots especially see it as a personal pantry, of course, which is why I would dearly love to get it dried and bagged quicker.'

Gretchen, who was very bored indeed, yawned volubly and gathered up her defunct game, reshuffling and laying out a new hand. Her sisters, used to her constant state of ennui, were unmoved, but Bernard felt a little wounded by her indifference.

Soon after, Klara, closely followed by the maid with tea, joined her daughters and Bernard in the library.

'Herr Schmidt?' asked Augusta, a few minutes later, her mouth full of buttery biscuit.

'Yes, Fräulein Mueller?'

'Do they have monkeys in the South Pacific?'

'No,' Bernard replied, picking up his cup. 'No monkeys.'

'Tigers?'

'No tigers.'

'Elephants?'

No, no elephants.'

'Pirates?'

Bernard laughed. 'No, no pirates either. Not in the way you mean, anyway.'

'Well, for goodness sake,' August exclaimed, looking terribly puzzled. 'Then what *do* they have in the South Pacific? Besides cannibals and coconut trees.'

'Oh, so many things,' replied Bernard, who had not by a long way finished his lecture series on the wonders of his adopted homeland. 'So many things.'

Looking at Bernard's strong square hands grasping his cup and plate, Marta thought that maybe if she tried very hard she could manufacture a desire for him. Certainly the thought of him didn't burn holes in her imagination, and his physical presence didn't make it difficult to catch her breath, but perhaps, after all that had happened, she no longer had the capacity to feel like this. At least he was interesting, and she wondered if a gentler response, led by the mind not the heart, might not be the way of mature love.

Gretchen yawned again. 'May I be excused?' she asked her mother.

'Oh, if you must,' replied Klara crossly, exasperated by the girl's complete lack of effort. Klara had decided some time ago that Gretchen was altogether too morbid for words and simply needed to cheer up and take an interest in society and in being young and carefree like other girls her age. It was all very well to droop around the house in a state of profound melancholy when there was only family in residence, but when one had guests, one should make a little more of an effort.

Upstairs in her room Gretchen opened the rectangular wooden box that contained her drawing materials and took out the little knife that she used to sharpen her pencils. She sat down on her bed, lifted her skirts and pushed down the stocking on her left leg. With the blade she made a small, shallow incision in the flesh of her thigh, gasping at the sting of the steel dividing her flesh, then sighing deeply, her whole body shuddering in relief, as the cut began to ooze blood. Her thigh was covered with scars, some historic, others still fresh, scabbed and raw. Tonight she would float, Gretchen thought, at peace as she sat and waited for the fog across her senses to lift and the arrival of the voice in her head that she knew was God.

Meanwhile, downstairs in the library, the conversation about the pleasures and perils of life in Neuguinea continued. And this is how Doktor Mueller, full of bonhomie after a lively afternoon in his mistress's bed, found two of his three girls, his beloved wife and Herr Schmidt from Neuguinea an hour later. They were hovering over the collection of maps once more, talking not only of Neuguinea, but also of other lands that Bernard had visited.

'Geography, geography. Excellent. Most interesting,' Egon said, wrinkling his nose happily, his approval obvious. 'How was the lecture?' he asked, turning to Marta.

'Oh, very interesting,' she replied. 'But there were naysayers in the crowd and sometimes that made it difficult to hear what Doktor Correns was saying. It was very obvious to me that many hadn't understood his research at all and were simply being reactionary. They didn't realise what a marvellous new understanding this is, nor how it will change science.'

'What this?' asked Bernard. 'Forgive me, I have been living on a plantation in the middle of nowhere for so many years.'

'The work Doktor Correns has done on the Gregor Mendel's theory on hybridity. I can't quite remember the name of it … Papa?'

'*G. Mendel's Law Concerning the Behaviour of the Progeny of Racial Hybrids*,' her father helpfully replied. 'Fascinating stuff. Though Mendel himself has long since gone to his maker, his work and name have lived on and the rediscovery of his research has changed the way we look at natural history every bit as much as the work of that English show pony Charles Darwin.'

'I was astonished that Mendel grew thirty-three thousand pea plants over a period of years to prove his theory. It's extraordinary really, isn't it, Papa?'

'Well, I've always said,' the doctor concluded, 'that science is application and commitment, with a pinch of genius thrown in for luck.'

Having said his piece, Egon bustled off in search of a drink and his bath. Outside the spring evening slowly ended and the city yawned and turned inwards on itself.

Three

✳ I like Herr Schmidt very much, I think. He is not like other adults such as Marta, who thinks I am spoiled and tells me so and is mean. Herr Schmidt is *very* nice for a grown-up.

Augusta, journal, 1903

Throughout the lengthening spring days Bernard frequently stopped by the house on Wipplinger Strasse, and by the time the trees were thick with new leaf, he was, for better or worse, comfortably ensconced in the Mueller family's daily lives. He was familiar enough to glance over Marta's shoulder one day while she was reading in the garden. Usually she read with utter absorption but with Bernard hovering around looking for distraction it was impossible to concentrate and she knew she should make an effort to be enamoured with this man for the sake of the experiment, if nothing else. Marta lifted her eyes from the page and smiled nervously. It was much more difficult to be confident without the support of her sisters. But the smile was all the encouragement the very bored Bernard needed.

'What's this?' he asked, sitting down opposite Marta and tapping her book with his index finger.

'*Sultan to Sultan*,' replied Marta. 'It's one of Gustie's and my favourites.'

'Is it a novel?' Bernard asked.

'Goodness no,' replied Marta, a little shocked. She generally regarded novels as more than a little frivolous. 'It's an account by Mrs May Sheldon of her journey from Mombasa to Mount Kilimanjaro in 1891.' She paused and turned the wedge of read pages back to the beginning of the book where there was a photograph of Mrs Sheldon. She sat in a beautiful room with a loosely bound manuscript in front of her on the table, on which she rested her elbow. 'She's a publisher and writer too, as well an explorer,' Marta continued, 'but it's the explorer part that interests us the most. She was the first woman to lead an expedition through East Africa and she did it with a degree of consideration to her native porters that had no precedent. In a 1000-mile trek she only lost one porter and that was because he was mauled by a lion.'

'Extraordinary,' said Bernard. 'It sounds riveting. Perhaps I should read Mrs May Sheldon's book.'

'I would certainly be more than happy to lend you my copy,' offered Marta. 'I've read it so many times I feel I know it by heart.'

'So you're interested in adventure and exploration?'

'Why yes!' exclaimed Marta. 'Isn't everyone?'

Bernard laughed. 'You may be right about that, Fräulein Mueller. Have you ever thought about undertaking such an expedition yourself?'

Marta sighed. 'Oh,' she said, 'sometimes I think of nothing else. But exploration takes money, of course, and while we're certainly comfortable, there are no resources available for such things as charting unexplored territories. Mrs Sheldon's expedition cost a small fortune. But I've been lucky enough to see something of Europe at least. I regularly take positions as a secretarial companion to various ladies and have found myself in places like Russia and Spain, though in recent times I've spent most of my time in Britain. I was in Scotland during the summer just gone. And once, some years ago, I spent a summer season at Lyme Regis, in Dorset, which has a remarkable history of fossil finds, including those by the Philpot sisters and Mary Anning, whom I admire very much.'

'That's rather unusual, isn't it?'

'I suppose so,' said Marta. 'But I couldn't bear though to sit around here, day after day, year after year, doing nothing. I need to think and see and do.'

'Quite,' replied Bernard, somewhat thrilled by Marta's passion.

'I would like to travel more, though, do things more exciting than taking tea at four and having sedate promenades by the seaside,' continued Marta. 'But it's difficult really to contemplate going anywhere in the faintest bit uncivilised in my present incarnation as an employee. No lady sadly ever wants to go to Africa or the Amazon to recover their health or take in the sights.'

'Your father tells me that you're something of a natural historian too, Fräulein Mueller?'

'And friend of science and a suffragette also,' Marta added proudly.

'And your lovely sister Gretchen, she is a suffragette too?'

Marta suddenly looked grave. 'No,' she said slowly, 'but I'm sure she would be if she could.'

'And where is she on this fine, warm day?' asked Bernard, who had been hoping, on a Wednesday afternoon, to find his intended paramour in a relatively empty house.

'Mama took her to the doctor and then they were going to have luncheon with a friend of Mama's whose people also come from Bavaria,' explained Marta.

Bernard's disappointment was palpable and he departed soon after, reluctantly clutching Mrs Sheldon's *Sultan to Sultan*. He could tell that Marta would expect him to talk about the narrative at length, just as his friend Royal Weston always did after sending him something to read.

A few times during the last weeks of the spring Bernard took Gretchen and Marta to dance in the pavilions in the city's parks where orchestras played into the night for the good citizens of

Vienna. It gave Bernard an opportunity to fly against his nature, and become uncharacteristically extravagant in both purse and personality, as he tried his best to flatter the sisters outrageously. Although the attempts were clumsy and mostly for Gretchen's benefit, Marta was, in her own way, enchanted. It was interesting to go to places where frivolity rather than learning was the order of the day, and in the company of a man. Before the advent of Herr Schmidt in her life Marta's Vienna existence outside of her family had consisted mainly of being on nodding acquaintance with a handful of women very much like herself, who attended the same sorts of events, such as public lectures, and haunted the same institutions of learning. Sometime they would flock together, and adjourn to a nearby café after a lecture, but not always. Intimacy was a mystery to them. They had all, to some degree, lost the habit.

During these outings with Bernard and her sister, Gretchen often lapsed into long unnerving silences that compelled the other two to fill the emptiness by talking to each other. It was, Marta reflected after a particularly lively conversation on the marriage practices of the natives of Melanesia, wonderful to be free of Augusta and her constant, unceasing need to vocally assert her existence. Bernard, albeit with motives entirely ulterior, also encouraged Marta to talk a little of herself and, inevitably, her sisters. Not that she minded: it had been a long time since anyone had simply wanted to listen to her. Bernard quickly noticed that, like most people, Marta forgot herself a little after a glass or two of wine, and told often very amusing anecdotes about her extended family. Most of the stories seemed to take place on Grandmamma and Grandpa von Tempsky's Bavarian estate, a Nirvana where children ran riot all summer, curtailed by neither lessons nor propriety, and every year there was an attempt to swim across the river and back by the young generation of cousins, both boys and girls.

'You were how old when you successfully attempted this?' asked Bernard, as they sat, with Gretchen, in a café drinking coffee. 'Fourteen?'

'Yes,' said Marta. 'I'm the youngest von Tempsky woman thus far to have completed this rite of passage. Though this year Gustie swears she's going to swim across the river and better my record by a year.' Marta smiled. 'I wish her luck in that endeavour.'

'So your mama, she has done this epic swim?'

'Oh, most certainly. As have most of my female relatives. For at heart we are women of the countryside, not the city.'

'And you, have you traversed this raging torrent, Fräulein?' Bernard asked Gretchen, who flinched under the directness of his gaze.

'No, no,' said Marta, leaning forward, unconsciously shielding her sister from Bernard. 'Gretchen is far too fragile for our rough and tumble. She is an artist.'

For just a moment, in the soft smoky light of the café, Marta looked almost beautiful. She was, Bernard had realised, curiously still and watchful, though not impassive like her sister. She managed, in the absolute and faintly apologetic containment that came upon her the moment she stopped talking, to retain a sense of energy, an evident desire to be pushed into action. Gretchen, on the other hand, had no enthusiasm for anything and looked most of the time as if on the brink of dissolving. The very few times Bernard had coaxed her into dancing she felt like an exhausted piece of silk in his arms.

If Bernard hadn't become so entrenched in their lives, and provided a modicum of a chance for Marta to secure herself a husband, which Liesl Baumgarten kept insisting to Klara wasn't beyond the realms of possibility, it was unlikely whether the Muellers would have invited him to share a few weeks of the family summer holiday in the country. Bernard had actually begun to bore the Muellers with his dissertations on copra. Did the man have no other topic of conversation? Naughty Augusta had begun to call him Baron von Copra, which made everyone laugh, including Marta, though she often defended him too. 'Herr Schmidt,' she would protest, 'is a good man and you, Augusta, are too cruel.'

However, Klara did extend the fateful invitation, though she found herself wondering, in the days that followed, whether she had made a great error of judgement. Liesl Baumgarten might sing her nephew's praises, but Klara had misgivings. Her sentiments were echoed by Egon, who went so far as to suggest that Herr Schmidt was something of a dunderhead. Still, as Klara comforted herself while she packed for the summer idyll, a potential husband was a potential husband, good, bad or indifferent. Klara sighed. She knew Marta would probably never love Bernard Schmidt and vice versa, and she also knew that her husband was right in his assertion that this man was entirely wrong for their clever girl, but Klara was a mother, and desired above all else to see her daughter happy and married, even if it did mean her going to a far-off island in the South Pacific.

In July Klara and her daughters, plus two of their four household staff, made their annual migration by train to Bavaria. Egon joined them a few weeks later when his summer sojourn from the museum began.

Bernard, having communicated his imminent arrival via letter a week before, sent a telegram on the 13th of August informing his hostess of his arrival at the small country rail station near the estate at 4.16 p.m. on the 15th. The arrival of the telegram set off another spate of Baron von Copra jokes from Augusta, much to the family's amusement. Even Gretchen, greatly restored by the sun and fresh air of the mountains, sometimes laughed out loud at Gustie's antics. Marta, Klara decided, would be responsible for the task of retrieving Herr Schmidt from the station.

So Bernard and his monotonous stories followed the Muellers to Bavaria. But Marta didn't mind, not at all, that she'd heard it all before. During his absence, she'd decided that she *had* grown fond of Bernard, and would make a real effort to look beyond the fact that he was a trifle dull and rather repetitive and perhaps not all that clever, and see if she could make this fondness she felt something greater, or at least deeper, than that.

The summer of 1903 was one of those summers of a thousand fictions: long sultry days filled with the lazy buzz of sugar sated wasps, the hollow pok-pok-pok of tennis balls against catgut and the relentless grumble of thunderstorms when the heat became too much to bear. Out in the fields the estate workers laboured in every hour of available light to harvest the bounty these ideal conditions had brought to the land. From dawn to dusk the kitchens were heavy with the delicious perfume of sugar and fruit, cooking and then cooling on the long wooden table in the shadows of the scullery. While the extended von Tempsky family played, talked and relaxed, all about them was activity. Alongside this seemingly ceaseless preparation for the long cold months there were various summer tragedies: Augusta failed in her attempt to swim the river and back, though two of her boy cousins succeeded; another of the boy cousins fell out of a oak tree while trying to rob a bird's nest and broke his wrist; one of the older grooms suffered an apoplexy from which it appeared he wouldn't recover; and the Muellers' schnauzer Bitte, with ruthless precision and speed, killed a litter of kittens belonging to one of the barn cats. Augusta, who had witnessed both the apoplexy and the murders, had been all but inconsolable for at least two days over the catricide, and had ignored Bitte completely for an entire week.

Bernard was in his element. The countryside provided a far more suitable backdrop for his masculinity, which had always appeared faintly incongruous in the drawing rooms and parlours of Vienna. In addition to striding around, riding horses and destroying assorted wildlife, Bernard was free to pursue the obviously reluctant Gretchen and found a newly captive audience for his stories among the tribe of predominantly boy relatives who descended upon the estate over the summer. Because there was attention enough, Bernard was blind to the Muellers', Marta excepted, obvious avoidance of his company outside of the communal meals. For Egon and Klara and even Augusta, it was very much a case of ennui. Gretchen, however, found Bernard's presence increasingly repellent. He was so big and smelly and animal that it made her skin crawl and on the odd occasion when he contrived to touch the back of her hand to make a point she pulled away. Yet Bernard remained wilfully myopic to this evident dislike.

Both Marta and Gretchen found escape from the incessant physical activity in their separate artistic endeavours. As they always had, the sisters painted in different parts of the castle. Two summers before, owing to the messy nature of her chosen medium of oil paint, Gretchen had taken over the atelier that a great-great-uncle with an artistic bent had established in one of the turrets. The room was cold even in the height of summer and smelled slightly of fungus, decay and madness, an attar that the rest of the family found at best oppressive and at worst migraine-inducing. Marta did much of the delicate watercolour work that her own small renderings of the natural world required at a desk in one of the castle's warm, modernised parlours. Much of her time, though, was spent outside, observing the minutiae of the natural world with both a botanist's and an artist's eye, happy in her own company. Quite often, when riding over the estate, Bernard would see Marta in the distance, often just sitting quietly, in her queer, still way, in the middle of a field or on the fringes of a copse. Once he had spotted her high in a plum tree in the orchard, sketchbook balanced on her knee, drawing a bird's nest and its almost fully-fledged inhabitants. And then there had been the occasion when he'd come across her wading through the shallows of a pond, almost completely soaked, with a large midwife toad clutched to her breast. She had taken it home, put in a terrarium and fed it flies and worms and morsels of raw veal. The ugly creature would get almost repugnantly excited when she leaned over its temporary home. Marta had drawn the toad in a number of poses during the following ten days before kissing it gently on the head and setting it free in the garden.

In the afternoons Marta would often climb the stairs to Gretchen's turret with perhaps a few sketches or a completed illustration to share. The two sisters would sit in one of the wide stone windowsills that looked out over the fields and forests. In the distance a church steeple rose above the huddled mass of a small, smudged town. And they talked, more often than not, quietly and peacefully of everything including God and fate and what that held in store for them. Marta was mesmerised by the canvases that Gretchen was producing this year, disturbing though they undoubtedly were, especially when compared with her earlier family portraits, which had been precise and beautifully detailed, but lacking in personality. Marta realised very quickly that this year her sister was incorporating her own inept drawings of plants and animals into these new and extraordinary oil paintings, and because of this she endeavoured to bring Gretchen increasingly more complex illustrations of the world beyond her tower.

Marta never noticed the droplets and smears of blood on the studio floor, so seamlessly did they blend with the inevitable splatterings of paint that Gretchen produced as she worked. She did, however, consciously start to shield her sister, and these new bizarre manifestations of her imagination, from the rest of the family and servants. Thankfully the many stairs to the studio kept the older family members at bay and the servants were more than happy to leave her meals at the bottom of the turret. There was much talk among the staff that summer about how odd Fräulein Gretchen, who most had known since birth, had become. But the conversation never went beyond the estate gates. The von Tempsky servants were very talented at keeping the family's secrets.

'You should paint landscapes, they're the thing,' suggested Bernard helpfully to Marta towards the end of his stay.

He'd been on the hunt for Gretchen, who seemed to appear with less regularity than the castle's rumoured ghosts, when he'd come across Augusta and Marta in the room where the latter liked to paint in the pale morning light. The youngest Mueller sister was lying on a rug eating a soft roll and chattering as Marta attempting to capture the exact nuances of a field poppy, which she'd picked that morning at dawn with the dew still upon it. This comment by Bernard was by no means new to Marta. Some suggested landscape, others still life and yet others watercolour portraiture, and previously her response to all such suggestions had been variously clever and cutting. Now, though, in an effort to be more feminine, she laid down her brush, tilted her head in that charming way she had seen Augusta affect when she wanted something and said, 'Perhaps you're right.'

'Oh,' declared Augusta, a little disappointed that Marta hadn't delivered her customary curt response to this much-voiced opinion. 'I think Marta's paintings are beautiful,' she added. 'Nearly-almost as good as Bauer's.'

'Is Bauer one of your school chums?' asked Bernard vaguely, systematically scanning the room in the hope that Gretchen was there somewhere, artfully disguised.

'Noooooo,' said Augusta, her tone saying rather a lot about what she considered a horrendous gap in Bernard's knowledge. 'He's an artist who went to Australia a hundred years ago with Captain Flinders.'

'Lieutenant,' corrected Marta gently. 'Flinders was a lieutenant when he took stewardship of the *Investigator*. Which proves that you don't know everything, Gustie, and shouldn't expect other people to either.' Augusta pulled a face. Marta turned her attention back to Bernard. 'The only reason we know so much about Ferdinand Bauer is because he's an Austrian and his extensive papers are lodged at Papa's museum,' she explained. 'Though I must say that Bauer's illustrative approach to the natural world is something of an inspiration to me.'

Bernard, who hadn't been listening, suddenly stood and said, far more awkwardly than he'd intended, 'Where is the lovely Gretchen this morning?' Augusta rolled her eyes and noisily slurped the last of her morning chocolate.

'Probably in her studio,' replied Marta.

'I must go up there and see this marvellous place that everyone talks of,' Bernard said, lighting a cigarette.

'Oh no, don't.' Marta was suddenly alarmed. 'She wouldn't like that at all. Gretchen isn't to be disturbed.'

'It smells,' offered Augusta, wrinkling her nose. It was unclear whether the remark applied to her sister's atelier or the burning tobacco. After Bernard left the room Augusta sat up and looked speculatively at her sister. 'You're being very nice to Herr Schmidt. He thinks he's in love with Gretchen, you know?'

'Yes,' replied Marta. 'But it doesn't really matter. But you must stay quiet, Gustie. Or everything will be ruined.'

Augusta held her index finger to her pursed lips. 'Shhhh.'

'Yes,' said Marta. 'Good girl … shhhh.'

The magnificent force of Bernard's totally misguided passion for Gretchen couldn't be held back forever; he would inevitably make his way up the hundred and four spiralling stairs of the tower where Gretchen was now almost permanently ensconced. How he could have thought it was a good idea was anyone's guess, but one Sunday afternoon, after everyone had wandered off to their own private locations after the intense early-day activity that involved church followed by a large midday meal with more then thirty people seated at the table, Bernard took the opportunity to slip away unnoticed to the older part of the castle. Opening the heavy wooden door that led to the staircase, he almost stepped on a tray of food placed on the floor of the tiny vestibule. He swore loudly, the words echoing back at him from the great stone walls, but the tray gave him an idea. Picking it up, he proceeded up the long spiral of the stairs to the very top.

'I brought your luncheon,' he cried in a hearty voice as he pushed the atelier door open with his foot.

Gretchen was curled up on the wide sill of one of the long thin mullioned windows, where in centuries past von Tempsky women had waited for their men to return from war. She turned slowly and looked at him. 'Herr Schmidt?'

'Bernard. Please call me Bernard,' he corrected. 'You didn't come to luncheon and I thought I would bring you a tray.'

Gretchen nervously licked her thin, dry lips. She remembered now who Bernard was, what the voice had told her about him. 'What do you want?' she said, looking away. 'Why are you here?'

'You need to eat,' he said, a little perturbed by the lack of welcome. Fräulein Mueller, he thought, seemed much more animated than was usual, though he would be the first to admit that he had little experience with feminine hysteria, the ailment from which Gretchen apparently suffered.

'I'm not hungry.'

'I'll just set it down here,' Bernard replied in soothing tones as he placed the tray on a wooden table thickly daubed with oil paint of every colour. 'Then you can show me your paintings.' Every canvas, and there were a great many, was either turned to the wall or shrouded in a paint-stained cloth.

'You want to see my paintings?' Gretchen asked, slipping out of the window bay and walking towards him.

To Bernard's surprise Gretchen was wearing only a nightdress of white cotton lawn and her feet were bare and blue, as were her hands and lips. 'Aren't you cold?' he asked.

Gretchen ignored the question and said again, 'You want to see my paintings?'

'Yes, very much,' said Bernard. The sight of Gretchen in such a flimsy garment, through which her childlike body could be clearly discerned, was deeply distracting, though not in an erotic sense.

'He wants to see my paintings, he wants to see my paintings, he wants to see my paintings,' Gretchen chanted softly, a sly smile on her lips and almost dancing as she approached a canvas in the middle of the room. She stopped, and with one hand on the cloth pulling it taut, she turned to him and said, in a voice resonant with strength and sanity, 'Are you sure, Herr Schmidt? It's not too late to leave. Nobody would blame you.'

'Whatever do you mean …?' Bernard started to say as Gretchen slowly pulled the covering from her current work in progress.

What he saw was so vastly unexpected and strange that it took Bernard a few moments to realise what he was looking at and utter the subsequent shocked oath. It was a full-length portrait of himself. The face in the painting was rendered in exquisite detail, as if the artist had taken a photograph and somehow managed to retain the exact colours of life. From the shoulders down an unclothed male body was hastily sketched in with charcoal except for the genital area, from which sprouted the long bud of a mauve lily, its petals just beginning to curl back and open, revealing the tips of the pistils and stamen. The implication was unmistakable. Gretchen had succeeded in capturing the sticky sensuality of the flower's sexual organs with orgiastic fervour. 'Do you like it?' Gretchen asked hoarsely, watching Bernard closely. 'I think the likeness is very good, don't you? My inspiration was Bacchus, the god of wine and pleasure.'

'Yes, yes,' said Bernard, finally jolted out of his stunned silence. 'Very lifelike.'

'Would you like to see another?' she asked. Bernard longed to say no, but already Gretchen was moving towards another painting that was still sitting on its easel. With great drama she tore off the veil. It was Marta, her face intricately rendered and seemingly smooth as glass, like Bernard's in the previous painting. The arms and most of the shoulders, as if unimportant, were simply slashed in with charcoal, though a ribbon of painted canvas bled down the neck to the figure's left breast where it bloomed once more into painted flesh, as if fed by the heart that beat beneath it. At the breast suckled the horny toad on which Marta's painted self looked down fondly, in a repulsive parody of the Madonna. So, too, did the tiny Christ child, as yet unfinished, who perched on the adjacent shoulder. Marta's left hand Gretchen had painted whole, the missing digit reinstated and the join between the real and the imagined obscured by a simple ribbon of bride's gold.

'I say,' protested Bernard, by now highly alarmed, 'I don't know about all this.'

'But you wanted to see,' taunted Gretchen. 'You said you did.' She began to run around the room, tearing the covering cloths from the paintings.

As he backed out the door Bernard caught glimpses of the canvases: the elderly countess with her head and shoulder studded with common butterflies, reaching down to birth a large brown river trout from her graphically rendered sexual parts; Augusta sitting like a child with her legs spread wide, offering the viewer the sight of a completely open clematis where the genitals should be; the count with a penis consisting of the female pistil of a tiger lily, committing an act of bestiality on his favourite Hanoverian broodmare, with diminutive centaurs, their faces those of the von ·Tempsky cousins, cantering around the feet and hooves of their sire and dam. It was all too strange. All too terrible. Without a word of explanation or even a goodbye, Bernard turned on his heel and fled for the door. As he rushed down the stairs he sincerely hoped that he would never again set eyes on anything so depraved. He needed a drink, or three, to steady his nerves. By the time he encountered a member of the family, Klara as it happened, he had quite recovered himself, and said nothing of the incident.

One hundred and four stairs above Gretchen returned to the painting of Marta. The voice was right: these paintings that it forced her to make were an antidote to evil. Only they could keep her safe. She picked up a brush and began to hum as she loaded the fine sable hairs with a colour the same blush as a newborn's skin. She stood with her head tilted to the side for a moment as she gazed at the canvas, before beginning to paint in the face of the Christ child sitting on Marta's right shoulder.

That night the castle was woken by screams and by morning it became clear to Bernard that Gretchen had had a turn for which the Muellers most definitely held him responsible, as Augusta had told her parents she'd seen Bernard leaving the tower that afternoon. But whether Bernard was responsible couldn't be known for certain. When the girl became herself again some ten days later she couldn't remember what had ignited the latest bout of hysteria and by then Bernard had returned, in something of a disgrace, to Vienna.

While Gretchen was locked in her hazy laudanum world, unable to see out or let anyone in, the family, with a few of the most trusted of the von Tempsky servants, had carried her paintings down from the tower and out into the orchard where, in the long golden gloaming of a late summer evening, they burned them all, except one, the portrait of Marta and the toad. That small canvas, a square, not all that bigger than a large book, Marta managed to smuggle away. She had argued against the destruction, saying that the paintings were extraordinary and to burn them was a desecration. But she was the only one. Watching the oily black smoke roil into the reddening sky Marta understood that a great wrong had been done. The next day the leaves started to turn in the heat of the dying days of the Indian summer.

Four

✳ I always had a passion for natural history, of course. Not only was there my father's association with the Naturhistorisches Museum in Vienna, of which he was a founding staff member, but my mother's family, the von Tempskys, numbered a few collectors, including one who was briefly employed by Peter the Great, as a collector of curiosities.

Marta, *Neuguinea Memoirs*, Heyward & Barge, London, 1949, p. 7

There was a distinct cooling in relations between Bernard and the Muellers after the family returned to Vienna at the end of the summer. Bernard continued to cultivate his friendship with Marta, though largely away from the house on the Wipplinger Strasse, which his Aunt Liesl had told him was quite acceptable, given Marta's age. Although Gretchen had returned to normal and was under the care of a new doctor who seemed to have made great progress with her, it had finally occurred to Bernard that the pretty Mueller sister was perhaps not entirely right in the head.

'The other one, Marta, she will make you a good wife,' counselled Aunt Liesl. 'All her expectations are long gone.'

'But I don't love her,' Bernard protested. The truth of the matter was that Marta's cleverness intimidated him and he didn't know if he wanted a wife who was obviously smarter than him, and far more learned.

'And you, my dear nephew, are far too old to be believing in fairy tales about love,' said Liesl. 'You need to settle, and the girl isn't entirely ugly.'

'No,' agreed Bernard. 'Not entirely.'

Looking intently at Marta sitting across from him late one afternoon a few days after this conversation, Bernard realised that his aunt was right. It was either throw in his lot with Marta or face the prospect of returning to Neuguinea without wife on his arm.

Frau Schmidt breathed her last on a crisp, golden morning in September. Although this tiny death had been many months in the making it was still a shock, and Bernard was surprised by how affected he was. There was also a realisation that it was indeed a season of endings. This chapter in his life was almost written. Bernard had increasingly put thoughts of Neumecklenberg and Gethsemane behind him through the long European spring and summer but now, as the dirt piled on top of his mother's last resting place settled and the nights turned cold, Bernard realised it was time to go home.

'So when will you go?' asked Marta.

It was a month or so after the funeral and they were walking across the Volksgarten towards the Naturhistorisches Museum, wrapped up against the newly arrived autumnal chill.

'I will leave soon, I suppose,' said Bernard with a sigh, as they neared the museum. 'There's some business to be finalised regarding the house of my mother but after that there's little reason to stay. I must return to Gethsemane. It's been nearly a year. Too long.'

'I will miss your company,' Marta said shyly as they climbed the stone steps of the building. And this was true. She hadn't fallen in love with Bernard, but she found his company uncomplicated and comfortable. She'd never had a friend before. Not like this. She'd thought the lady novelist she'd accompanied to Spain all those years ago in search of 'love and romantic atmosphere' had been more her friend than her employer. But that had proved not to be the case at all. It had simply been another one of the authoress's fictions.

'Yes,' agreed Bernard, his tone suddenly jolly. His aunt had given him another good talking-to only the night before, urging him to make more of an effort to woo the oldest Mueller daughter properly. 'We have become such friends, haven't we?' he continued, trying to work up the courage to take this particular conversation just that bit further.

But Marta wasn't listening. 'This way,' she said briskly. She led him past the great halls of the museum's galleries, through an innocuous door and down a narrow flight of stone stairs, until they reached a much humbler part of the institution. Earlier in the week she'd arranged for Bernard to be shown his own contribution to the museum's collections in situ. Bernard was slightly put out when it dawned on him that his Neuguinea artefacts weren't on display but buried away in the museum's basement, condemned to languish in the darkness of closed drawers.

'When I was a girl, before the museum was opened, Papa would leave me down here for hours,' Marta said. She laughed. 'Once,' she continued, 'he went home without me and Herr Weber, whom you are about to meet, took me home on the tram.'

Herr Weber, the keeper of the storerooms, was sitting at his desk writing in one of his many ledgers when Marta and Bernard entered his domain. He looked up, peering myopically through his spectacles at the two figures approaching, not realising at first that the woman was Doktor Mueller's eldest daughter, for whom he had developed a great affection since making her acquaintance as a girl over two decades before.

Then the little man's face lit up. 'Aha, it's you, I think!' he exclaimed. 'Fräulein Mueller!'

'Yes,' said Marta warmly. 'Were you not told that we were coming, Herr Weber?'

'Perhaps, perhaps,' he said, rising from his desk and wiping his inky fingers on the front of the buff-coloured twill dustcoat. This was an old habit, judging from the various stains on the garment. Once he was ostensibly de-inked, though his fingers were permanently dark with the stuff, a degree of formality came over the custodian. 'Fräulein Mueller, it's a pleasure to welcome you and your gentleman friend to my humble sanctum,' he said, bobbing his head in a deferential fashion. Weber's delight in seeing Marta was obvious. It was also clear to Bernard that the affection was entirely mutual.

'What is it you wish to see today, Fräulein Mueller?' asked Weber.

'We've come to see human remains from Neuguinea that Herr Schmidt gifted in the spring,' replied Marta.

Weber went to a shelf loaded with hand-bound ledgers, making a happy noise when he found the one he required. 'Yes, see here,' he said running a thumb down a column of entries on a page towards the back of the tome. 'Herr Bernard Schmidt of Neumecklenberg – a dozen human skulls, Tolai, from Neupommern?'

'Yes,' replied Bernard, 'that's correct.'

'Right, come, follow me, let us go in search.' He shuffled off with surprising speed into the shadowy territories of the storeroom, with Marta in hot pursuit. As he followed more slowly, Bernard noted that the odd little man was wearing carpet slippers.

Marta looked over her shoulder. 'Come along,' she said as if he Bernard were a small, sulky child. This wasn't far from the truth: he would much rather be sitting in a warm café, embraced by the conviviality of the living, than prowling around a cold, dark tomb looking at dead things.

Along the dusty, dark rows of shelves and drawers they travelled, the conversation between Marta and Weber becoming more muted and intimate as they penetrated the heart of the miniature city of cabinetry. Looking up, Bernard was unnerved by the huge glass jars placed on the very top of the wooden stacks that rose above them like the great forests that they had once been. If Bernard had perhaps been a cleverer man he would have made this connection, but the most prevalent emotion he was experiencing was extreme repulsion at the contents of the jars, in which animals were suspended in preserving fluids of every kind. Death, time and chemicals had given the creatures colours they'd never achieved in life. Boiled to their essences, suspended in viscous syrups, they had attained the saturated hues of overripe fruits. In spite of his horror Bernard was vividly reminded of the endless jars of preserves at the von Tempsky estate, shining jewel-like and rich from the shelves of the dark stone pantries. But the nearest museum jar caught in a thin shaft of dust-moted sunlight revealed not a bounty of apricots or apples packed with cinnamon quills, but a night monkey, its imperfectly preserved flesh slowly dissolving into a crust of scum on top of the embalming fluid. The primate was crunched painfully into too small a container, its long limbs tucked under the recognisably humanoid head from which the eyes had vanished, dissolving into the potent brew in which it marinated. The tracery of its veins and arteries was revealed by the alizarin that filled them. A little further along was a veritable coven of bats and the carcass of a whole shark, perhaps sixty centimetres long, its cartilage contorted as it curled upwards towards the surface of its very own sea of glycerine. Bernard shuddered and quickened his step so that he caught up to the other two as they rounded a corner of the stacks in the heart of the room.

'Here we are!' cried Weber. 'Let me see, what was that number?' He peered at the numbers on the drawers. 'Aha! This is the one!' he exclaimed, bending down to open a drawer perhaps thirty centimetres from the floor. The twelve skulls in their bed of cotton batting shone wanly in the cool grey light, the eye sockets deep shadows, darker than death.

'Look, Bernard.' Marta plucked a small white envelope from where it had been slotted between the skulls and, extracting the provenance lodged within, began to read. 'One dozen, twelve, human skulls, Tolai ...' Marta paused. 'Did I say that correctly?'

'Near enough,' said Bernard.

'One dozen human skulls, Tolai in origin,' continued Marta. 'Taken from a native burial ground on the north-east coast of Neupommern, German East Neuguinea, 1903. Collector, Herr Bernard Wolfgang Schmidt of Gethsemane Plantation, Neumecklenberg.'

She handed Bernard the provenance so he could see the words, his name, for himself. Clutching the slip of paper, with its information neatly recorded in Weber's plain hand, Bernard found himself oddly moved. As though, in a small way, he did actually matter. That he was part of history. The trio stood and looked down at the skulls for a few moments, each wondering what else there was to say. The silence was as heavy as grief and it was something of a relief when Weber, suddenly galvanised into action by something only he could hear, abruptly retrieved the provenance from Bernard, tucked it in its envelope and dropped it back in the drawer.

'We shall have a little tour, shall we? Like when you were a girl,' he said to Marta, firmly slamming the drawer shut. 'Come along then, let's hunt for treasure,' he continued briskly, clapping his hands and scuttling off towards the back of the room.

'Come along, Bernard.' Marta tapped his leg with her umbrella. 'There's not a moment to lose.'

'These recently arrived from a museum in America.' Weber stopped suddenly and pulled out a drawer to reveal row after row of black and white beetles bigger than a man's hand, which had been affixed to a board with ordinary house nails. 'Our American colleagues, as you can clearly see, have a much more *primitive* approach to display than we here at the Vienna Naturhistorisches Museum.'

'Yes, how extraordinary,' observed Marta. 'Certainly not how we do it here at all.' Both looked askance at each other, delighting in their mutual sense of horror and superiority at the collection practices of institutions beyond civilised Europe.

'Those are big blighters, aren't they?' Bernard observed, peering over Marta's shoulder. 'We have ones like that in Neuguinea. Rhinoceros beetles, we call them. Scourge of the copra farmer, let me tell you. I'll send you a few if you would like, once I return to my plantation.'

'I'm sure any further contribution you could make would be an invaluable addition to our holdings,' said Weber politely, though with a little smirk, as he closed the drawer. 'Come along.' He shot off again.

At the far end of the storehouse flocks of birds, shot, stuffed and mounted on twigs, were perched in seemingly random order, caught in repose, in flight and everything else in between. Here the dust that Weber couldn't see lightly coated every surface and cobwebs were draped from wing to beak, from talon to feather, from species to species, down to the floor. Under the still and silent aviary was a cross-section of apes of many kinds, all in various stages of decay. Glass eyes had popped out and been lost, white cotton stitching could be seen and hair drifted to the stone floor on which the primates sat in a perpetual, unobserved moult. The primate troupe payed no heed to the improbable pride of lions, tigers and cheetahs, mangy and mostly toothless, caught static in mid-stalk nearby.

'A gallimaufry of gimcracky,' said Weber, kicking a disintegrating hyena with unnecessary violence as they passed.

Marta paused for a moment and apologetically patted the hyena on its head. She looked across at Bernard, who was obviously perplexed by Weber, and smiled. 'He's quite the eccentric,' she whispered sotto voce. 'I like him enormously.'

'Ah, now these you'll rather like, I think,' said Weber. He opened a number of large shallow drawers that were filled with the carcasses of parrots of every variety, from the bright red and metallic greens of the South American quetzal and Australian rosella to the sulphur-crested cockatoo with its snowy white plumage and bright yellow cockade.

'How beautiful they are,' sighed Marta, gently stroking the feathers, laying the odd ruffled one flat again in its natural fall. 'So sad, though, that they should have to die in order to live forever.'

'These are a recent acquisition from a collector in the Tanganyika,' cooed Weber, revealing an enormous drawer densely packed with whole flamingos, which were not just pink but white and apricot and tangerine too. The birds' curious upside-down beaks were tied together with the cotton strings, on which hung the card tags bearing their identification numbers. 'You can tell that they are freshly preserved by the existence of the eyes,' Weber said. 'After death the eyes decay first.'

'I remember you saying that to me years ago,' Marta said wistfully. 'I always thought it was such an interesting thing to know.'

When they left the storehouse perhaps an hour or so later Marta casually trailed her outstretched fingers along a glass-topped case full of eggs, but because she kept walking she never saw the beautiful way in which the three striations, made in the thick dust by her fingertips, allowed the soft light to stripe the brittle shells in their nest of cotton wadding.

'How I would love to travel like Maria Merian and Mrs Sheldon did,' said Marta later as she and Bernard sat drinking coffee and apple brandy in a coffeehouse overlooking the Ringstrasse.

'Which one was she?' asked Bernard.

'The Dutch artist who went to Surinam with her daughter in 1699 to paint its flora and fauna.'

'Ah yes,' replied Bernard. 'I remember now.'

As always, the visit to the museum had woken Marta's desire to do something extraordinary and important with her life. 'But in a simple uncomplicated way,' she continued. 'Like Merian, not Mrs Sheldon and her hundred native porters. Not to conquer, or prove a point, but simply to observe and paint the plant and animal life of a far-off exotic land.'

'So exploration on the scale of Mrs Sheldon doesn't interest you?' asked Bernard, who had spent the whole summer ploughing through *Sultan to Sultan*. But he had enjoyed it tremendously, and told Marta so: Mrs Sheldon had a good story-telling style.

'Only in books,' laughed Marta. 'I'm much more of a natural historian by nature anyway. My ambitions are actually rather humble.'

'And why don't you?' asked Bernard. 'Travel as you want to? You could perhaps find a way?'

Marta looked uncomfortable. Nobody had ever come out and asked her this question. 'I think,' she said slowly, 'I think it's really because I'm afraid. I think about the possibilities and then it all becomes such a monumental undertaking in my head that I begin to wonder at my own ambitions.' She stopped, then laughed. 'Maybe Augusta and I should go with you to Neuguinea, and I can chronicle the flora and fauna of that country.'

'Then why don't you?' said Bernard. 'Come with me to Neuguinea? Would that be so outrageous? Ladies frequently visit the colony for one reason or another.'

'Because what would people think? If you were a relative perhaps, then such a visit would be appropriate, but under the circumstances … though what a magnificent opportunity it would be.'

Bernard lit a cigarette and thought for a minute, his aunt's strident instructions loud in his subconscious. 'Why not marry me? Come to Neuguinea as my wife?' The words came out in a rush, but were comprehensible nevertheless.

'Are you proposing to me, Bernard Schmidt?' Marta asked playfully, fully expecting this to be a joke, a harmless speculative jest by a not very sensitive man.

'Yes, no … I don't know. It just seems to me that you would like to go to Neuguinea and we get on tolerably well, perhaps even feel some affection towards each other. And I have no wife and you no husband.'

'Yes,' replied Marta, adding the measure of brandy to her coffee. 'We are both alone in the world and peaceful enough in each other's company as you say. That is true.'

'And would it be so bad,' asked Bernard, 'to be married to me? Many a marriage has been built on flimsier foundations than friendship and neither of us is as young as we were. You never know, it might all be a great success.'

'A great success,' murmured Marta, a little taken aback. Apart from those initial few weeks of their acquaintance when she had attempted to cultivate the potential of a romance between them, the possibility of marriage hadn't occurred to her. That they had become friends was surprise enough. But perhaps Bernard was right: they *could* make a successful union based on mutual affection, tolerance and, if she was honest, basic human need. And how wonderful it would be to start all over again on a clean new page. Escape beckoned like a newly opened door. 'A success,' she said again, trying the notion out for size. She turned to Bernard, her dark, handsome eyes glittering in the lamplight. 'Yes, you may be right. May I think a little on this, Bernard, before I make my decision?'

'Of course, of course,' he replied. 'There is, after all, much to consider.'

When they parted, in deference to the new, if undecided, nature of their relationship, Bernard bent clumsily forward and kissed Marta farewell on the corner of her mouth, though he'd been aiming for her cheek.

❋ ❋ ❋

The news of Bernard's proposal didn't prompt as much joy in the Mueller household as it might have six months before. Even Klara, who was desperate to marry off her eldest, had arrived at a distinct antipathy towards Bernard. Egon was quietly devastated by the news and Gretchen uninterested. The only person even mildly excited was Augusta. Klara blamed Liesl Baumgarten: she was sure her friend had pushed her nephew towards this outrageous declaration, which, to her horror, Marta was considering. 'But do you love him?' Klara asked, when the family gathered in the parlour the next day to consider the proposal.

'Yes, of course,' Marta replied, lying only a little to her mother and herself. 'In my own way.'

'And does he profess to love you?' asked Egon, his brow knitted with worry.

'Oh yes, Papa, we speak of nothing else,' Marta said smoothly. 'We shall be very happy with each other, I'm sure. And in these modern times Neuguinea isn't so very far away.' So with that Marta's parents had to be satisfied.

Marta and Bernard married less than a month later, giving neither the bride nor the groom much time to reflect on the nature of their relationship. Bernard was pleasantly surprised by the avidity with which his new wife took to her marital obligations in the bedroom. Marta's enthusiasm for lovemaking didn't make Bernard fall in love with her, but it certainly piqued his interest and inspired him a little too. It had never been like this when he'd laboured away on top of whores who feigned a scant interest, or Gloria, who didn't even bother to pretend that she found his erotic endeavours anything other than a necessary evil. It never occurred to Bernard that Marta might have come to their marital bed in a less than pristine state.

Two weeks after the wedding Marta waved goodbye to her family and the newly married Herr and Frau Schmidt took the train down to Trieste on the Italian coast. There they boarded a passenger liner, which would take them to Australia. They were shown to their first-class suite of rooms on the upper deck by the purser and invited to dine that night at the captain's table. Ensconced in splendour, the Schmidts sailed across the Mediterranean all the way to Cairo.

When they returned to the ship from a final afternoon's Egyptian sightseeing, they were greeted at the top of the gangway by the purser, who informed Bernard that his and Signora Schmidt's belongings had been moved down to a second-class cabin as per instructions. As they walked to their new and inferior accommodation, Marta was stony-faced but Bernard didn't notice. He was pleased to have given up their suite to a wealthy

American, especially since he'd been offered a cut-price rate on the new cabin in recompense for this inconvenience. That night, sitting across the table from her husband in the second-class dining room, Marta wondered, for the first time, whether she had made a terrible mistake. This was real, as real as the sandcastle of salmon in cucumber aspic that was melting on her plate in the North African heat. This was her life. And just for a moment she wanted to put down her knife and fork and flee into the darkness of the Egyptian night.

By the time the vessel had slipped down the Suez Canal and sailed out into the Gulf of Aden, Marta, who had conceived only days after the wedding, was felled by nausea every morning. In spite of the sun she had caught in the Mediterranean and Egypt, she was as pale as a winter pear. Bernard, who knew little about babies, put his wife's queasy stomach down to seasickness. One morning soon after their vessel crossed the equator, Marta woke with her lower belly wracked by an almost continuous cramping. She was alone, Bernard having dressed and gone to breakfast without waking her. He spent as little time as possible in their cabin, which was small and reeked of vomit. The blood came soon after, thick and dark with clots, though nothing she could discern as having once been the beginning of a life. Marta hadn't mentioned her suspicion that she was pregnant, so neither did she talk to Bernard of the miscarriage. As they were leaving Mombasa a few days after she lost the baby, Bernard commented how much better she was looking now that she'd found her sea legs. And it was true. She'd stopped bleeding, her breasts had returned to their normal size and no longer ached, and the nausea had disappeared completely.

The passenger liner, travelling via Colombo, reached Fremantle, on the south-western tip of Australia, in early January 1904. After a few days in Fremantle the ship continued its journey, pushing its way through the choppy oceans of the Great Australian Bight, then stopping briefly in Melbourne before sailing across the remainder of Bass Strait, out into the Tasman Sea and up to Sydney. Bernard had planned a stay of a few weeks in Sydney so that his new bride could recuperate from the long journey and he could do business. After all, he'd been away from his beloved plantation for close to a year now and Gethsemane would be in serious need of supplies, especially things like bed linen and china, of which he had never had much need. For the most part, their time in Sydney passed uneventfully. During the day Marta shopped and looked at the sights such as they were and Bernard procured more masculine requirements and met his agent and lawyer on a number of occasions. He would return to their hotel in the late afternoon ebullient and full of bonhomie, ready to dine and dance with his wife.

The ship that was to take them from Sydney to Neuguinea was considerably smaller and much less palatial than the vessel on which they'd reached the edges of the Pacific. Marta had her birthday on board the SS *Katarina Georgescu*, turning thirty-four but a day's sail from Neupommern and the settlement of Herbertshohe, where they were to spend a week or two until a passage could be found to Neumecklenberg. The arrangements for their sojourn in Herbertshohe had been made by Bernard's great friend, the legendary Royal Weston, about whom Marta had heard so much.

Five

The first time Royal Weston saw Marta was through a telescope. Of course he didn't know for sure, as his eyeglass swept the row of passengers along the rail of the *Katarina Georgescu*, that the tall, dark woman was his friend Bernard's new wife. She looked … well, frighteningly capable really. Not a beauty, by any means, but very striking. Royal grunted in satisfaction as Bernard walked into the circle of focus. *So it is her, eh. Bernard's brand-new German missus. Let's hope she stays and puts an end to this nonsense with Gloria.*

The blur of land that Bernard said was Neupommern had come slowly into being on the edge of the horizon a little after dawn. Within a few hours the land mass had begun to take on shape and a huddle of volcanoes on the far right of Neupommern could clearly be seen rising abruptly from the water. Bernard had told Marta that Neupommern, on its south-east coast especially, was defined by its volcanic cones. The largest of these volcanoes was the active cone that Bernard said was called Tawurwur. It stood like a sentinel on the far point of the island, a long ribbon of smoke and ash winding up from its summit and into the endless blue ache of the sky. One of the other passengers, a Methodist missionary who'd been out in Neuguinea for many years, told Marta that the natives rather cleverly viewed the collection of volcanoes around Simpsonhaffen as being related, a mother and her daughters, as indeed geographically and geologically they were.

They sailed up the coast of Blanche Bay, keeping close to land. Bernard pointed out first Cape Gazelle, where Royal Weston lived, then Vunapope, the main Sacred Heart mission in the area. Marta was amazed by how uninhabited the land seemed to be. The villages and mission stations Bernard had indicated were no more than hastily wrought scribbles along the thin pale sliver of the coast.

'And this is Herbertshohe,' Bernard said proudly as the *Katarina Georgescu* turned inland towards a comparatively substantial settlement. 'That white bungalow on the eminence there is the hotel where we'll be staying.'

'We've arrived!'

'Yes, Liebling, we have.'

'At last,' sighed Marta.

Herbertshohe, the main settlement on the eastern coast, was a collection of whitewashed single and two-storeyed bungalows strung prettily along the cliff face under the coconut palms. Only the land seemed unmoved by the fierce midday heat, which leached the colour and solidity from everything else and reduced it to a shimmering, gaseous haze. Many of the buildings of Herbertshohe curiously resembled the alpine chalets and guesthouses of Marta's homeland. This she hadn't expected: to be reminded so poignantly of home by the sight of mere architecture in the wilderness. In Marta's imagination Neuguinea had been cast in shades of darkness, yet looking upon it for the first time she saw only light: the gleaming buildings; the cool white cotton clothing of the expatriates waiting on the main wharf; the pearly lustre of the road up to the township; the white-hot glare on the pale, salt-bleached boards of the wharves; and the milkiness of the pristine sand that hemmed the foreshore. And because Bernard had thoroughly prepared her for the worst, Marta found that she was somehow enchanted with this strange place, a brave banner of civilisation against the all-encompassing vastness of the land, the sky and the sea.

As they came alongside the Herbertshohe wharf, Bernard drew Marta's attention to the small group of people standing on the secondary pier, obviously belonging to the hotel, that jutted out from the base of the eminence rising abruptly to the north of the main wharf.

'There's my good friend Royal Weston.' He pointed to a tall, but slight figure dressed much like the other expatriates, in crisp white cotton, but with a farmer's hat rather than the panamas and solar topees that his companions were wearing. He was surrounded by a group of natives so black that their skins gleamed like obsidian in the sunlight.

Royal Weston, who had handed his telescope to one of his natives a few moments before, was now smoking a cigarette and watching as the *Katarina Georgescu* prepared to dock at this smaller wharf first; Marta and Bernard's luggage had already been hauled out of the hold. As the boat came alongside, Royal caught Marta's eye, smiled and lifted his extraordinary hat, made from dried and plaited coconut fronds, to reveal a thatch of dull apricot hair. 'Welcome to Herbertshohe, Mrs Schmidt,' he said in English.

Herr Weston, Marta observed, as she looked down at his upturned face, wore a faintly bemused expression, as if he'd just been told a rather good joke. He was also, Marta thought, rather a handsome man. This was something Bernard definitely hadn't mentioned in his many stories about his friend.

'Bernard, good to see you, old chap,' continued Royal, again in English.

'Ah Royal, my great friend,' replied Bernard. 'I have returned. At last. So you see.'

'Not before bloody time, old man.' Royal spoke laconically. 'How like a Kraut to bugger off chasing women while his plantation falls to pieces.'

'You exaggerate, I'm sure,' ' answered Bernard, clearly amused by the abuse.

A few minutes later they disembarked, introductions were made and Marta explained, for what seemed like the hundredth time since she'd left Vienna, that she spoke perfectly adequate English, even if it was heavily accented. 'I also speak French, Italian and a little Spanish too.'

'Gosh, that's clever. You'd think after being surrounded by the bloody Hun for the last five years I'd be fluent by now,' offered Royal in quasi-apology. 'But it's still something of a mystery to me, I must confess. Though I understand enough to get along. And I speak a little Swahili, if that's any consolation.'

Marta gazed with almost childlike intensity at her husband's best friend. Like the natives he stood with, Royal seemed absolutely unaffected by the heat. His linen suit was still crisply starched against the devastating humidity and he looked cool and relaxed. As far as Marta could tell, Herr Weston's only concession to the tropical climes appeared to be his odd hat and the sandals he wore instead of the boots or white canvas shoes that Bernard seemed to favour.

'Extraordinarily comfortable,' explained Royal, seeing Marta's look of surprise when she spotted his unconventional footwear. The Australian wriggled his toes. 'Have to watch out for snakes, though. Little blighters love nothing more than sinking their fangs into a fat pink toe.'

It was the toes that did it: there was something so deliciously playful about that simple action of wriggling them that made Marta laugh out loud. 'I think, Herr Weston,' she concluded, 'that you are something of a prankster.'

'Oh no, not at all,' demurred Royal, who was thinking with some pleasure that Mrs Schmidt had very fine eyes. 'At best I am an amateur oddity. A dilettante, isn't that so, Bernard?'

'Oh,' said Bernard, 'you know what your problem is, Royal?'

'What's that, old chap?'

'That you're too clever for your own good.'

'Yes,' agreed Royal. 'That's been said before.'

At Royal's side was a native with cicatrix-seamed skin the colour of midnight, holding a scarlet velvet cushion with a white pith helmet on it. 'Your topee, old man,' Royal continued, with a distinctly theatrical flourish. 'You left it at my bungalow when you departed and I know for a fact that this one is your favourite to wear when shouting at lazy kanakas.'

Bernard laughed and, with great ceremony, removed his panama, handed it to one of Royal's natives and retrieved his topee from the cushion. As Bernard put it on, Royal said something to his assembled natives, who grinned toothily, and chorused back in the same unintelligible patois, though their reply was obviously appreciative of the fine figure Bernard now cut.

How strange, Marta though, recognising the slight element of cruelty in Herr Weston's little performance, but looking anew at her husband. Who would have imagined that the addition of something as banal as a hat could state so completely who you were in this world?

Tickled by the sight of Bernard looking so much the colonist, Royal smiled. 'Welcome home, Bernard,' he said kindly, resting a hand briefly on his friend's shoulder. 'It hasn't been quite the same without you.' Both men knew this was something of a lie, but Bernard felt quite emotional nevertheless.

Royal then turned to Marta and took her arm. As he did so she caught the unmistakable musk of his body, rich and earthy, so different from Bernard, who always smelled faintly sour and milky, like the dairy on the estate in Bavaria. 'Are you all right, Mrs Schmidt?' asked Royal, looking at her in slight alarm. 'You swooned a little, I believe, and you're suddenly quite pale.'

'It must be the heat,' said Marta. 'I feel quite incredibly odd, I must confess. Light-headed, short of breath, and my heart is doing the most extraordinary things.'

Royal laughed. 'That sounds a little like love.'

'Does it?' asked Marta, genuinely surprised. 'I wouldn't know,' she continued, not really thinking about what she'd said.

'Yes,' said Royal. He immediately understood that this was no love match between his friend and this tall, slim woman with her funny, crooked smile and hoarse laugh. 'But just in case it *is* the heat, let's get you to the hotel.' He turned to Bernard. 'I'll leave you and the natives to sort out the luggage and I'll get your good lady wife to the hotel before it rains. I'll see you in the bar.'

'It's going to rain?' exclaimed Marta incredulously, now quite recovered from her odd little episode. She looked at Royal as if he was completely mad. The dense, sticky heat was stultifying. It felt as if someone had thrown a steaming hot, wet blanket over her whole body. The sky stretched above them as an endless canvas of blue with nothing more than a gathering of cloud haloed around the grumbling volcano to the north.

'Oh my goodness, yes,' Royal replied, as they walked towards the steps that led up the cliff face. 'We need to get you inside. It's going to pour. The hotel is very pleasant. Visitors to Herbertshohe are constantly amazed at the sumptuousness of our lives out here. They arrive fearing a hut in a cannibal village.'

'Are the cannibals still a threat?' Marta asked, curious rather than fearful.

'Oh yes,' replied Royal with great candour, 'though not so much now and it tends to be the native missionaries sent into the hinterlands rather that the white men of God or us planters who cop an end in a cauldron.'

'Why?'

'The plantations and the big mission stations are mostly coastal, and we wait for the natives to become civilised enough to come to us, after the missionaries have had a go at them. By that time they've been taught that God doesn't like them to eat us. There also seems to be quite a lot of evidence that they don't really like eating the white man. Our flesh, my local plantation kanakas tell me, is sour.'

'You said native missionaries?'

'Yes, yes. They're from other Pacific nations where the God-botherers have been ensconced for a long time. The theory is it takes a native to convert a native. It's got nothing to do with self-preservation on the white man's part.' He chuckled slyly. 'There's not much love lost between me and the church, though I like the people. Especially the nuns, who do so much for the children.'

'Bernard tells me you paint, Herr Weston,' said Marta as they began their ascent.

'I'm not very good,' confessed Royal. 'People tend to laugh at my paintings, but yes, I do daub a little.'

'And what is your genre?'

'Oh portraits,' replied Royal. 'I paint ghastly pictures of kanakas mostly. The kind of thing a six-year-old would be ashamed of, Bernard will tell you. Terrible things really.'

'You're too modest, I'm sure,' said Marta.

'And you, Mrs Schmidt, do you have an interest in the fine arts?'

'Botanical illustrations are my oeuvre,' replied Marta, a little self-importantly.

'Ah, so you're something of a lady naturalist. You're in good company here. Everyone in Neuguinea is mad on natural history. You must meet Richard Parkinson.'

'So I hear,' replied Marta. 'Bernard has spoken of him, and of Queen Emma too.'

'Ah yes, a great lady.'

'Indeed,' agreed Marta. 'So I've heard.'

'That's my storehouse there,' Royal said as they paused at the top of the steps to catch their breath. He was pointing at one of the more modest buildings, perhaps a dozen or more dwellings to the left of the hotel. 'Very small,' Royal explained. 'I haven't been here for long, so I still have just the one plantation, not like the consortiums such as the Neuguineakompagnie or Norddeutsche Lloyd, who seem to want to own the whole colony.'

The small hotel was the most highly decorated of all the buildings built on the cliff overlooking the harbour. Its deeply shaded wrap-around verandahs were abundant with lattice and fretwork and, most charmingly, it had four square turrets complete with steeply pitched roofs for snow that would never fall. Like the other buildings that made up the Herbertshohe township, it was perched on triangular whitewashed concrete piles as tall as a man to allow air to circulate beneath the dwelling and also to lessen the accumulation of malaria-carrying mosquitoes.

'Those are the living quarters of the hotel.' Royal pointed to the main building. 'That one next to it is the dining room and Trinkhalle.' From the latter came the sound of men's voices and raucous laughter. 'There's quite a crowd in,' said Royal, turning to indicate the three other ships anchored out in the harbour. 'Your stay should be most convivial. You'll learn we make our own fun out here.' He led Marta into the blessedly cool gloom of the hotel.

Marta already was beginning to wonder what her husband and Royal Weston, one so utterly masculine and visceral and the other so distinctly effete and definitely cerebral, could possibly have in common, apart from coconuts and location. But she had little time to ponder this as a few minutes later she found herself being whisked up stairs by a pair of Asiatics with the Bavarian hotel manager's promises of a bath and a pot of tea ringing most invitingly in her ears. Royal disappeared in the direction of the Trinkhalle.

When Marta opened her room's french doors out onto the verandah she discovered that the light had suddenly turned a deep, rich violet and a few moments later the predicted deluge arrived.

Waking a few hours later, having fallen into immediate rain-soothed slumber after she'd bathed, Marta discovered that the day was coming to a blazing end. The downpour had been and gone like a dream, leaving the colours of the sunset to paint the room with brief celestial fire. On the bedside table stood a jug of water covered by a net weighted with beads, and two glasses. She drank most of the water, gulping greedily until she felt the approaching migraine, caused by dehydration, go into retreat. Wearing only a thin cotton muslin dress, soft and much laundered, Marta walked out onto the verandah. Standing unobserved, as darkness fell like a theatre curtain, she looked out into the first night of her new life.

Six

✳ I miss you very much, Mama and Papa are worried and Gretchie is sad. She hasn't taken me ice-skating once this winter, not like you used to. And Bitte has a growth and must be shot Papa says. Though he promises that we will get a new puppy.

Augusta, letter, c.1904

Royal, with Bernard, had drunk the night away, but, as promised, he was in the lobby bright and early the next morning to take the Schmidts to his plantation at Cape Gazelle. As they approached Royal's pony and buggy, the land started to shake and from within the hotel came the sound of breaking glass and china.

'Mein Gott!' gasped Marta, grasping Royal in her panic.

'There, there, Mrs Schmidt,' said Royal comfortingly. 'It's only a guria. Dime a dozen here.' The tremor faded and the land became still once more. 'See,' he said. 'All over now. Nothing to worry about.'

Marta, embarrassed, released her death grip on Royal. What on earth had made her cling to him rather than Bernard?

'Yes,' continued Royal, handing her into the buggy's front seat, 'here on our eastern coast they're a daily occurrence. Something to do with the volcanoes, I've been told.'

The buggy was pulled by a fine-boned horse that was barely more than a pony. Used to the plump Haflinger ponies and heavy warmbloods of her homeland, Marta was intrigued by this creature, which reminded her more of the half-starved ponies she had seen in Cairo. It looked as though it could barely hold itself upright, yet trotted effortlessly along the white road leading out of Herbertshohe in heat that would have flattened most equines. She voiced her amazement to Royal, who explained that it was an Arabian crossed with a Macassar pony, bred by a Captain Macco of Ulul-Nono plantation on the island of Neumecklenberg.

'Neumecklenberg?' asked Marta, grabbing onto the name that had become so familiar in the months she'd known Bernard. 'Is this plantation near Gethsemane?'

'Not so far,' replied Bernard, who was nursing something of a sore head and bilious stomach. 'Ulul-Nono is our northern neighbour. We share a boundary.'

'Does he have a wife?' asked Marta.

'No,' replied Royal. 'But Emma is determined that he should marry one of her girls and is being none too subtle about it.'

'How is Frau Kolbe anyway?' asked Bernard.

'Her health isn't good. There's talk in the colony that she will sell soon, which is making the consortiums happy.'

'Why?' asked Marta.

'They don't want individuals like us and Emma to have too much power or land,' replied Royal. 'And Emma has both in spades.'

'It's all politics,' observed Bernard gloomily from the buggy's back seat.

'Oh indeed,' agreed Royal. 'And *that* we should never forget.'

The humidity, which had blanketed the coast the day before, had been blown away by a breeze that was beginning to build out at sea. The water glittered in the morning sun, and from the trees that lined the side of the road came the raucous squawks of birds, and the flash of their gaudy plumage, which Marta had previously seen only in museums or rendered on parchment. How beautiful it all was, this place called Neuguinea, though the volcanoes, lurking behind her, *were* a little unnerving.

A few minutes later, perhaps only a kilometre or so from Herbertshohe, they rounded a bend to see a cluster of some dozen and a half white buildings, including what was obviously a church, nestled beneath the ubiquitous coconut palms.

'Oh, yes, I saw this place when we were coming into Herbertshohe yesterday,' said Marta. 'I noticed the church especially. It's called Vuna something, isn't it?'

'Vunapope, yes,' clarified Royal. 'Mission station.'

'What denomination?' asked Marta.

'Catholic,' said Bernard, rousing himself. 'Are they Sacred Heart, Royal?'

'Yes. Sisters of Our Lady of the Sacred Heart. French. Not German. You can tell by the haphazard manner in which they've arranged their buildings. Krauts do everything in a straight line.'

'French?' asked Marta, amused.

'Yes,' said Royal, glancing at her and smiling. 'Used to be plenty of them around these parts before the Germans arrived. But your lot mostly saw them off, eh Bernard?'

'Can't abide the Frenchies myself.' Bernard belched loudly and thumped his chest with his fist.

'Oh look,' cried Marta, 'look at the church. It's so large.'

Royal and Bernard merely smiled, both well used to the sight of often elaborate church buildings, seemingly transplanted from European villages complete with bell towers, and placed, if not in the middle of the jungle, then in close proximity to it.

'This is the main Sacred Heart mission for this area,' explained Royal, slowing the pony to a walk as they passed through the collection of wooden buildings that stood on both sides of the road. Down in the bay Marta could see a small wharf stretching its long thin finger out into the still azure of the sea. Word travelled fast and by the time they'd passed through the mission they were being followed by a procession of native children. On the outskirts of the station three nuns were waiting to gather the children back into the benign dictatorship of God. Royal hauled the pony to a halt and introductions were made, though it was hard to catch the convoluted names of the nuns as the children had surrounded the carriage and were chirping away. It took a few moments before Marta realised that they were begging. Royal put his hand in his pocket and pulled out a paper bag of sweets.

'You spoil them,' said the nun to whom Royal handed the bag for distribution later.

'Impossible,' said Royal. He slapped the reins on the pony's back, startling it back into locomotion and causing the children to pull back like a startled flock of sparrows.

When Marta looked back over her shoulder, the children were lining up on the side of the road, waiting for the nun to dole out Royal's treasure. 'How do they survive?' she asked.

Royal laughed. 'The children or the church?'

'The church, of course.'

'Like the rest of us. They have plantations, large and profitable ones. And many of the inland mission stations, in the rainforest, have sawmills. There's much need for timber here, as you can imagine.'

'So who else owns all these coconut trees?'

'Some plantations are privately owned – the smaller ones, like those worked by planters such as Bernard and me. The bigger plantations that cover hundreds and hundreds of hectares are owned by consortiums and by people, like Queen Emma, who got in early before the German administration limited the size of plantations. For example, all this land from Herbertshohe to here belongs to a German consortium, the Neuguineakompagnie. Then everything between here and my plantation on the point of the cape belongs to Mrs Kolbe.'

'The famous Queen Emma,' said Marta. 'She sounds like a remarkable woman.'

'And a very rich one,' chuckled Bernard, cheering up as his heartburn started to abate. 'Incidentally, you, dear wife, have been summoned to Gunantambu for an audience with the Queen. There was a note at reception this morning.'

'I don't understand,' said Marta.

'Emma wants to inspect you, m'dear. Make sure you're up to scratch,' said Royal.

'Really? Mein Gott, how terrifying!'

'No,' said Bernard. 'Don't tease her, Royal. Like any good monarch, Emma simply likes to know who's in the colony and what their attachment is to Neuguinea.'

Within the hour they reached Royal's plantation. The bungalow, a variation on what Marta now understood was a type, was a long, low white building, elevated by concrete piles. It had wide verandahs and expansive gardens. But what made it special were the stunning views on either side of Cape Gazelle, out across the York islands and Neumecklenberg beyond, and the long avenue of casuarina trees planted twenty years before by the original plantation owner, a Dutch bachelor who had since returned home to seek a cure for his gonorrhoea. A purple morning glory – a *Convolvulus* something, Marta thought – ravished the front of the house.

'Oh, it's lovely,' said Marta as they arrived at the front steps and a few natives appeared out of nowhere to take possession of the pony and buggy. 'Perfectly charming,' she concluded, after Royal had led them up the stairs and into the huge central room of the bungalow.

'Yes,' agreed Royal, looking around with obvious satisfaction. 'We do ourselves rather well out here. Keep up standards, etcetera.'

When Marta's eyes adjusted to the changing light she realised that the panelled walls of the room were liberally hung with brightly coloured unframed paintings and the floor was strewn with African animal skins. She would have liked to pause and look at the paintings but already Royal was moving briskly across the room towards the open french doors. 'Have you been to Africa, Herr Weston?' she asked as they stepped out onto the verandah.

'Yes,' replied Royal. 'I spent a few years in Mombasa with my brother Jupiter, working for the Imperial East African Company.'

'How interesting.'

'Actually, yes, it really was.' Royal took them down to the shady far end of the verandah, where bamboo blinds had been closed against the sun. 'Now I'm sure she'll be down here, she usually is ... Rebecca?' But there was no answer.

Along this easterly aspect of the bungalow's verandah were four other sets of open french doors: an office, two bedrooms, the modesty of their interiors protected by the drawn lace curtains, and finally, to Marta's delight, a room that was obviously a library. She was about to ask Royal about his literary interests when he began shouting again.

'Rebecca! Rebecca! Where are you, woman?' he bellowed.

'I was resting,' came a petulant voice from the shadows, where Rebecca Weston was lying on a cane divan with a moistened wad of white cotton over her eyes. 'There's no need to shout, Royal. I'm not one of your natives.' The hard round ball of Rebecca's pregnancy protruded obscenely from her thin body like a tumour.

Marta wouldn't need very much time in Rebecca Weston's company to understand that Royal's wife was not a happy woman. Immediately after introductions were made the diatribe began. The servants, the snakes and spiders, the natives, the food, the lack of diversions, the missionaries, the hardships, the heat, the boredom – all of it was cause for discontent. Even before tea had been brought and drunk, Marta was beginning to wonder if she'd made a terrible mistake coming here. Perhaps it was the pregnancy that made Rebecca dissatisfied with everything. Or maybe she was simply the type of person who would never be content.

'And then there's that awful incident at St Paul's,' said Rebecca, pushing away the toddler, Thomas, who was attempting to climb on her lap. The boy, who had inherited his father's faded marmalade hair and pale, milky skin, had woken from his afternoon sleep and been brought out by a native girl to be admired by the visitors and was already bored and demanding. 'Those poor women,' continued Rebecca, oblivious to her son pawing at her skirts. 'They said they never stood a chance against the natives.'

'What incident?' asked Marta, looking to Bernard, then Royal.

Both looked a little shifty. Royal had filled Bernard in the night before on the massacre at the Sacred Heart mission station in the nearby Baining Mountains a few months before. They had thought it wise to keep this information from Marta as long as possible, but it was inevitable that she would soon hear about the brutal slaying of both priests and mission sisters. Royal just wished the information were coming from someone a little more moderate in their views. It was amazing how quickly his wife had turned into a shrew. Not that he blamed her. Not at all. The fault was entirely his.

'The natives turned on the mission,' explained Rebecca, her voice laced with hysteria. 'Nine lost their lives. Nine! Who's next? Us? We're not that far away from St Paul's. We could be next.'

'There, there,' said Royal, picking up and comforting his son, who was now sobbing pitifully in the face of his mother's complete lack of interest. 'You're overreacting, Rebecca. We're quite safe here.'

As they left a few hours later, Marta was able to look properly at Royal's paintings. They were raw and simplistic, approximations of human forms made up of thick blocks of primary colour. 'I see you are a disciple of Monsieur Gauguin,' said Marta, who liked them very much. 'A modernist.'

'Yes, yes,' agreed Royal enthusiastically. 'I was very saddened to hear of his death last year. I met him you know, a few years ago, when I was still deciding where in the Pacific to settle, and I went up to the Marquesas for a look. Extraordinary painter, but a bit of a bad hat with the native ladies.'

Marta smiled. 'Surely you gossip, Herr Weston!'

'Perhaps I do,' Royal replied, raising an eyebrow.

The audience with Emma Kolbe the next day was not as nerve-wracking as Marta had feared, once she had got over her hostess being seated on a throne of cane on the verandah of Gunantambu. Emma was a commanding presence, to say the least, even if her legendary beauty was almost lost in the rolls of flesh that padded a body once said to be the finest in the whole of the Pacific. The Queen smoked as she talked, a cigar of foul-smelling native tobacco she'd had sent from Samoa. Across the harbour to the east the dark masses of the Duke of York Islands, where Emma's Neuguinea story had begun could be seen. To the north was Simpsonhaffen and its family of volcanoes, where the first stages of a new expatriate settlement had just started. If one went up into the hills behind her plantations, Emma told Marta, the start of the new road connecting Simpsonhaffen to Herbertshohe was a visible scar in the verdure above the lone brave white square that was the newly built Norddeutsche Lloyd Line depot house.

When Emma rang the bell to have the teapot refreshed Marta noticed her hostess's hands for the first time. Short-fingered, swollen with fluid, they were decorated with rings, the bands of which cut noticeably into the flesh. It was just one of many things that spoke of Frau Kolbe's ill-health. Time had not been kind to the Queen. She had aged quickly in the torpid climate of the tropics, on a diet of quinine, ill-fated love and French champagne. These days Emma no longer looked for her own reflection when she passed mirrors. It reminded her too awfully that she was no longer the tempestuous teenager who, in full evening dress, had dived off a ship anchored in Apia Harbour and swum successfully to shore.

'My husband Paul, who is German, will be sorry he missed you,' said Emma, after a wizened native wearing a many-buttoned long white linen coat had brought out a kettle of steaming water and deftly made another pot of Earl Grey. 'Vienna is one of his favourite cities. I think he would like to talk of it to you.' The great lady paused. 'He wants us to sell up and leave here,' she continued, 'but don't tell them.'

'Who?'

'Anyone,' Emma said. 'Don't tell anyone.' And Marta never did, though the rumours around the colony were rife.

Before Marta left she was given a guided tour of Gunantambu. Emma proudly showed her the hot water system in the bath-house which, like the kitchen quarters and her sister Phoebe Parkinson's bungalow, was located discreetly in the many hectares of manicured gardens. The chatelaine of Gunantambu also pointed out the various objects of interest such as the credenza, desk and leather chair that Robert Louis Stevenson had given to her father Jonas in Samoa many years before, and the personally signed picture of the Kaiser, for which Emma showed considerably more enthusiasm. The house was lovely, of that there was little doubt. The shrouded verandahs and lowered wooden venetian blinds created a golden half-light that reflected off the polished timber floor and cast stripes of pale sunlight throughout the white painted interior. Large, beautifully faded and worn oriental carpets were thrown across the floors. Perched on tables and shelves were vast crystal and porcelain vases filled with exotic flowers, from large, brightly coloured trumpets with petals soft as a baby's skin to long fragile stems clustered with delicate, waxy, translucent orchids the size of the fingernail on the smallest finger on a small woman's hand. Standing in these rooms, just for a moment Marta understood how civilised existence here could be, and that the vast, the dangerous and the unknown were best not dwelt upon.

'How was the Queen?' Bernard asked that evening as he and Marta joined Royal at the bar of the Herbertshohe Hotel dining room before dinner.

'Charming but sad too,' replied Marta. 'But Gunantambu … I now have great expectations of Gethsemane. Is it half as grand?'

'If only,' replied Bernard. Marta's face fell. 'Not to worry, Liebling,' he continued. 'We'll be very cosy, I'm sure. We'll add to the main house as the children come and before you know it, Gethsemane will be easily as wonderful as Gunantambu.'

Royal, on his fifth gin of the evening, did his very best not to look too sceptical at this claim.

✳ ✳ ✳

That night, long after most people, native and expatriate alike, had succumbed to sleep, Queen Emma sat before the mirror in her bedroom unpinning her coils of grey wiry hair. A single candle guttered at her elbow, casting a soft and reverential light. She hoped she hadn't been unwise in telling Bernard Schmidt's new German wife that she would probably soon leave these islands and this house. She sighed. It was all for Paul. *Paul.* It was well past midnight and he hadn't returned to Gunantambu. And she knew he wouldn't come home or offer an excuse tomorrow for his absence. He had a mistress, of course. He was the kind of man who would always keep a woman if he could.

Emma had told Marta her secret because she'd wanted to hear how the words sounded when spoken as part of an ordinary conversation. It was easier to tell a stranger in a strange land about this idea that her husband Paul had planted in her head. Emma had always thought she would be buried here, in Neupommern, in the family mat-mat beside her slain lover, the Dalmatian captain Agostino Stalio. She had always imagined that Paul would lie on her other side and that the three of them would march together into the afterlife. But perhaps … perhaps this was not to be so. All she could do was pray that they wouldn't bury her somewhere cold. She had never liked the cold.

Her marriage to Paul had been strategic – a means of working within the German administration, and thus furthering her empire for herself and her family – but it didn't mean she didn't love him. Emma sighed. Her beloved empire, her one true love since Stalio's death thirteen years ago. Now Stalio, he had loved her as a man should love a woman. All the years of work, first with Farrell, who had taken her and her son Coe away from Samoa and her first husband Forsayth, then Stalio and now Paul, at her side. She'd buried her dead here in this land, and wept for the living, and now Paul wanted to leave. He was pushing her to sell up, abandon her family and this place for a comfortable bourgeois existence in Mosman, New South Wales. For their health, he argued, though Emma would truly never believe that. She knew Paul was lonely and found life on the island tiresome, in spite of his wife's fortune and his latest paramour.

She sighed again, then blew out the candle. Outside the full moon cast a silvery light across the sea and somewhere in the darkness a night bird cried out. It sounded like a woman's scream.

Seven

A ship sailing for Sydney arrived at the end of the week, and Rebecca Weston, complaining every step of her walk down the wharf, and accompanied by Thomas, boarded the vessel that would take her home to have her second child. Marta, who had been compelled by her sex and the friendship between their respective husbands to spend more time than she wished in the company of Royal's wife, was quietly relieved to see her leave.

His wife wasn't returning after the baby was born; this Royal knew as he watched her embark without looking back. The pregnancy provided a convenient excuse for her to return to her people in Tasmania. Right up until the moment, a month or so before, when she had caught her husband engaged in a deviant act with a young Buka boy from the plantation, Rebecca had intended to have her second child at the mission station at Vunapope under the watchful eye of the nuns.

It had been a shock, walking into the bath-house and seeing her husband with his trousers around his ankles and his cock buried to the hilt between the boy's buttocks. She had always assumed that her marriage, though admittedly lacking in passion, was in relatively good heart. It never occurred to her that her own husband was prey to the same evil temptations as his brother Jupiter, who was widely known among the Christian expatriate community in Mombasa as a rampant sodomite who was going to burn in hell for his misdeeds. But everything that she believed to be true about Royal, whom she had loved, had instantly turned to ashes in her mouth. Staying on was untenable. Not only would her pride not bear it, but her church, and her assurance of Christian salvation decreed that everything that her husband did was against God. She feared the taint of his sin, as if his depravity would infect her and the children by mere approximation. 'You repulse me, and with a child too,' she had hissed at Royal many times as she waited for a vessel to take her back to Australia.

Royal had refrained from pointing out that the boy had been well used by others before he'd come to his own notice and certainly seemed to have no problems regarding the use of his anus or mouth as a receptacle for male genitalia. Well, one didn't say things like that to a very angry wife who was about to take your children away forever. He certainly thought it, though, even as the placatory words – 'an anomaly', 'a moment of madness', 'never again' – were coming out of his mouth.

The marriage was over, even if, in those last days together, both Royal and Rebecca were at pains to pretend that it wasn't. Royal wasn't overly distressed by his wife's departure, for who could blame her? She deserved better. He'd hoped that marriage and family life would cure him of this hunger for young black boys, but all around him was a daily parade of temptation, and he'd given in many times since his arrival here in 1899. The most recent encounter, however, was the first time he'd been caught. Even as he'd pulled his cock out of the boy and rebuttoned his trousers, Royal had known his marriage was over. And what a relief it was. He would miss his son, though. Now almost three, Thomas, with his shock of carroty hair, was turning into quite a character and Royal was extraordinarily fond of the little bugger. So it was with something of a heavy heart that he waved goodbye to his little family.

✳ ✳ ✳

Rebecca Weston may have departed, but there was no escaping the opinions of the expatriate women Marta met over the remaining week of their stay in Herbertshohe. All were eager to offer advice to a Neuguinea novice and thus Marta got her first real taste of how things were in this inward-looking, self-contained society.

'You'll be so lonely out at Gethsemane all by yourself. Not like here where we have each other. So lonely, so lonely, so lonely …' The women cooed like native pigeons as they sipped their medicinal gin and tonics.

'What will you do? You'll go mad with no one to talk to. Bloody bonkers!' added a trio of Australian women, who were more forthright than their English and European counterparts. 'Gethsemane is bloody miles from Kavieng. And your neighbours on both sides are confirmed bachelors.'

'There's a definite social order here,' Marta wrote to her mother towards the end of the stay in Herbertshohe. 'Well, among the women, anyway.

Many of my fellow German sisters, for example, parade their minor titles, real or otherwise, in a manner I suspect they never would back home. It's so clear that they wish to place themselves a little above the Australians and, of course, the women here of mixed native and European blood, who are in mainly the many relatives of Queen Emma, whom I mentioned in my last letter. In truth I rather like the Australian women, *and* the Queen's nieces, who are a merry bunch and rather exotic in appearance. The Australian women are often a little uncouth in their manner and means of expression, but I enjoy that about them. Well, you know how I feel about airs and graces.

It seems I may have escaped contracting a malarial fever as the season is almost at an end. Apparently the rains dry up after Easter, though the danger hasn't completely passed. I'm longing for the rains to end, I must admit. One is constantly being caught by these deluges that arrive without notice, drenching all in their wake. Then the sun comes out and the earth begins to steam and is hot beyond all imaginable possibility, completely enervating, but smells wonderful and rich. Almost delicious, though I'm sure Papa would snort at *that*.

Marta's admiration for the Australian women wasn't without foundation. They were, on the whole, strong, thickset women with sun-raddled faces and large, capable hands. The type who pushed a brat out every two years without turning a hair and could arrange an impromptu dinner for twenty with a few shouted instructions to their well-trained native staff. The kind who flourished out here where social conventions didn't matter so much: they drank with their husbands, glass for glass, without the slightest hint of self-consciousness. They liked a joke, bawdy or otherwise, and were more comfortable than their German neighbours with the handful of half-caste women who were part of their society.

Marta especially liked Frau Ettie Kaumann, whom she had met at Kuradui, when Emma's sister, Phoebe Parkinson, hosted a ladies' tea towards the end of the first week of Marta's stay in Herbertshohe. Ettie, whose father was Emma's brother, Willie Coe, was just a few years younger than Marta and already looked very much like her aunt Emma, though not nearly as formidable. Marta and Ettie instantly gravitated towards each other out on the Kuradui verandah as the gathering conversed, ate little fish-paste and cucumber sandwiches and drank weak, amber oolong from Spode teacups.

'You speak very good English, Frau Schmidt,' Ettie said.

'Thank you,' replied Marta. Marta repeated what she'd told Royal on the wharf.

'How very accomplished of you,' said Ettie, with a hint of laughter in her voice when Marta concluded.

'I'm sorry.' Marta was suddenly anxious. 'Did I sound ridiculous and pompous?'

'No, not at all. I'm teasing you. Do you think you're going to like it here?' Ettie continued as she and Marta leaned on the verandah rail and looked out to sea.

'Yes,' said Marta. 'I rather think I will. Well, if I can get used to this heat. I must confess I find it ridiculously hot.'

'It's the humidity. It makes it worse, but that will be gone soon and you'll adjust.' Ettie stopped and looked appraisingly at Marta, who was wearing a fitted long-sleeved dress that buttoned all the way up to her chin. 'And your clothes too, Frau Schmidt, they're all wrong for the climate. You're in the islands now and you should dress as we do for informal occasions.' Ettie plucked at the cotton of her voluminous white cotton shift, which did nothing for her figure.

'Yes,' said Marta. 'My ridiculous clothes. You're right. I'm in the Pacific now, and all the conventions of the Western world, not to mention fashion, need to be rethought.'

'Or we could just go shopping tomorrow and find you something more suitable,' Ettie said.

And true to her word Ettie had appeared at the Herbertshohe Hotel the next morning and taken Marta to the Forsayth and Co. store.

'It's rather big,' Ettie said doubtfully, as Marta stood in front of her at Emma's store with the Mother Hubbard billowing around her like a half-inflated hot air balloon.

'But ones that fit around here,' Marta explained, pointing at her inadequate bosom, 'fail to fall much below my knees.'

'Yes,' said Ettie, 'I see your problem. You're ridiculously tall and thin, aren't you?'

'The bane of my existence,' sighed Marta as the voluminous dress slid off one bony shoulder.

'Never mind,' Ettie consoled her. 'Emma's Chinese tailor can take them in for you.'

Less than twenty-four hours later the remade dresses, laundered, ironed and wrapped up neatly in brown paper, arrived at the hotel for Marta. Also included was a note from Ettie, inviting her and Bernard to the Kaumanns' plantation for a few days.

Like all plantations on the northern coast of Neupommern, Kurakakaul had no road access – though the German administration was in the process of rectifying this – and therefore had its own jetty, from which trade and social traffic came and went. Fritz Kaumann, waiting with a trio of native houseboys, was obviously pleased to see Bernard, though he barely glanced at Marta.

In a letter to Gretchen, who was in a sanatorium having what Klara's latest missive described as 'a rest', Marta described Ettie's husband as best she could for her sister's amusement.

An odious man, you know the sort, disagreeable and suffering from bad digestion and ill-humour in equal measure, like Monsieur Chevalier who taught you piano for a whole excruciating year and who you claimed was much in love with me. I discovered later that Herr Kaumann had just recovered from a bout of malaria and was suffering from ringing in the ears, an after-effect of the illness, so perhaps he had cause to be such a bear with a bad head.

Fritz Kaumann may have been arrogant and overbearing but Ettie was South Pacific hospitality personified. Included among the guests at Kurakakaul were, unsurprisingly, a number of other Coe girls, all of whom, like Emma, were descended from that vigorous begetter of children, Jonas Coe. It was obvious that Ettie was particularly fond of Marie Allen, who was not much more than a girl, with the mark of her island heritage very much on her. The mother of this Coe girl, Marta would discover, was one of the offspring from Jonas' fifth marriage. Recently arrived from the Solomons where her mother and stepfather lived, Marie was staying with her aunt Emma at Gunantambu. Talkative, merry and quick to laugh, Marie reminded Marta painfully of Augusta – whom she had thought she would be happy to see the last of.

There was another Coe woman there, an older one who was not a part of the clique of giggling girls. This was Gloria, who had been sent to East Neuguinea two decades before, when it was little more than a collection of huts, for Emma to bring into line. The stories of Gloria's conduct over the years were so numerous that even Marta had already heard of her. With her beauty, if not her appetites, somewhat diminished, wild Gloria, once the scourge of Apia owing to her penchant for bar brawls and rough men, had become as bitter as the quinine powder they all quaffed. Although Gloria had been blacklisted from many plantations, including Gunantambu, because of her constantly outrageous and antagonistic behaviour, Ettie was always happy to include her cousin and her gargoyle of a husband in her house parties. It was also clear that Marie, young and easily impressed, was rather taken with the family's bad hat.

'This woman Gloria,' Marta told Gretchen,

has been waging a war on Frau Kolbe since the Queen used her as payment on a gambling debt to a man who is rumoured to be the ugliest in the entire South Pacific. It is said that even before a stick of dynamite went off in his hand, taking an eye, half his face and shattering the hand holding the explosive, he wasn't overly endowed with handsomeness. He sits behind his wife, in the shadows, occasionally pawing at her with his claw in a begging way like an animal. The repulsion she feels is clearly evident in her face. And the clothes, my dear ... now I know little of fashion, but surely one shouldn't wear purple satin and diamonds, real or paste, before luncheon. Really, she's quite eccentric, like a character in a book. I almost wonder if I like her.

On the second day of the Schmidts' stay with the Kaumanns, an outing to a local sightseeing spot, an ancient native burial ground, was arranged for Marta's edification.

'You're not faint-hearted, are you, Frau Schmidt?' asked Fritz Kaumann over the breakfast table that had been set up on the verandah.

'No,' replied Marta. Human remains were hardly alien to her after the many hours she'd spent in the storehouses of the Naturhistorisches Museum with Herr Weber. 'Not at all,' she continued, calmly spreading jam on her toast.

'I can vouch for that,' added Bernard, who was making short work of the repast Ettie's house staff had laid out.

'There's a boat coming in,' said Ettie as she walked up the steps to join her guests. She'd been down at the wharf buying fresh fish for dinner.

They all turned as one and looked down the long sweep of the lawn to the sea as a small trade vessel putted into the Kurakakaul wharf and a lone white-clad figure leapt out.

'It's Royal Weston, I think,' said Fritz Kaumann, who was well practised at gazing at far-off objects and deciphering the riddles created by distance and heat. At these casually spoken words Marta felt a sudden, clenching pain in her chest, followed by a quickening of her heartbeat and a distinct lightheadedness. Perhaps it was something she'd eaten or the dreaded malaria fever after all. Bernard *had* said that the onset of delirium was one of the first symptoms. It never occurred to her that she was suffering from the disease the French call coup de foudre.

'I think you're right,' said Bernard, shielding his eyes against the bright morning light. 'It *is* Royal Weston.'

'Oh, it is too,' said Phoebe Parkinson who, with her husband Richard, had arrived the night before, coming in on the trade boat that had taken Gloria and her husband out. 'How lovely.'

'What ho,' called Royal cheerfully as he came up the bungalow steps, his straw hat in his hands.

'Herr Weston,' said Ettie, rising to greet her guest. 'You must be famished. Sit, sit. Eat.'

'Ever the hostess,' said Royal. 'You're too kind, Mrs Kaumann, and looking particularly ravishing this morning.'

Ettie rolled her eyes. She'd known Royal since he'd first arrived in the territory and this banter between them was all part of their ritual. Watching Royal flirt outrageously with her friend, Marta experienced once again the non-specific physical pain she'd felt a few moments before. It felt as if an invisible hand was squeezing her heart and lungs. Not that she felt sick, not at all. Quite the opposite, in fact. She felt oddly ebullient, as if champagne, bubbly and foamy, filled her veins. It was probably the fever. She promised herself she would go and see the German doctor at Herbertshohe when they returned the following day.

'Are you having fun, Mrs Schmidt?' asked Royal as they waited for the native boy to bring the plantation cart around to the front of the house. The carriage was too small for the six who had decided to go to the burial ground: Richard and Phoebe Parkinson, Ettie,

Marie, Royal and Marta. Fritz Kaumann was tinkering around with the idea of producing desiccated coconut and Bernard was interested in seeing the shredding machine that his compatriot had made.

'Yes,' Marta replied. 'I really am. Everyone has been so nice and welcoming, and I'm so much more comfortable now that I have some appropriate clothing.'

'Yes,' laughed Royal. 'But then it's always struck me that ladies' fashions are hopelessly impractical.'

'I have a secret yen to wear trousers,' confided Marta.

'You suffragette!' exclaimed Royal, a single pale eyebrow rising dramatically to punctuate his point and drawing Marta's attention to his unusual eyes. Rather than the pale blue his colouring suggested, Royal Weston's eyes were hazel, but more golden than brown, like a lion's. We would have dark-eyed children, thought Marta, that keen student of Mendel. The thought was an odd amalgamation of utter logic and complete irrationality.

After half an hour of travelling inland the cart halted in the shade of a tropical almond that was smothered in St Thomas bean. The dropped seed pods of the vine crunched underfoot as the sightseers walked into the rainforest, following a well-worn track that wound around the vast, spreading buttress roots of the tallest trees. High above in the canopy, birds that truly must have descended from paradise competed vocally as they flitted from branch to branch. Because it was early March, many of the orchids were in their final stages of bloom, their multiflowered stems milky pastel-hued blurs of light among the intense verdant shadows of the forest. The palms, like the orchids, had also revelled in the long season of near constant rain, and had great fountains of inflorescence cascading down their trunks. The further the visitors travelled inland, often climbing rudimentary steps cut roughly into the clay. The mud underfoot became stickier and trickles of water quickly turned into small streams.

'Almost there,' said Royal encouragingly, though only Marta was struggling with the climb. The Parkinsons, by far the oldest in the group, were putting the rest to shame; Mrs Parkinson was even able to chat non-stop with Ettie behind her. Eventually, after what seemed like hours, but in reality was not much more than thirty minutes, they rounded a bend where Marta could see, partially obscured by the foliage, a vast lead-grey limestone cliff face that appeared pockmarked like the surface of the moon as seen through an observatory telescope. As they climbed the last stretch to their destination, a gleam of ivory in the mud caught her eye. It was a femur, half buried, the ball of the knee-joint washed clean by the thread of water that had exposed it. A few steps further and another skeletal fragment, a human skull, revealed itself. A patina of lichen bloomed on the domed top of the head, almost obscuring the gaping fissure that was a mute testimony to the killing stroke of a stone axe possibly centuries before. An emerald tree skink, head cocked in such as way as to suggest that it was watching the intruders, was curled like a smile inside the empty eye-socket of the skull. There was a flicker of green and the skink vanished, its brightness swallowed up by the forest. In spite of the warning provided by the scattering of bones, Marta was unprepared for the macabre entirety of the native boneyard. Cadaver after cadaver was stuffed into shallow cairns in the cliff face, turned to stone by the incessant leaching action of the lime. The ossuary of perhaps two hundred bodies or more, frozen in time, was appalling, yet strangely beautiful.

'Mein Gott, how extraordinary,' gasped Marta. She was breathing heavily and a haze of sweat frosted the downy hair of her upper lip. 'Truly, truly, extraordinary. The degree of preservation, amazing,' she continued, stopping and inspecting a semi-mummified body. She was suddenly reminded of the storehouse at the museum in Vienna, and if a native equivalent of Herr Weber had appeared out of the rainforest she wouldn't have been even remotely surprised.

'I knew you'd be interested,' said Ettie.

'Do the natives still bury their dead here?' asked Marta.

'Not to my knowledge,' replied Richard Parkinson, stroking his long, greying beard. 'Besides, it's been plundered so many times by people exactly like us that it's hard to see the natives still regarding it as a tambu place.'

'Tambu?' asked Marta.

'Taboo,' translated Ettie.

'But I do think,' continued Richard, 'that the ground had been abandoned long before the arrival of the white man. It has the feeling of a past civilisation. An unrecorded time.'

'It's very beautiful,' said Marta, gazing up in wonder. Some of the higher cadavers, the more ancient ones, were nothing more than crumbling bones, the limestone no longer preserving but consuming those last physical remains.

Beside her Marie shivered. 'I think it's ghoulish. I don't think I'll never become used to it.'

'That's because you're young,' Phoebe said, not unkindly. 'As you get older things like death become a more natural part of living.'

'Just like the Egyptians, really,' Royal said to Marta, immediately appealing to her intellectual curiosity. 'Roughly the same kind of preservation process, I gather, but the natives use the land itself to do the work. Clever of them, I've always thought.'

Marta reached out to touch the stretch of grey skin suspended between a corpse's cheekbone and chin. To her amazement, the skin, which she had assumed would feel like leather, was actually petrous to the touch. This place of bones, she realised, was no different from a European churchyard except that the bodies themselves became their own memorials and headstones.

Royal and Marta sat together in the cart for the ride back to Kurakakaul.

'What happened to your finger, Mrs Schmidt?'

'Blood poisoning. A long time ago now. The tip of a rose thorn – stupid, really, that something so minor could cause so much damage. By the time I was seen by a doctor it was too late and all they could do was amputate.'

* * *

That night Marta slept heavily, after the long walk and three glasses of wine, and dreamed vividly of the native burial ground. The ossuary would haunt her dreams occasionally in years to come, but never with the clarity it did that night.

Eight

✳ 27 November – I wonder what kind of monster I am that I can so easily leave behind everything that is supposed to matter.

Marta, journal, 1903

Preparations for the ball had thrown Emma Kolbe into a flurry of happy activity, much to the relief of her girls, who'd thought their matriarch had been rather melancholy in recent months. Champagne was unearthed by the gallon from the Forsayth and Co. storehouses, and at Gunantambu's kitchen quarters, Emma's younger sister Phoebe and the pair of Chinese–Malay cookie-boys planned and provisioned for the festivities.

Emma and Phoebe weren't the only ones galvanised into urgent action in preparation for the party. From Webberhaffen in the north, to Simpsonhaffen beneath its smouldering volcanos, to Cape Gazelle in the south to the Duke of Yorks and Neumecklenberg in the east, men were instructing their houseboys to clean and press their dress whites and women were busily reworking their hopelessly out-of-date evening dresses.

Marta had decided to wear her most summery gown. She knew she looked utterly unalluring – the dress, a soft ivory with pink embroidery, needed a lush, creamy blonde, not a heavy-browed scarecrow with very large feet – but she didn't care. She would have quite happily worn one of her cotton Mother Hubbards if she'd been able to. Although everyone she met endlessly assured her that she wouldn't notice the heat so much after a while, that seemed unimaginable.

Marta and her escorts, Bernard and Royal, were late for Emma's soiree. Royal's carriage pony had come up lame that afternoon with a bruised hoof and another had to be acquired from a neighbouring plantation, which had taken some time. The trio arrived a few hours after festivities had begun, long after nightfall with the gibbous moon already high in the velvety sky. The sight of Gunantambu as they trotted towards it, all lit up, with the music and laughter that poured out its open doors and windows pushing back the tropical night, caused Marta to shiver involuntarily, though it wasn't cold. Once they'd apologised to their hostess for their tardiness, the Schmidts and Royal drifted around the party. Marta quickly realised that, with glass in hand, Royal was in his element. He had the easiness of a natural social animal and it was obvious that he was well known and liked by all. Where Bernard stepped back, Royal stepped forward, dragging Marta by the arm to join him. How easy it all was when you were with someone like this. Much to her own surprise Marta found herself chatting away with … well, everyone, while Bernard hovered behind her.

'Do you know that Queen Emma presides over a native divorce court?' a young Danish woman, the wife of one of the plantation managers, asked, sotto voce. 'You may be shocked to hear it, but matrimony in New Britain is not entirely the domain of the missionaries and Mrs Kolbe is all in favour of swapping spouses. Her father, they say, kept six native wives in Apia and the Queen herself lived in sin for many years with two of her lovers.'

'How extraordinary,' laughed Marta. 'I shall remember that if I ever tire of my own husband. Perhaps Mrs Kolbe could design a better union for myself than I have done.' The Danish woman looked quite shocked at this.

But Bernard, who was listening, laughed. 'I shall have to be careful then, won't I?' he said.

'Yes,' agreed Marta playfully. 'That would be wise.'

'That's the ticket, Mrs Schmidt,' added Royal.'Keep old Bernard here on his toes.'

Such scandalous exchanges were a rarity. For the most part the conversations at the gathering were an extension of those Marta had already heard on the verandahs of Neupommern. How bad, or mild, the gurias had been in the proceeding days was a favourite. And it *was* extraordinary how quickly one got used to the land and its grumbles and shakes. After just ten days she barely noticed them any more. The massacre at the Sacred Heart mission in the Baining Mountains still had some feeling nervous, but it was evident that for many, especially the men, the murder of the Catholics was already fading into Neuguinea history. There were also a few outraged and mostly bemused murmurings about Gloria's temerity in turning up at the party when they all knew she had been blacklisted from Gunantambu, for Emma loathed her, and with good reason.

Another well-worn topic of conversation was the development of Simpsonhaffen on the northern end of Blanche Bay under the shadow of Mother and her Daughters. Already Norddeutsche Lloyd had drained the mangroves and established a wharf and a bungalow for their company offices on the foreshore. The volcanoes were a menacing presence, but the company men were finding the area all but clean of mosquitoes and the malarial fevers that they carried, and the harbour was pleasingly deep. Now the Neuguineakompagnie and the other consortiums were also in the process of moving their own administrative headquarters from Herbertshohe to Simpsonhaffen.

'Sad really,' Royal said to Marta as they strolled out onto the verandah for a breath of air and to wait for Bernard, who had gone to replenish their drinks. 'Herbertshohe will wilt and fade if we all go to Simpsonhaffen and I rather think the new place won't have the same character. However with the trade in copra increasing, and bigger ships coming and going, the colony really does need a deep sea port, volcanoes or no volcanos.'

'How much of a threat do the volcanoes pose?' asked Marta.

Royal smiled. 'Much more than any of us will care to admit. A volcano is a volatile creature and this, m'dear, is a violent land. Perhaps even more than we know.'

The Schmidts and Royal were in deep conversation with Richard Parkinson about his recent establishment of a botanical garden in the rich volcanic soil at the nascent Simpsonhaffen settlement, when Gloria, chattering loudly, sailed past on the arm of a German naval officer. She was clad in an extraordinary amount of parrot-green satin which still somehow contrived to keep her bosom bare, and around her throat was a heavy necklace of what appeared to be topazes but could have been paste. Blue and green peacock feathers were secured in her hair by a large glittering clip worked in the shape of an open fan. She looked, Marta thought, quite amazing and rather beautiful, as if the rest of the women in their sedate pastels were the ones who'd got it spectacularly wrong. Gloria was also made up like a faded actress, which caused some tongue-clicking, especially among the nuns. As always, her scarred husband was following in her wake, like a strange, surreal hybrid of a lady's lap dog in a Velasquez painting.

'Who is that woman?' Marta asked. She already knew, of course, but was curious to hear what Herr Parkinson had to say on the matter, related as he was to Gloria by marriage.

'One of ours, I'm afraid, as I'm sure you know,' explained Richard, smiling through his bushy beard. 'She's sailing a little close to the wind, though.'

'Why?' asked Marta.

'She was definitely *not* invited to tonight's festivities,' he replied. 'Though she knows now she's here Emma won't ask her to leave. Not in front of everyone …' Richard shrugged. After all, bad behaviour of both a social and carnal variety was hardly a novelty in the lives of the extended Coe family. It was the South Pacific way and Richard had learned not to judge. 'Ah,' he continued, 'there's Phoebe, at last. I must join her.' He turned to Marta. "It's been a pleasure, Frau Schmidt. I hope we meet again soon.'

'Come and stay with us at Gethsemane,' suggested Bernard, who was pleased beyond measure that the very respected Parkinson was showing him such favour. He was glad, though, that Marta had been there to provide most of the conversation: Herr Parkinson always made him feel like such a dunderhead.

'Yes, perhaps I will,' replied Richard. 'I have much work still to do in Neumecklenberg.'

'Well, it's settled then. You will stay with us,' said Bernard. 'When you come.'

'You've made another conquest there,' said Bernard as Richard Parkinson walked away.

'Really?' Marta was genuinely surprised. Perhaps, she mused, standards were lower here and her novelty qualification enough for some social success.

Out on the lantern–lit verandah couples were waltzing sedately to a gramophone record. In the middle of this array of wilting evening dresses and starched dress whites was Gloria, dancing with the naval officer. Her husband was conspicuous by his absence. It was obvious that Gloria was very drunk, as were some of the handful of other younger ladies, much to Marta's, but nobody else's, shock. Even the Queen was noticeably intoxicated. No one, though, was drunker than Gloria, who seemed very determined to make a complete spectacle of herself. Marta couldn't tear her eyes away as the woman wrapped herself like a python around the young officer, much to his discomfort. If she had unhinged her jaw and swallowed him whole none of the gathered company would have turned a hair, Marta was sure.

'The Queen married her off to old ugly face quick smart and sent her off to the Yorks with him to become a good little German hausfrau. Not that that's worked, as you can see,' said Royal, seeing the direction of Marta's gaze.

'No,' said Bernard in a forced jolly tone meant to suggest that it didn't hurt him at all to watch Gloria cavorting so outlandishly. 'No, same as ever.'

'Cheer up, old man.' comforted Royal.

Whatever does he mean? wondered Marta briefly, but she had drunk too much champagne and the question escaped before she could ponder its implications.

Bernard turned to Marta. 'It's time we went home, I think,' he said.

'But we've not even danced,' protested Marta. 'You can't want to go yet.'

'No, no, Liebling. Not home to the hotel. Home to Neumecklenberg. Home to Gethsemane. It's time.'

'There's a trader heading for Kavieng, going out on Monday morning,' said Royal. 'Would you like to see what I can do?'

'If you could,' replied Bernard. 'I've neglected Gethsemane for far too long. I need to introduce my two great loves to each other.'

'Oh!' said Ettie, who had just joined them. 'That's so romantic, Herr Schmidt. It's inevitable that you must leave Neupommern, but I shall miss you, I think, Frau Schmidt.'

'And I you,' replied Marta warmly. 'And call me Marta. All this formality seems odd out here.'

'I couldn't agree more,' said Ettie. 'And you will call me Ettie.'

'Splendid!' Marta was thrilled that she had made a friend. And so easily too. For the first time she felt as though she fitted in.

'I have come to steal you away,' continued Ettie, tucking Marta's arm under her own. 'You must meet my sister Dolly. She's the most scandalous one of my generation.'

'More scandalous than Gloria?' asked Marta as they walked into Gunantambu's main room.

'Oh, her!' snorted Ettie. 'She's older than us.'

'You are wicked,' said Marta approvingly.

Long past midnight, Marta, who hadn't set eyes on Bernard for almost an hour, excusing herself from a discussion on which natives made the best house servants – the Malagan from Neumecklenberg took it by a nose – and went in search of her missing husband. Bernard was nowhere to be found inside and not a soul, it seemed, had seen him since earlier in the evening. Marta walked down into the garden to continue her search. She was, she realised, quite, quite drunk. She who had been horrified at the other party guests levels of intoxication only a couple of hours earlier, was now just as compromised and it made her laugh quietly to herself. It was the oddest thing, she thought as she walked across the lawn: everything was hazy and dislocated, like a dream. Many of the younger people had spilled out of the crowded bungalow and were drifting through the gardens, taking advantage of the privacy offered by the play of light and shadow from the flaming torches. The razor-sharp giant clam shells that Emma had had placed around the perimeter of the house, to keep thieving natives at bay, gleamed like teeth in the gaping maw of a phosphorescent deep-sea monster. From Gunantambu's gardens came the rich, sweet perfume of jasmines and honeysuckles, as exotic as oils from the Orient. In such a setting, on such a night, and distinctly intoxicated, it was possible for Marta to believe in anything. Even her own capacity to love. Eager to share her epiphany with her husband, she set about the task of finding him with new purpose.

She saw the green of the dress first, made insect iridescent by the light of the flickering torches. A flash, a scrap of colour among the native almond trees and ngaio deeper in the garden where the shadows were richer. Then Marta heard the laugh. Haughty, throaty and somehow ancient, as if for the one who laughed so mirthlessly there were no surprises left in this world. Marta froze in the shadow cast by a giant jacaranda and watched as Gloria emerged from the clotted darkness of a hibiscus copse that flourished around one of the Gunantambu guesthouses. The trollop was saying something over her shoulder to an invisible companion. So shocked was Marta by Gloria's utter lack of propriety as she strode across the lawn with her skirts hoisted high, displaying bare feet and legs, that she failed to notice the woman's previously unseen escort following her at a decorous distance. With the moon behind them and the torches offering an inconstant light, it was some moments before Marta realised that Gloria's companion was Bernard.

Gloria and Bernard were more than halfway across the lawn before they noticed Marta standing by the jacaranda, watching them. Scarcely faltering and perhaps even lifting her skirts a little higher, Gloria sashayed up to Marta, paused for a moment, looked at her rival's set jaw and rigid mouth and laughed in her face. Marta noted grimly that Gloria's hair was tumbling down from its elaborate arrangement and that the spray of feathers and gaudy jewelled clip had disappeared. Taking just a moment to ostentatiously adjust the front of her dress, from which her generous breasts were about to escape, Gloria swept off in a manner that could only be described as triumphant, leaving Bernard and Marta standing facing each other in the moonlight.

'Liebling,' Bernard said, picking a hibiscus leaf out of his hair, 'what are you doing out here?' It sounded like an accusation.

'Looking for you,' Marta replied.

'Well, here I am,' he countered, twirling his moustaches and attempting to turn on the charm. It was a woeful effort.

'What were you doing with that woman?' Marta asked, her moment of clarity about the nature of love forgotten.

'Helping her with her husband,' replied Bernard smoothly. 'She's an old friend. I've known them both for years. Poor chap had passed out in the garden. Too much to drink. She needed me to help drag him to their guesthouse.' It sounded so plausible, though if Marta had thought more closely she would have understood that Gloria and her husband were the last people who would have been given one of the coveted Gunantambu guesthouses. And Bernard's words didn't really explain the loss of Gloria's stockings and shoes, though that could easily be put down to the woman's rampant exhibitionism. So, largely because she wanted to, and it was that kind of evening after all, Marta decided that perhaps Bernard was telling her the truth.

That night after they had returned from the party at Gunantambu Bernard and Marta made love in a gentle, exhausted manner and Marta conceived for the second time, though it would be another twenty-one days before she would suspect as much.

＊ ＊ ＊

The next morning, with a throbbing head and queasy stomach, Marta picked Bernard's clothes up off the floor while he bathed, singing a German folksong more loudly than was necessary, in a tub behind a screen on the verandah. There was something heavy in one of the pockets of his white dress jacket, which was covered in yellow pollen. Marta slid her hand into the pocket and wrapped it around a shape she hadn't expected to encounter. Pulling it out and holding it up to the light, Marta recognised it instantly. It was the clip Gloria had been wearing in her dark hair. Without hesitation Marta walked quickly to her trunk and hid the trinket, which she could now see, in the unforgiving light of a new day, was only cheap paste. Later she was amused to catch Bernard searching his clothes from the night before.

When she asked him what he was looking for he replied, 'Nothing. Nothing at all.'

Nine

✳ Although my family was not poor, I chose to go out into the world and earn a little of my own keep. Owing to the exemplary education that my father had endeavoured to give me, I sought positions that required a fair degree of secretaryship rather than mere fetching and carrying. My first position, when I was just eighteen, was in England, with a lady novelist. Other positions followed, and I was lucky enough to find myself returning to England on another two occasions to spend summers in Dorset and in Scotland. In Dorset I was but a stone's throw from where Mary Anning had found her 'fish-lizard' dinosaur – ichthyosaur – half a century before. Looking back, that part of my life seems so long ago.

Marta, *Neuguinea Memoirs*, Heyward
& Barge, London, 1949, p. 7

A day and a half after the party the Schmidts took passage on the *Ann Pistacchi*, a small trade steamer, leaving Neupommern and its many volcanoes and constant earth tremors behind. As the new day dawned, they sat together in front of the bridgehouse of the pungent little vessel as it chugged out of Blanche Bay and towards the Duke of York Islands. The steamer made good time across the glassy waters of St George's Channel and up around the Yorks, following the western coast of Neumecklenberg north to Kavieng. Marta was particularly delighted by the coral atolls strung across the jade and indigo surface of the ocean. The trader captain, however, had quite another opinion. 'Those pretty corals,' he told Marta as she attempted to wax lyrical, 'they'll rip the hull out of a boat as quick as look at you.' This did nothing to dampen Marta's enthusiasm, though from then on she held her tongue.

The *Ann Pistacchi* reached Kavieng in the late afternoon, nosing slowly into port around the little islands that punctuated the harbour. Looking down, Marta was delighted to discover that although the coral-clad ocean floor was many fathoms below, the water was so crystalline that much of the life it contained could be clearly seen. Bright blue angel fish and their close relatives, the daffodil yellow butterfly fish, both chevroned with silver and black, flitted back and forth with vast schools of slender fusiliers. Among the anemones nestled in the corals, clown fish the same burnt orange as koi, but extravagantly banded with white and black, hovered around their living, undulating homes. There was so much to take in, Marta thought, as a school of glittering blue, yellow and silver damsel fish flickered into view and vanished again as quickly as a magician's sleight of hand.

'Bernard, this is just wonderful.' She looked first at her husband and then to the land where, among the coconut palms, fish poison trees, casuarina and pisonia, were signs of a well-established expatriate settlement and busy port.

During the hour that the *Ann Pistacchi* spent in Kavieng doing business, the Schmidts strolled up the casuarina-flanked road from the harbour to the township, stopping only for a cool drink in the bar of the Kavieng Hotel before returning to Bagil Wharf. There was just an hour or so of daylight left when they boarded the vessel for some of the overnight leg of its run to Namatanai, the other main trading depot on Neumecklenberg. It had been arranged that the Schmidts would be dropped off at the Gethsemane wharf, which the *Ann Pistacchi*'s captain expected to reach a little after nightfall. The wharf was something of an anomaly on Neumecklenberg's eastern coast, which was made up almost entirely of sheer cliffs bordered with dense barriers of sharp, hard corals. Gethsemane's harbour existed only because of its unusual depth, which made it worth the trouble of dynamiting away the corals that grew over the mouth of the entrance.

The *Ann Pistacchi* made poor time down the coast, battling against the newly arrived trade winds that Bernard said were a sign that a big blow was coming in fast. The dusk had been and gone before Bernard, on the prow with the mate, who was holding a lantern, sighted a familiar landmark: two coconut palms entwined on the point before the entrance to Gethsemane's harbour. He shouted and the captain, standing with Marta on the bridge, nodded, happy that they had reached the bay before the storm struck. The first spits of wind-driven rain were already splattering against the roof and windows of the bridgehouse and the captain knew they had only minutes to spare. Once alongside the wharf the Schmidts were hurriedly bundled off the vessel. Bernard clutched a lamp, and in his other hand he held a small valise of the bare necessities, which included not much more than a few tins of food and a bottle of schnapps. The rest of their belongings would be unloaded by the mate and the cabin-native when the storm had passed.

'Come on, Liebling,' Bernard whispered in Marta's ear, his lips forming a soundproof seal against the building cries of the wind and crashing sea. 'Not far now.'

Then, as if someone had turned on a great faucet above, the rain arrived, falling in great wind-chased sheets that soaked them in seconds. Without looking back to where the *Ann Pistacchi* was already pushing off, Marta and Bernard stumbled down the wharf through the torrential rain, pushing against the wind that tore at their clothes. Marta's hair was pulled almost instantly from its pile on top of her head to snake over her shoulders and down her back in thick, drenched coils. Above the wharf there was a track up to the plantation's bungalow, its entrance barely discernible in the darkness and density of the shoreline foliage. Up the path, awash with flash flooding, they struggled. More than once Marta fell into the river of mud beneath her feet but hauled herself up and continued without complaint.

Then, all of a sudden, there it was. Gethsemane. The house Bernard had started to build almost a decade and a half before and never quite got around to finishing. The feeble light of the lamp revealed two tall white concrete piles framing the wide concrete stairs that led up, beyond the pool of light, to what Marta assumed correctly would be a verandah and then a front door. The sight thrilled her a little, though she was sincerely hoping, as she followed Bernard up the stairs, that this house, now her entire world, wouldn't simply be picked up by the hand of God and dashed mercilessly back against the land before she'd even had a chance to see it in daylight. Bernard pushed open the door and they fell into the frowsty interior, panting, drenched with sweat and rain, liberally bespattered with mud and completely exhausted. Gethsemane's houseboy, Masta Raus, knowing of Masta Schmidt's imminent return, had left everything as it always had been, so Bernard, even after such a long absence, knew on which tables there would be lamps. Moving swiftly, he lit one after another, illuminating the sparsely furnished interior of the central room with a soft glow. Despite her fear, for the storm was still building in intensity, Marta was enraptured.

'I knew instantly,' she would write in her memoirs many years later, 'that Gethsemane would be my best and my most enduring love. And because of that I never once regretted my decision to come here, to Neuguinea, to live amongst the cannibals and coconuts in the time of quinine, in spite of everything that happened both before and after the war.'

The cookhouse, with its fires extinguished because of the wind, was out in the garden in any case, so they ate cold food from tins that night, using heavy silver flatware that Bernard unearthed from a drawer. The next morning Marta would notice how tarnished the knives and forks they had used were and shudder in faint horror.

Later, lying in bed with Bernard snoring like a walrus beside her, the sheets damp and sticky with humidity and the noise of the storm all around her, Marta thought she would never sleep, and yet she did. Almost instantly. She woke just the once in the night, confused and disorientated. The rain had stopped and the wind had moved on so that an eerie quiet, strangely louder than the tempest, seemed to have fallen. And yet when she listened there was the sound of the nocturnal insects who were tentatively creeping out into the dripping darkness and setting up their stridulating orchestras of rasping music, joining the cacophony of croaking amphibians, the cries of the night birds and the incessant drip-drip-drip of water on the boards of the wide verandah outside and, of course, Bernard's breathing, now teetering on the brink of snores. All seemed well at Gethsemane so Marta closed her eyes and slept once more, dreaming of nothing she would be able to recall the next day.

With the Schmidts finally packed off to Neumecklenberg, Royal was finally freed of his hosting duties. He stocked up on provisions at Herbertshohe and slowly headed south to Cape Gazelle. He had barely been home since Rebecca had gone and a slow ache of longing settled into his bones as familiar landmarks came and went. The sun was setting when Royal rounded the final corner of the casuarinas avenue and saw his house. Tomai was waiting in the garden by the stairs, the sunset painting his ebony skin with fire.

As they embraced Royal buried his face in the curve of the Buka boy's long, slender neck, inhaling deeply. Tomai smelt of the earth, its very essence. 'My boy, my boy,' Royal murmured, his voice choked with emotion and desire, his cock already hardening as he ran his hands greedily down the boy's back, stroking the silky ribbons of the keloids that welted the hot black skin. And for the first time in years he felt an immense sense of peace.

Ten

✳ The land in East Neuguinea more than resisted our efforts to conquer it, it visibly pushed back. I always felt that we were there under sufferance and the moment we abandoned the country it would simply sigh and remake itself exactly as it had been before we arrived.

Marta, *Neuguinea Memoirs*, Heyward & Barge,
London, 1949, p. 218

By mid-morning, when Marta woke alone, the sun had been out for hours and the humidity had already crushed any hint of coolness out of the day. The thin cotton sheet had been dragged down the length of the bed, leaving Marta's breasts and most of one leg uncovered for all the world to see if it had wished. She hurriedly dragged the sheet back over her body and looked to the windows, expecting to see a host of leering native faces peering in at her pale nakedness. But there was no one, just the bright crimson of the bougainvillea that grew up the verandah: an explosion of colour that cast a pink saturated light across the white walls and pale wooden floors. Each flower was a perfectly formed paper lantern, like the ones she'd seen in a Chinese emporium in Sydney. Bernard may have left the bed but his scent remained and Marta breathed in deeply, savouring the slightly rank maleness of spilled semen and sweat. Marta touched her belly. The skin was cool and tight under her fingers and she wondered whether a child had been conceived the night before when they'd made love in the madness of the storm. She didn't know if she really wanted a child, but Bernard did, and it seemed like the next logical step. If she did have a baby, would she be able to love it? Would she somehow find that capability in herself, or would her maternal instincts fail her again?

Marta threw back the sheet, and climbed down from the bed, which was a high wooden creation with a coconut fibre mattress. A disintegrating book propped up a short leg. Just for a moment Marta revelled in the feel of her own unclothed skin before bending and retrieving her damp and filthy chemise and Mother Hubbard from the bedroom floor where Bernard had dropped them the night before. The clothing clung unpleasantly, clammy against Marta's skin, but this did little to quell her excitement as she pushed open the bedroom door and walked barefoot through the house she had seen the night before only in disparate puddles of artificial light.

Used to the stuffy overcluttered rooms of Vienna, Marta was still unnerved by the emptiness of homes here in Neuguinea, and the bungalow at Gethsemane was emptier than most. However, though not as palatial as Gunantambu or many of the other long-established plantation homes she had visited in the past fortnight, the house was more than adequate, and in truth lacked only a woman's touch. It mattered not that the windows were bare or that there was an odd leak here and there, nor that the floorboards were unpolished and warped in some places because they'd been insufficiently cured before laying or that there were just four rooms. By building up high over the harbour rather than next to the sea, and clearing a minimum of the rainforest from around the dwelling, Bernard had ensured that, if nothing else, Gethsemane was a cool haven from the relentless, punishing heat of the tropics. It was the building's one and only element of genius.

Finding no kitchen in the bungalow, Marta concluded that, as with most Neuguinea houses, the cooking quarters were outside in the garden. As she had suspected, behind the bungalow was a shack constructed of corrugated iron with a smoking chimney at one end. Sitting outside it were two Oriental men. Knowing nothing of the language of the East, or Neuguinea for that matter, Marta pointed at the coffee pot sitting to the side of the hearth inside the shanty and said 'coffee' first in German, then in English. Fortunately they understood her perfectly and moments later she had a substantial drinking vessel made of enamel-covered tin, filled with what she would soon learn was bitter locally grown coffee from Toma, up in the hills behind Herbertshohe. There was no milk and the sugar, in a treacle tin beside the stove, had a few dead ants in it which, she discovered, tainted the liquid unpleasantly with the acid they secreted. With her mug in one hand and a farinaceous tea biscuit, which the men had insisted she have, in the other, Marta wandered back across the lawn to the house. On the verandah, she settled into a cane chair and looked with pleasure over the descending canopy of the rainforest to the harbour below. The shallow waters of the lagoon silently echoed the empty deep azure of the sky above: the *Ann Pistacchi* had unloaded the Schmidts' supplies and luggage and sailed before first light.

As Marta sat on the verandah at Gethsemane for the first time, waiting for the coffee to wake her properly and the sun to dry her damp clothes, another layer of her Neuguinea experience was spreading itself over the map of her past. So inevitable was this process of new memory covering old cartography, that, in years to come, she would struggle to recall the first third of her life in the northern hemisphere – the mineral smell and taste of Vienna fog; the blossom on the fruit trees in spring; the loudness of the city; the sound of her own footsteps on the marble floor of the Naturhistorisches Museum when she walked through the galleries to her father's office; and the time in Gibraltar and the following winter, when she was sequestered in the castle on her grandparents' Bavarian estate. Marta would never forget the food, though, the butter and cream and venison and chocolate and ice cream and foie gras. And the fruit and vegetables they never saw in the tropics – strawberries; early-season plums; plump, furry peaches, warm with sun; glorious Hungarian apricots, perfect, small and sweet.

The tastes of an almost forgotten homeland would come unbidden to her tongue, and she would find herself hungering for them so much that she was almost brought to tears.

All around her the rainforest, the skies and even the rafters of the bungalow roof exploded and hummed with the activity of creatures, both seen and unseen. Strange birds swooped from tree to tree, chattering among themselves and shrieking their hosannas into the skies. A bright green lizard, its body no bigger than Marta's smallest finger, scuttled across the boards of the verandah, its tail absent, left somewhere else to distract a predator. It stopped near her feet, opening and shutting its golden eyes in slow contemplation. And the reptile might have stayed there, if it hadn't caught, through the sensitive pads of its feet, the seismic hum of human approach and scuttled abruptly away. A few seconds later Marta heard voices and looked expectantly in the direction of the bush-shrouded path that led up from the harbour. Yes, there it was, Bernard's voice as he chivvied a handful of natives carrying their belongings and supplies up the hill from the wharf. Marta was relieved that Bernard was back. After the months of living with strangers at close quarters on various vessels and in hotels, she found the lack of human habitation at Gethsemane more unsettling than she'd expected.

'Frau Schmidt,' shouted Bernard in German as he appeared out of the foliage, followed by a procession of natives. He was red faced and large circles of sweat soaked the underarms of his white suit. 'I bring you treasure from the other side of the world.' Bernard strode up the stairs and swept Marta up into his arms, his moustaches tickling her ear as he whispered an endearment that she didn't quite catch and most probably wouldn't have believed in any case.

'Bernard! Put me down,' Marta gasped, also speaking in their native tongue, which was something of a joy after two weeks spent conversing almost entirely in English. 'What will the servants think?'

Bernard roared with laughter. 'They'll think what I want them to think,' he said, but returned her to terra firma all the same. He looked over his shoulder and barked something that caused the porters to drop their loads at the foot of the stairs and scuttle back down the track. He turned back to Marta. 'Find a clean dress and put your boots on, I have a surprise.'

Even the effort of finding fresh clothing caused sweat to trickle down Marta's spine and between the twin apples of her buttocks. There was a slight sting as the salt in her sweat came into contact with chafed skin. It was the heat, Bernard had told her, that caused the rust-coloured prickly rashes, the bane of every white person in the tropics, to bloom like noxious flowers on tortured skin. By the time Marta had put her boots on, fossicked through one of her trunks at the bottom of the stairs for a clean Mother Hubbard and gone back inside, Bernard was seated on an ornately carved oriental throne, one of only four chairs in the entire house, drinking his first schnapps of the day.

Bernard drained his glass. 'Ready?' he asked, speaking once again in English. After so many years in the colony it had become more comfortable than his mother tongue.

'Yes,' Marta replied, also in English.

'Excellent.' Bernard stood and took the dress from her, stuffing it into a native bag made of woven coconut fronds.

Outside, in the noonday sun, the land smoked and steamed as the rain from the night before evaporated back into the sky from which it had come. Marta staggered as they left the shadow of the bungalow, suddenly light-headed from the press of heat. Bernard took her arm and asked, 'Are you unwell, Liebling?'

'No, no,' replied Marta. 'It's just so hot. For a moment I felt faint, but I'm sure it's nothing. I'm all right now.'

Still holding her arm, Bernard led Marta around the back of the bungalow, past the kitchen quarters and across the patch of coarse grassed lawn to a break in the foliage and the beginnings of a track. As they stepped once again into shadows, the rainforest swallowed them in its cool dripping, embrace. But the feeling of relief was short-lived as the path began to climb steeply upwards and any illusion that this was a gentle stroll vanished completely. The perspiration poured down Marta's body, soaking the bodice of yesterday's dress, and a blister was forming on her left heel as her wet wool stocking creased and began to rub. Oblivious to her distress, Bernard was happily pointing out various examples of flora and fauna, using their generic or native names, barely looking behind him.

'Bernard! Bernard! Stop, stop right now,' Marta shouted some twenty minutes later. Bernard turned to gaze upon his wife, who was standing with her hands on her hips, breathing heavily. Her inadequately secured hair clung to her sweat-beaded and flushed face. 'For the love of Gott, show a little mercy and slow down,' continued Marta. 'I can't keep up, Bernard. It's too much. It's the heat, I'm not used to it. I must catch my breath and then we can proceed at a more moderate pace, I think.'

'I'm sorry,' Bernard said, thinking, in a rare show of intuitiveness, that this was perhaps not the time to point out a huge tree python that was draped on a branch overhead watching them impassively, its forked tongue flickering in and out of its mouth. 'Here I am dragging you through the jungle, not thinking … I am a Dummkopf.'

'We just need to slow down,' said Marta, feeling a little more reasonable in the face of his obvious contrition. 'Is it much further?' she added, her tone softer now.

'No, not at all. Just a hundred metres or so. Not far at all.'

'Then lead the way,' said Marta. 'But slower, Bernard.'

'Are you sure, Liebling?'

'Well,' replied Marta, squaring her shoulders. 'I've come this far, haven't I?'

True to Bernard's word, the tall trees of the rainforest soon began to thin noticeably and more and more sunlight pierced the leaf canopy above, painting the floor of the jungle and its nascent undergrowth with shifting gold. Butterflies flitted through the filtered sunlight. Then, as Marta and Bernard rounded a bend in the path, the rainforest abruptly opened out into a clearing where the most beautiful and welcome sight that Marta could possibly have imagined was waiting for her: a tree-shaded pool fed by a small waterfall that tumbled from the rocks above.

'See,' said Bernard triumphantly, 'wasn't that worth the walk?' In spite of her considerable discomfort, Marta was completely lost for words. 'Magnificent, isn't it?' Bernard continued, leading the way across the clearing to the pool's edge.

'Oh mein Gott, look at that, how beautiful.' Marta gasped as she realised that butterflies hovered in their thousands across the surface of the water like a vast, exotic, undulating carpet. 'How marvellous it was,' she wrote that night in her journal, 'to see them so vividly alive, even if those lives are unimaginably short, rather than speared on fine wires and arranged in false flight inside a museum cabinet.'

'Sit, sit,' said Bernard, leading her to a flat-topped rock at the pool's edge. Kneeling at Marta's feet, Bernard unlaced her boots and pulled off her stockings. He clucked with concern when he saw the bloody, smeared skin on her left heel.

'We'll have to look after that,' he said. 'The slightest scratch can go septic so easily out here.'

'Really?' replied Marta, examining the raw patch on her heel. 'But it looks so unimportant.'

'Believe me,' her husband said. 'See this.' He rolled up the left sleeve of his shirt past the elbow and showed her an old faded scar the size of a Vesta box, which she had noticed a number of times and been too shy to ask about. 'This was a mosquito bite once. It happened when I first came here and didn't know about such things. You mustn't scratch. Insect bites, those are the worst. They can turn bad overnight.'

Marta nodded guiltily. Only that morning she had been furiously tearing with her fingernails at the mosquito bites that covered her legs. With Marta's boots and stockings removed and her clean dress, in its native bag, stowed under a sheltering rock, Bernard turned his attention to the garment his wife was wearing.

'What *are* you doing?' said Marta as he started to unbutton the front of the shapeless cotton dress. Their previous encounters of the flesh had taken place in the privacy of their bedroom and the lights had been extinguished well before any disrobing had taken place. 'I can't. What if people see? What if someone's watching?'

'Nobody's watching. The natives think the place is tambu, bewitched,' said Bernard, taking one of her hands in his own. 'Besides,' he continued, taking a fold of skirt fabric between the thumb and index finger of his other hand, 'you can't bathe wearing this. It's hopelessly impractical.' Bernard, with rare insight, recognised the moment of capitulation in his wife's eyes and quickly set about divesting her of her outer layer of clothing before she could change her mind. He gently pulled the bodice from her shoulders, exposing her small high breasts, which he found incredibly erotic, especially shrouded by the gauzy, sweat-stained cotton lawn of her chemise. An ugly rust-coloured heat rash had spread over her breastbone and up the left side of her neck. He bent his head and gentle kissed the inflamed skin. 'The water will help soothe this,' he promised. 'Now stand.' He helped Marta up so that the dress fell around her feet, like a wind-torn flower. 'There, isn't that better?'

Although the frosting of mist created by the waterfall was so wonderfully cool that she nearly shuddered with delight, Marta had never felt so exposed and instinctively shielded herself from her husband's gaze with her arms and hands. Scrambling clumsily to the edge of the pool, she slid into the water, crying out as the icy water hit her overheated flesh and the raw spot on her heel. Moments later, bare as a newborn, Bernard joined his wife in the water, swimming with slow, easy strokes out into the centre of the pool, where she floated, treading water while the butterflies made an agitated frenzy of colour above her bobbing head. Without a word, Bernard closed in on his wife until his body was brushing against hers almost imperceptibly as the effort of staying afloat moved them backwards and forwards like seaweed catching an ocean current. Marta looked down through the endless, sun-spotted chartreuse depths of the pool. Through the glaucous haze their naked bodies looked as if they were carved from restless jade.

A tremor of desire, a want that Bernard had proved particularly adept at igniting in her, revealed itself in the altered quality of Marta's breathing as Bernard pulled her towards him, wrapping his arms around her waist so that she could succumb entirely without fear of drowning. Weightless in the water and tethered to him, she moved like a length of wet silk, completely at the mercy of the movement of liquid around her and the will of her husband. As Bernard drove his tongue into the moist depths of her mouth, Marta grunted – a primal, organic noise that came from the bottom of her belly and rose up through her throat, travelling from her mouth to Bernard's own.

The sound, which would have mortified Marta had she realised she'd made it, excited Bernard tremendously and he hurriedly dragged his wife back to the edge of the pool. With one arm under her bent knees and the other around her shoulders, he lifted Marta out of the water and carried her to where the grass was long and soft. The cotton of Marta's chemise had been rendered transparent by the water so that her cleft and her breasts, with their cold hard nipples, were clearly visible through the cloth. Moments later it was all over. Their unconscious, uninhibited cries still echoed through the jungle as they clung to each other panting, waiting for their heartbeats to ebb.

Nothing had prepared either Marta or Bernard for the chemistry between them and it was one of the very few parts in her life that Marta would never talk of to anyone, and on the odd occasion when she felt herself compelled to write in her journal of this carnality that Bernard inspired in her, she would neatly tear the page out of her journal and burn it. Sometimes she wondered if it *was* love, this physical hunger that they had for each other. Perhaps for some this was how love manifested itself. And for a while this was enough.

* * *

Marta lost the child conceived on the night of the ball at Gunantambu, in the ninth week. It was so uneventful, this loss of an unrealised life, no more than a heavy bleed, that she decided to save her tears for other sadnesses and said nothing to Bernard.

Eleven

✳ I am quite recovered from my first attack of malarial fever. You mustn't worry it's a commonplace enough occurrence, and Bernard was terribly good as a nurse and fed me the hateful bitter quinine dissolved into schnapps three times a day until the fever broke. He says the attack was mild and that I have now required a degree of immunity from the illness which I know Papa is sure to laugh at and say that *that* is an old wife's tale. However this is what the colonists believe and much of science and exploration is after all, anecdotal as you have often said, Papa.

Marta, letter, 17 March 1905

Egon Mueller was tremendously tickled as his wife read out the latest letter to arrive from Neuguinea, to the family in the library. 'Our Marta. Yes,' he said to Klara. 'She has a good mind.' He stopped and sighed. 'But Bernard …'

'Yes,' agreed Klara. They had both noticed that Marta wrote almost doggedly of the sky and sea and everything in between, but very little of herself and her marriage. The letters were neither happy nor sad; in fact they were precisely as Marta herself had been for so long now. Her parents had hoped that her insistence on marrying Bernard was the result of some sort of hopelessly rose-tinted love, that their eldest daughter had shaken off the inertia that had seized her heart. But no, here it was, page after page of proof that she may have been sweltering in the tropical heat, but was as frozen as ever. 'What happened to our little girl?' Klara would mourn, as if she didn't know the reason.

'But I like Bernard,' protested Augusta, not understanding why Egon and Klara pulled such long faces. 'Just because he's not clever …you know clever isn't everything.'

'No,' said Egon very emphatically. 'You're right, of course, my little maid. It's not everything.'

'But it's something,' concluded Klara.

✳ ✳ ✳

With Bernard away from the bungalow most days and Masta Raus and the cookie-boys melting away like lard on a hot tin plate come afternoon, Marta was often completely alone in the house and very quickly found herself left with an increasingly evident pocket of emptiness that she had to fill. Most women out here had children to occupy the endless stretches of time in their lives. Marta supposed motherhood would happen to her too, when her body deemed it should, and soon enough she would be writing letters to Ettie and her mother complaining that she would do anything for a bit of peace and quiet. The decorating of the house had been tremendous fun, much more so than she'd expected, not being particularly domestic in nature. Her quest to procure items that would make her and Bernard's lives considerably more comfortable had involved countless letters, to Royal Weston especially. The most wonderful thing Royal had found for her was a cast-iron bath with claw feet. It had been criminally expensive, but Marta had discovered, having taken over the surprisingly well-kept plantations accounts, that Bernard was considerably wealthier than he'd ever let on, and would become even more so, as the plantation, one of the first to be established, was just coming into the peak of its production. She doubted whether her husband had ever really spent his money on anything beyond basic survival, so the bath was purchased without consultation – Bernard had nearly choked when he saw the price entered in the books – and a bath-house of native construction was built in the garden at Gethsemane. And now every afternoon Masta Raus lit a fire beneath the washing copper and filled it with water, so that by nightfall the water was wonderfully warm for their baths.

The only decorative note in the entire place had been an unframed portrait hung above the desk in the room Bernard used as his office, obviously painted by Royal Weston, of Bernard in his dress whites and solar topee, the rainforest hovering behind his right shoulder. Like the paintings Marta had seen at Cape Gazelle, this was rendered in bright blocks of primary colour, on thin, slightly warped wood. Only the desk in the office and painting had survived her purge. The bed, the four rotting chairs and the homemade table had all gone out the door to be shared among the plantation staff.

Marta's writing, too, both in the many letters she sent off to Neupommern and Vienna and the detailed daily entries in her journal, had conspired to keep her more or less entertained since her arrival in Neuguinea. But her impressions, for she couldn't think what else to write about other than what she saw in front of her, were beginning to pall with repetition. One day in the territory, Marta was discovering, was much like the next and the distractions were few. In short, she realised one day, a year after her arrival in Neuguinea, that she was bored. Her grand project à la Merian had been preying on her mind of late. After all, her heroine had managed to complete her project in just two years, and yet here she was, with half of that time gobbled up, and not even started.

It was hard to make a beginning, thought Marta, stretching voluptuously before placing both her feet firmly on the boards of the verandah where she'd installed a newly acquired bamboo chaise lounge, when one has all the time in the world. With the recent cessation of the rains, plants had begun to flower in profusion and the wildlife had been compelled into a frenzy of activity. It was a sign, she concluded as she stood up, that she should do something about the task she'd set herself back in Vienna when she had decided that she would accept Bernard's proposal.

When she and Masta Raus had unpacked the things that Marta had carried with her halfway across the world from Vienna, the drawing folio, pencils, paper and paints had been stored away in the small room at the back of the bungalow that served as the plantation office. It didn't take more than a few moments to find them.

'Oh no!' she exclaimed as she opened up the oblong boxes of paints and pastels. All the art materials were dried out and crumbly and the pencils and charcoal looked distinctly chewed. Drifts of powdery colour sifted together like colour-saturated desert sand through the interiors of the various boxes. Marta licked a finger and touched it to the violet disc of a colour that was more or less intact. The synthesis of colour and moisture stained the pad of her finger, proving that all wasn't entirely lost.

Marta spent the remainder of the afternoon sitting on the top step of the bungalow, conserving as much as she could. The oils were completely ruined – the cockroaches had chewed through the lead of the tubes and eaten the colour inside – and a great many of the watercolour discs had dried to dust and were visibly disintegrating as she disturbed them. But she managed to save enough to start with. That evening she would write to Royal, appeal to him as a fellow artist, to aid her in her task of procuring new materials.

The first line on a page, when Marta picked up a pencil and began to draw the next day, was tentative. Three strokes later the flaw created by the first touch of lead to paper was fully revealed and she started again, on the same piece of paper. Soon enough both sides were covered with steadily improving illustrations of the waxy frangipani flower, with its clean, uniform lines, that sat on the table in front of her. Marta looked at the drawings with some pleasure, relieved that the little talent she possessed hadn't totally deserted her but had simply grown a little creaky from lack of use. They weren't wonderful drawings by any means, but they were definitely a step in the right direction. It had been, she decided, a productive morning. So much so that all through lunch she itched for Bernard to go back to the plantation so that she could attempt a large-scale drawing of a more complex and colourful flower, perhaps a hibiscus, with a view to tinting it with the remaining watercolours.

Finally he left and Marta set up her painting things on the dining table found on a rare trip to Kavieng, in the central room of the bungalow where, with the afternoon sun slanting in, the light was best. On the completion of her first specimen painting, a mauve hibiscus with a blood-red stamen, Marta ran a critical eye over her own endeavours, seeing only the inadequacies and none of the charm that the somewhat clumsy watercolour contained. Although the pencilled outlines of the flower were competent enough, the colours were not true – the purples too deep, the greens too bright – and the paint had dried with a slight grittiness due to its compromised quality.

Marta had just tucked the dry painting into her folio of foxed and mildewed drawing papers when Bernard returned to the house. The afternoon had quickly and quietly trickled away. She joined Bernard on the verandah, sitting on the top step of the concrete staircase, as he poured them both water tumblers of schnapps and quinine-enhanced tonic, from the newly acquired drinks trolley. There was no ice: the freezer box had run out of kerosene a few days before.

'Thank you,' Marta said, taking the glass from him. She closed her eyes and leaned back against the balustrade.

Bernard sat in the shadows of the eaves, having had enough sun for one day, and together, in a peaceful sleepy silence broken only by the sounds of the rainforest, the Schmidts watched the day die. While the last fiery streaks of colour painted the sky the colours of molten earth, the bats took flight, their squeaks shattering the peace as they took to the night skies in search of sustenance.

'The natives say they make good eating,' Bernard commented as the last of the bats vanished into the incoming darkness. Marta, who found the thought quite revolting, made no comment. 'Captain Macco from Ulul-Nono called in today,' Bernard continued. 'A message came over his wireless yesterday afternoon that the Parkinsons are at last to come to Gethsemane. To honour us by staying for a few days.'

✳ ✳ ✳

The Forsayth and Co. steamer, which the Parkinsons had borrowed from Emma Kolbe, docked at the Schmidt plantation wharf one afternoon a few weeks later. Much to Marta's delight, the Parkinsons were accompanied by Ettie and Marie Allen. The guestroom at Gethsemane, now filled with a bed bought from a sold-up German plantation owner on Neumecklenberg's western coast, was taken by Ettie. The Parkinsons had arranged for themselves and Marie to stay with Captain Macco at the considerably more palatial Ulul-Nono a few kilometres away.

The excursion to Port Breton, to look at the few architectural remains of the Marquis de Rays' folly, had been Ettie's idea. She had discovered over the dinner table at Gethsemane on the second night of their visit, that Marta had never seen the ruins of La Nouvelle France.

'Such an interesting story,' sighed Phoebe.

'Yes, yes, fascinating, isn't it?' agreed Captain Macco.

'Were you at Ulu-Nono then?' asked Bernard.

'No,' Macco replied. 'I was still with Hernsheim, at the Finschhaffen station.'

'Those poor people. They would have died without Emma and Captain Farrell,' continued Phoebe. 'I remember when the survivors were brought out from the settlement – they were mere shambling skeletons. A week or two more and I doubt any of them would have made it. Such a scandal.'

'And so thoroughly swindled out of their money,' added Ettie, cutting into a sweet potato and popping a chunk delicately in her mouth.

'When did this happen?' asked Marta.

'Maybe twenty years ago now,' Richard Parkinson replied. 'That that would be right, wouldn't it, Phoebe?' 'Longer,' said his wife. 'It was 1882, I think, when Emma and Farrell took them off.'

'Yes, it would have been,' agreed Macco. 'It was '87 when I resigned from Hernsheim and bought Ulul-Nono and the de Rays affair was by then considered old history.'

'And the marquis himself, he was there?' asked Marta. 'Leading his people?'

'No, no,' laughed Richard. 'That's the best, well, the most dreadful part really. The man had never left France, had never even seen the land on which he proposed to create this settlement. If starvation hadn't killed the colonists, the malaria and dengue would have. It was a madness, it really was.'

'And these people paid the marquis for the privilege of going there?' asked Marta.

'Yes,' replied Richard. 'I've always rather admired him on that count. It shows tremendous business acumen.'

'Oh Richard!' exclaimed Phoebe, 'how could you? The man was a fraudster of the worse kind. People lost their lives or their loved ones because of him.'

'He ended up in an insane asylum, didn't he?' asked Bernard, who was happily ploughing his way through an entire roasted fowl.

'That's the popular belief,' replied Richard. 'However I understand he was tried in France on a myriad of charges relating to the fraud, found guilty and spent six years in gaol.'

'How interesting,' said Marta. 'And you say it's just a short trip down the coast?'

'Yes,' said Richard, 'half a day's sail, no more.'

'So,' said Ettie, looking very pleased. 'It sounds to me as though an excursion to Port Breton is in order.'

The next morning, as dawn was streaking the skies, Ettie, Marie, the Schmidts and the Parkinsons, on board Emma's steamer, were well on their way down the coast of Neumecklenberg to Port Breton. They arrived just before midday, anchoring offshore in a sheltered bay. The crew lowered a clinker over the side, into which they carefully climbed, via a rope ladder. With the main company disembarked on the sliver of white sand at Irish Cove, the clinker returned to the ship to bring over the steamer staff and the provisions for their picnic. After exploring the few remains of the settlement – a number of scattered bricks stamped with the marquis's initials, the millstone and water-race – they sat on blankets spread over the sandy soil, beneath the coconut palms that fringed the bay. Marta fell into conversation with Richard, who was preparing to go for a walk before lunch to look, as he had many times before, at the local flora, to see if there was anything he had missed and needed to collect for the botanical gardens in Rabaul. The gardens, which he had established only two years before, already abounded in specimens that he had gathered and nurtured, and had gained a degree of maturity that would have taken years, if not decades, to achieve in a northern European climate.

'May I accompany you on your walk?' Marta asked. 'I'm something of an enthusiast of natural history and enjoy painting specimens, though my talent is small. I've been lucky enough to have Maria Sibylla Merian's *Metamorphosis Insectorum Surinamensium* as an inspiration – my father had one in his personal library. I've also been able to peruse Ferdinand Bauer's collected works, which I admire very much, a number of times at the Vienna Naturhistorisches Museum.' She *was* boasting, she knew that, but Marta was desperate to impress upon this learned man that she wasn't entirely stupid, even if her husband had a tendency to obtuseness.

'So,' said Richard, stroking his long beard. He was rather taken by Frau Schmidt's fervour. 'Perhaps you wish to paint the creatures and flora of Neuguinea as Merian did in Surinam.'

'Well …,' started Marta, with a tone of protest in her voice as if this thought had never occurred to her.

'Now, now,' said Richard, 'don't be disingenuous, Frau Schmidt. It's an admirable idea and I'm very much impressed by admirable women with admirable ideas.'

Marta pulled a self-deprecating face. 'My own drawings thus far have proved to be vastly humbled by those of artists like Merian and Bauer. However, I am undaunted and have just taken delivery of new art supplies from Sydney, courtesy of Mr Royal Weston, so at least I should try.'

Richard smiled. 'I have great faith in you, Frau Schmidt. I think you will contribute as much to natural history as Merian.'

Pushing through the undergrowth, following a track made years before by the Nouvelle France colonists and kept relatively clear by the not infrequent invasion of expatriate tourists like themselves, the pair spent a highly enjoyable hour wandering around a small area of the rainforest, not far inland from where they had landed. Charmed to have such an astute and avid listener, Richard started peeling back the layers of the natural world of Neuguinea so that Marta could see a little at least of this wonderful, verdant land that he carried always in his heart and mind and dreams. He pointed out birds, lizards, gigantic spider webs with their makers poised in their very centres, lazy watchful snakes in the branches above and beckoning parasitic blooms.

When the visitors boarded Emma's steamer a few days later to return to Herbertshohe, Richard promised that he would send Marta some books on South Pacific natural history as soon as he was home. As the steamer disappeared from view Marta felt an intense wave of happiness. She knew she'd made a great friend in Ettie, and even Royal Weston, and now she hoped she could number Richard Parkinson in her cadre. There was something about this land, she thought, walking up the hill to the bungalow, unconscious of how unaffected she was by the heat. Something that made knowing people so much easier.

After the Parkinsons and Ettie had left, Marta wrote in her journal:

It has occurred to me how little Bernard and I know of each other. And the fault is not entirely his, I must admit, for although he is most definitely not the most garrulous of men, I haven't been entirely dedicated to the task of extracting his story from him. What are the things I know about him that I can't see with my eyes? Not very much, I'm afraid. I will have to coax him, I think to reveal his true history.

As it happened, Bernard was more than happy to divulge the details of his past life to his wife once she took the time to sit with him and ask – embarrassingly happy, in fact. It had never occurred to him, until Marta asked, that he himself would be a compelling subject on which to pontificate. Finally, he had something to say to his new wife that didn't appear to make her eyes glaze over – well, initially at least. Some weeks later Marta was beginning to regret her decision. For in spite of being sent off to East Neuguinea in the early days of the colony, as a junior clerk in the employ of Hernsheim and Co., it appeared that Bernard had lived a life notable mainly for its complete unremarkability, though perhaps it *was* a little more fascinating than he made it seem. His story-telling style took the glister off even the odd snippets that were potentially interesting, such as how he'd first met Captain Macco, who arrived in the colony a few years after him to work for Hernsheim. Even his discovery of the little deep-water bay that suddenly made his land viable, and the waterfall in the hills high above where they now sat, all this richness Bernard somehow made dull. And oddly enough, the more he polished them, the less shiny these anecdotes became, worn relentlessly away by the monotonous tumble of words.

Poor Bernard. There was much more he might have told her, had they both been different people. About his terror at being sent away to school when he was eight, just days after he'd been forced to look upon his father's body in an open casket; how he'd been mercilessly bullied by the other boys for wetting his bed, an affliction he'd largely overcome in his senior years at the academy when he, the tortured, became the torturer. Not that his heart was ever in it and this, too, had set him apart from his peers. Bernard was not one of life's social animals, or leaders, by either example or force. Everything would always be hard for him. He'd thought, after leaving the academy without a backward glance, of following in his paternal grandfather and father's footsteps and buying a commission, but that had come to nothing. If being in the army had been entirely about war and killing, perhaps Bernard would have considered it more seriously, but he knew from his father's example that the wardroom would be just like school, and although he would wear the uniform of an officer, he never would really have the respect it should afford him. He also could have told Marta of the sense of freedom he'd felt the day he'd signed the contract at the Berlin offices of Hernsheim and Co. and collected the ticket that would take him to the other side of the world; how he never doubted that he'd made the right choice, no matter how miserable the pay and conditions promised to be. This was a clean canvas, a new start. A chance to be nothing more than who he was. None of this Bernard told Marta.

Nor could he, for obvious reasons, tell his wife that he'd loved each and every whore he'd paid over the previous two decades, how their obvious ennui, as he slapped away at their unresponsive cunts, had excited him immeasurably. Nor about his passion for Gloria, how the more cruel she'd been, the more he'd desired her. But of course he couldn't speak to Marta of these things, any more than he could tell her how she made him feel when she looked right through him as he spoke.

Twelve

Because it had been so very dry for so long, in a strange way Marta no longer remembered what rain was like. It seemed as if it *never* rained here, just south of the equator. Except ... yes. She remembered now. That first night she and Bernard had arrived here. Oh, how it had rained. Every other downfall since had simply become part of the fabric of her existence. Four years, Marta thought. I've been here four years. Where has the time gone?

Since her arrival at Gethsemane Marta had conceived twice that she knew of and lost both pregnancies in the first months. If she'd been a more fanciful woman, Marta would probably have seen it as God's will and subsequent punishment, but logic told her that something had gone irrevocably wrong with her reproductive system, and caused her womb to evict Bernard's babies one after another. Marta was for the most part philosophical about these losses. It wasn't as if she could even imagine herself as a mother. Babies and children had never held any appeal for her. Augusta had been five years old before Marta could bring herself to really acknowledge her existence. Her barrenness bothered Bernard, though. He wanted children. A whole tribe of little Baron and Baroness von Copras running around, shouting at natives and listening in riveted silence to their father's words of wisdom. The thought, however, made Marta shudder. She was always a little relieved when her monthly bleed arrived with the new moon and with it the knowledge that her routines, the way she'd organised her life, could carry on as before.

Royal had responded promptly to Marta's request for art supplies and the correspondence that had begun during the decorating of the Gethsemane bungalow had continued and expanded into the realms of philosophy and scientific theory. He also sent her books from his expansive library, which they would gleefully dissect slowly, letter by letter. Marta had occasion to reflect, on more than one occasion, that Royal was far better read than she – and, if she was completely honest with herself, a lot less pompous about it. Bernard thought nothing of the correspondence between his wife and best friend. And why would he, knowing, as he did, of Royal's predilection for his own sex.

Ettie Kaumann also wrote regularly, first from Neupommern, and, in this last year, from Europe, where she was travelling with her aunt Emma and Paul Kolbe, who were seeking a cure for their various ailments in the health clinics and sanatoriums of Europe. While her aunt and step-uncle were admitted into one of these institutions Ettie had journeyed to Vienna and called upon the Muellers.

'What a delight it was,' she wrote to Marta, 'to finally meet your people and see the house you grew up in. You're right about Augusta, she *is* very like Marie, whom Emma sent to boarding school in New South Wales to put a polish on her when we left for Europe last year. Sadly I didn't get to meet your other sister, Gretchen. Your charming mother said she was unwell and confined to her bed.'

A letter from Klara had arrived a few days after Ettie's, reiterating much of what Marta's friend had said, with the addition of an assurance that although Gretchen had been unwell during Frau Kaumann's visit, she was now quite recovered – a lie, as it happened – and a postscript from Gustie about how exotic Frau Kaumann was, and was it true that she was a South Pacific princess? Marta had laughed at that, though she supposed, in many ways, that Ettie, who was obviously Emma's heir apparent, was indeed royalty of sorts.

So although Marta's days didn't have a great deal of variety, she was actually more than happy with the slow rhythm they'd acquired over the years. There was her work, not just painting the specimens, but also observing them in their natural habitat as Richard Parkinson had encouraged her to do. Sometimes she *was* bored, and occasionally even lonely, but not often enough for these two states, which seemed the natural order of human experience, to be of possible concern. She'd even grown used to Bernard and the big, noisy way he filled up a room, and was attempting to be less judgemental about his intellectual limitations, and far more appreciative of a decent man trying to do his best. Because, without a doubt, all that Bernard did was well intentioned, within his own mind at least, and free of malice.

They'd fallen into the habit of going for long walks, in the late afternoon, unless it was pouring with rain, either along the coast or up to the waterfall in order to bathe. Marta, fully acclimatised and fitter too, found she kept up with her husband easily now, matching him stride for stride. During these walks, Marta would inevitably collect one or two specimens, usually floral in nature, to paint the next day, carrying the delicate blooms home carefully in her hands so as not to bruise their petals.

However, in spite of her successful acclimatisation, the heat that characterised the dry season of 1908 was another matter altogether. No one could remember it ever being so brutally hot. Even the natives were suffering: you could see it on their parched faces. The rainforest around the house at Gethsemane and up on the foothills and mountains remained, to the casual observer, as verdant as ever, though Marta had noted how much the undergrowth had shrivelled and died away as the trees, with their gigantic exposed buttress roots, had sucked every hint of moisture from the ground, leaving nothing for their shallow-rooted companions. Even the waterfall, fed by a subterranean spring somewhere deep beneath the earth's surface, was diminished by the long dry. It was covered almost entirely now by a thick blanket of butterflies, which had migrated there as other water catchments dried up and disappeared.

On the plantation itself, that vast expanse of flat land planted two decades before with row after row of *Cocos nucifera*, the grasses between the palms died and were bleached to ghosts of themselves by the relentless glare of the sun, though the coconuts themselves were seemingly unaffected by the conditions, locked into a continuous cycle of flowering, fertilisation and fruiting. But at least the mosquitoes, the plague of the Pacific, had almost entirely vanished. Their larvae, however, lay thick and oily on the surface of any hint of contained water, a meniscus of hibernation, waiting for the rains to arrive again, bringing them back to life.

Spontaneous fires that appeared out of thin air become increasingly frequent throughout the colony, and the smell of smoke was enough to strike fear into the heart of any planter. Drying sheds, bungalows and entire native villages burned to the ground.

'It would only take one spark,' Bernard told Marta, when he was holding forth on the subject, which he did often, and the drying shed, the plantation or even their bungalow could vanish in a cloud of smoke and the consuming crackle of flames in no more than a few minutes. The coconut palms were safe – the grass was so thin and dry that any flame would have to travel quickly in order to stay alight – but the plantation buildings were becoming increasingly combustible as even the essence of moisture was leached out of their organic materials. Each day Bernard looked at the sky and fretted volubly. He had organised for hessian sacks to be soaked in seawater at the start of each day. Once sopping, their fibres swollen and heavy with moisture, the sacks were laid around the foundations of the bungalow and various plantation buildings. Two near-naked piccaninnies were put in charge of replacing the sacks around the bungalow as they dried out. Scurrying around like two little ants, dragging the sodden sacks that weighed almost more than they did, up the hill from the shore, hour after hour they worked in the hot sun with Bernard roaring helpful advice at them from the verandah. Advice, Marta noticed, that the children, like their parents and other adult natives on the plantation, blithely ignored. The sight of her husband – ridiculous man! – with his chest puffed out, mercilessly bossing a pair of seven-year-olds around was altogether too much for Marta. Such a little Kaiser in his own kingdom. Baron von Copra indeed, she thought, amused, but just slightly irritated too. Augusta had been right. And that, too, was a source of abstracted annoyance.

Surely, Marta thought, one afternoon in early November as she lolled on the chaise on the verandah, fanning herself with an ivory fan Royal Weston had given her the Christmas before, surely it must rain soon. She sighed. It was so very hot and she lacked even the energy to read or draw or write. Bathing was the only thing that brought any comfort and soothed the scarlet rashes that covered her and Bernard's bodies. Not down at the lagoon, which the warm sea currents had turned tepid as bathwater, but up at the pool beneath the waterfall, which hadn't lost its subterranean chill, where they would float until they turned blue with cold.

Marta decided that she would go up to the waterfall now, by herself, rather than waiting another hour or two for Bernard to return. He can join me later, she concluded, snapping her fan shut with a satisfyingly loud clap.

She left a hastily scribbled note under the bottles on the drinks trolley, where Bernard was sure to find it, and with a lightness of heart set off. Without her husband to constantly hurry her along, Marta stopped often to peer into the sunlit depths of the jungle, taking her role of lady naturalist rather seriously. There was much to see: birds with feathers far more wonderful that anything that had evolved in Europe; lizards of every variety with skins that were intricate mosaics of colour; snakes barely visible as they wrapped themselves around branches that their scales replicated perfectly; sullen toads skulking under foliage at the path's edge; butterflies playing in the sunlight that pierced the leaf canopy above, their wings like stained glass. And then there were the spiders, resting in the centre of their intricate vibrating webs, waiting for their prey to blunder into their silken ambushes.

A large black and royal-blue swallowtail butterfly alighted on the sleeve of Marta's dress as she neared the waterfall and would not be shifted from its chosen perch. And because she was so enchanted by this living corsage Marta had almost stepped out into the clearing before she noticed a grey horse tethered and grazing on the still lush grass around the pool. It wasn't the one they used to pull the carriage and which Bernard rode periodically – that was a stocky chestnut mare, one of the famed Macassar ponies bred by Captain Macco. Marta knew this pretty horse, with its distinctive dappled body, dark legs and long silky mane and tail, but she couldn't remember from where.

The sound of voices from the pool caused Marta to pull back into the shadows as if she was an intruder, not the proprietress of this little piece of paradise. She recognised one of the voices, Bernard's, which surprised her: at this time of the day he was always down at the drying sheds. The other was a woman's, somehow familiar. Then Marta remembered where she'd seen the horse.

Some months before, shortly, in fact, after the rains had stopped, they'd been invited to visit the new owners of the neighbouring plantation to the south. It had been previously been the property of a solitary German called Konig, who hadn't encouraged visitors. That had been easy when there was no road, but the beautiful new highway that was being built under the titular auspices of Franz Boluminski, a district officer with the German Colonial Service, which would eventually run from Kavieng to Namatanai, had made such previously isolated plantations accessible. However the chance for social intercourse wasn't the only motivating factor in the Schmidts' acceptance of the invitation. The stories of the Millers and their financial excesses had kept Neumecklenberg agog for months. There was even a rumour that Ames Miller had shipped a pair of giraffes all the way to East Neuguinea, such was his extraordinary wealth and desire to please his wife, who, it was rumoured, was very beautiful.

The journey from Gethsemane took a little under half an hour and soon enough the horse drawing the Schmidts' carriage was trotting briskly along the Miller plantation driveway towards a large, newly built white bungalow that had something of its own flavour and style. Many years later, while studying crocodiles in Queensland. Marta would finally understand from where Ames Miller had taken the inspiration for his own dwelling. As they pulled up in front of the house, a trio of chattering sulphur-crested cockatoos alighted upon the thick, succulent branch of a nearby frangipani tree.

'Hello,' cried a man, coming out onto the verandah. His accent was Australian, similar to Royal Weston's, but coarser. 'You've arrived. Lovely! The boy will be here in a moment to take your horse.' He turned and shouted back into the depths of the house, 'The Schmidts are here, old girl. Get the billy on.'

Marta, though becoming inured to Neuguinea eccentrics, was a little taken aback by the informality of their unshaven neighbour's manner and attire. Ames Miller was wearing a distinctly grubby cotton shirt that was faded and badly frayed around the cuffs and collar, and an equally tatty pair of trousers, held up with a piece of string. His feet, stained with years of ingrained dirt, were bare, the heels horny and as cracked as dried-out mud. As Miller ushered them up the stairs of the bungalow, Marta brushed past him and caught the man's pungent, unwashed reek. He smelled, she thought, recalling the animals on her grandparent's estate, distinctly billy-goatish. But it wasn't entirely unpleasant. The cockatoos, perhaps sensing a departing audience, started bouncing up and down on their perch and shrieking furiously, a high-pitched tantivy that fractured the still air and halted the trio of humans in their tracks.

'They're terrible show-offs, as you can see,' said Miller, raising his voice to be heard above the raucous cackling. He walked back to the edge of the verandah and waved his arms. 'Bugger off, you lot. Go on. Shoo! Bugger off.'

The birds obliged, taking to the air. Marta, Ames and Bernard watched silently as the parrots drifted between the plane trees, pandanus and frangipani that rose from the newly established lawn, around to the kitchen at the back of the house.

'How wonderful it would be to fly,' observed Marta.

'Yes, I've always thought that it would be the very best thing to have wings,' replied Miller. 'When Pamela and I were on our honeymoon we had an opportunity to go up in a hot air balloon. Simply spectacular. If you ever get the chance, take it.'

At this point Pamela Miller, wondering what was taking her husband so long, appeared on the verandah. 'For goodness sake, Ames, the Schmidts must be dying of thirst. Bring them inside immediately,' she instructed. Marta was pleased to note that the stories of their hostess's amazing beauty were greatly exaggerated. Pamela Miller was, however, beautifully dressed in a pale white dress that was not dissimilar to Marta's own garment, but somehow better cut and of far superior fabric, and on her feet she wore soft white kid slippers like a ballerina's, which struck a feminine chord in Marta and which she immediately coveted.

Pamela Miller, English and in her early twenties, was fine boned, pretty, pleasingly plump and creamy skinned. She was in many ways quite ordinary, but somehow the combined effect of all her ordinary parts was aesthetically pleasing, giving her an aura of beauty she didn't perhaps actually possess. She was without obvious fault or flaw and somehow that was precisely what stopped her being a great beauty. Ames, an Australian descended, he said, from convicts, though Pamela rolled her eyes at that, was at least a decade, if not two, older than his wife.

As a boy newly out of short pants, Ames had set off on his own and become an opal miner who had struck it rich twice, first by finding the seam, then by selling his opal licence. Suddenly richer than he'd ever imagined, Ames had spent the next twenty years travelling the seven seas and all the territories between and voraciously reading books. Two years before moving to Neuguinea, he'd had been home in Australia, and exploring the possibility of settling in Melbourne, when he'd met Pamela Sneddon by chance on the train to Bacchus Marsh and had been smitten on sight. Pamela, for her part, hadn't been convinced at all.

Pamela had been in Melbourne for three years, having followed her father from England to Victoria once he'd given up his missionary work in China, and taken a parish in Bacchus Marsh. Joining her father in Australia was to be her big opportunity, but things hadn't quite worked out as she'd hoped. She ended up working as a teacher at a little school in St Kilda. Temperamentally she was ill qualified for teaching, which she saw merely as a means to an end – to pay her board and feed her need for the expensive French skin emollients that she bought from the chemists in Lonsdale Street, which was also home to all the city's best brothels. The pupils repulsed her with the malnourished, rank smell of their hideous little bodies, the near-constant presence of impetigo sores on their faces and the lice in their filthy hair. It was only when she was back in her clean little room, massaging those soft white creams into her dry pale skin, that Pamela felt the anger at her life begin to dissipate. On Sundays, with her skin smelling of roses and violets, she would walk the gilded tree-shrouded streets of Toorak and wonder what it would be like to be rich.

Once their courtship had begun in earnest Pamela began to accompany Ames and his agent on his visits to various properties, one of which, it was hoped, would entice the former to buy and settle. What she saw in the course of these excursions made Pamela's mouth water. Her beau might have been distinctly shambolic but it was obvious, mainly because of his calm acceptance of everything that was shown him, that he was a very wealthy man. On one of the farms they'd visited, in the Yarra Valley on the outskirts of Melbourne, as well as flock of albino peacocks from Ceylon, there had been two dozen or so delicate Arabians of every colour behind white painted fences and in the cool shadows of the property's stables. Pamela had been mesmerised by the sight. Horses were one of the many things she missed from her past existence, when she'd spent the school holidays under her uncle's roof in Kent. The whole family had ridden and so little, almost-an-orphan Pamela had ridden too between terms at the half-rate boarding school where she'd been deposited, at the age of eleven, after her mother died. So when, barely six weeks after they'd met, Ames got down on bended knee and asked the big question, avarice and sloth and the memory of those long, happy rides with her cousins, made Pamela look past his eccentricities and say yes.

Although quick to the altar, Ames wouldn't be hurried in his decision on the matter of their future and subsequent abode. He consulted his banker and, strangely enough, his Chinese astrologist too. The former said, 'Buy, you fool, anything you like', while the latter urged caution and spoke in enigmatic tones of far-off lands. Two months after they'd wed Ames had returned to the hotel where he and Pamela had been ensconced since the nuptials, and announced that he'd bought them a home at last. Pamela hadn't been pleased to discover that her husband had purchased a copra plantation on an island in East Neuguinea. A number of heavy objects were thrown and some words, which Ames was shocked to discover that his wife knew, were employed at length to express exactly what she thought about her husband's decision.

Ames had left for Neumecklenberg soon after to see exactly what he'd bought. Pamela had gone reluctantly to her father's home in Bacchus Marsh until she knew that a house at least awaited her before she threw her life away completely and followed her husband as convention dictated she should. This had proved fortuitous. Despite having lived on the property since well before the turn of the century, the previous owner of the plantation hadn't advanced his living quarters much beyond the bush hut he'd built there when he first arrived. A judiciously placed lit match cleared the site and the building of a new house, and auxiliary buildings, started the following day. With money at his disposal Ames was able to build his wife a house that rivalled the German residence in Kavieng in size and luxury. It took almost a year to complete and a further six months after that before Pamela finally agree to leave civilisation and join her husband. She'd been making his life a living hell from the moment she'd stepped off the boat, though the Schmidts were not yet privy to the level of discord in their neighbours' marriage.

After a rather good luncheon and an hour or so of idle chat on the verandah, looking out towards the sea, Ames suggested that since the heat of the afternoon had abated, a tour of the plantation might be in order. As on most plantations, the garden boasted a handful of guesthouses and the ubiquitous cooking quarters with their incumbent Oriental cookie. Ames had struck gold with his cookie, whom he'd recruited, complete with wife, children, parents and assorted other relations, from the best of the shanty noodle houses that had sprung up in Rabaul's fast-developing Chinatown. There was also a mown grass tennis court, the lines burnt out with lime, and a stand-alone hexagonal bungalow, bigger than the guest chalets, and complete with its own verandah, in which Ames kept his extensive library and where he'd installed a camera obscura. The moment Ames closed the shutters of the room and a small piece of the world outside appeared on the white painted disc on the floor in the middle of the room, Marta craved a camera obscura. As Ames cranked the lever that positioned the aperture on the roof, different views of the sea, rainforest and garden swam past, the colours beautiful and real in a way that a photograph could never be.

'Pamela's department', as Ames put it, was the bloodstock, half a dozen Egyptian Arabians, five mares and a newly weaned colt, which she intended using as the foundation of her breeding enterprise. As they approached the stables the horses, seeing their mistress, began to call out, alerting the dozing native horse-boy. Pamela's favourite, a dapple-grey called Chantilly, was brought out so that she could be admired in her entirety. The horse-boy was obviously scared of the mare, with her rolling eyes and flared nostrils, and Marta didn't blame him. The creature in front of her bore no resemblance to the sunny-tempered Haflingers and gentle

Hanoverians of her limited equine experience. Once clear of the stable the mare reared up, striking at the air, causing Bernard and Marta to step back in alarm. When the horse finally touched solid earth with all four hooves, Pamela quickly stepped in, taking the halter rope from the boy and dismissing him. He scuttled off in obvious relief.

'The natives are scared of them, you know,' Pamela said as she caressed the animal's head. 'The horses. That's why I'm never afraid to ride by myself, even in the rainforest. They wouldn't dare come near me.'

Because they wanted to reach home before dark, Marta and Bernard declined an invitation to join the Millers for supper, and headed home to Gethsemane. Bernard was talkative on the journey, clearly impressed by the Millers and their money. Marta wasn't so sure.

The next day a native arrived at Gethsemane with a note and a white sulphur-crested cockatoo perched on his shoulder. Marta opened the missive, thinking that the bird was a gift from Bernard. 'Perhaps you can teach it to speak German. Regards A.I.M.,' the note read. It took Marta a few moments to realise who A.I.M. was.

✳ ✳ ✳

Marta was just about to step out of the shadows and into the meadow around the waterfall in order to greet the Millers, when she was arrested by a feminine shriek, a great splashing and the sight of Pamela climbing out of the pool without a stitch of clothing on, followed by an equally naked and fully tumescent Bernard, who proceeded to chase her around the clearing, much to the alarm of her horse, who snorted and skittered out of the way.

'Stop it, Bernard,' protested Pamela breathlessly between contradictory giggles of encouragement. 'We're scaring Chantilly.'

But Bernard merely growled like a big, golden lion and kept up the chase until he caught Pamela, dragging her down onto the grass. And, unaware of their audience, Bernard and Pamela Miller made love with tremendous vigour and a good deal of moaning. When Marta heard the horribly familiar cry of triumph that Bernard emitted as he spilled his seed, she turned and hurried as fast as she could down the path back to the bungalow, so utterly preoccupied with what she'd witnessed that she was unaware of dropping her native bag, containing a book, bathing sheet and clean dress, in the middle of the path where light and shadow came together.

In many ways she wasn't shocked. Men had mistresses, Marta knew that from the conversations she'd been privy to among her older female relatives and her mother's friends. Even her darling Papa had been conducting an affair with a colleague's wife for who knows how many years, with the tacit knowledge of the magnificent Klara.

Marta's discovery of her father's long-term infidelity had occurred one autumn afternoon when she was out shopping with her mother and had caught sight of her father leaving a hotel with the woman on his arm. Marta might have called out a greeting, if she hadn't clearly seen the look on Egon's face as he leaned in and whispered something in the woman's ear that made her laugh.

At that moment Klara dropped her shopping. 'Oh, look what I've done,' she cried out in irritation. 'Help me gather up this mess, Marta, before it's all ruined.' When the last paper bag of shell buttons and skein of embroidery silk had been retrieved, and the two women had straightened up, Egon Mueller and the woman were gone.

'That was Papa,' Marta said to Klara.

'Yes,' Klara had replied. 'And Frau Straussman.' Her mother's tone had told Marta everything she had *not* wanted to know about the secret lives of her parents.

This prior knowledge did little, however, to comfort Marta as she hurried home, her mind in turmoil. The only thing she felt was the immense, crushing weight of betrayal that had settled in her chest. It puzzled her that it hurt so much, and in such a physical way too. Her heart really *did* feel as though it was grievously wounded. Why? She understood that she probably didn't love her husband, not in the way a wife should. And yet it felt as though her heart was being destroyed, squeezed to fleshy pulp by an unseen hand. It wouldn't be until much later, when Marta happened across a number of books on psychoanalysis, that she would look back and understand what she'd felt in those first days of knowing. That it wasn't her heart but her pride and her sense of self, what Jung and Freud viewed collectively as ego, which had been broken into a million little pieces.

Collapsing on the stairs of the bungalow, breathing heavily from her rapid descent, Marta desperately wanted all this to be a bad dream, but the harsh rasp of her breath and her stinging cheek where a thorny branch had raked her face in her flight down the hill were palpable reminders that this was all too real. Perched on the balustrade of the verandah, watching Marta intently as she tried to order her thoughts, was the sulphur-crested cockatoo Ames had sent over three months before.

'Oh, go away, you ridiculous creature,' shouted Marta, waving her arms. Taking the hint, the bird flew off, drifting down over the tree canopy to the harbour. Watching the parrot disappear, Marta wondered what on earth she was going to do. She thought of her mother and her stoic acceptance of her father's infidelity. I need time to think, she realised. And plan for the future.

When Bernard returned to the bungalow later than usual, only a few minutes short of darkness, his wife was sitting on the top step waiting for him as she usually did in the evenings. He came a little warily, searching for signs of anything at all on Marta's face. He had discovered the little bag of possessions on his walk down from the waterfall and hadn't quite known what to make of its presence so unnervingly close to where he'd recently fornicated joyfully with Pamela Miller. He'd hidden the bilum in the hollow of a tree at the edges of the garden where the garden native would find it and return it to the bungalow via Raus, without raising even a flicker of interest. When Marta greeted him with a small smile, Bernard was encouraged in his hope that he hadn't been caught out after all. He bounded up the stairs and headed towards the drinks trolley. There, still under the bottles, was the note Marta had written earlier that afternoon. Extracting the short missive and reading it in the failing light, Bernard knew things would never be the same again. The thought didn't exactly break his heart for, fool that he was, Bernard had fallen for Pamela Miller, and had begun to ponder idly the prospect of divorce.

Dinner was a desultory affair, with Marta refusing even to look at Bernard and barely eating. Before they retired, the Schmidts sat on the verandah and smoked in a dense, impenetrable silence as they floated apart from each other in the Neuguinea darkness, singular as islands. The wind from the north-east had picked up since nightfall and out on the horizon lightning flashed in a sky that was low and dark with building cloud.

'There'll be rain before morning,' Bernard predicted, desperate to break the glacial impasse.

A mere twelve hours before, such a words would have been cause for joy but now they were nothing more than dust. Marta made no reply, instead rising and making her way indoors and to bed. Some minutes later Bernard followed, walking past the door of the guest room without noticing that it was uncharacteristically shut. Marta wasn't in the bed they'd shared for the past five years but, thinking nothing of it, Bernard stripped and laboriously climbed in under the mosquito net and between the thin cotton sheets. He quickly fell into a deep exhausted sleep and it wasn't until he jolted awake over an hour later that he realised that Marta still wasn't there. Fearing the worst, that she'd been murdered by natives or snakes or both, he leapt from bed in order to search the bungalow and grounds if necessary, starting with the guestroom. As he twisted and turned the handle and pushed at the unyielding door, the realisation slowly dawned on him that his wife intended to punish him for his infidelity. That she would take away the one thing that held them together.

Later that night both Marta and Bernard, in their separate beds, woke to the sound of the steady drumming of rain on the iron roof and the cacophony of animal life celebrating the breaking of the drought. By morning the rain had moved on across the sea and the long dry days continued into December.

Thirteen

✳ Even after I had witnessed the phenomenon year after year, those first few days after the dry broke and the trade winds brought in the warm, wet rain were always extraordinary to me. How quickly the constant precipitation and suffocating heat restored the lushness to the grasslands of the plantation and the verdant shadowy depths of the rainforest behind the bungalow at Gethsemane. It was almost as if one could sit on the verandah and witness the foliage was closing, inch by inch. How long, if left, would it take for the land to swallow us whole?

Marta, *Neuguinea Memoirs*, Heyward
& Barge, London, 1949, p. 28

Bernard knew it was his own fault. There was no getting around it, no matter how long he sat on the verandah in deep rumination watching the rain fall in great leaden sheets from the sky. *Stupid!* There had been no need for Marta to ever know, and it wasn't beyond the realms of possibility that he might have actually been able to manage a wife and a mistress reasonably successfully, as countless men before him had done. But his treacherous heart had intervened, and it wanted only Pamela. It had led him to make careless mistakes, such as meeting his mistress at the waterfall, a place often frequented by his wife. Pamela! From the moment he saw her … well, it wasn't all that different from the way he'd felt all those years ago when Gloria had began to waltz in and out of his life. He hadn't thought he'd ever feel like this again. There had been his feelings for Gretchen, of course, but it was her untouchable beauty that had intrigued him, nothing so base as the lust aroused in him by Gloria and now Pamela.

He hadn't said much more than ten words to her and had been shocked when Pamela had touched him, under the cover of the tablecloth, as they'd eaten lunch the day he and Marta had visited the Miller plantation. To his embarrassment he'd hardened immediately as her questing hand had travelled lingeringly over his crotch and she'd smiled at him, a sly little smile, full of promise. She had so consumed his every thought that a little over a week later, when she rode up to the drying sheds at Gethsemane, dressed in a man's cotton shirt and jodhpurs, with the morning sun flaring behind her, Bernard wondered if she was something conjured up by his inflamed imagination. It was all he could do, as she alighted from her grey mare and stood boldly in front of him, her eyes brazen as any whore's, not to take her there and then in the dust and filth and stink of burning coconut, with the natives watching. Neither of them had suggested going up to the bungalow where Marta sat, not even for a drink. Instead Pamela had made Bernard show her the copra-smoking machine he'd invented.

'Wonderful,' she'd murmured appreciatively as he'd explained its workings and benefits in intricate detail. Within an hour the tour of the drying sheds and labour quarters was complete and Bernard had come to the end of his monologue and was suddenly at a loss as to what to say next. After a long and very pregnant pause, he'd been about to invite her up to the bungalow for lunch when Pamela had beaten him out of the starting blocks and suggested Bernard saddle his own horse and accompany her to Gethsemane's gate. In the shadow of the rainforest, close enough to Boluminski's road to hear the sound of the natives' voices as they walked past, words had ceased to matter as Pamela had allowed Bernard to unbutton her shirt and rub his face in her chemise-covered breasts. 'Wonderful,' she'd sighed.

After that they'd met whenever they could up at the waterfall, from where a native track led through the rainforest and down to the next valley where the Miller plantation lay.

In the days that followed the discovery of his infidelity Bernard waited for his wife to say or do something – anything. But other than locking her door and herself against him, Marta had done little but become ever more detached and unresponsive. And it was beginning to dawn on Bernard that if he wanted that fire lit, and indeed he did, for in his neighbour's wife Bernard had finally found someone who effortlessly eclipsed – no, obliterated – his long-held feelings, the memorial to Gloria he had painstakingly constructed over two decades, he would have to do it himself. He hadn't told Pamela yet that Marta knew, though he had seen his mistress twice since his infidelity had become revealed. A nagging little voice in the back of his mind voiced an insistent doubt, but how could Pamela *not* feel the way he did? It was she, after all, who had sought him out, had instigated the affair. If not for love, then what else? He would ask Pamela to marry him the next time they met, he decided. This union he'd made with Marta was beyond reconstruction. What was done was done. Disentangling themselves from spousal obligations would take some time, certainly, but it wasn't beyond the realms of possibility. Marta would probably go back to Vienna. Back home to her family.

Leaving Bernard and returning to Vienna *had* occurred to Marta in those long nights when she lay alone in her bed and fretted on the future. But again and again she came back to the same realisation: she didn't want to leave Neuguinea. There was her work to be considered, and her passion for this country. Neuguinea suited her very well; it was the only place where she felt she fitted in, not as a wife, but in her own right. In many ways it *had* been the new beginning she'd hoped for, and the thought of abandoning this place she now thought of as her home and returning to Vienna was untenable. And there was another reason too, if she was completely honest with herself. Royal Weston. Again and again, Marta's thoughts came back to Royal. It was ridiculous, she knew, to cast him in the role of lover when he'd shown not the slightest hint of any affection beyond friendship, but in these upsetting times, her mind, usually so obedient, went exactly where it wanted to.

But, above all else, Marta needed to be practical. She'd come to the conclusion that the best thing for her to do was divorce Bernard and take a little house in either Herbertshohe or Rabaul. He would have to pay her an allowance, and that would keep him, if not exactly poor, then not rich either. Marta didn't feel particularly vindictive towards her husband or the whore – well, perhaps there was some animosity towards Pamela Miller – but she didn't want to make it easy for them either. What Bernard had done was wrong and he needed to be punished for that a little before she would let him off the hook. Yes, she would be quite happy, Marta thought, living on the east coast of Neupommern. She was sure Royal Weston could find her a little house, and how lovely it would be to see Ettie when she came to town. It had also occurred to her that she could take on some of the care of the still nascent botanical gardens at Rabaul, which had been left without a custodian by Richard Parkinson's unexpected death the year before.

So she would set Bernard free, Marta decided. Eventually. When he asked. And she *would* make him ask. It was his dirty work and he could clean it up all on his own. She was damned if she was going to help him as she knew he wanted her to. How long would it take him to work up the courage to follow his own heart and desires? She enjoyed watching Bernard squirm, pinned by nothing more than her mocking gaze. He was craven, and she hated this about him, even more than his infidelity, but not nearly as much as his stupidity.

Bernard did propose to Pamela Miller as he'd promised himself he would and she laughed in his face. 'Don't be ridiculous, Bernard,' she said, 'I'm already married. Go home to your wife.'

Pamela had punished him for this display of need too. For six long weeks she failed to make their habitual weekly rendezvous at the drying sheds where they'd begun to meet now the rains had come. Then, one rare fine day in February, she reappeared, all smiles and her flesh even more abundant and luscious than Bernard remembered. Neither spoke of the possibility that they could be together as man and wife. Bernard had learned his lesson. Soon after it became obvious that Pamela was with child and although Bernard found his mistress's expanding body incredibly erotic, Ames had forbidden Pamela to ride so their trysts, like that year's rains, came to an end.

Soon after Marta noticed that her husband's affair appeared to have come to an abrupt halt and she pondered on the reason for this as she sat writing up the notes she'd decided should accompany her illustrations. All was revealed a few weeks before Easter when Ames Miller, on his way back from Kavieng, dropped in at Gethsemane and announced that Pamela was five months pregnant. He thinks the baby's his, Marta concluded, as she studied Bernard's face intently.

Bored and frustrated by Pamela's disappearance from his life, Bernard would sit in the shadows on the verandah when he returned to the bungalow in the afternoons and watch his wife as she waited for the bats to take to the deepening skies And he would wonder why she stayed, why she chose to say nothing. It seemed odd to him that he felt so dissatisfied when everything had worked out to his own advantage. Not that he really had a mistress, or a wife, any more. Bernard missed his wife more than he expected. It was if Marta's vitality had evaporated in the heat of last year's long dry. They spoke only as much was necessary – often mere three-word requests and answers. He even missed her condescending attempts to educate him, which had once annoyed him profoundly. The only time she seemed genuinely excited, reflected Bernard sourly, was when a letter or parcel arrived from Royal.

'So what did Royal have to say for himself?' Bernard asked one afternoon after Captain Macco, fresh from Kavieng, had dropped some mail off at Gethsemane.

'Nothing much at all,' replied Marta. 'You know how he is.'

'You're fond of him, aren't you?' Bernard observed slyly.

'You're not suggesting that there's anything between us, are you, Bernard? Because I assure you there isn't,' said Marta tartly.

'Oh, I know there's nothing between you and Royal, Liebling. He's a fruit. A queer.'

'What an earth do you mean?' asked a perplexed Marta.

'He likes young black boys. Always has.'

'But he was married, and has children,' protested Marta, her devastation palpable.

'And that's why she divorced him.' Bernard ploughed on, actually appalled at how much his words had obviously hurt Marta. All the mean-spirited revelation had done was make him feel slightly shabby and very small. 'You didn't know, did you?' he continued, his voice kinder.

'No,' said Marta. 'No, I didn't.'

'I'm sorry,' Bernard said. And he truly was.

'Whatever for?' replied Marta. 'It's not as if it's any business of mine.'

✻ ✻ ✻

And just as Marta kept her own counsel in far-off German Neuguinea, so too did the inhabitants of Wipplinger Strasse. It had been a dire year for the Muellers, culminating in Gretchen attacking her mother with a palette knife and her very own teeth like an enraged animal. Although Gretchen hadn't truly hurt Klara, the attack had been unprovoked and sufficiently violent for Egon and his wife, in consultation with Gretchen's doctors, to commit their daughter to an asylum. There was, in those long, dry and strangely noncommittal conversations with the men in white coats, no talk of her ever coming out again. It was unspoken but clearly understood that the days of relative calm and sanity had gone. The first time Klara had visited Gretchen, making the journey by train out to the asylum in the countryside, her daughter had been curled up on the floor of her cell, oblivious to the whispered calls of her mother, crouched beside her in tears.

After she left Klara had sat on a hard wooden bench at the small deserted railway station in the winter cold for a very long time, with her eyes closed and her hand on her heart. But Klara would go back, time and time again, unable to give up the shred of hope that one day the doctors would have good news when she arrived at the asylum door.

Marta was lucky enough to escape an attack of malaria during the months of perpetual rain, though Bernard wasn't. For ten days, just as the rains were ending, he took to his bed, alternately shivering and sweating as the fever rampaged through his bloodstream. Marta, because she didn't trust Cookie or even Masta Raus to do it correctly, prepared the draughts of quinine powder dissolved in schnapps herself, always adding lime juice to cut the bitterness of the cinchona powder and the punch of the raw, potent spirit. Early on in Bernard's illness, as she prepared the antidote, it occurred to Marta that she could simply poison her husband and solve all her problems. The thought amused her enough to become a recurrent theme in her musings on the state of her marriage and never failed to make her smile. Soon enough the quinine began to do its work and the fever retreated. Bernard's skin took on a yellowish hue in response to the quantity of the drug in his system, though this was accredited to the sickness rather than the cure.

Bernard had harboured hopes, as his health improved, that there had been a thawing in relations between him and Marta, for she'd nursed him diligently, and to his delight this did prove to be the case. Slowly they began to talk again, perhaps even more thoughtfully than they'd ever done before.

'Are you and Pamela no more?' Marta asked suddenly one evening shortly after the rains had come to an end.

'Yes,' replied Bernard, trying not to sound too heartbroken. 'It has ended. A few months ago now.'

'Why?' asked Marta. 'And don't say because of me, Bernard. I couldn't bear it if you did.' Bernard didn't say anything for a long time, simply stared at his hands. 'Oh!' exclaimed Marta at last. 'She won't leave Ames?'

'No,' said Bernard, looking up, his face stricken. 'She says it's because of the baby, but it's more than that.'

'The money,' guessed Marta.

Bernard nodded. 'I'm not rich enough for her.'

It was odd, Marta knew, but seeing Bernard so dejected, wiped away much of her own hurt. Now she only pitied him. 'You do love her, don't you?'

'Sometimes I think more than life itself. But it's pointless. And over. It's over now.'

'Would you like me to stay?' asked Marta.

'Yes, yes, I would.' Bernard's voice was filled with gratitude. 'If it wouldn't be too awful for you. I *would* like us to be friends again, at least. And it's finished now with Pamela. I promise you.'

So Marta stayed. But she didn't return to his bed.

❋ ❋ ❋

Ames Miller dropped by the drying sheds at Gethsemane in early August on his way to see his new son, who'd been born the night before in the hospital at Kavieng, unable to resist the opportunity to brag and strut around like a bantam rooster.

'Congratulations, my friend,' Bernard said, with a heartiness he didn't feel. There would be no Bernard junior to carry on his legacy in Neuguinea. 'I have no cigar, but I do have a little schnapps,' he continued, taking a hip flask from his jacket pocket. 'We toast your newborn, yes. A son. A boy to continue your name. I envy you, my friend.'

'You and Marta should have children,' Ames said, taking the flask from Bernard. 'Women, they get lonely out here. They need children.'

'Yes,' said Bernard, gloomily. 'You're probably right.'

The sun was almost directly above the land when Bernard returned to the house with a ravenous appetite and the Millers' news. Marta shrugged, and made no comment, her face as expressionless as a piece of unmarked paper. Bernard had a sudden compulsion to hit her – hard. Beat her until something – rage, fear … anything – rose to the surface and finally erupted. The moment passed as quickly as it had come upon him, and, slightly ashamed of himself, Bernard turned away from his wife and went to pour himself a tumbler of schnapps.

'You drink too much,' said Marta, as Bernard tossed back the entire contents of the glass.

'Yes,' replied Bernard belligerently, pouring another three fingers, 'I probably do.'

Marta shrugged again and went back inside.

One afternoon in the early new year, the Millers drove over in the automobile, the first in the colony, that Ames had recently shipped to Neumecklenberg from Sydney at great expense.

'Tally-ho,' Ames cried, tooting the horn, as he barrelled around the corner of the final stretch of Gethsemane's driveway, heading at unwavering speed towards the bungalow. Bernard and Marta flinched as the auto skidded across the sand, then heaved a collective sigh of relief once the dust settled and it became evident that their neighbour hadn't driven clean under the house. 'Forgot where I'd put the brakes,' laughed Ames. 'Still getting the hang of the thing.'

Pamela, with the baby on her lap, was pale and silent, her face frozen in a rictus of fear. The baby-meri in the back, however, who'd been volubly expressing her terror at the Masta's dreadful driving throughout the entire journey, leapt out the moment the auto became stationary, shrieking like a great demented bird.

'Oh, shut up, you silly moo!' said Ames, climbing out of the vehicle and going around to the other side to help his wife, who seemed incapable of moving. 'Come on, old thing,' he chivvied, taking his son, who promptly started wailing, though not as loudly as the baby-meri.

'So it's finally arrived then, my friend?' Bernard came down the stairs, grinning at the sight of the vehicle.

'Last week,' replied Ames happily, thrusting the screaming baby at the howling baby-meri. 'Isn't she a beauty?' Both men raised their voices to be heard above the bedlam. At this point Pamela had finally released her death grip on the door of the auto and was trying to open it. Ames broke away from his conversation with Bernard, opened the door and offered Pamela his arm.

As he pulled her to her feet Pamela leaned against her husband and put her mouth up close to his ear 'If you ever drive like that again,' she hissed, 'I'll leave you and the baby too.'

'Oh, it wasn't all that bad, was it?' protested Ames, but Pamela was already walking away towards the bungalow, where Marta waited at the top of the stairs. The baby-meri, following Pamela, sensed that her own moment had passed and finally stopped her squawking, though the baby didn't. The two men turned back to the automobile and who knows how long they might have stayed, admiring its splendid lines and marvellous engine, had Pamela not put a stop to it.

'Ames,' she snapped, without even turning to face him.

With a sheepish look on his face, Ames fell obediently into line behind the baby-meri. Reluctantly Bernard, too, joined the others on the verandah. He'd been rather hoping to go for a spin.

Five-month-old Timothy Miller wasn't the most attractive baby Marta had ever seen. Still without much in the way of hair on his bony head, the little mite was covered from head to toe in a deep scarlet-coloured heat rash.

'Oh, he takes after you Ames,' said Marta, though, in her opinion, the baby actually resembled no one in particular.

'Do you think?' asked Pamela, glancing uninterestedly at her first-born, now being bounced energetically by the baby-meri, sitting on the floor of the verandah. 'I've never seen heat rash like it. Poor little soul,' continued Pamela, taking a gin and tonic rattling with ice from Bernard. 'I leave him near naked most of the time. It's the only thing that helps. Dreadful. If he didn't leak so much I'd divest him of his nappy too.'

After finishing his drink Ames suggested he and Bernard go for a drive, leaving Marta and Pamela sitting across from each other without very much to say. It was an uncomfortable hour of observations that led nowhere, concerning the weather, children and the difficulty of getting good native help. Both women became distinctly more animated when the sound of the vehicle's engine was finally heard in the distance. The auto sedately reappeared around the bend of the driveway, with Bernard at the wheel, and drifted towards the bungalow, coming to a gentle halt at the foot of the stairs.

'My old mare can walk faster than you drive, Bernard,' teased Ames as the two men got out of the vehicle.

'Slow and steady wins the race,' replied Bernard.

'Not that slow it won't,' said Ames.

'Ready to go then are we, my love?' asked Ames, seeing Pamela already standing at the top of the steps.

'It's been lovely,' Pamela said stiffly to Marta.

'Yes,' agreed Marta. 'Perfectly lovely.'

Because Marta didn't accompany the Millers to their automobile she failed to see both the look that passed between her husband and Pamela and the fleeting moment when their fingertips brushed in silent conversation.

A few weeks later Marta knew that Bernard had resumed his affair with their neighbour. The signs were all there: the random disappearances, the fishy reek of sex on his skin and, most of all, the extravagant attentions he paid her when he returned to Gethsemane after being unavoidably detained in Kavieng overnight. To her own surprise Marta found that her knowledge of the revived affair less important than the fact that Bernard thought she didn't know. That cast aspersions on her intelligence and *that* Marta truly did find offensive. And he'd stopped slumping outside her door, begging and crying to be let in, on those nights when he'd drunk too much.

Fourteen

✳ 3 May 1910
  Vienna

Dear Marta,

It's with a heavy heart that I write to confess that things haven't been so well with our darling Gretchen. The doctors at the sanatorium tell me that she will never come back to us from that place. She doesn't speak any more or appear to hear, though fortunately she is not violent like some of the other unfortunate souls, and seems happy enough to spend her days drawing. But in truth, dear daughter, our Gretchen was never really the same after you married Bernard and went away …

Although it wasn't her mother's intention, her words evoked in Marta not only intense feelings of impotence in the face of tragedy, but also of guilt. How easy, sometimes, it is to leave – to walk away from pain and hurt and bad memories. For Klara was right, it *had* been during that last summer, before Marta had married Bernard, that Gretchen had begun her final fall into the deep frozen pit from which they couldn't extract her. Perhaps even back then, Marta had known that she could only save herself, that already Gretchen was lost to this world.

The letter had compelled Marta to unearth Gretchen's only surviving painting, which she'd hidden in the bottom of a trunk.

She'd never shown the painting to Bernard, somehow knowing that he would never understand, that the portrait was too real, too emotional, too mythological for his ignorant eye. Looking at the mould-spotted canvas, Marta was struck again by its beauty and skill and wondered, not for the first time, if Gretchen had sold her sanity to the devil in return for this afflatus that had flowered for but a single season. In her own tragic summer, spent with the lady novelist in the Mediterranean, Marta had forfeited her finger, but for what? It had been hard to see the thing inside her, then no bigger than an apricot, as a blessing. As she rewrapped the painting Marta thought of that time, long ago, when she'd been not much more than a girl, and had first ventured out into the world on her own.

The summer of 1889 was the second that Marta had spent as a companion to Miss Sophia Constantinelli, a freakishly tiny lady novelist who, though only a decade older than her, had written a number of novels that Marta secretly thought were horrendous. Fortunately for the authoress, however, the book-buying ladies of the bourgeoisie in no way shared Marta's opinion. As a consequence Miss Constantinelli had become vulgarly wealthy from her pedestrian prose, social inaccuracies and wandering, yet titillating, storylines. Marta had been employed by Sophia's publishers in the vague hope that a secretary would keep their writer's worst excesses and inaccuracies in check, especially now that Sophia had embarked on a novel, historical in style, in order to silence her many male critics.

It had become increasingly evident to Marta the year before that there was no question of her correcting any of the many wildly inaccurate allusions to history and classicism of which Miss Constantinelli was so awfully fond, but in which, oddly, she had no real interest. The secretary's job, as far as Sophia was concerned, was to write out her manuscripts in a legible hand because it was so terribly difficult to keep it all neat and tidy when the muse was upon one. At least, Marta thought grimly as she deciphered her employer's dreadful handwriting, when Miss Constantinelli set her novels in England in the present time they had a native authenticity that even someone as self-centred as she – 'I need only my imagination' – couldn't fail to bring to the page. Despite requiring only her imagination, Miss Constantinelli had arranged to spend the summer touring the Mediterranean looking for a suitably attractive location for the latest novel. This was the only reason Marta had returned for a second time.

The authoress, accompanied by Marta, marched around the ruins first in Italy and then in Greece, sighing volubly at each new crumbling temple, marmoreal and gleaming under the hot bright sun.

'It's not how I imagined it at all,' she complained to Marta, her disappointment palpable. After these encounters with the past, Sophia would take to her bed, as if made ill by such ancientness, and start scribbling furiously. It was obvious to Marta that her employer was much happier in her bed, with the shutters closed against the bright Mediterranean sun and the interminable reminders of the past with which these countries appeared to be littered. But inevitably, by the time they reached Athens and the second month of their Grand Tour, even Sophia had become a little jaded by her own company.

'Tarquin's coming tomorrow,' she told Marta one afternoon after they'd returned from sightseeing. 'I've had a telegram. Thank goodness. I'm beyond bored.'

Tarquin, 'Quin', Grubb, was the lady novelist's younger brother. His name was actually Terence: Tarquin was yet another of Sophia's affectations, fabricated entirely to distance both siblings from their humble past. Marta had met the brother a number of times when he'd visited Sophia's damp dilapidated house in Kent the previous summer, complaining about gambling debts and straitened circumstances. He was, like his sister, remarkably short in stature and, rather rotund. Seeing them together, perambulating around the overgrown grounds, Marta was reminded immediately of Tweedle Dee and Tweedle Dum from *Alice's Adventures in Wonderland* and the thought caused her some private amusement. Marta rather liked Mr Grubb. He was kinder and less self-absorbed than the capricious and demanding Sophia, and was constantly apologising to Marta for her appalling behaviour. But he was also lazy and easily swayed by his sister. Even when they were very small, Sophia could get Terry, as he was then known, to do anything she asked.

Marta was relieved that a diversion was to arrive in the next day or two. The more disappointed Sophia became with her Grand Tour, the greater her petulance and random tantrums became. Just the week before, when Marta had suggested that perhaps the Sistine Chapel, which they hadn't yet visited but Sophia had read about in her Baedeker, didn't have a place in a Roman – or was it Greek? – tragedy, her employer had, in an inconsolable rage, thrown an empty teapot at her, though the missile had fallen well short of Marta, standing by the door.

Tarquin duly arrived and the trio travelled by coach up to Bologna, then headed south-east from there to Venice, which Sophia proclaimed damp and smelly and nothing like the Venice she'd conjured up in her own mind over the previous winter. After five days she declared that she'd done all the research she needed on the floating city. Not even the opportunity to meet Henry James could induce Sophia, who'd never heard of the gentleman in any case, to stay a day longer. Milan was their next destination, where they stayed for ten days as the 'muse had descended' and Sophia took to her bed to write. In her absence, Tarquin and Marta, both tourists to the core, visually ravished the place.

Once Sophia's fervour of creativity had broken, they moved on, trailing reams of scribble-covered paper, to Monte Carlo, where a suite of rooms had been taken for the remainder of the summer. Sadly Monte Carlo didn't prove to be a good choice. Sophia was unhappy with the accommodation, which was outrageously expensive and very small, and nor was she overjoyed at Tarquin's habit of disappearing into the casinos come nightfall. Within the month, much to the landlord's ire, she abandoned the lease without a second thought.

'He shouted at me,' she told Marta and Tarquin as they left hurriedly. 'Something about contractual obligation. Silly man. I gave him a signed copy of *Persephone Undone* and *that* silenced his protests, as you can well imagine.'

Eventually they ended up in Spain, where Sophia fell in love with a shambolic hacienda on the outskirts of Valencia. Once settled in the most cavernous and gloomy of the bedrooms, Sophia took to her bed, in the company of the Italian greyhound Lucinda and the halitotic Pekinese Alfred, who had accompanied their mistress on her summer sojourn, to begin the serious work of writing her new novel. Exactly what the perimeters of that narrative would be even the writer couldn't say for certain in these early days: all she could do was wait for the muse. 'I write as if in a trance, you know,' she'd told Marta — and anyone else who would listen — countless times. 'I hear voices from the other side, who speak to me in a tongue that only I can decipher.' With Sophia ensconced in her bed for most of the day, Marta and Tarquin were left with much time on their hands. They fell into the habit of ordering a carriage and going into the city to look at the flamboyant architecture, a blend of Moorish and high Gothic, all built from the pale local stone, and eat the saffron-infused paella that Sophia wouldn't allow to be served at their dinner table. She distrusted all foreign food, except French, naturally.

Occasionally, however, Sophia would come up for air, demanding a bath and summoning her brother to her side in order to make plans.

'So what tickles your fancy, Soph?' asked Tarquin who was perched on a stool beside the bath in his sister's bedroom.

'Don't call me that,' she admonished gently as she slowly soaped her arms with a large sponge. 'You know I don't like it. And I don't like you very much when you speak in that common way.'

'But it's who we are.'

'No, it's not,' she said tartly.

Tarquin sighed. 'So what do you want to do?'

'A picnic, I think,' Sophia replied, splashing her brother playfully. 'In the country. Will you arrange it for me, Quin? I would ask Marta but she's proving less than helpful.'

'She's your secretary, not your maid,' Tarquin reminded her.

'Details, details,' said Sophia standing up abruptly, the soapy grey water cascading down her naked body, and extending an imperious hand so that her brother could hand her a bath sheet.

They were all in good spirits an hour or so later as they set off, with Tarquin driving the little pony and carriage he'd procured, up into the countryside behind Valencia.

'It's rather pretty, isn't it?' observed Sophia in slightly surprised tones, looking around from beneath the shelter of her enormous hat and ornately trimmed parasol. 'Not green like England, of course, but definitely possessing its own picaresque charms, don't you think, Tarquin?'

Marta coughed apologetically. 'I think,' she said slowly, 'you'll find that the word is picturesque.'

'Oh,' laughed Sophia, 'but I say it in the French way. So much prettier, don't you think?'

'But …,' started Marta.

'It is lovely,' interpolated Tarquin, skilfully diverting the conversation back into more tranquil waters. 'But really, Soph, you should come into town with us and look at the buildings and visit the galleries. Most marvellous paintings.'

Sophia yawned, not even bothering to cover her mouth. 'Oh my darling Quin,' she laughed, 'you know how I loathe old buildings and art. It's history I love. Real men doing real things. Not pretty pictures and churches, but love, passion and desire!' she declared vehemently.

'Calm down, old thing,' said Tarquin, looking over his shoulder to where the two women sat side by side. 'You'll do yourself a damage carrying on like that.'

Eventually they came to a length of the riverbank that Sophia deemed 'picaresque' enough on which to lunch. It was blissfully cool there, under the trees that grew along the edges of the Turia, and once Tarquin had spread the mackintosh cloth and then the blanket on the grasses, Sophia flopped down with a sigh and unbuttoned her bodice far more than was decorous.

'Gosh, what a frightful din,' she observed, cocking her head to one side and listening to the noise of the cicadas from the trees. 'I do wish they'd shut up.'

Marta was busying herself with organising the lunch, which had been packed into baskets that morning by the hacienda's cook, who specialised in pallid English food.

'Delicious!' declared Sophie, greedily eating one bloater paste sandwich after another. 'I knew Cook would understand what it was I wanted. Remember when we were children, Quin? The picnics that we used to go on and the marvellous lunches that Cook used to pack us?'

'Yes,' said Tarquin, though no such thing had ever taken place. The estate where they'd grown up had been grand, but it had never been theirs. Their father, Victor Grubb, had run his lordship's racing stables and stud, and Sophie and Terry had attended school in the village. Much good it had done the future Miss Constantinelli who, in Marta's opinion, was as close to illiterate as a writer could be. Tarquin was a little disturbed by his sister's compulsion to make up things regarding their respective and mutual biographies. But he knew better than to question her fictions, for his sister was inclined to fly into rages and sulk for weeks, refusing to give him money. As far as Tarquin was concerned, if his sister wanted to fabricate entirely new lives for them, why not? As long as she kept writing and her novels continued to be eaten alive by her admirers, Sophie Grubb could be anyone she wanted to be.

'I think I'll take the dogs for a walk for a while,' Marta said, rising after lunch.

'Don't be too long,' said Sophia. 'Remember I must return to the grindstone in order to keep us all in the manner to which we've become accustomed.'

Late the next day, when she came to collect her employer's daily scribbles for transcribing, Marta was pale and listless enough for even Sophia to notice.

'What's wrong with you?' she asked.

'It's most odd,' said Marta as she crawled around the foot of the bed retrieving the unnumbered pages that constituted Sophia's daily output, 'but I don't feel well at all, and my finger is aching terribly.'

'Your finger?' asked Sophia, who was sitting up in bed feeding shortbread to the dogs. 'What did you do to your finger?'

'I pricked it with a thorn from a rose I picked on my walk yesterday. It drove right in, as you can see,' said Marta, showing Sophia the red and swollen ring finger on her left hand. There was a dark, bruised heart where the thorn had punctured the skin. 'I extracted it, but I fear some residue may remain and is causing the inflammation.'

'Oh it's nothing,' said Sophia, barely looking. 'A scratch.'

'I think I should go and have it looked at by a doctor,' persisted Marta. 'It throbs terribly.'

'But you can't!' exclaimed Sophia. 'I need you here. There's transcribing to be done immediately if we're to have food on the table next week and beyond.'

Marta knew this was a lie but capitulated to Sophia's will. It was easier and her employer was probably right. The finger did hurt so much, though, and she did feel terribly queer. Perhaps a good night's sleep would put everything right.

That night only Tarquin and Sophie were seated at the dinner table, Marta having taken to her bed.

'Such weakness,' complained Sophie. 'I can't abide illness, as you well know, Quin. I don't even know why my publishers foisted this woman on me. I'm a writer. Why would I need someone else to do it for me?'

'I'm sure it's nothing,' said Quin, finishing up the last of his chicken consommé. 'Miss Mueller will be back to her usual efficient self tomorrow. Probably a touch of the sun. It was very hot yesterday.'

'I feel restless,' said Sophia. 'Going out yesterday has proven to be my undoing, and rather than fight my distraction, I think we should go away, all three of us. Seek out fresh fields to inspire me. The day after tomorrow we should leave. A change of location, a little holiday, is what we all need. Just for a few days, a week no more, then we shall return here for the last of the summer.'

'And where shall we go now?' asked Tarquin petulantly. He was tired of this constant movement.

'To Morocco,' she replied. 'We shall go to Gibraltar and from there catch a vessel across the straits. A native vessel, perhaps. With an Arab crew,' she continued, already seeing herself, much taller and slimmer, attractively turbaned and draped in a white fluttering – no, undulating – garment, standing on the prow of some half-visualised vessel. 'I'm sure the food will be appalling, but think … *think* of the atmosphere. The poets love the place, naturally, not that *that's* any testimony.'

A good night's rest hadn't proved to be the cure-all for Marta's malaise. She rose shakily from her bed the next morning, feeling worse than she'd done the day before. She barely noticed the dull throb of her finger, which matched her heartbeat, as her head ached interminably and she could barely even open her eyes, and although her skin was hot to the touch, she was cold, so cold. But she soldiered on, doing as much of her employer's packing as she could before giving in and retreating once more to her bed.

'Do you think we should summon a doctor?' said Tarquin after Marta had left.

'Don't be ridiculous, Quin,' said Sophia, throwing things haphazardly into an open trunk. 'It's probably just women's problems. No concern of a doctor. Besides, there's no time. The train leaves at dawn tomorrow.'

By the time they'd arrived at the finest English hotel in Gibraltar three days later Marta had been drifting in and out of consciousness for several hours and could barely muster the energy to climb the stairs to her room.

'How inconvenient,' Sophia said as she tucked into a very good piece of unseasoned boiled beef with mustard sauce.

'I do think we should summon a doctor, Soph,' said Tarquin. 'I really do think Miss Mueller is very ill.'

'Oh, I'm sure she's not,' said Sophia. 'Miss Mueller is obviously constitutionally weak. Probably because she's so tall. And don't call me Soph. You know I deplore that name.'

'It's the one our mother gave you,' said Tarquin.

'*Her!*' exclaimed Sophia with a derisive snort. 'What did she ever do for us?' She'd never forgiven her mother for marrying down the social scale, instead of up. Imagine throwing away the chance to make something of yourself by running away with Victor Grubb, an estate worker. In Sophia's imagination her mother had been an aristocrat rather than the genteel daughter of a reasonably prosperous farmer. 'I don't care at all about her, nor the name she gave me. Now be a good boy, Quin, and ring for the waiter to clear these plates and bring us more claret. I have quite a thirst tonight. It must be all the travelling.'

By the time they reached the dessert of floating island pudding, which Sophia insisted a non-existent nanny had made superbly throughout their childhoods, the siblings were very drunk and attracting outraged glares and mutterings from their fellow diners.

'Get a bottle of liqueur or port from the waiter, Quin,' ordered Sophia. 'And coffee too, and maybe some petit-fours, and have them sent up to my room.'

When Tarquin, having carried out his sister's bidding, entered Sophia's room, she'd divested herself of some of her layers and loosened her stays and was propped up in bed against a mountain of pillows. The french doors were open, and the gentle sound of the waves floated through them.

'I looked in on Miss Mueller,' said Tarquin as he sat down on a chair just inside the french doors and lit a cigarette. 'I couldn't rouse her, though.'

'Perhaps she's simply a deep sleeper,' said Sophia, 'though why she would be tired is anyone's guess. She's barely lifted a finger for days. I have a good mind to deduct her pay.'

'No Soph, I think she's really ill.'

Sophia had been about to dismiss his concerns when there was a soft knock at the door. 'Come,' she commanded, making no attempt to cover herself as the waiter entered. 'Oh look, Quin!' exclaimed Sophia, clapping her hands with glee at the sight of the petit-fours. 'How delicious.'

'But Soph ...' protested Tarquin.

'But nothing,' his sister replied. 'Come and lie down on the bed with me and drink your port and coffee. Come on, come now, come to Sophie,' she coaxed. Tarquin did as he was told, positioning himself at the foot of the bed facing his sister. 'No, no,' she said. 'That won't do, Quin. Come and lie beside me.'

'Oh Soph, why?' protested Tarquin as he reluctantly did as he was bid.

'Poor little man,' cooed Sophia, gathering his head in her arms and pulling it to her hot, sticky breast. 'Such a grumpy bear. There, there. Let Mamma Sophie make you all better.'

'Mamma Sophie always make it better,' replied Tarquin in a little childlike voice as he started to nuzzle like an infant at her breast.

'Yes, that's right,' continued Sophia, swiftly unbuttoning his trousers and taking his stiffened member in a practised hand. 'And you're Mamma Sophie's brave little soldier, with his pee-wee all standing at attention. Mamma make all your grumbles go away, shall she?'

Abruptly Tarquin rolled, turning his back on her. 'It's wrong, all this, Soph, you know that.'

'Only to people who don't understand.'

'Soph … '

'Do you love me?' asked Sophia petulantly.

'Of course I do, Soph. Always,' he replied dutifully.

'I don't believe you. I think you're deliberately cruel to Sophie and will need a spanking.'

But Tarquin refused to be drawn into the game. He sat up, stuffed his flaccid cock back into his trousers and hastily rebuttoned his flies. 'I'm going to check on Miss Mueller.'

'Again?'

'Yes. I'm worried about her.'

'I suppose I should accompany you,' grumbled Sophia, rolling off the bed, 'so people don't talk. It's rather late to be entering an unmarried woman's room.'

'Good thinking,' said Tarquin. 'And for the love of God, Soph, make yourself a little more decent.'

Sophia rather reluctantly buttoned her bodice and picked up the lace mantilla she'd been using as a shawl. 'Happy?'

'Yes, much better,' said Tarquin.

When they failed to rouse Marta, Sophia let them into the room, which was dimly lit by a turned down lamp. Marta lay still and unresponsive in her bed, not stirring as the pair approached.

'See, I told you, Soph.'

'Is she dead!' enquired Sophia with more relish than was necessary.

'No, no, she's not,' replied Tarquin, laying his hand against Marta's neck, 'but she's boiling up.'

Marta, Marta. Do you hear me?' he asked, gently patting her face. 'Come on now, wake up, wake up.'

'Marta groaned and her eyes fluttered open. 'Tarquin,' she said faintly. 'What are you doing here? Is there a fire?'

'No, I was just concerned. Are you feeling all right?'

'Yes of course,' replied Marta. 'I'm just very tired.'

'See!' exclaimed Sophia as Marta lapsed back into unconsciousness. 'Nothing to worry about. If she's still sick in the morning, we shall get the doctor.'

'If you're sure,' said Tarquin reluctantly.

'Completely,' assured Sophia, studying Marta's inert form. She looked speculatively at her brother. 'You like her, don't you?'

'Yes,' he admitted, 'I do.'

'You could make love to her, you know.'

'What? Now?' Tarquin's soused brain was trying to process what his sister was suggesting.

'Yes,' said Sophia. 'She'd never even know.'

Tarquin had drunk enough claret not to be overly shocked by what his sister was proposing. She'd always been a perverse, prurient little thing. 'Soph, sometimes I think you go too far,' he observed mildly. For she couldn't be serious this time: what she was proposing was more than a scandal, it was a rape.

'No, but really … Quin, do you think you could?'

'No. I won't do it. It's abhorrent.'

'I'll give you money. A hundred pounds,' she coaxed.

'Don't be ridiculous, Soph.'

'I'll buy you that house you want so much in Mayfair.'

Tarquin had tried, to no avail, to convince his sister to buy a Georgian townhouse in the spring just before she'd left for the continent. 'Really?'

'If you let me watch like I did when I bought you that whore in Whitechapel,' she added. 'Then yes, I'll make that house yours.' So Tarquin did as he was bid, out of habit and out of greed. It was all over in a few minutes.

They had amputated Marta's finger in the naval hospital where the concerned doctor Sophia had finally summoned had immediately sent her. With the infection literally sliced from her body, Marta started to rally and by the time Tarquin and Sophia returned from Morocco – 'The stench, you can't believe the stench and the cruelty. Their animals are nothing but skin and bone' – Marta was sitting up and was looking much her usual self, albeit greatly etiolated, not unlike the Moroccan animals for which her employer had such empathy.

'They say I almost died,' Marta said to Tarquin. 'I can't imagine. And all because of a rose. They say it poisoned my blood.'

'You should have said something,' Sophia said, putting a small box of Turkish delight on the table beside the bed. 'Before it was too late.' She looked speculatively at Marta's lightly bandaged hand. 'You'll never marry now, for you have no finger on which to put a wedding band,' she observed, seemingly without malice.

'Shush,' pleaded Tarquin. 'Just for once, Soph, hold your tongue.'

'I will not!'

'Let me tell her,' said Tarquin who, in the course of their three days in Tangier had, like Sophia, concluded that it was time to go home. The Grand Tour hadn't been a success; now Sophia wanted to sit by the fire in her house in Kent and eat hot buttered toast and drink good English tea.

'No,' said Sophia. 'It is for me to say, not you, Tarquin. *I* employ Miss Mueller, remember. We've come to say goodbye. I tire of the continent and wish to return home. I haven't enjoyed our travels one bit, I must confess, and I don't know why people insist that the Mediterranean is quite the place to visit. I found it all rather dreary and far too hot. I wish I'd spent the summer at home. I'd have got much more done. We start our journey back to England tomorrow.' Sophia opened her voluminous tapestry and velvet bag and extracted an envelope, which she put down next to the Turkish delight. 'Here are your wages up until the day you came here, which I think is most generous of me as you were worse than hopeless during the last week of your employment, and there's also enough there to buy you a second-class ticket back home to Vienna. I regret to say that I won't be offering you a position in the future, your work not having been up to the standard that an important writer like myself requires. I rather think I can make greater progress and be truer to myself without your continuing

'…' – Sophie wanted to say interference, but understood that that was probably one bridge too far – 'involvement in a novel of this nature and significance.'

'Oh,' said Marta, 'I more than agree that you need to follow your own path, Miss Constantinelli, and I wish you luck and success in the future.'

'Oh,' said Sophia, with a tinkling little laugh that wasn't her own, 'I don't need luck. Luck is for those without a talent as precious as mine.'

'I've telegraphed your parents,' added Tarquin, 'and told them you've been ill. I understand your father is coming here to escort you home.'

'Papa?' asked Marta, looking happier than she had in months.

'Yes,' he replied. 'He should be here in the next day or two.'

'Well,' interrupted Sophia, 'I think that's all there is to say. Come on, Tarquin. I don't want to be late for tea at the hotel. I wish you well in the future, Miss Mueller, and as much as I would like to say it was a pleasure having you in my service, it truly wasn't. So goodbye.' And with that Sophia marched out, Tarquin following close behind.

A few minutes later one of the naval hospital's few female civilian nurses came into Marta's room with a note. 'The young gentleman asked me to give you this,' she said, handing Marta a piece of paper on which was written, 'I'm sorry'. Marta was puzzled. Herr Grubb had always been very kind and certainly didn't have anything to apologise for. The next day Egon arrived in Gibraltar, exhausted, but delighted to find his daughter alive.

✳ 31 June – Three Cups Hotel Lyme Regis. I found S.C.'s newest novel, or it found me. There was *Moroccan Moonlight*, leering at me from the window of Lyme Regis' best bookshop. But I bought the wretched thing, out of curiosity I admit, to see what the ridiculous woman had done with all that dreadful prose I had dutifully transcribed as we travelled. I took it back to our hotel, where Lady Jane fell on it with a fervour that surprised me. It transpired that my elderly employee was quite the devotee. 'Miss Constantinelli's best yet,' Lady J. said when she returned the tome to me late the next day, having devoured it. Imagine my surprise when I finally open the novel, in the churchyard of St Michael's, and began to read, to discover the narrative was set in present-day Spain and Gibraltar. And as I read and reread those final lines in my room, long past midnight, I wondered at the miracle of Sophia's momentary visitation of prescience. How had she known? The next morning after breakfast I went down to the Cobb and threw the wretched book out into the depths of the dark Dorset Sea.

Marta, journal, 1891

Miss Sophia Constantinelli published her continental novel, in which two of the three main characters were obviously much more attractive versions of herself and her brother, to hisses of scorn from the critics she'd so hoped to silence. Still it had sold by the cartload and the subsequent royalties had been a satisfactory emollient to her injured pride. She continued to write, to the derision of the men of literature, but had followers enough for such opinions not to matter. She never married and died quite happily a virgin in her seventieth year. Tarquin Grubb, like his sister, never married. After returning from the Continent in 1890 he became something of a recluse, and would blow his brains out in the library of his beautiful Georgian townhouse in Mayfair just before the Great War. He left a note that said only, 'I'm sorry', which confused his few friends who were of the opinion that he'd lived a blameless, almost boring life. At his funeral Sophia rather tactlessly pointed out, during a two-hour eulogy in which she talked primarily about herself, that he'd never been the happiest of people.

Fifteen

✳ Cassowary [figs 67 to 69] The cassowary is an extraordinary bird. Shy and solitary, it avoids human contact. The female cassowary is polyandrous and has many mates whom she leaves to sit the nest and raise the young while she goes off in search of fresh conquest. It is quite a delight to come across a male cassowary in the wild, grunting and hissing at his little following brood of three to five chicks. Unfortunately the natives hunt them for meat and I fear the tenure of the cassowary here in Neumecklenberg, where numbers are low, has not much more time left to run.

Marta, *Neuguinea: Flora & Fauna*,
Wolff & Grunwald, Vienna, 1923, pp. 95–6

'And so it has come to pass,' Marta wrote in conclusion to a letter she was penning to her family towards the end of 1910. 'The Queen is leaving her kingdom as she told me she would when I first came to the colony.' Marta looked up from the page and frowned: she could hear Bernard crashing around the bungalow, swearing loudly. He was so maladroit, which she supposed was a result of his now gargantuan size. The German doctor at Kavieng had advised restraint in all things, especially diet, when Bernard had consulted him about the gout, constant indigestion and cantankerous bowels that had become the bane of his existence. It was the diet, rather than the sobriety the doctor had recommended, that was making Bernard even more irritable than his inflamed lower intestine. Marta sighed. She wished he'd just go to bed. Everything in Bernard's life these days seemed either a personal affront, an attack or, at the very least an event, that required a fair amount of shouting to soothe. He was unhappy, in spite of the resumption of his relationship with Pamela Miller, but his misery was entirely of his own making, so Marta hadn't a lot of sympathy. If he didn't cheer up soon, she thought, tapping her pencil against her teeth, and stop trying to be such a bully, she might leave him after all and go and live in Rabaul. Unable to concentrate, Marta threw down her pencil, opened the door and glared around the corner.

'Mein Gott, Bernard, *what* is the problem? What is the reason for this unholy racket?'

The news of Emma's quitting of the colony had arrived at Gethsemane in the form of a letter from Ettie, who'd returned to Neuguinea with her aunt and Paul Kolbe earlier in the year and was back at Kurakakaul. The doctors of Europe, according to Ettie, had offered no hope of a cure for the Kolbes, only palliative care as they rolled down the slow incline of chronic ill-health towards death. Marta had written back immediately, teasingly raising the possibility that Ettie would succeed her aunt and become the new queen of Neuguinea, which she knew would make her friend laugh. But even as she'd written these fond words, Marta had known that the time of kings and queen of this tiny outpost was all but gone. As Royal had told her in one of his many missives, copra was about business now, not colonisation and empire building.

A few weeks later Captain Macco rode over to Gethsemane. Emma had wired him about the possibility of hosting a reception at his plantation early in the new year, and to do so he needed Bernard's co-operation. Bernard was a little miffed that Emma Kolbe had chosen Ulul-Nono rather than Gethsemane, though it made much more sense. The captain may have been a bachelor, but his plantation, which he'd established soon after Bernard had begun to develop Gethsemane, but with distinctly more capital, was a show place and an ideal location for a large gathering, serviced as it was by Boluminski's road and Gethsemane's wharf, if Bernard would agree to its use.

'So she's really going then?' asked Bernard, who had hitherto dismissed the news out of hand as women's gossip.

'It appears so,' said the captain, who had the most glorious pair of beeswaxed moustaches and always smelled faintly of horse. 'The Queen has sold the lot to HASAG, Whalen's company.'

'Even Gunantambu?' asked Marta, wondering, not for the first time why the captain, who was rather attractive, was still unmarried. Just for a moment she considered what it would be like to be mistress of Ulul-Nono, then laughed silently at herself. She was no more in love with Macco than she was with Bernard, but she *was* a little attracted to him on this hot December afternoon as they sat on the verandah and drank schnapps. She missed the physical aspect of marriage: sometimes, especially now Bernard had resumed his affair, she wondered if in fact she wasn't the loser.

'Yes, even Gunantambu,' replied the captain. 'Whalen is champing at the bit to move in.' He paused and picked up his drink. 'It's something of an end of an era, though, I must say.'

'And what of Mrs Parkinson?' asked Marta.

'Well,' laughed the captain, 'Emma's trying to get her to sell Kuradui, which HASAG sorely want, sitting as it does right in the middle of their holdings, but I have a notion that Frau Parkinson isn't going to budge.'

✳ ✳ ✳

Travelling in Emma's small but comfortable trader, and accompanied by Emma's favourite servants, the Kolbes, Phoebe Parkinson, Marie Allen and Ettie arrived at Gethsemane five days before the party at Ulul-Nono. Although the Queen was travelling with a retinue, the 'ladies in waiting', Marie excepted, had disembarked at Kavieng, from where they were transported to various plantations to stay for the duration of the Neumecklenberg leg of the grand farewell. And for that Marta was grateful. One of the things she'd grown to love about Gethsemane was the quiet, so it was a relief to see only

173

a small group step off the boat and onto the wharf at Gethsemane on a Tuesday in the early February of 1911.

'Oh Ettie,' said Marta, taking both of her friend's hands in her own. 'How lovely to see you again. It's been *too* long. I have missed you.'

'And I you, Marta,' agreed Ettie. 'Do you remember Marie?' she asked, turning to her much younger cousin.

'Yes,' replied Marta, 'I do. But you weren't much more than a child the last time I saw you. And now here you are, all grown up and so pretty too.'

Marie blushed. 'You're very kind, Frau Schmidt.'

'You've been at school in Australia, I believe?' continued Marta.

'Yes' agreed Marie. 'In New South Wales, learning how to be a lady. Though Aunt Emma says she doesn't know how successful that's been.'

Because Ulul-Nono didn't have a harbour anchorage like Gethsemane, Emma had chosen to base her personal steamer at the Schmidt plantation and travel, with the party provisions she had brought, up Boluminski's road to the neighbouring plantation by horse and carriage and Ames Miller's shiny new automobile, which she had commandeered. In spite of this steady stream of traffic through the plantation, Bernard and Marta hardly felt like hosts at all. The Kolbes and Ettie had decided to sleep onboard the trader and Phoebe, who was helping the captain with the party preparations, had arranged that she and Marie would stay in one of Ulul-Nono's many charming guesthouses. Gethsemane, apart from its wharf, was largely redundant, which pleased Marta but left Bernard feeling a little left out. As a result it hadn't taken much gentle bullying from Phoebe to press him into service and soon enough he was her lieutenant.

Even Emma, who'd left the bulk of the organisation to Phoebe, barely spent barely a moment at Gethsemane, occupied in visiting nearly all the plantations in close vicinity, one by one, to say her goodbyes. She did, however, confirm one afternoon, as she and

Phoebe paused a while on the Gethsemane verandah to catch their collective breath, that the HASAG company director, Herr Heinrich Whalen, who had planted Maron Island, and rather famously also made a substantial fortune in the trochus shell trade from which buttons were made, *was* to move into the Gunantambu bungalow after she'd left. It was quietly said, as if it was a small thing, but the Queen's sadness was etched into her large, soft face: more than anything else, the bungalow was representative of Emma's domain.

Phoebe, sensing her sister's need of distraction, beckoned to Emma's major-domo and whispered something in his ear. The native nodded and trotted off down the steps to the pathway that led down to the harbour. A few minutes later he returned carrying a large brown paper-wrapped parcel, which he gave to Phoebe.

'Richard wanted you to have these,' Phoebe said without ceremony, handing Marta the heavy square package. 'He always meant to give them to you himself but somehow …'

It had been almost four years since Phoebe had put her husband to his final rest in the family mat-mat, under the trees he'd planted so many years before when they'd first arrived from Samoa. It had all been so unexpected, a horse and buggy accident. The loss, this rupture in her life, still caused Phoebe obvious pain.

'Thank you,' said Marta, laying the package on her lap and untying the string. 'Herr Parkinson was very kind to think of me.'

Included in the dozen of so books that Richard had left Marta was an annotated manuscript of his book, *Dreissig Jahre in der Südsee*. 'You see,' he had written in German on the cover page, 'there is a little of Merian in all of us, even old scientists like me. Kindest regards – RP.'

It was dated just a few days before his accident. Stroking the paper cover of this, the most precious of Richard Parkinson's gifts, Marta was visibly moved. 'This is very generous,' she said, 'thank you. They will remind me of him always. He was a good man.'

That night the visitors and Macco joined the Schmidts for dinner. They all drank a little too much of the champagne that Emma had bought, and for the first time the Queen talked of her decision to sell up and leave Neuguinea.

'The world is changing. All of this,' she paused and gestured, 'soon all of it will be gone. We Germans,' she said, though Emma, like Phoebe, was only German by marriage, 'need to be careful and wise.'

'Whatever do you mean?' asked Marta, who understood that Frau Kolbe was leaving because it was the wish of her husband, a charming well-fed flatterer, with an eye for the ladies and a profound and oft-voiced dislike of the tropics.

But in answer to that question Emma merely adopted an enigmatic expression and resolutely changed the subject back to the party, now two days away. Macco, who'd been sitting at the far end of the table talking avidly to Marie, was compelled to join this conversation. Seeing his obvious reluctance to abandon his courtship, because it was obvious already to the assembled company that the pair were smitten, Marta felt a sharp twinge of jealousy. Her eyes had never sparkled like Marie Allen's, she thought sadly. But Marta was wrong: they had sparkled and occasionally still did, but she'd convinced herself that she'd forgotten joy, that it had become an elusive talent.

Word of the celebrations at Ulul-Nono had gone out throughout the colony and people travelled from far and wide to attend. A Forsayth and Co. trading ship made a special journey from Rabaul and Herbertshohe loaded with party-bound passengers disembarking at Kavieng and Gethsemane. Among the passengers leaving the vessel at Gethsemane was Royal Weston, who'd been invited to stay by Bernard.

'Where will he sleep, Bernard? Did you think of that?' asked Marta when her husband had informed her of this arrangement only an hour or so before Royal arrived. She had a point. The bungalow had never grown beyond its original four rooms.

'Royal's like a cat, he can sleep anywhere,' Bernard assured her. 'Don't you worry about him.'

But it wasn't the lack of a spare bed at Gethsemane that bothered Marta. It was Royal himself. Since Bernard had revealed Royal's secret, Marta had been unsure how she felt about him. So much so that she hadn't answered his last few letters. In fact she barely read his letters any more: every affectionate laughter-filled word mocked her, made her feel like a fool.

'Are you going to sleep in *that*?' asked Marta, as she watched Royal lash up a string hammock under the eaves of Gethsemane's verandah.

'Absolutely, Mrs Schmidt,' he replied. 'They're very comfortable. I will have to borrow a mosquito net, though. I've brought a change of shirt, a bottle of single malt, a tin of beluga and a painting for you, but no mosquito net, I'm afraid. It was a question of priorities.'

'You have caviar,' Marta said, her eyes lighting up.

'Ah,' said Royal. 'About the caviar she's excited, but my artistic masterpiece, in that she has no interest.'

'Yes, but caviar!' giggled Marta. 'You can't blame me, Royal.'

It was interesting: until the moment that Royal had appeared at the foot of the steps and smiled up at her, she'd thought she would be repulsed by him, but all she'd seen was her friend, a boyishly charming man who made her laugh and talked to her in a language she understood. With Royal, nothing, whether spoken or written, was lost in translation. Nothing. No wonder she smiled the moment she saw him.

'All the way from Russia,' Royal replied. 'You'll have to provide the schnapps, though.'

'But show me the painting first,' said Marta.

Royal pulled a small oilskin-wrapped oblong, not much more than twenty by twenty-five centimetres, out of his satchel and handed it to her.

'Oh, how lovely!' exclaimed Marta. It was a painting of Bernard and Masta Raus, just their heads and shoulders, one so white, the other so brown. Behind Raus were the white boards of the bungalow, and backdropping Bernard was the impenetrable green of the rainforest. 'You are very clever, Royal.'

'I've always thought so,' said Royal. 'But you, m'dear,' he said, 'are the only other person in the world who knows it. Sadly my genius is lost on the masses.'

Marta laughed. 'I wouldn't go quite that far.'

'Oh, but you should,' replied Royal cryptically. 'You should.'

They ate the glossy grey fish eggs, so deliciously salty, with hard-boiled eggs, smeared onto water crackers that hadn't quite gone stale.

'So how's your painting going?' asked Royal, after they'd exhausted the latest colony gossip. 'The oils and brushes I sent you recently, they were adequate? My agent tells me they're the best than that can be had. I'm only an amateur dabbler, as you know – a piece of wood and some house paint is all I need – so I wasn't entirely certain what you required.'

'Oh goodness, yes. More than adequate. Beautiful, in fact. Your agent's right, I'm sure the colours *are* the very best. I'm not entirely convinced of about this venture into oils, but I've charged myself with at least playing with them for an hour or two each day. It's a very different medium from my more usual watercolour, and I need to develop the technique.'

'So you're busy then?'

'Oh, very' replied Marta. 'In addition to the paintings themselves, I need, of course, to be constantly gathering subjects.'

'Ah,' said Royal. 'And this is perhaps why you haven't being replying to my letters of late. You are engrossed in project à la Merian?'

'Yes,' said Marta, seizing the convenient excuse. 'Yes, that's it exactly.'

'Good,' replied Royal. 'I was beginning to think you were cross with me.'

'No, no, no.' Marta's denial was emphatic. 'Cross with you, Herr Weston?' she teased. 'Never.' And that was true. She hadn't been cross, merely unnerved.

Royal scooped the last of the caviar onto a cracker and handed it to Marta. 'You're a little drunk, I think,' he observed, sitting back in his chair and looking at her. They'd swallowed rather a lot of schnapps.

'Oh!' exclaimed Marta. 'How can you tell?'

'Your eyes,' he said. 'They're shining like stars, or diamonds, well … something glittery anyway. Sorry, not much of a poet, I'm afraid.'

'You old flatterer,' Marta protested, blushing a little.

'I do my best,' said Royal as he lit two cigarettes, giving Marta one. 'Can I see what you've been doing?' he continued. 'After all, I've let you laugh at my ghastly daubs.'

'No,' replied Marta, 'not yet. Maybe later when I've improved. I'm terribly amateurish still.'

'As you wish,' Royal replied. 'Though I suspect, Mrs Schmidt, that you're a better artist than you give yourself credit for.'

✳ ✳ ✳

The day of the party started in torrential rain but by early afternoon a wind had picked up and had chased away all the rain clouds and the humidity. It was still hot but not unpleasantly so. Over at the Ulul-Nono labourers' quarters near the drying sheds the sound of drumming could be heard as the afternoon began to wane, and the smell of roasting village pig, a pair of which had been gifted to the plantation workers by Emma so that they too could enjoy themselves, drifted over towards the plantation house. By nightfall the bungalow and garden at Ulul-Nono were full to overflowing.

'Yes, I can see your problem,' mused Reverend Miles Ford from the Wesleyan mission in Kavieng. Having discovered that he was a keen amateur natural historian, Marta had been talking to him at length about her difficulty in obtaining specimens of deep-sea shells and fish. 'You need to get some pet natives on to it,' Ford continued. 'Don't do it yourself – terribly dangerous. Don't want to end up as bait for sharks, not a pretty young thing like yourself.'

'Yes,' agreed Marta, amused at being called both pretty and young in the same breath. She was distracted, however, having glimpsed beyond the Reverend Ford's shoulder, a few moments before, Bernard, bending purposefully over Pamela Miller, who was in the first flush of her second pregnancy. Her husband was in very real danger of falling into his mistress's expansive cleavage. Then, as quickly as it opened, the gap had closed and Bernard and his whore were swallowed up once again by the crowd. 'I've been told that many of the deep-water shell varietals are actually poisonous,' Marta continued distractedly. 'But they're so beautiful that I want to paint them very much.'

'Yes,' agreed Ford, 'very pleasurable to paint I would think, though not my interest, of course.' He had earlier revealed to Marta that he was 'a bird man'.

'Yes,' replied Marta. 'Though their translucency, that shine, is difficult to capture in watercolours, and would perhaps be better served by oils. My primary difficulty, though, as I said, is the shells that I find have long been abandoned by their creature and the colours are always rather faded.'

'Ahh,' said Ford. 'Yes, there's nothing like a live specimen to which the amateur natural historian can apply the correct method of killing and preservation.'

'It all seems rather bloodthirsty.' Marta mostly resisted killing God's creatures, even if it meant that her subjects often flew, crawled or scuttled away before their portraits were completed.

'The amateur natural historian cannot be squeamish,' advised Ford robustly. He was at his happiest when eviscerating some hapless bird of paradise that only hours before had been hopping from branch to branch in the rainforest. Curiously, he always felt, in the moment when he took a bird's life, rather closer to God than perhaps he should have.

'And you say the natives will go out into the ocean and collect for me if I ask them?' Marta asked.

'Well, you'll need to pay them, in coin or tobacco. They won't do it out of any sense of the greater good or indeed even science. I have paid dearly for some of my most magnificent bird specimens, the ones that were brought alive and flapping to my door by kanakas,' Ford added. 'They're quick to learn what you want if you're paying for the specimens. People underestimate the kanaka. But he's clever in his own way.'

And with that, the man of God excused himself to refresh his glass, leaving Marta standing on the bougainvillaea-shrouded verandah, watching a handful of people dancing on the torch-lit lawn to music provided by a gramophone, which a young native boy wound before each new record was played.

'Come dance with me, Mrs Schmidt,' said Royal, coming up behind Marta and laying a hand on her shoulder. For the brief moment it was there, the hand felt, to Marta, solid and real and, best of all, right.

'Yes,' she replied, surprising herself. 'Yes, I would like to dance very much.'

To their mutual delight, Marta and Royal, danced together well, as did Captain Macco and Marie, who were still getting on splendidly, much to Emma and Phoebe's obvious satisfaction. Sometime after midnight Marta found herself sitting with Ettie on the bungalow steps, discussing Marie and Macco's courtship.

'I do love a good love story, don't you?' said Ettie.

'Oh yes,' agreed Marta fervently, though she didn't really care one way or the other.

'I see a wedding in our future,' Ettie prophesied.

Marta laughed. 'My mother used to say such things. Claimed she always knew when something of a romantic nature was up.'

'And did she?' asked Ettie.

'No,' said Marta. 'She was *always* wrong.'

'And what can you see for yourself in the future, Marta?' laughed Ettie.

'Only my bed and a good night's sleep,' Marta replied, yawning widely. She suddenly felt very old and profoundly exhausted. It was time to go home. But rather than finding Bernard and their transport after she'd bid Ettie goodnight, Marta decided that she would walk home, following the native track lit now by the full moon that hung bloated and low in the night sky. She skirted a couple talking in that urgent undertone of arguing lovers; genuflected, mentally at least, to the Catholics and Wesleyans who were smoking and quietly talking under the fish poison trees; and finally passed a young girl, a Parkinson granddaughter perhaps, sitting despondently on the grass beneath a frangipani, sobbing in a heart-rending manner that was difficult to resist. However, with the call of the sea coming in like a promise from the east and the thought of her cool, clean, white bed, Marta paid the girl no mind, and walked on, following the ribbon of silvery soil, worn clean of any growth by the pad of native feet, that wandered through Ulul-Nono's plantation.

It took over an hour but eventually Marta saw the shadows of the pair of entwined coconut palms on the point and realised she was almost home. The native village near the drying sheds was dark and silent, the cooking fires settled to sulky embers. As Marta walked by, a curly-tailed dog barked once, twice, then slunk back to its lair. She had just rounded the corner on from the drying sheds and into the bay below the house when she was arrested by the sight of a lone figure sitting on the end of the wharf smoking a cigarette. A man, Marta could tell by the outline of the sitter's body, but not Bernard. It wasn't until Marta was a few strides away from the end of the wharf and the figure had turned at the sound of her footsteps that Marta was sure it was Royal. She sat down beside him.

'How are you?' he asked, flicking the spent end of his cigarette into the sea.

'Drunk and tired,' she admitted.

Royal sighed. 'Me too.'

'I was surprised to see you here. I thought you'd still be at the ball.'

'I got bored,' Royal replied.

'What are you doing out here by yourself? Fishing?'

'Fishing, yes. Very funny. Fishing for malaria maybe. The mosquitoes are murder.' Royal pulled his cigarette case out of his pocket, opened it and offered it to Marta.

'What a week it's been,' Marta said, leaning in as the Vesta flared. 'I will be pleased when everyone goes home and life returns to normal.'

'How are you and Bernard?'

'Aside from the fact that he's been having an affair with Pamela Miller for the two years, surprisingly well,' Marta replied.

'Ah,' said Royal. 'I wondered whether you knew.'

'You *were* fishing!'

'Yes,' laughed Royal. 'I probably was. But let me say, m'dear, you don't appear overly upset by Bernard's infidelity.'

'I don't know if I even am,' confessed Marta. 'Even in the best of times we were hardly a love-match.'

'Then why did you marry him?'

'I don't think I ever really intended too,' admitted Marta. 'But the chance to travel, to expand my horizons, protected by the conventionality of marriage, was too wonderful to resist. And, to be honest, I don't know if I even really believe in romantic love or its transformative powers.'

'Oh,' sighed Royal softly. 'That's so sad.'

'Really?' said Marta.

'Oh yes,' he said. 'To love is everything.'

'But life isn't a romantic novel or a fairy tale.'

'Oh yes it is,' replied Royal, flicking his spent cigarette into the sea. 'And we need to believe in a happy ending or there'd be no point going on.'

'Ha! How maudlin you are tonight, Royal.'

'It's the full moon.'

'And the liquor,' Marta said, standing up. 'Don't forget that.' She stood for a minute looking at the moon, dragging the last few puffs of smoke out of her cigarette. 'Don't stay out here too long or the mosquitoes will suck you dry.' Then suddenly she bent down and gently kissed Royal on the mouth. His lips were soft and dry and he tasted of whisky and tobacco. The moment was fleeting – a brush, a touch, nothing more, before she straightened up again. 'See,' she said. 'A kiss is just a kiss, Herr Weston. It doesn't have the power to transform.'

That night, when Bernard returned home from the party, he found his wife waiting in his bed. But when he woke the next morning she was gone again. But sometimes, after that, when he least expected it, she would come to him at night, under the cover of darkness, and without a word passing between them they would make love.

No one who attended the party at Ulul-Nono was at all surprised when, six weeks later, it was announced that Captain Macco and Marie Allen would marry. For Emma the union was especially gratifying, the last marriage that she would arrange for one of her girls. Perhaps it *was* time to go and sit like a fat, old lady on the verandah of her handsome, comfortable home in Mosman, with her son Coe Forsayth near at hand and Paul at her side. She would miss Phoebe most. Then Ettie.

Sixteen

✳ It's impossible to know what to do with her. I am quite at my wits' end, I must confess. One simply gets too old for such emotional upheavals.

Klara, letter, April 1912

Augusta, indulged to the core, had in adulthood found her own path, and her particular talent was people. Bright, garrulous and completely lacking in self-consciousness, she drew all to her: men, women, children and animals. School, which was a torture for Gretchen, had proven, as it had for Marta some years earlier, to be Augusta's natural habitat, albeit for completely different reasons. Throughout Augusta's adolescence the house on Wipplinger Strasse had been filled with young people's voices as Augusta brought home friends and assorted strays. And her parents had encouraged it, hoping, in a small way, that some of Augusta's joy would magically rub off on the increasingly melancholic Gretchen. It never occurred to Klara that Augusta would do anything other than marry well and with ease at the first possible opportunity. After two such difficult daughters, she was surely owed a child who would do all the normal things.

But Augusta had never, as far as Klara knew, harboured a romantic affection for any of the young gentlemen in her endlessly shifting entourage of friends. It had been at Augusta's twentieth birthday soirée, in 1910, that Klara realised she knew hardly any of the guests. These new people were older and shabbier, they didn't laugh easily and their faces had none of the softness of privilege

185

to which Klara was accustomed. Gustie had changed lives without either her or Egon noticing. It was, Klara had thought dryly, time she had a talk to Augusta about the company she was keeping.

'She claims to be a suffragette and socialist,' Klara had written, the day after this conversation, 'and says she's been offered a position, which she intends to take, in one of the trade unions. It's hard to know which is the worst of the three.'

But it was more than the embracing of proletariat political causes that concerned Klara. At the party Augusta had constantly gravitated towards an older man, a senior member of some trade union or another. He was nearer Klara's age than Augusta's, but the look in her daughter's eye, the sway of the hips, the way she held herself, with her head tilted to the side when she talked to Herr Hennecke ... well, it was unmistakable. Klara also knew that there wasn't much she could do about the infatuation. It was probably just a schoolgirl crush and her fears had faded a little over the succeeding months when it became evident that Herr Hennecke was entirely absent from the group of strange people with which Augusta seemed most inclined to spend time. There *was* someone, though.

'Well,' continued Klara's letter of early 1912,

it transpires that Augusta has been conducting an affair with this man, this communist, who, my dear, might I add, is married, for over two years now, if her journal is to be believed. We confronted her with this and she was completely unrepentant. She spouted some nonsense about becoming his second wife when the revolution comes. My hand itched to slap her when she said that, I can tell you. We sent her off to the estate immediately, of course, but the little minx ran away at the first possible opportunity, saying she would rather die than be separated from her lover. Such nonsense! And now the gentleman, it seems, has left her, and she has spent the past month sobbing and refusing to eat, saying her heart is irrevocably broken. Of much more concern is the ruin of her reputation. Who will have her now?

'Mein Gott!' said Marta as she read this. She was shocked, and a little impressed too, but not entirely surprised by the news. Gustie had always been flighty.

The only saving grace in the whole sorry affair is that it hasn't resulted in a child and for that I'm eternally grateful. I don't know what else I can do other than exile her to Neuguinea with you. It is time, my dear, for you to do your duty by Augusta. Neither your father nor I has the energy or heart to deal with her, and I fear if we don't send her away it will all end very badly, if not this time then at another juncture in the future. She is wild, willful and beyond our control. You *must* take her. You *will* take her, Marta. On this there is no negotiation.

As she'd written this, Klara had thought of Gretchen in her small white room at the sanatorium and knew she couldn't traverse the emotional peaks and valleys of another imprisonment. And really Neuguinea was probably Augusta's only chance of making a marriage. Marta had always said how thin women were on the ground in the territory.

I have found a family for her to travel with as far as Australia, and Augusta has reluctantly agreed that she will join you in Neuguinea. The ship sails in eight weeks with Augusta on board, with or without your permission, and for goodness sake, Marta, you *must* find her a husband.

Marta checked the date on the letter: a little over seven weeks had elapsed since it was written. Any day now, if everything had gone according to plan, her sister would be setting sail. Of course Gustie was welcome. And her mother was right, it *was* time that she did her duty by the girl – well, woman, for Gustie was all grown up now, the same age Marta had been when ... well, all that was history now.

'So she is to come here? To live?' said Bernard one evening, a month or so after Marta had received her mother's letter, to which she'd replied with a confirmatory wire. She'd seen no need to discuss Augusta's imminent arrival with Bernard before now. She knew he wouldn't say anything – he wouldn't dare – so had merely presented him with a fait accompli. 'For how long?' he asked, as he gnawed on a chicken leg.

'Perhaps forever,' said Marta. 'Mama wants me to find her a husband.'

'Shame Macco's been snapped up at last,' said Bernard.

'Yes,' said Marta. 'I thought that too.'

'We'll have to build another room,' continued Bernard, between mouthfuls, 'unless of course … '

'I was thinking of two new rooms,' Marta said, cutting her husband off at the marital pass. 'I've done some drawings. I'll show them to you after luncheon.'

✳ ✳ ✳

'Marta, Marta!' The shouts came from a frantically waving figure, standing on deck next to one of the ship's officers. 'Here! Marta, here!'

Marta, who'd availed herself of Ames Miller and his auto to come into Kavieng and retrieve Augusta, smiled, then laughed and waved back. Judging by Augusta's enthusiasm and volume, Marta thought wryly, she hadn't changed a bit, disgrace or no disgrace. The *Tui Robust*'s wooden sides scraped against the wharf and the crew scurried about making the ship secure. Augusta was at the head of the queue when the gangway was finally lowered, champing at the bit like a portly young pony on a hunt field. Once the all clear was indicated by the officer of the watch, Augusta charged down the gangway and seconds later was hugging Marta, her head fitting neatly beneath her sister's breasts, and gabbling away in German. There was a faint wave of laughter from the handful of passengers following Augusta down the gangway: few hadn't been charmed by the diminutive Fräulein Mueller's exuberance and energy during the overnight voyage from Rabaul.

'Gustie, Gustie, slow down,' Marta protested, fighting her instinctive reaction to push away this warm, slightly pungent mass of soft human flesh. 'Catch your breath, you silly girl,' she continued, extracting herself from her sister's sticky embrace. She held Augusta at arm's length. 'Let's have a look at you.'

The two Mueller women stood, temporarily silenced, and gazed at one another. 'Gustie, you're all grown up,' Marta observed in wonder. 'Though you're still as tiny as ever.'

'Well, of course I've grown up!' exclaimed Augusta. "I'm a woman now. And you … you've got old.' Reaching up a tentative finger, she touched the deep lines that scored Marta's face. 'You look like the painting of Grandmother Mueller that hangs in the hall at home.'

'Do I?' said Marta.

'Oh yes,' said Augusta. 'Remember, the miniature, in the hall beside the dining room door? We used to giggle about what a grim old witch she looked – not that you are … '

'How are Mama and Papa?' asked Marta, who wasn't at all offended by Augusta's tactless comparison.

'As can be expected,' Augusta replied. 'Mama wrote to you of my scandal, I assume?'

'Well yes,' replied her sister. 'How could she not? And *how* could you, Augusta? I mean, really! What were you thinking?'

Augusta giggled. 'You sound just like Mama,' she said, distinctly unchastened. 'I was in love with him. There was quite a to-do about it all. Lots of yelling and tears. And I really did think I would die when he threw me over. He left, you know. The party found him job in the Munich office and he left me. It was odd, though, how quickly I started to feel better and in fact by the time I boarded the ship in Italy I felt quite myself again. Isn't that the oddest thing? The heart really can heal itself.'

Marta raised an eyebrow. It was clear that Augusta had made a splendid recovery. 'It almost sounds as though you enjoyed the whole débâcle,' said Marta dryly.

'Oh, but I did in the oddest kind of way,' explained Augusta, linking arms with Marta. 'I really did. I was so bored, and it *is* the most exciting thing that has ever happened to me *and* I got to come to Neuguinea too, so that I could see for myself the cannibals and coconuts that Bernard spoke of at *such length*.'

'But Augusta, the consequences, think of the consequences. Many would regard you as soiled goods.'

'Oh that,' said Augusta complacently. 'Mama said it probably wouldn't matter out here and that you'd be able to find me a husband.'

Marta had to concede that her mother was probably right on the first count, though she wondered how on earth she was expected to marry Augusta off. The place *was* crawling with bachelors, but the few men she knew were married or, as in Royal's case, otherwise inclined. Perhaps Ettie and Royal would be able to help her with this endeavour, for surely between them they knew everyone in the colony.

'Oh look,' Augusta said. 'Look, they've started unloading. What a relief. I'm longing to get out of this heat.' Beads of sweat trickled down her bright red face and the underarms and neckline of her slightly soiled, white dress, were soaked. Augusta held a hand to her flushed cheek beneath her straw boater. 'Is there anywhere I can sit? Is it safe?' She looked longingly down the length of Bagil Wharf towards the casuarina trees growing along the shore, under which a group of kanakas were squatting on their haunches, chewing betel nut.

'Oh, yes, yes. I'm sorry,' Marta said, a little flustered. 'Silly of me keeping you out here. So unnecessary. But look,' she turned and pointed down the wharf, 'here's Ames and the auto now.'

'Ames?'

'Ames Miller. He owns the plantation to the south of us. He's taking us to Gethsemane. He has an auto — terribly handy, so much faster than a horse and carriage. It's the only one on the island. He's a nice chap.'

'He's a bit of a sight,' observed Augusta, taking in Ames' shambolic attire as he strolled up the wharf towards them.

'Oh,' replied Marta blithely, 'one gets used to what a scarecrow he is. He's an Australian, and they put on airs by not putting on airs. He's very rich, you know. Lovely auto too. I rather covet one for myself. He doesn't speak German, though.'

'I have been practising my English on the way over,' Augusta assured Marta.

'Fräulein Mueller,' cried Ames, sinking into a deep, clumsy curtsey. 'Ames Miller, chauffeur extraordinaire at your service. Welcome to our humble island.'

Augusta giggled.

'Oh Ames, thank Gott,' said Marta, speaking once more in English. 'Could you please take my sister to the auto while I organise her luggage?'

'Splendid plan!' Ames said. 'Follow me, Fräulein Mueller, the auto's just over there, under the trees. We'll have you at the Kavieng Hotel in a jiffy. Bit of a tiffin before we head for home, I think.'

'Is it much of a journey to Marta's plantation? I keep wondering when the end will come to all this travelling,' said Augusta, her English slightly hesitant.

'A little further,' said Ames, as he helped Augusta into the back seat of the auto. 'An hour or so more, along a splendid road with the wind in our hair, and we'll be at Gethsemane.' A few minutes later, with two natives carrying Augusta's luggage trotting behind her, Marta joined them. 'A quick tiffin at the hotel, old girl?' asked Ames.

'Mmm,' agreed Marta, 'yes, lovely.'

Augusta took her hat off and fanned herself with it. 'I didn't realise it would be so hot here. How do you bear it, Marta?' she asked, still speaking in English, as she plucked at the soaked bodice of her high-necked dress. 'You should have warned me,' she continued as the engine spluttered into life, then settled into a rhythmic putt-putt-putt as Ames manoeuvred it into gear and pushed down on the accelerator. After that conversation came to a standstill. It wasn't until a few minutes after they'd been decanted at the foot of the hotel steps that Augusta could speak again. 'Does he always go that fast?' she asked in German as the two women entered the building with Ames trailing behind them.

'Sadly yes,' replied Marta. 'Though I must confess I find Herr Miller's recklessness rather exhilarating.'

Ames Miller's driving wasn't greatly enhanced by the three gin and tonics he'd quaffed at the hotel bar, but as Marta and Augusta were a little tipsy too, it somehow mattered less. For Augusta the last leg of her journey to Gethsemane passed in a blur of nausea, coconut trees, clouds of white dust and the outraged squawks of chickens fleeing from the auto's path. By the time Ames swung off the road and roared up Gethsemane's driveway, Augusta was feeling distinctly ill.

'Home sweet home!' cried Ames, applying the brakes with unnecessary violence so that the vehicle slid sideways over the sand and shell, heading towards one of the bungalow's concrete piles. Fortunately it was brought to a sudden halt by the low stone wall that edged the driveway.

'You're going to come to grief in that thing one day, old man,' said Bernard, as he wandered down the bungalow steps.

Augusta, though delighted to see Bernard of whom she had very fond memories, was also a little shocked at his appearance. He was so *fat*. Not just plump, not just a little overweight, but positively gargantuan. How could someone change so much in ten years?

'Little sister,' said Bernard. He took one of Augusta's hands and leaned in to kiss her on her forehead. The smell of his breath, sour with indigestion and decaying teeth, did little for Augusta's roiling stomach and woozy head. 'Welcome to paradise.'

'Hello, Bernard,' replied Augusta faintly, swaying a little. The ground seemed to be shifting beneath her feet and her vision had gone hazy. Then she bent over and threw up on her brother-in-law's boots.

'Mein Gott!' exclaimed Bernard, clearly repulsed, though the contents of Augusta's stomach amounted to little more than thin bile dotted with chunks of the pineapple she'd eaten for breakfast.

Marta started laughing. 'Oh, you poor thing,' she said, taking Augusta's arm and half-carrying her up inside, leaving Bernard standing there with vomit-splattered boots and trousers. 'It's the heat,' continued Marta. 'I was exactly the same when I first arrived. You'll get used to it.'

As Augusta was settled into the chaise on the verandah and poured a glass of tepid water from the jug on the drinks trolley, Bernard stalked off around the corner of the house to clean himself up. 'Raus, Raus,' he bellowed. 'Kissem was–was he come.'

'So tell me,' said Marta, in a too bright voice, 'how did you find Herr Weston?' Royal had taken care of Augusta during her stopover in Rabaul. 'Did he look after you well? Did you like him? Such a dear friend. Did he ask after me?'

It had taken Augusta a week or two to realise that Marta and Bernard didn't exactly present a united front. Strangely enough, though, it wasn't the separate bedrooms that had alerted Augusta, for that was hardly unusual, but the way Marta looked right through Bernard as if he wasn't even there. Something had obviously gone very wrong since the couple had left Vienna, but Augusta, wise now in the way of people, knew that it would be prudent to hold her tongue. She would have to wait for Marta to come to her. Though who knew how long that might take? It was obvious she preferred to work on her illustrations or wander around the jungle than spend time in the company of others. Even her own scandalous affair, which Augusta had expected to be a frequent topic of conversation between them, had warranted no more than the faint telling-off that Marta had delivered at the wharf.

It had taken just small one thing for the puzzle of Bernard and Marta to become complete. Everything, the reason for Marta's simmering anger and oblique coldness, and Bernard's apologetic mien, was revealed to Augusta in the moment she bent down to shake hands with three year-old Timothy Miller, when he visited Gethsemane a few months later with his parents and eighteen-month-old brother Jonathan, and found herself gazing into her brother-in-law's eyes.

Seventeen

Life at Gethsemane would have been very lonely for Augusta had it not been for Marie Macco at Ulul-Nono. As Marta and Ettie had both observed, the two young women had much in common in terms of age and temperament, and Macco, too, approved of the friendship. Renowned for his generosity, he gave Augusta a pretty bay pony on which, most days, she rode over to Ulul-Nono via the native track that joined the two properties, leaving Marta to her unnerving and protracted silences, which, she told Augusta, meant she was thinking. And as far as Augusta could tell, Marta seemed content enough, though the same couldn't be said of Bernard, who was clearly miserable. It was impossible for Augusta, who so valued the heart, not to mourn for what she found at Gethsemane. Bernard had betrayed Marta, and Augusta couldn't understand why she consciously chose to live, seemingly happily, without love. Sometimes, Augusta felt, Marta was nearly as mad as Gretchen, though in a completely different way.

Gretchen took her own life a year and a half after Augusta left Vienna. Klara's sad missive telling Marta and Augusta of the tragedy arrived a few days before the Easter of 1914.

There had been some improvement in Gretchen's condition over the years, spells when her affliction retreated and she could walk and talk a little. Although cause for quiet hope among her family and doctors, these spells of semi-lucidity left Gretchen with the terrifying knowledge of her insanity. Somehow she'd slipped out the asylum building unnoticed the day after Christmas, when the staff were slow and drowsy from seasonal excess and festivities, and wandered out into the snow and down to the orchard, where she'd hanged herself from an ancient apple tree. The staff had found her a few hours later, suspended beneath the branches, like a dreadful icicle, twisting in the chill wind.

'Her feet were bare,' wrote Klara, her tears smearing the ink. 'She wasn't even wearing shoes. Nobody saw her go. Nobody noticed until it was too late.'

Reading that awful, sad, letter, Marta shivered, thinking of her sister walking through the snow in order to finish the madness, to make it go away forever. In a small way, she thought she understood.

In the days following the arrival of the news, there was talk of Augusta returning to Vienna, but it was too late, they all knew that. Gretchen's death did have at least one positive outcome: it brought Marta and Augusta together for perhaps the first time in their lives as they turned to each other for comfort and to honour Gretchen's memory. It was inevitable, in these hours when they sat together quietly and talked of happier times, that Marta would eventually remember Gretchen's portrait, which she'd carried halfway across the world and hidden away a decade before.

'Ugghh! That's hideous! Disgusting!' exclaimed Augusta, who had never seen any of the paintings that Gretchen had produced during that summer. 'I don't know how you could have kept it! You should burn it, Marta.'

'Never!' said Marta, protectively drawing the oilcloth wrapping back over the picture. 'I think it's a magnificent painting and I like it very much.'

'But Marta,' cried Augusta, 'it's so lewd and depraved. Your breast is bare. And that hideous creature and the way you're looking at it. And the Christ child, well, that's just blasphemous. How could you love such a thing?'

'Because I do,' said Marta, unruffled. 'It's art, Gustie. All a matter of taste. Besides, the nude is a perfectly legitimate subject.'

'Yes, yes,' protested Augusta, 'but they're not real people, are they?'

Marta laughed. 'Well, I think they may have been at one time or another. Besides, I think the painting is meant to be religious in nature and Gretchen has depicted me as some sort of pagan Virgin. The child sitting on my shoulder is meant to represent Christ, I think, as you said, and the toad … I don't know, perhaps sin. We'd been to look at the religious paintings at the Kunsthistorisches Museum that spring, when Gretchen was still well, and she'd been very taken with them, as well she might, for they were extraordinarily beautiful. I remember that day – she was so excited and alive, and I thought, hoped, that Gretchen's sadness was on the wane and she would be well again.'

'So sad,' said Augusta, tears trickling down her cheeks.

'Awful.' Marta left her sister sitting on the verandah quietly sobbing, wanting to secrete the painting away in the large new room that was her study, before Bernard came home from the drying sheds.

Gretchen's suicide wasn't the only death in Europe in 1913. In July of that year the Hamburg office of HASAG, which had bought out Frau Kolbe's Neuguinea interests, received a telegram from Queen Emma, who was in Monte Carlo, having travelled there from Australia only a few weeks before to nurse her estranged and dangerously ill husband. The wire, sent two days after the fact, informed HASAG that Paul Kolbe had died in a Monte Carlo hotel. What Emma's telegram didn't say was that he was living as a married man with another woman at the time. Kolbe's death might not have raised much more than a ripple of interest in the colony if the first telegram hadn't been followed a few hours later by another from the hotel manager informing HASAG that Frau

Kolbe had also died, and what did her European agent want to do with the two bodies that he now had in his hotel. It was the height of the summer season and the rooms were needed.

The colony was electrified by the news of the double deaths and rumours were rife. Emma's son Coe Forsayth wrote an article, published in the *Sydney Morning Herald* near enough to a week after his mother's demise, explaining that Paul Kolbe had died on the 19th 'from Brights Disease and heart failure, and his decease evidently accelerated Mrs Kolbe's death, which took place from heart failure on the 21st'.

No one believed it, of course, not for a second. It was much too banal a way for a character like Emma to go. Besides it was hardly a secret that the Kolbes had barely been man and wife since they'd left Neuguinea in 1909. HASAG's owner, Wahlen, had seen the Queen only two months before her death when the passenger liner taking her to Europe had stopped in Rabaul for recoaling. He'd tried to convince her to return to Australia, as had Royal Weston, both arguing that Emma owed Paul nothing and that her own health should be foremost in her mind. In truth both men had been very well aware of just what Emma might find in Monte Carlo. But Emma had always had a blind spot when it came to her men, as Royal had often pointed out, and wouldn't be deterred.

At Gethsemane Marta, Augusta and Bernard each favoured a different version of what had happened in Monte Carlo. Augusta, who'd never met the Kolbes, naturally went for the most dramatic and popular scenario, which involved Emma discovering her husband living with another woman, poisoning him and, wracked with guilt, taking her own life thirty-six hours later. It was her age, thought Marta, shaking her head in disbelief: the young do so like things to be exciting.

Bernard's version involved Emma, seeing her own end in sight, using the last of her strength to smother Paul so that her riches would go to her family, not Paul's German relatives, who'd always looked down their noses at her and referred to her as 'the large Creole'.

Marta, however, reached the sensible conclusion. She knew from the letters she'd received from Ettie over the years that neither Paul nor Emma was well. Back in 1909 the pair had been patients of the Frankfurt clinic, which had sent them both away, saying that there was nothing further they could do to help and that all either could do was wait for death. It didn't seem unreasonable to Marta that Emma, exhausted from her journey and made fragile by her husband's latest betrayal, would collapse and fail to rally when Paul died.

As a measure of Wahlen's respect for Emma, he arranged for the Kolbes' ashes to be bought home to Gunantambu and interred in the family mat-mat, in the country she loved, surrounded by the people she'd always thought of as her subjects.

The Schmidts and Augusta took passage on a trader with a number of other expatriates, German and Australian, who were travelling to Herbertshohe for Emma's last farewell. There was almost a carnival atmosphere on board the *Ngaire Belle*, as it sailed through the night, packed to the gunwales. There was barely room to sit, so even catching forty winks was out of the question. Not that anyone minded. Hip flasks of scotch, schnapps and gin were freely passed around, and little of the legendary animosity between the Germans and Australians was evident. Everyone had a story about Emma and that was social glue enough. Herbertshohe was already a swarming mass of activity when the *Ngaire Belle* arrived in Blanche Bay the next morning. They had to wait for over an hour before they could tie up alongside, such was the queue of vessels waiting to dock and disembark.

'Bernard, old man, over here,' shouted Royal, weaving his way through the crowd on the wharf. 'I thought you'd never arrive. Hell of a turnout, though. Emma would be very pleased.'

'I've never seen so many people in Herbertshohe!' exclaimed Bernard, looking around in amazement. 'There can't be a white man left on a plantation in the whole of the colony!'

'Extraordinary,' agreed Marta. 'Royal, lovely to see you again.' She held out her hand to her friend, who shook it firmly. 'And you remember Augusta?'

'Of course,' said Royal. 'We had a merry day or two, didn't we, Miss Mueller?'

'Of course we did, Herr Weston,' agreed Augusta, though she'd actually found Marta and Bernard's Australian friend a little strange. He was far friendlier, for example, than Augusta thought one should be with a native servant. When she'd mentioned this to Marta, her sister had laughed and said something about this simply being Royal's way and that she, too, had found him a little odd when she'd first made his acquaintance.

'Have you got much luggage?' asked Royal.

'No,' replied Bernard, hefting a carpetbag on high. 'Just a few bits and pieces. We return home tomorrow.'

'Were we able to get rooms at the hotel?' asked Marta as she climbed into the carriage.

Royal laughed. 'Not likely with all this lot in town,' he said. 'You'll stay with me out at Cape Gazelle. It's a bit of a journey, but we'll endure, I'm sure.' He slapped the reins gently against the pony's back. 'The whole shebang for Emma doesn't start until midday, so I thought we'd go to the hotel and see if we can't find some breakfast.'

By midday the party atmosphere at Herbertshohe had reached fever pitch as everyone, expatriate and native alike, gathered at the foreshore in front of the offices Emma had built at Ralum. A few minutes after twelve o'clock Herr Wahlen in his automobile, with Coe Forsayth sitting beside him, holding two metal urns on his lap, drove slowly through the crowds to the start of the road from Ralum to Gunantambu. The cortege fell effortlessly into a hierarchal formation. The hearse, for want of a better word, was followed by Emma's huge extended family, then the incumbent German governor, with various senior officials in the administration falling in behind him like chicks behind a mother hen, as in death they accepted and honoured Emma as they never had in life. Expatriates, planters and company people, both German and Australian, trod as one in the wake of officialdom. Then came the natives. Too many to count, they brought up the rear, drumming and wailing with grief as the funeral procession slowly made its way past Gunantambu to the mat-mat in the foothills over looking the harbour a mile or so inland from Emma's old residence.

A concrete slab, not more than a couple of metres from the elaborate memorial Emma had erected for Captain Stalio over two decades before, had been prepared on Wahlen's instruction, and it was around this that the mourners gathered and a silence fell.

'Emma Eliza Coe Forsayth Kolbe was a remarkable woman,' began the Wesleyan minister.

When the burial service came to an end Coe Forsayth, Emma's only child, though she'd always counted all her many siblings' offspring as her own, stepped forward and held up the pair of urns. 'They're not marked,' he said, his voice cracked with emotion. 'I don't know which is my mother. But she was a big woman and this,' he continued holding one of the urns aloft, 'is the bigger container.'

There was a ripple of appreciative laughter from those who'd heard and understood. Coe Forsayth then kissed the urn that he'd decided was Emma and gently placed it in one of the holes in the concrete slab. Into the other indentation, with much less ceremony, he placed the other urn, the one that held Paul Kolbe, who'd never wanted to be buried in this 'godforsaken place'. Emma may have lost countless battles with her husband, but she won the war, when hardly any of it mattered any more and they were both nothing but ash and fragments of bone.

The vast undertaking of feeding the multitudes who descended on Gunantambu had fallen to Phoebe. It was right, she thought, as she hurried back to Gunantambu with her own house servants, and Wahlen's too, that she should organise this last and most important act of Emma's grand goodbye. Besides, it was good to be busy. Although Phoebe had grieved for Emma in the weeks before her beloved sister had arrived home as ash, the ceremony had made it feel so immediate again. *Her wonderful sister was no more.* When Emma had sold up, many had considered it the end of an era, but not Phoebe. But this, she thought, as she walked briskly through Gunantambu's garden, this *did* mark the end of something. First Richard, now Emma. *Who would be next?* Suddenly Phoebe felt very old.

Marta threaded her way through the crush of people, many of whom she didn't know, looking for Ettie. She eventually found her friend sitting under a jacaranda tree behind the bungalow with her sister Dolly, who was famous for being a tearaway in her youth, having once publicly horsewhipped a German naval officer.

'Ah Marta, I'm so pleased you came. I did hope you would,' said Ettie, rising and embracing Marta.

'My condolences,' said Marta. 'I'm sorry. Your aunt was an extraordinary woman.'

Dolly, who'd remained seated, laughed. 'It's sad, and yet right that we're celebrating,' she said. 'Ettie and I were just saying how much Emma would have enjoyed all this.'

'Goodness yes,' replied Marta. 'She did love a party, didn't she?'

'This is my sister, Mrs Dolly Messenger,' said Ettie.

'Yes, I remember,' replied Marta. 'I think we met once, years ago when I first came to Neuguinea, at a ball, right here.'

'Yes, I remember,' replied Dolly. 'You're Frau Schmidt from Gethsemane plantation. When we met, you'd just married Herr Schmidt and were newly arrived from Germany.'

'Yes, that's right,' agreed Marta. 'How clever of you to remember.'

'Sit, sit,' said Ettie, sitting down beside Dolly once more and patting the seat of the bench. 'I've just had the pleasure of meeting young Augusta again.'

'Ah,' said Marta. 'The naughty Augusta.'

Ettie laughed. 'Not such a bad thing.'

'No,' agreed Dolly. 'I believe we've all been guilty of high spirits at some time in our lives.'

Marta suddenly felt oddly depressed at these words. She'd buried her own high spirits long ago.

'They really do seem to have hit it off,' observed Ettie as Marie, with her pet sugar-glider Suki on her shoulder, and Augusta walked past, their arms linked, giggling and whispering like schoolgirls.

'They *have* become great friends,' agreed Marta.

'Giggling Gerties,' said twice-married Dolly. 'That's what my English husband would call them.'

'They'll grow out of it,' Ettie said. 'We all did eventually.'

Eighteen

✳ Sometimes I wonder if I stayed in Neuguinea simply because I could not imagine any other life. And by then I had found myself so enamoured of Gethsemane that none of it seemed to matter any more.

Marta, foreword, *Neuguinea Memoirs*,
Heyward & Barge, London, 1949, p. 5

War! It was all they talked of on the verandahs, at the hotels and down at the wharves, as news of unrest in the northern hemisphere continued to arrive in the colony, consuming page after page of newsprint. Europe, all the papers were saying in early 1914, was a powder keg waiting to blow. Bernard, like other patriots of similar ilk, tried to join the German East Neuguinea Reserve, rather fancying the idea of himself in uniform, and was bitterly disappointed when he was turned away after being told he was unfit for service owing to his less than svelte psyche and gout, attacks of which left him hobbling. He sulked for days, shouting unnecessarily at the plantation natives and more than once telling Augusta, of whom he was usually so tolerant, to hold her tongue.

With all the talk of unrest, and two noisy people in the house, Marta found herself withdrawing more and more into the quiet spaces she made for herself both physically and in her own head. She walked a lot, and spent longer and longer periods of time in the study, rather than joining her husband and Augusta on the verandah. She tried not to be irritated by the random explosions of noise that echoed constantly around the bungalow: the crash of a dropped book; the sound of Bernard scraping his chair back as he got up from the table; Augusta out on the verandah mindlessly repeating 'Pretty boy, pretty boy' to the sulphur-crested cockatoo, which pertinaciously refused to speak. The only time none of the noise and the intrusions seemed to matter was when she was painting or writing.

Ten years she'd been here, she thought as she critically assessed the illustrations she'd completed, and read the notes she'd inscribed beneath them. Although what she had didn't, in her opinion, amount to overly much, she *could* see a steady improvement. A recent series of illustrations she'd done of Marie Macco's dear little Suki, for example, she considered rather fine. But on the whole the paintings still weren't good enough yet to be seen by anyone other than herself. Like mould, that insidious black canker that grew on any surface not constantly polished by the touch of human fingers, self-doubt plagued her. Why was she bothering? *It was hubris, no less, no more.*

Bernard never did get to witness the beginning of the war. Just six weeks before the assassination in Sarajevo, which ignited half a decade of bitter conflict, he managed, quite by accident, to kill himself, taking three of the plantation's best natives with him.

Bernard was by no means an explosives novice. He'd been dynamiting the passage every three or four years since his arrival in 1889, and it had become an occasion of great excitement, especially among the local natives, and always commanded something of an audience. Despite the access now provided by the new road, Bernard liked to provide a safe harbour for wandering ships caught on the coast by inclement weather. He liked the fact that Gethsemane was a familiar word on captains' lips. There wasn't a great deal that Bernard did well, but blowing things up was definitely one of them.

Ames and Pamela Miller, proving that neighbourliness was still stronger than the very real possibility of war between their respective countries, had come over to witness the dynamiting, with their boys, who now numbered three, another having been born six months before.

'Did you never want children, Marta?' Pamela asked slyly, stroking the shiny golden head of her first-born.

'No,' said Marta. 'No, I never really did.'

'Poor Bernard,' said Pamela. 'Men always want children.'

Marta had to actively resist pushing her down the bungalow steps.

After lunch, Bernard having calculated that this was when the tide was at its lowest ebb, they proceeded down to the wharf, where natives from the plantation and nearby villages had begun gathering since mid-morning.

'Ha ha!' laughed Bernard. 'The kanaka, he likes an explosion as much as the next man.'

The Millers, Marta and Augusta walked through the throng to the end of the wharf, where four seats had been placed a few minutes before by Masta Raus.

'Excellent, excellent. Such fun,' Ames murmured to himself. Once seated he pulled out his cigarette case and offered it around. All three women took one, leaning in as Ames struck a Vesta. Marta was a little surprised at how expertly Augusta drew on her cigarette. Baby Peter Miller, sitting on his mother's lap, screwed his eyes up against the smoke she blew down over his head. Out on the exposed coral wall, Bernard, followed by three natives, walked out towards the passage. Marta was just about to turn and say something to Ames, exactly what she would never be able to remember, when she distinctly heard Pamela softly say to her eldest, who was sitting at her feet, 'Wave to Papa, Timothy. Wave to Papa.'

'And they're off!' cried Ames, causing Marta to return her attention to the performance out on the water at the very moment that Bernard, running back into shore, tripped and crashed onto the coral like a felled oak. Had he been a fitter or younger man, perhaps he would have been able to scramble to his feet and keep going, but instead he floundered about impotently, unable to rise. On the wharf they clearly heard his terrified voice as he called out to the natives who'd been fleeing just ahead of him.

'Help me, help me,' he begged, the raw fear in his voice so palpable it made their blood run cold. The three Bukas hesitated, then turned back for their masta, sealing their own fate with Bernard's.

There was a curious stillness, as if the whole world was holding its breath, then a massive thump as the charge blew and Bernard and the natives disappeared in a cloud of water and white coral fragments. For some seconds after the explosion Marta fully expected to see Bernard emerge from the haze of destruction, alive and whole, crowing about his achievement. It wasn't until she registered that Pamela Miller was screaming hysterically in her ear and that the natives were wailing and shrieking in horror, that she realised something had gone terribly wrong.

By the time Marta had run along the ridge of coral from the shoreline to where she'd last seen Bernard, the spotted moray eels and jaw fish and a vast school of blue and green fusiliers were cleaning up what little remained of the four men. She watched in faint horror as fragments of human tissue drifted into the banks of anemones on the deep-water side of the reef. Staring into the bloodied sea, still cloudy with coral dust and shreds of human existence, it finally occurred to Marta that Bernard was dead. Really, really dead. She wouldn't see him tonight or tomorrow morning or next week or ever again. And what she felt then, gazing into the water at the awful beauty of the opportunists of the sea hunting for the last morsels, was nothing. She would mourn, certainly, in the days that followed, primarily for the untimeliness of her husband's end, for although he hadn't been a good man, nor had he been a bad one. He hadn't deserved to die before his own, largely blameless life had been blundered through in its entirety. But that was all. Augusta was far more devastated, but then she was young and inexperienced and bound to be affected by witnessing such a violent end.

✳ ✳ ✳

'Who on earth?' said Marta, who was sitting on the verandah entertaining the Kirchners from Kavieng, who had come with their Australian governess, Miss Sommerhoff, to pay their condolences. She' d just turned to chase away the sulphur-crested cockatoo, which had turned into something of a beggar, when she'd noticed a solitary figure strolling up the road from the drying sheds to the bungalow. 'Who is that?'

'Ah, Herr Weston, I think,' said Herr Kirchner, whose eyes were better than Marta's.

'Oh, so it is!' Marta exclaimed, in a tone far too cheerful for one so recently widowed.

'How good of him to come. But he and Bernard were very dear friends.'

'How did you get here?' Herr Kirchner asked, after Royal had been given a seat and a drink.

'Came over last night,' Royal explained. 'Soon as I heard about poor old Bernard. Arrived this morning and was having breakfast at the hotel when who should wander in but Macco. I cadged a lift with him as far as Ulul-Nono and shanks' ponied it from there.'

The assembled company, except for Miss Sommerhoff, looked a little perplexed. 'Shanks' pony?' ventured Augusta.

'Walked,' clarified Royal.

'Well, why didn't you say so in the first place?' said Marta. 'Really, Herr Weston.'

After the Kirchners had left, taking Augusta with them for a stay in town, and all the words that could be spoken about Bernard, his achievements and ridiculous death, had been said, Royal and Marta, having eaten early, sat on the verandah waiting for night to fall.

'Do you want to sell up and leave?' asked Royal.

'I don't know,' replied Marta. 'Do I have to?'

'No, not at all. Remember we have a precedent of women plantation owners in Neuguinea. The question is, though, do you want to stay?'

'Where would I go if I did sell?'

'Not back to Austria,' said Royal. 'The war is very close. Word has it that it will only be days before that fuse is lit, and this side of the equator seems the safest place to be right now. You could go to Australia. That would be my advice if you did want to sell up.'

'And if I don't?'

'You'll have to learn how to run a copra plantation.'

'Is it a difficult business?'

Royal smiled. 'Not especially. Bernard managed it, after all.'

'Well,' concluded Marta, 'I have much to think about then.'

'I'll give you a fair price if you sell,' promised Royal and left it at that.

'How did you and Bernard become friends?' Marta asked a few moments later as Royal lit two cigarettes and she topped up their tumblers with the cognac he'd brought with him.

'Through Emma Kolbe. When I first came here in 1898 she suggested that I talk to Bernard since the only good land remaining was here in Neumecklenberg.'

'But you didn't buy here in the end.'

'No,' Royal replied. 'Making a killing wasn't really my main interest, and I fell in love with the Cape Gazelle place, though it cost a pretty penny. Emma was always rather cross about that. She'd coveted the plantation herself but I pipped her there.' He stopped and smiled at Marta. 'All seems like such a long time ago now.'

Herbertshohe was Royal's first port of call the first time he came to German East Neuguinea. After booking into the newly built Herbertshohe Hotel, a handsome establishment overlooking Blanche Bay owned by a gentleman from Bavaria, Royal strolled down the slim white waterfront road to Ralum in order to make the acquaintance of Frau Emma Kolbe, the legendary Queen Emma, who was rumoured to be the best business mind in the Pacific. Royal hoped she would be generous and truthful about the possibilities the territory presented, and the problems that might arise because he wasn't German.

'Some of them are a little superior,' admitted Emma, as she and Royal sat in her offices drinking black tannic pekoe from Spode cups. 'Especially the government men. However a bureaucrat's a bureaucrat in any language, isn't that so, Mr Weston? But the company men who work for the consortiums are a nice bunch, as are the many individuals who've established plantations out here.'

'So it's a sound place to invest in.'

'Oh yes, Mr Weston,' said Emma, with a twinkle in her eye. She did so like a handsome man, even if he was a fruit, as the man sitting opposite her most definitely was. 'There's much money to be made, but not here – over there, on Neumecklenberg.' She pointed to the landmass across the ocean to the east.

She explained about Boluminski's road and told Royal about Bernard Schmidt and Captain Macco. 'You should meet Herr Schmidt and the captain, I think, listen to what they have to say.'

'Yes, perhaps you're right,' said Royal. ''What about existing plantations, here on Neupommern, do they ever come up for sale?'

'Occasionally,' replied Emma evasively. 'Though they generally change hands without notice of sale. The consortiums, you know, are always looking to expand their holdings, and plantations here are expensive, Mr Weston.'

Royal shrugged. 'But I'm not looking to make my fortune.'

'Then why are you here?'

Royal smiled. 'To be honest I really don't know. Looking for somewhere to call home, I suppose.'

'Good,' said Emma. 'Because you need to be here. You have to tend your investment. The kanaka needs guidance. You can't leave him to his own devices. The Bukas are relatively trustworthy but

211

the Melanesians run away back to their villages at any provocation or try and eat you. Asiatics are the best, if you can get them. I use them on my plantations to run my labour lines. In short, Mr Weston, this isn't a place to bury your money in the ground unless you're prepared to be here to see it grow.'

'I understand,' Royal replied, looking out the window of Emma's office just as a half-naked Buka walked past. 'It's not so bad, here, is it?' he asked.

'I've never thought so,' said Emma, 'but you do have to fall in love with the place. Life here isn't without its hardships.'

A few days later Royal caught a trader to Neumecklenberg to meet Captain Macco and Bernard Schmidt. Within a few hours of making their acquaintance at Macco's plantation, Royal found himself thinking how much he liked them. They were easy and relaxed, obviously not inclined to stand on ceremony like the Germans, and the English too, if he was honest, he'd encountered in Mombasa. Macco, who was garrulous and quick-witted, proved to be a bountiful source of gossip. Bernard Schmidt, however, was a little more reserved, not contributing greatly to the conversation and more interested in his dinner than in talking. Subsequently it came as a surprise to Royal the next morning, as the three breakfasted, when Bernard extended a stumbling invitation to Royal to come and stay a few nights at his plantation, Gethsemane. 'Macco thought of it,' he clarified, seeing the look of bewilderment on Royal's face. 'It was Macco's idea.'

'I would invite you to stay on here, Herr Weston,' explained the captain smoothly, 'but I have pressing business in Neupommern. I leave you in good hands with my friend Bernard, though, and I shall return soon. Maybe I shall see you before you leave?'

The bungalow at Gethsemane proved a humble affair, but Royal was comfortable enough on a camp stretcher in the large empty room at the back of the house.

'So what bought you here, Bernard?' Royal asked after they had spent a long day at Gethsemane's drying sheds talking about copra, and were relaxing on the verandah drinking schnapps as the light fell out of the day.

'I came to Neuguinea because I thought I would be happy here, and stayed on because I was. I'm not the most socially skilled of men, as you probably have noticed,' said Bernard candidly, 'and this solitary bachelor existence suits me very well.'

'That makes sense,' said Royal,

'I'm not a greedy man Herr Weston, but nor am I an exciting one. By coming to the colony I could be my own man, my own not very interesting self.'

Royal laughed. 'I don't know if your truth is all that different from my own and everyone else's.'

'I'm very ordinary,' said Bernard, 'but it makes for a peaceful life.'

'But what about a wife? Do you wish to marry? Have children?' asked Royal casually, resting an enquiring hand on Bernard's thigh.

'What woman would want to come here?' asked Bernard, gently but deliberately removing Royal's hand. 'Though yes. I *would* like a wife very much. There was a woman once, but she married someone else.'

What woman would want to come here? Bernard's words resonated constantly in Royal's head for the remainder of his time in the territory and in the weeks that followed as he drifted east from Neuguinea across the Pacific, stopping at Rotuma Island, Apia in American Samoa and then made his way via Caroline Island to Tahiti and the Marquesas. As Emma and Bernard had said, these places, with the exception of Samoa, offered fewer opportunities. He *was* tempted, though, by Tahiti. There was something especially languid and intoxicating about those islands but he couldn't see Rebecca being happy there. Tahiti was even further away from Tasmania than Neuguinea.

His South Pacific travels completed, Royal returned to Neuguinea and based himself once more at the Herbertshohe Hotel. He was investigating the possibility of purchasing an already established plantation with a fine house near Kavieng, when he heard a whisper that a very good plantation at Cape Gazelle, on the southern tip of Blanche Bay, was for sale. He also heard that Emma Kolbe had set her sights on it, as had the Neuguineakompagnie, which was the only consortium that dared to go up against the Queen. Royal, unaware of the potency of these undercurrents, borrowed a horse the next morning and blithely trotted out to Cape Gazelle. He liked what he saw and offered the saturnine owner a price he couldn't refuse. By the time it became known that an Australian had bought the Kushel plantation at Cape Gazelle, Royal himself had long since returned to Tasmania to retrieve his very reluctant wife, who was rather enjoying what Launceston had to offer and wondering why they didn't just stay there with her parents on the apple farm. There was even a little house at the bottom of the orchard. But Royal was having none of it. He refused to live his life under the beady judgemental eye of God.

Emma Kolbe was distinctly frosty with Royal for some time after he and Rebecca set up house at Cape Gazelle, but eventually she relented and in years to come she wouldn't even remember how she'd lost one of the best plantations in the territory to a parvenu who dared defy her.

Next day, while Royal was taking stock of the plantation at Gethsemane, which he had to admit was in very good shape, Marta, for a reason she would never be able to remember, went to her mending basket and took out a large pair of shears. They were a little blunt and spotted with rust but they would do the job she required of them. She stood in front of the small, silvered mirror that hung crookedly on the back of the door to her room and, without once looking her own reflection in the eye, unpinned her long dark hair, with its few new ribbons of grey around the temples, and cut it so short that the blunt irregular ends brushed her strong jawline. Stepping over the hanks of shorn hair that lay on the floorboards, she walked across the hall to Bernard's bedroom. Opening the door of her husband's wardrobe, Marta was surprised to find herself suffused with emotion, as Bernard's smell washed over her.

Because she was nearly as tall as Bernard, Marta found that the few items of clothing which had survived her first husband's early years at Gethsemane, when he had been a lean and hungry young man, fitted her rather well. She selected the least mildewed shirt and trousers to wear immediately and dropped the remainder on the floor for Raus to collect for laundering. Once dressed, Marta looked at herself in the distorted mirror on the inside of the wardrobe door in Bernard's room and thought, without vanity, that she actually looked not entirely ridiculous.

'Goodness, what have you done?' was the first thing Royal said when he returned to the bungalow later that afternoon and found his hostess, with her shorn head, bent over an illustration of a huntsman spider that she was delicately colouring.

'It was hot,' Marta replied. 'Too hot to have so much hair so I cut it.'

'It is hot,' agreed Royal. 'Let's have a look?'

Instinctively, Marta put a shy hand up to her hair and turned slowly this way and that, so that she could be admired. Although it lacked the vivacity of a younger or more beautiful woman, the gesture was so deeply rooted in her gender that she didn't even realise she'd, that it mattered to her that Royal should care how she looked.

'It suits you very well,' Royal concluded. Of her trousers and shirt Marta offered no explanation and Royal requested none, primarily because, for the first time in the decade that he'd known Marta Schmidt, she looked utterly right.

The next morning Royal departed from Gethsemane, having arranged a ride with Ames Miller, who was driving into Kavieng.

'If you need anything, anything, just let me know, Marta,' he said as he climbed into the auto. 'You are my friend as much as Bernard was.'

'Thank you,' Marta replied simply. There was nothing else to say.

When Augusta returned at the end of the week, having been successfully distracted from her shock by the Kirchners, she was momentarily rendered speechless, perhaps for the first and last time in her life, at Marta's appearance. But once she had recovered, Augusta ventured the very welcome opinion that Marta looked 'wonderful, just like a suffragette'.

In the days and weeks that followed Bernard's death, Marta thought about Royal often and not always innocently. It was ridiculous, she knew, but the thoughts came unbidden. Even though she had Augusta for company, she was, Marta realised, terribly lonely and had been for a very long time. She hungered to talk to someone who really understood her. She missed her father.

Nineteen

✳ Some wag jokingly called the Great War in our little South Pacific colony
the 'Copra War' and in the way of all things possessing a modicum of wit,
the sobriquet stuck. By 1918, however, it had become a chilling accurate
description.

Marta, *Neuguinea Memoirs*, Heyward
& Barge, London, 1949, p. 157

Although nobody had talked of anything else in the preceding
year, the war, when it did arrive, was still something of a surprise to
the colony. It was the speed with which events in Europe reached
the South Pacific that took them all unaware. Within a month of
the declaration, the German Empire, in East Neuguinea at least,
had fallen with little more than a whimper of protest.

The news that, on the 12th of August, the Australian navy
had entered Blanche Bay and sent in landing parties to destroy
the telephone services in Herbertshohe and Rabaul, arrived at
Gethsemane within hours. Captain Macco had picked up it on
his wireless and ridden over to bring Marta and Augusta up to
date on the latest developments. Within the week he was back
again, accompanied by Marie, full of talk about further drama in
Neupommern.

'The administration in Rabaul have retreated to consider their
options,' he said, shaking his head in disbelief, shocked, like so
many, by how quickly the German resistance was crumbling.
'They've gone inland to Toma.'

'Dr Haber too?' asked Marta, referring to the colony's governor.

'He was the first to leave,' snorted the captain.

'Will Neumecklenberg be next?' asked Marta.

'Almost certainly,' replied Macco. 'This isn't over by any means.'

Suddenly afraid, Augusta shivered in spite of the bright, dry heat. She reached out and squeezed Marie's hand. Her friend turned, smiled and gave Augusta a reassuring squeeze back.

'But why?' asked Marta. 'Why us? The war is in Europe. It's their concern, not ours.'

'It's the plantations,' explained Macco. 'They want our copra.'

'But these plantations are our homes and livelihoods. We have nothing else.'

'Yes,' agreed Macco. 'It is of serious concern. I think, though, their interest is largely in those territories owned by the consortiums, where the personal cost would be minimal.'

'Let us hope,' observed Marta.

'Indeed,' agreed the captain.

Having severed the telephone lines and put on a show of force in Rabaul and Herbertshohe, the Australian naval men had departed. Nobody truly knew what would happen next and more than a few prayed fervently that this was the beginning and the end of the war for the colony. The waiting was the worst. By early September all hopes of an uneventful war in Neuguinea were quashed when a combined Australian military and naval force, two thousand strong, landed and occupied Herbertshohe and Rabaul in a single morning. The Copra War, as it would become known, had now begun in earnest. Having taken the two main centres on Neupommern with such ease, the Australians had a quick lunch, then confidently marched inland along the Bitapak road that led to the German wireless telegraph station. There the German Reserve, which numbered nine commissioned officers, fifty-two NCOs and regulars and two hundred and forty native soldiers, put up a good defence for a few hours, in spite of being seriously outnumbered, but all too soon it was all over and the death toll stood at six Australians, one German and thirty natives. The German Reserve was rounded up and marched off to Rabaul under armed guard to await a decision on their fate.

Just two days later, on the 13th of September, Royal attended the ceremony marking the official beginning of the military occupation of the colony, though the incumbent German administration hadn't said a word about surrendering. After returning home to his house on Rabaul's Namanula Hill, where he was semi–permanently based these days, Royal suddenly felt compelled to sit down and write to Marta.

Shortly before three we all gathered in front of the German residence, forming a square around the flagpole, which has been bare since the administration high-tailed it off into the mountains to Toma a month ago. The British military men and the native police, who have quickly changed their allegiance to us conquerors, formed three sides of the square, the fourth being made up of the Australia military, mainly naval, and the residents of Rabaul, naturally enough, arrived in droves to witness the changing of the guard. There was something of a sense of occasion about the whole thing, even among the Germans, which may change later for your compatriots once the shock wears off and they realise that they are actually in an occupied state. Frau Ettie Kaumann came along, as did, unfortunately, her husband, who behaved very obnoxiously and did little to endear himself to anyone by singing the German national anthem as 'God Save the King' was played by the Royal Marine band, which was jolly good and very rousing. Ettie asked to be remembered to you with great affection and promised to write to you soon.

But I digress. At 3 o'clock the White Ensign was hoisted up the staff and as the troops saluted, the naval warships in the bay fired their guns twenty-one times, which was rather magnificent actually.

I appreciate that this is *not* the news you want to hear in these uncertain times, but I can reassure you that there is no desire to harm the German nationals in these parts and you're not in any physical danger. I have talked with Major General Holmes about this matter and he assures me that, apart from ascertaining who is in the colony, there's a strong desire to keep the existing, very efficient system in place. I'll write again soon, I promise, when I know more.

Because Marta hadn't been to town since shortly after Bernard's death, her mail, weeks of it, had been given to Ames Miller when he'd collected his own, and he subsequently dropped it off on his way home from Kavieng. Their Australian neighbour hadn't, however, stopped for a drink as he was in the habit of doing. As she watched him race away in a cloud of white coral dust, Marta realised that Ames had been unable to look her in the eye. It was, she thought, as if he was slightly embarrassed.

'Did Herr Miller's behaviour strike you as odd?' she asked Augusta, who was sitting at the back of the verandah, well out of the sun.

'No,' said Augusta, looking up from her own mail, a letter from an old colleague in the Communist Party in Vienna telling her that Dimitri, her lover, had divorced his wife and married the daughter of a comrade much higher up the food chain. 'In what way?'

'I thought he seemed uncomfortable,' replied Marta. 'I wondered if it was because of the war.'

'But that's silly, isn't it?' said Augusta, who was pleased to discover that the mention of Dimitri hadn't pained her in the slightest. 'The Millers are our friends.' Both women knew this was stretching the truth somewhat: neither of them liked Pamela Miller, and understood implicitly that Ames' wife returned the favour.

'Yes,' said Marta, sitting down. 'They're our friends.'

'Who's *your* letter from?' asked Augusta, changing the subject to prevent her sister from brooding on the perceived slight from Miller, which Augusta *had* noticed.

'Royal,' Marta replied as she slit open the envelope with a none too clean thumbnail. 'At least he isn't letting this ridiculous war interfere with our friendship.'

'What news?' Augusta asked a few minutes later when Marta lifted her head from the short missive and sighed softly.

'Nothing we don't already know, but it appears that the administration has now surrendered. Royal says the Australians' battleship shelled Toma, where Haber and his fellow officials were holed up.'

'But what does it mean?'

'I don't know, Gustie,' Marta replied. 'I truly don't. We'll just have to wait and see what happens.'

Quietly, through September and into October, the expatriate settlements dotted around the islands of East Neuguinea began to be taken over by various small Australian detachments, their numbers augmented by the secondment of the native constabulary previously been attached to the German Reserve. Friedrich-Wilhelmshafen was occupied on the 24th of September, the landing party marching through the settlement unchallenged and hoisting their standard up the administration's flagpole. They stayed briefly, conducting a census of those German nationals still in the area before leaving a handful of men and two officers, and carrying on with their march across east New Guinea. Kavieng and Namatanai were next.

The first Marta and Augusta knew of the occupation of the two expatriate settlements on Neumecklenberg was when Ames Miller drove up to the bungalow at Gethsemane on the morning of the 17th of October.

'Hallo Ames,' said Marta, coming out onto the verandah to greet him. 'Lovely day.'

'Frau Schmidt, I would like to ask you and Fräulein Mueller to accompany me into Kavieng,' said Ames, standing at the bottom of the steps.

'Why?' asked Marta.

'By order of the military occupation I have been asked to bring you into town,' replied Ames.

'What's going on?' Augusta had joined her sister.

'I think Ames is taking us prisoner,' replied Marta calmly. 'That is what you're doing, isn't it, Ames?' At least he had the grace to look embarrassed. 'And what will you do if I refuse?' she continued, deeply amused by her neighbour's formality.

'I will shoot you,' said Ames calmly. It was probably a joke, but Marta would never be entirely sure.

'This is ridiculous. You know that, don't you, Ames?' Marta protested as she and Augusta got into the auto after being allowed to gather a few personal items.

'Yes,' he said. 'Yes I know, but I'm just following orders, you understand.'

'Then the very least you can do is tell us what this is all about.'

'Well, that's the thing. Actually I can't. As of two months ago, you're the enemy. For me to say anything to you would be tantamount to treason, I should think.'

'Oh, what nonsense!' exclaimed Marta. She was entirely fed up with the war already.

'Are we being taken prisoner? Really?' asked Augusta tremulously from the back seat.

'Yes,' replied Ames, brusquely. 'That's exactly what's happening. Sorry about that. I'm sure it won't be too bad a time for you. I've been told to take you to the hospital.'

The main street of Kavieng was swarming with uniforms. Civilians were thin on the ground, but all the non-German trade stores were open for business as usual. A Union Jack fluttered from the flagstaff outside the German residence.

The Kirchners and Maccos were already at the expatriate hospital when Marta and Augusta arrived. Miss Sommerhoff, though Australian and exempt, had elected to stay with her German employers during their internment and look after the children. Nobody knew exactly what was going on and tense words were exchanged between Captain Macco and some Australian officers before it became evident that all the German owners of plantations that flanked Boluminski's road were being brought in.

One day passed, then two. It wasn't unpleasant at the hospital and they were well fed, but nerves were jangled by uncertainty. No one would tell them anything and rumours that started as grains of sand grew into entire islands of untruth. Some began to wonder if they would ever see their plantations again. There were one or two comments on Marta's short hair and masculine attire from some of the older women, but most were too caught up in worry even to notice. Besides, as Frau Kirchner pointed out over a hand of bridge on the second afternoon of their imprisonment, Frau Schmidt cut a sporty figure as she strode around the hospital grounds, bored and frustrated. 'But then she's very slender,' she concluded, as she and Miss Sommerhoff took another trick.

'So slender,' agreed the others. 'Like a reed.'

Marta may have been irritated beyond belief to be cooped up and kept entirely in the dark, but most of her compatriots reacted with stoic good humour. For surely it was all just a gigantic mistake. The handful of younger folk like Augusta came together like mercury, their laughter and excited chatter silvering the air around them. For them, this was a chance to have some fun. Soon enough, they would probably all go back to their plantations and it would be months and possibly years before they met again. New alliances were inevitable.

'Fräulein Mueller appears to have made a conquest there,' observed Frau Kirchner to Miss Sommerhoff as Augusta wandered past them with Wolfie Hoffmann, whose father owned a large, well-established plantation just north of Namatanai.

'Yes.' Miss Sommerhoff pulled some mending out of her workbasket. 'I rather thought so too.'

'I didn't even know that he'd come home,' continued Frau Kirchner. 'I was led to believe that he now lived in Melbourne.'

'He was visiting the old place, I believe, and had been intending to take a position back in Melbourne in the new year. Though what will happen with that now ...,' said Frau Uechtritz, who was sitting with them.

'He's a solicitor, is that right?' asked Miss Sommerhoff.

'Yes, dear,' clarified Frau Uechtritz. 'I do believe that's what his mama said.'

'This is driving me mad,' Marta said to the trio as she stamped up the verandah steps. 'I just tried to go for a walk down to the harbour and a poltroon in a uniform ordered me back when I got to the gates. He waved his gun at me. Imagine.' She paused and grinned. 'That's the second time this week some man has threatened to shoot me.'

Finally, on the morning of the third day, a Major Louden gathered them together on the hospital verandah.

'It has been decided,' he said, 'to let you all return to your plantations for the time being. Although the colony has been officially placed under military occupation, it serves no purpose for the German citizens of New Ireland, as Neumecklenberg is now known, to be prevented from carrying out their duties on their plantations and, until otherwise advised, the status quo will remain.'

'But what of the copra?' asked Herr von Grunig, who had a holding on the west coast.

'Every endeavour will be made to see that trade and shipping carry on as usual,' the major replied. 'However, I must point out that though you are all being permitted to return to your plantations, you are the enemy and, as such, any subversive behaviour on the part of German nationals will be observed and swiftly dealt with.'

'So you are going to spy on us?' exclaimed Herr Kirchner.

The major smirked. 'Yes, that's exactly what we'll be doing. There'll be detachments posted all over the island and any hint of insurgence will be crushed.'

'Outrageous!'

'Ridiculous!'

'I'll never call it New Ireland. The place will always be Neumecklenberg to me.'

'And me.'

'And me too!'

'Mein Gott! What next?'

But the major ignored the murmurs of protest. 'You are free to leave,' he said.

'And how will we return to our plantations?' asked Herr Uechtritz.

'That,' the major concluded, 'is a problem you'll have to solve among yourselves.' And with that he walked away.

The Australians were true to their word. When a few of the more vocal German plantation owners made themselves vexatious enough to warrant being arrested, they were shipped off to Rabaul. Lauri's Cinema on Mango Street, in the middle of town, where only a year before the entire expatriate community had sat happily watching films from America, had been turned into a prisoner of war camp. This unsettled many, and the Germans became more watchful of their non-German neighbours, whom they'd previously always thought of as friends. *There were spies everywhere.* The sense of unease Marta had identified in Ames Miller spread throughout the colony. As the last weeks of the dry season continued into October, tensions grew as tinder dry as the land, requiring only an opportunistic spark to ignite an inferno. It was young Wolfie Hoffmann, who had decided that, war or no war, he was going to court Fräulein Mueller of Gethsemane, who brought the news of Reverend Cox's beating at Namatanai.

'So when did this all happen?' asked Marta, horrified at what Wolfie had just told her.

'Two afternoons ago, on the 26th.'

'The German doctor and some of his friends just barged into the mission at Namatanai and beat Reverend Cox until he was unconscious?'

'Indeed,' replied Wolfie. 'And they say that the attack was particularly vicious. There were six of them.'

'But why?' asked Marta. 'He's a man of the cloth.'

Wolfie shrugged. There had been talk among the Germans at Namatanai about Cox being a spy since the first days of the occupation. He'd become very chummy with the Australian officers and was often seen sitting on the verandah of the bungalow that had been turned into an officers' mess.

Once Cox had recovered a little he drafted a bitter letter of complaint against the men who had beaten him and sent it to Colonel Holmes, who was heading the military occupation, in Rabaul. Ten days later the perpetrators were rounded up by the military, taken by boat to Rabaul and tossed in with the other German troublemakers behind the barbed wire strung around Lauri's Cinema. To their surprise, stories of the attack had even reached here and they were greeted by the other prisoners as something akin to folk heroes. After the officers of the Namatanai detachment had investigated the incident and duly filed a report, the order was issued for the attackers to be publicly beaten on the Rabaul parade ground. The German doctor, who was given thirty strokes with the cane, lost consciousness long before the punishment was completed. His compatriots took twenty-five strokes each. Given his tender age, the doctor's young medical assistant, who had accompanied the older men to the mission, was given a mere ten strokes. Pondering on this news, which had arrived at Gethsemane courtesy of a letter from Ettie, Marta had cause to think that perhaps this land, this marvellous place, rich in malaria, kanakas and coconuts, was no longer a German colony. That their time here was over.

By the close of the year, neighbours were enemies. Although logic told them that they were still the same people they'd been before the war, mistrust had all but rubbed out those memories and allegiances. They had forgotten that once, they had spent hours in conversation at the Herbertshohe Hotel's Trinkhalle, raced their horses against each other on the course at Rabaul and played cricket and tennis together. Many of the German nationals, for good reason, began to feel as if they were no longer working their plantations for themselves, their consortiums or their empire, but for the Australians and their British king.

Marta who, like her compatriots, nursed an unspoken hope that the might of the German Empire would prevail, continued to work Gethsemane as if it were still her own. She couldn't have done it without Captain Macco, who would send a wagon over to Gethsemane's drying sheds every six weeks or so to pick up the plantation's copra and take it with his own to the copra barges waiting in the port below the Kavieng township.

In the early days of running the plantation, after she'd watched the bats take to the night sky, Marta would sit and drink schnapps, too exhausted even to talk to Augusta, who had effortlessly taken over the management of Gethsemane's bungalow and garden. Marta's journal and drawing folio remained unopened, sometimes for weeks. To her surprise, Marta found she enjoyed this sometimes physically punishing regime. Never had she felt more useful, more peaceful in her mind, and she began to understand the pleasure Bernard had derived from the relatively simply task of making copra. Letters from Vienna arrived spasmodically as the war progressed. Both she and Augusta found these much-inked envelopes particularly unnerving as they always expected them to contain bad news. One von Tempsky cousin, a bright young naval officer, had already been lost when his battleship had been torpedoed in the Atlantic only a few weeks into the war. In spite of this sadness, Klara and Egon seemed in good spirits. Their lives had become more austere, and considerably smaller, but so too had everyone else's.

13 September 1915
Kurakakaul, New Britain

My Dear Friend,

What joy it was to receive a letter from you just the other day, I hope you and your sister are well and holding up under the strain of this dreadful occupation.

My, how I laughed when I read of your travails in your new incarnation as a lady copra planter, as I too have found this occupation thrust upon me due to my husband having to return to Germany a few months ago. Undoubtedly you have heard that he had been making a nuisance of himself and the new administration all but threw him out of the colony. I'm sad to say that this is all completely and entirely true. Fritz, on Mr Royal Weston's advice, left soon after the rains finished in April. He is back in Berlin, where his people come from, but nonetheless seems still able to be vexatious from a distance and has been writing me long lists of instructions on how to run Kurakakaul in his absence. Me! Who has coconut oil, not blood, coursing through my veins.

Like you, I have discovered that although the days are long, the principles of copra are relatively simple and certainly I have reason to believe that the natives are happier with me in charge. I have outlawed flogging, which of course all my neighbours say will lead to disobedience, though *I* have seen no evidence of this. I urge you do the same and discard this abhorrent practice. Both Mother and Aunt Emma always said that you only discipline when absolutely necessary, and like children the kanaka responds to firm kindness. Firm words, Mother says, are all that are needed, and if that fails, wash your hands of the whole sorry business and send the culprit back to his village.

Ettie went on to describe her recent visit to Rabaul where she had found little changed on the surface, though the Germans were outnumbered by the Australians and British. She had also run into Royal, who had taken her out to lunch.

We had the most interesting conversation about the situation as he sees it in regard to plantations nominally in German ownership. I say nominally, for in spite of Father being German I feel a stronger tie to Mother's family and consider myself to be a daughter of the Pacific not the Fatherland. However, Mr Weston tells me that there is a strong possibility we will be divested of our holdings if Germany loses the war, regardless of how Samoan or American we might consider ourselves to be. I sincerely hope that he is wrong; I can't imagine what any of us would do if we had our beloved plantations taken from us. Where would we go? Not Germany, that much is certain. We would never be welcome or happy there.

My only note of thanks is that Aunt Emma doesn't have to witness this whole sorry business. Now, with the vantage of hindsight, I wonder if she had known something was up all those years ago, when she sold out to HASAG and urged Mother to do so as well. I worry most for Mother, for she says she will never leave here, even if the new administration takes Kuradui from her. She says: 'I will live in a grass hut with the kanakas if I have to'. And indeed I rather think she would.

Marta folded the letter. The plantation, she now understood, was a lumbering but infallibly efficient beast. Its greatest strength was the sheer simplicity of how it functioned. It had taken her approximately a year to realise that she didn't have to spend every waking hour down at the drying sheds looking over her native labour line's collective shoulder. It all worked entirely satisfactorily without her monitoring its every breath and heartbeat. She'd come to the point where she felt she could paint again in the afternoons, when the heat of the day was at its most savage. The next day, she finally picked up her brushes again.

Twenty

✳ Of all the strange and extraordinary items from the natural world that I have encountered, the most intriguing have been the creatures broadly classified as Nautilidae [figs 8 to 10], of which I have identified four striated varietals in Neuguinea. Into this family also fall the *Argonauta nodosa* [figs 11 to 14] or paper nautilus, which is common to these islands and frequently found washed up on the sand in various bays along the coast. Because these shells truly are exquisite jewels, nothing quite prepared me for my first sighting of the cephalopod [fig. 15] that lives inside these calcareous, multi-chambered shells. It is nothing less than a miniature kraken, complete with numerous waving tentacles, a gaping maw, and two cold little holes for eyes in its grotesquely enlarged head.

Marta, *Neuguinea: Flora & Fauna*, Wolff & Grunwald, Vienna, 1923, pp. 23–4

When, late in 1916, Royal came up with his plan to save Gethsemane from expropriation, he was acting partly from self-interest. If the fortunes of war turned, Australian planters like himself could just as easily find themselves without a coconut to their name. The occupation depressed the hell out of Royal but it *did* have its good points. For example, he enjoyed the company of Colonel Samuel Pethebridge, his new neighbour, who'd replaced Holmes as administrator, but the undercurrent of suspicion and dread saddened him. He liked the Hun, he truly did. They were funny folk, but once you got used to them, they were great company. He missed the old days when one of his greatest pleasures was to go to the Trinkhalle at the Herbertshohe Hotel, and listen to his Kraut friends' and neighbours' vast repertoire of patriotic songs. He'd always envied them their absolute knowledge of who they were, even in the middle of nowhere. His parents had always considered themselves to be Irish, though they would both be buried in Australian soil. But because he'd been born in a clean, white room with a view of the Yarra River, Royal supposed he was an Australian. Yet that wasn't right either, because he felt, deep in his bones, that he belonged here in East New Guinea. Because it was here that he was true and free of the guilt that had plagued him for so long.

There had been other encounters over the years, other men, black and white, but it was Tomai who had finally inspired in Royal something that could only be love. He'd noticed the boy around the plantation, observed the special way in which he was treated by the other Bukas on his labour line. It wasn't until later, after he'd brought Tomai into the house and the boy had brazenly offered himself to Royal, that the penny had dropped. Royal hadn't been prepared for the intensity of emotion that Tomai had evoked in him. It was something far beyond the hunger he had for the black boy's body, his taut, shiny skin and the long, thick cock that jumped and twitched at a mere look or the slightest touch. It, love, desire – whatever it was called – swallowed Royal whole, eating him alive, bones and all. He carried the boy's very being with him as an ever-present ghost that only he could see. But in spite of this Royal was lonely. To his great surprise, he missed his brother Jupiter, who had joined a British infantry regiment in Kenya as a guide for the duration of the war.

So here he was contemplating what he thought he would never do again: the possibility of marriage. In truth, Royal wanted a foot in each camp. It was all very well to curry favour with the military administration, but he needed to be able to keep on side with the Germans too, just in case. Shortly before Bernard's untimely death, he and Royal had discussed the possibility of merging into a single, ostensibly nationless, company that could ebb and flow with the tides of the imminent war. Royal had gone so far as to have the papers drawn up by his lawyer and delivered to Bernard. Marta had found them, unopened in a drawer in the office, after the occupation, and by then it was too late. All German land title in the colony had been frozen, which left only marriage as a means of making an asset-based alliance. Royal didn't tell his Buka lover of almost two decades of his plan to marry and bring not one, but two women, to the house on the Namanula Hill. It never occurred to him that he should.

✳ ✳ ✳

Augusta, who was reading on the verandah, heard the chug of an engine a few moments before a boat rounded the point and nosed its way into the channel that led into the lagoon below Gethsemane. A trader meant much-needed supplies, but also the possibility of mail!

The courtship between her and Wolfie Hoffmann had been erratic at best since they'd returned to their respective plantations. They'd hardly seen each other, since those heady first days, as social gatherings, of Germans at least, had faded into oblivion since the occupation. However, this enforced separation had only stoked the fires between the two young people, who communicated their passionate love for each other via letters.

Augusta put down her book and hurried inside to find her sister. 'Ah, there you are,' she said, poking her head into the office where Marta was painting. 'There's a trader down at the wharf. I'll go if you like.'

'I'm almost finished,' said Marta, opening a drawer of the desk at which she sat and taking out a sheaf of bank notes, which she gave to her sister. 'I'll join you in a moment. Don't let Cookie and Raus buy everything they see. You know how they are. And shut the door as you leave.'

How odd, thought Marta, picking up her brush once more. Traders were a rare commodity these days; this vessel might well be one of the last to dock at Gethsemane's wharf. She'd been to look at the coral barricade only a few days before, and realised that the lagoon was close to inaccessible once more, that this strange gorgonian creature of the sea that was alive, but ostensibly stone, had silently grown over the wound in its side.

Marta knew she should go down to the disintegrating wharf immediately so as not to hold up the captain, but having achieved the exact shade of green she required to reproduce the colour of the land snail shell she was painting, she bent back over her work. It wouldn't take more than a minute or two to finish the illustration. Once the watercolour dried she would use a fine sable brush dipped in Indian ink to follow the pencil marks that delineated the contours and shape of the shell under the green–apple wash. In subsequent illustrations of the shell she would add a view of the creature that generally inhabited the structure, and another exposing the delicate fluting of the shell's mouth. Absorbed again, Marta failed to notice the passage of time and it wasn't until the door of the study opened that she was even aware of anybody being in the house.

'Bernard?' she said, without thinking.

'No, silly,' said Augusta in amazement, 'it's Herr Weston.'

'No!' said Marta, turning to greet their visitor.

'Afraid so,' said Royal, who was leaning against the doorframe, hat in hand.

'Hello Royal,' she said smiling. 'How lovely to see you. Did I say Bernard?'

'You did.'

'How strange,' said Marta, dropping her brush into the jar of cloudy water at her elbow. 'Oh, the trader,' she continued, hurriedly pushing back her chair and standing. 'He'll want to go.'

'All done,' replied Augusta. 'He didn't have much apart from Herr Weston.'

'Any mail?' Marta asked.

'Only for me,' Augusta replied, triumphantly waving a letter.

'And judging by your face, it would be from young Hoffmann?'

'Yes, yes, it is.' Augusta was incandescent with joy.

'Excellent,' said Marta. 'You can read it after you've asked Cookie to make us some coffee. Please?'

'So how are you, Mrs Schmidt?' Royal lifted a pile of books off the other chair and sat down.

'I'm well,' Marta said, settling back into her chair.

'What are you doing there?' Royal asked, as Marta attempted to nonchalantly slot the newly completed illustration into her folio.

'Something. Nothing,' she said.

'I don't believe you,' Royal replied. 'Something is never nothing, Marta.'

'It's just a drawing of this,' she said, carefully picking up a *Papustyla pulcherrima*, a very common Neuguinea land snail. Marta held it up to the light, where it glowed a ravishing green.

'Show me,' commanded Royal, his hand outstretched. Marta placed the shell on his open palm. Royal laughed. 'No, your picture of it.'

'It's not very good,' Marta apologised as she handed over the illustration. The paint had dried almost as quickly as Marta had applied it, so that the colours had a vibrant, immediate quality that was served well by the pale-wheaten background provided by the heavy buff paper.

'It's very beautiful.' Royal took in the delicacy of the colouring and the sure stokes of fine, dark pencil of the preliminary sketch that gave shape and depth to what would otherwise be nothing more than a wash of colour on a blank page. 'I had no idea you were so talented, Marta.'

'Not really,' protested Marta. 'Our sister Gretchen was the painter. I'm merely an amateur. Nothing more. No, Gretchen was the true talent. Such a shame. Such a waste … '

'What happened to her?' asked Royal, his interest instantly piqued.

'She died,' said Marta, 'just before the war.'

'Was she ill?'

'Yes,' replied Marta brusquely. 'An illness of the mind. She took her own life. '

I'm sorry,' said Royal, taking his cigarette case out of his satchel. 'Unforgivable of me to stir up sad memories, m'dear. I apologise.'

'There's no need to apologise,' said Marta. She took a cigarette and leaned forward so she could catch the flame of the struck match. 'Poor Gretchen. She was so very beautiful. Bernard was much more in love with her than he was with me. If he was here he would say it was so.'

'Surely not,' said Royal, who'd always thought that his friend Bernard Schmidt had vastly underestimated and undervalued his wife.

'He thought I didn't know, but I always did. And I was so glad when she rejected him because I knew then that if he wanted a wife he would have to choose me. You know, I thought I could make myself love him and vice versa, in the beginning. But that's not possible, is it? You can't learn to love someone.'

'Enough of the past,' Royal said, refusing to answer the question. 'I'm here to talk of the future.'

Royal's odour, Marta noticed, was completely different from Bernard's. Her husband had always smelled slightly rank – of poor digestion, rotting teeth and sour sweat. Royal, on the other hand, though pungent after his long trip, smelled, to Marta at least, utterly delicious. And for a moment, as she inhaled in his distinctive attar, she was overcome with a wave of desire so intense that her whole body ached from the force of it and she could scarcely breathe. Then Royal moved back in his chair and the feeling vanished as quickly as it had come upon her.

'You all right, m'dear?' asked Royal. 'You're very flushed.'

'Sorry , I suddenly felt faint. You were saying …' Unable to recall the conversational thread, Marta turned even pinker.

'I came here to talk of the future. What you're going to do about Gethsemane.'

'Yes, I was rather afraid that that's why you were here,' said Marta, recovering her composure. 'Ettie Kaumann says that you have the ear of Pethebridge.' There was a hint of accusation in her tone that wasn't lost on Royal.

'You have to trust me, Marta. Bernard was my friend, as are you. I want to help you, you have to believe me. The on dit is that if the war goes Britain's way the first thing on the bargaining table will be Germany's colonies and the lands of its expatriate citizens. Yours included.'

'And yet,' Marta said sadly, 'Gethsemane is my home. Bernard bought the land, planted the coconuts and built this house and still somehow this isn't enough to safeguard our ownership.'

'Yes,' agreed Royal. 'War and its spoils pay little heed to the plight or greater good of the individual.'

'But what if Germany and her allies triumph?'

'Touché, m'dear. Then perhaps I, as a citizen of one of Britain's dominions, will lose everything that *I've* worked so hard for. War doesn't play favourites.'

'Is there anything we can do about this, or is the situation hopeless?'

'Well,' said Royal, standing and flicking his cigarette butt out the window, 'that is what you and I have to decide. But come on, let's go and find that coffee.'

They found Augusta in floods of tears, the pages of her letter lying abandoned on the floor of the verandah.

'What on earth?' said Marta crossly. *How like Augusta to make a scene because they had a visitor.*

'It's Wolfie,' sobbed Augusta. 'He … he … he's gone to Rabaul in search of passage to Valparaiso or Santiago. He says he's going to try and join a German naval ship from there.'

'Is that young Hoffmann?' asked Royal, unperturbed by Augusta's tears or Wolfie's show of patriotism.

'Yes,' said Marta, looking around for the coffee. 'Oh, for goodness sake. You didn't even ask Cookie for coffee, did you?'

'As it happens, I did,' her sister replied, as Cookie rounded the corner of the house carrying a rattling tray. 'You're so mean, Marta. In fact I don't think I can bear being with you another moment.'

'I tell myself it's her age,' observed Marta as Augusta, having retrieved her letter, flounced off down the steps and into the garden. 'I had rather hoped that young Hoffmann would marry her and that would be the end of it.'

'I'm sure he will when the war's over and he's proven himself.'

'If he does succeed in joining the navy he might not come back,' reasoned Marta.

'It's unlikely he'll even gain entry,' said Royal, 'and it's a little more involved than simply turning up on the day. The boy obviously reads far too many adventure stories.'

'Well, I shall be very cross if he does get killed.' Marta picked up the silver coffee pot. 'If he doesn't come back and marry her, I'm going to send her back to Germany.'

'Is it really all that bad?' asked Royal. 'Having her here? I'd have thought you'd enjoy the company.'

'I do enjoy her company,' confessed Marta, 'silly though she can be at times. But there's nothing here for her, except Wolfie Hoffmann, the possibility of marriage and maybe a plantation. If there's any such thing as the Hoffmann plantation after the war.'

The next morning Royal went down to the drying sheds and caught and tacked up the horse that pulled the Gethsemane carriage. It was still cool and the mare frisked a little beneath him, though she must have been twenty if she was a day, as he settled into the saddle. He remembered vividly Bernard telling him, years ago, soon after he'd bought her from Macco, that she was a little cold-backed. As he rode around the plantation where already the labour line was at work, and later when he inspected the drying sheds and quality of the copra, Royal was quietly impressed. Marta was doing a very good job of running Gethsemane and there appeared to be neither dissent nor discontented murmurings among her natives, all of whom enquired after the Missus. If she'd been one of his managers, reflected Royal, who'd been quietly extending his own empire beyond Cape Gazelle over the years, and had picked up a further two plantations, one in Friedrich-Wilhelmshafen and another on Witu Island, he would be well pleased and perhaps even inclined to give her a raise. But then Marta had always struck him as being more than capable. In some ways she reminded him of Emma, but without the latter's weakness for men and liquor.

'You've done well,' Royal said when he returned to the bungalow shortly before luncheon and found Marta sitting at her desk painting a paper nautilus, as intricately pleated as origami and the size of a man's spread hand. 'The place is in good heart.'

'Thank you,' said Marta. 'Though really it's not that difficult. I mean, here am I, spending a whole morning on my own pursuits safe in the knowledge that the place runs all too well without me.'

'Well, I did say to you that copra wasn't a particularly complex business.'

'Indeed you did,' said Marta, rinsing the fine paintbrush she was using to tint the portrait of the *Argonauta argo*. The water in the jar turned albescent as Marta stirred it with the brush. 'Though it did take me a good while to realise that.'

'So what are we to do?' asked Royal. 'About Gethsemane?'

'I was rather hoping you had all the answers,' said Marta, as she loaded her brush with colour. 'Isn't that why you're here?'

'I *have* come up with something,' confessed Royal. 'Though how successful it will prove to be, I have no real idea. It's a means by which we are both protected, regardless of the outcome of the war.'

Marta lifted her head from the page, and in that moment of inattention, carelessly let too much colour escape the brush. It spread well beyond the edges of the pencilled in form of the shell that wasn't really a shell, but the egg pod of the species that had hardened into a brittle carapace once removed from the sea.

'I'm listening,' Marta said, frowning.

'You and I,' said Royal, reaching over and covering one of Marta's hands with his own, 'we should marry. Make an Australian–German alliance.'

Marta started laughing. 'Honestly? Well, that's just too ridiculous for words.'

'Yes,' replied Royal. 'Truly ridiculous. But there's no other way, as far as I can see.'

'Couldn't I just sell Gethsemane to you?' Marta asked. 'For no money at all, and you could sell it back to me after the war.'

Royal shook his head. 'Marta, the day German Neuguinea capitulated to the Allies, all sales and transfers of land title were frozen. I can't buy Gethsemane from you, not for all the money in the world, nor can you even give it to me. It's no longer yours.'

Although Marta did indeed know this, it still shocked her to be told that she didn't own her home. With this endless status quo it was so easy to forget how things really were. 'Surely there's some other way? That's just too ridiculous. You're my friend, certainly, but my husband?'

'There's no other way,' Royal said. 'We have no choice and we have to act soon. Don't think of it so much as a marriage as a business arrangement.'

'So we would marry and then carry on with our separate lives. Augusta and I would stay here?'

'Ahh, no. Not while everything is in such a state of flux. It would be wiser if you and Augusta came to Rabaul. Present a united front and all that.'

'But Gethsemane?'

'I have a good manager I can put in here,' replied Royal. 'That's the least of our problems.'

'And it's the only way?'

'To be honest, m'dear, I don't even know if getting married will be enough to safeguard both our interests. But I'm willing to try anything at this stage. Buggered if I'm going to let a bunch of idiots in Europe take away what's mine.'

Marta sighed. 'I suspect you're right. It just seems so unfair. This isn't our fight. I came here as Bernard's wife, not to expand Germany's cause in the Pacific and *this* is my home now. Here, at Gethsemane.'

'I know, I know,' said Royal, 'and sadly it's small independent planters like you who will suffer the most. The company men, having lost nothing, will simply make the long sail home. New Guinea will be but a chapter in their lives.'

'Then I suppose there's no other way.'

'Good girl,' said Royal. 'I knew I could count on you to see reason. But there *is* just one other thing.'

'What?' asked Marta.

Royal started to tell her why his marriage to Rebecca hadn't been a success.

Marta cut him off in mid-sentence. 'I know. It doesn't matter. I understand.'

'Did Bernard tell you?'

'Yes,' said Marta. 'And you have a … a friend?'

'Yes,' said Royal. 'But it's discreet, I promise you.'

'And there's no other way?'

'No, m'dear, there really isn't,' replied Royal, taking her hand again and giving it a reassuring squeeze.

Marta avoided Royal all the following day, disappearing from the house shortly after dawn. If she'd been a less clever woman perhaps she would have leapt at the chance to marry a man she desired, fully believing in her ability to change the object of her affection. But Marta knew it was more complicated, that love wasn't transformative, any more than people were capable of changing. Love had that kind of power only in fairy tales and there was no place for fairy tales in *her* life. At dusk she returned to the bungalow, famished and dehydrated. Pausing at the bottom of the steps, she looked up at Royal, who was waiting for her. 'I've made my decision,' she said without joy or embellishment. 'I will marry you.'

'We can divorce later, after the war. It may only be for a few years, and would it be all that bad? I like to think that we're good friends.'

Marta smiled. She remembered Bernard saying almost the exact same thing years ago in Vienna when they were courting. And look how *that* had turned out.

Over dinner that night they told Augusta, who was not at all surprised. It was obvious to her that Marta was a little in love with Royal Weston, and she adored the idea of abandoning Gethsemane, which she'd decided was the most tedious place on earth. 'When can we leave?' she asked, impatient to get to Rabaul, where, by faint chance, Wolfie might still be cooling his heels. She was sure she could persuade him to stay, induce Royal to give him a nice safe job.

❋ ❋ ❋

A juvenile tree python had begun living in the hot, dark space between the ceiling and roofing iron of the bungalow a year or so before Bernard had died, though Marta had never told him about it, as he was quite frightened of snakes and would have in all likelihood killed it. Three years later it was still there. Marta sometimes found it curled up in a patch of sunlight on her desk among her papers, happy to stay there as she worked around it. She had witnessed its growth and its metamorphosis from daffodil yellow to acid lime with the onset of maturity. She'd formed a degree of attachment to the reptile. It wasn't exactly a pet, but nor was it completely a creature of the rainforest.

A few days after it had been decided that she and Royal would marry, Marta went into the office after breakfast and found a large, incomplete sliver of newly shed snakeskin, which had floated onto her desk sometime in the night. Marta picked it up carefully and rubbed its friable ophidian silkiness gently between her thumb and finger, as if feeling a fabric, and thought about what she'd decided to do. She knew she was making another unsuccessful marriage, and wondered at the wisdom of yet another such choice. The decision was entirely cerebral, for as much as she desired Royal, the voice in her head told her that it wasn't possible, and never would be. As she placed the delicate snakeskin in an old cigar box of Bernard's, she hoped that, by agreeing to marry Royal Weston, she'd done the right thing for herself, for Augusta and, most of all, for Gethsemane. At least she *liked* him, and she couldn't honestly say that that had always the case with Bernard. But as for love, she knew it was impossible. They both were who they were and there was no changing that. She'd made her decision and now it was time to go, to start something new. It was almost exciting.

But she would miss Gethsemane.

Before she left Marta went up to the waterfall one last time, to say goodbye to Bernard; at the very least she owed him that. At Royal's suggestion, she had built a memorial of stone and concrete to her husband there a few months after his death. Standing in the middle of the clearing, with the afternoon sun slanting across the grass and water, Marta delighted anew in what lay around her. The lowest branches of the mango trees were now too high for her to pluck a perfect specimen of fruit as she used to do when she came up here in the early days of her marriage. Instead she had to content herself with combing the ground beneath for a mango that had fallen recently and with the minimum of bruising. The paper wasps floated around her, drunk and sluggish on sugar from the rapidly decaying fruit. Finding a mango that pleased her, Marta approached the pool. The cloud of butterflies hovering over the water reacted to her arrival by rising higher above the surface of the pool, a massive squadron of incessant moving colour, waiting to take flight if the danger became more pronounced. Sitting down on a rock at the water's edge, Marta stripped the skin easily from the fruit with her fingers and, holding it in both hands, ate it in great mouthfuls, taking pleasure not only in the taste but in the juice that ran down her chin and bony wrists, staining the rolled-up sleeves and front of her shirt. And in this way, without needing to do anything dramatic like shedding her clothes and slipping into that cool green water or shouting her own name to the heavens as a declaration that she, Marta, still lived, she made her peace with Gethsemane and with Bernard. As she squatted at the water's edge to wash the mango juice from her hands Marta was momentarily taken aback by her own reflection. Sometimes she forgot she was almost fifty. She sighed, allowing herself a brief moment of regret for her vanished youth, such as it was. Then, after washing her hands, she stood and walked across the clearing to the memorial she'd built for Bernard on the escarpment looking out to sea.

'Sleep soundly,' she whispered, laying the palm of her hand against the sun-warm stones. 'I'll be back one day.'

As she was packing up the last of her belongings, Marta came across the gaudy hair clip she'd discovered in Bernard's pocket years ago, after the ball at Gunantambu. Holding it up to the light, where it shone dully, Marta marvelled that such a thing had once held the power to hurt her. Later that day she threw it on the fire in the cooking quarters while Cookie and Raus were out fishing. The flames consumed the entire bauble, ersatz gemstones and all.

Twenty-one

Mr Royal Weston, plantation owner of New Britain, and Frau Marta Schmidt, widow of New Ireland, were pronounced man and wife at Royal's residence on Namanula Hill, above Rabaul and its harbour, in December of 1916. Although they were supposed merely to be a means to an end, the wedding festivities got well out of hand as, for the first time since the beginning of the war, many put aside their national differences and were more than happy to celebrate this marriage. Some, though, were puzzled by Royal's choice of bride, especially those mamas with daughters younger and prettier than Marta Schmidt, who considered Royal Weston something of a catch. The reception was initially a little stiff and contained, but as night fell and more champagne was drunk, the guests talked as friends and neighbours once more. In fact the only person who was truly down in the mouth at the nuptials was Augusta, who made a pretty bridesmaid in spite of her long face and tear-swollen eyes. Wolfie Hoffmann had sailed for South America just hours before her arrival in Rabaul the week before.

'He's gone forever,' Augusta had declared, when Royal had delivered the news.

'Don't be so ridiculous, Gustie,' Marta had replied, fervently hoping that this wasn't the case.

At the close of the marital festivities the bride and groom went to their separate bedrooms in the palatial residence that Royal had purchased a decade before, closing their respective doors behind them. And so the marriage began.

* * *

Hearing shouts and crashes from behind the bungalow shortly after lunch a month or so after the wedding, Marta and Augusta, carrying their cups of coffee, went to investigate and discovered the garden natives digging holes in a vague square towards the rear of the garden.

'What an earth?' exclaimed Marta.

'Look, here's Royal now,' said Augusta, who'd been alerted of her new brother-in-law's approach by the soft scrunching noise of his gelding's unshod hooves on the coral of the driveway.

'Oh, so it is,' said Marta, turning around and spilling half her coffee in the process. 'What's the meaning of this, Royal?' she asked.

'I'm building you an aviary as a wedding present, m'dear,' replied her husband. 'My gift to you, in way of thanks.'

'Goodness, how romantic,' sighed Augusta, completely missing the jaundiced look her sister gave her. 'You're so lucky, Marta.'

'Yes, well,' said Marta, draining her cup. 'Thank you, Royal. Augusta's right, this is an extraordinary gift.'

''I'm only building the aviary,' Royal said. 'You, m'dear, will be responsible for filling it and for the care of your creatures, so maybe in time you will curse me for this … albatross, for want of a better word, around your neck. I thought it would help you with your ornithological studies. Allow you to get up close without killing the poor blighters. I'm told birds of paradise are actually eminently tameable. And make rather good pets.'

'And I could set them free when I'm finished with them,' said Marta, warming to the idea.

'If you should so wish,' agreed Royal. 'Splendid thought.'

'I still think it's romantic,' said Augusta as the sisters walked back to the bungalow.

Marta suddenly smiled like a new bride. 'Yes, you're right,' she conceded. 'It *is* romantic.'

'Now you'll have to give him an equally spectacular gift,' said Augusta.

'I will?'

'Yes, of course.'

'But what?' said Marta. 'Where on earth would I find something like that anyway? China Town? The Carpenters' store on Mango Street?'

'You'll think of something,' Augusta said cheerfully.

'I wish I shared in your belief. I shall fail at this, I'm sure,' fretted Marta. 'I've never been any good at gifts.'

But Augusta wasn't listening. 'I wonder if there's mail?' she said, looking down on the harbour where three vessels were newly docked at the main wharf.

In years to come, when she caught a moment of profound tenderness between her husband and Tomai, and felt utterly unloved, Marta would walk out to the aviary, sit among her birds and count the ways that Royal did really love her, in his own way. He understood her. 'He gave me,' she would write many years later in her memoirs, 'the courage to know myself.' She would never write about how she missed being truly touched each time Royal stroked her cheek or squeezed her hand.

Not all the mail that came up the hill each afternoon from the port throughout 1917 was from Wolfie in Valparaiso, though the young man wrote to his beloved every day. Letters from the house on Wipplinger Strasse continued to arrive much as they had in peacetime, though a little more slowly. The war, now in its fourth year, had bought a new austerity to Klara and Egon's lives, but they were bearing the privations with a patriotic stoicism. Although the mails were fairly reliable, it was still brave of Egon to carefully wrap up his precious copy of Maria Sybilla Merian's *Metamorphosis Insectorum Surinamensium* and entrust a chain of strangers to carry it halfway across the world to an island in the South Pacific; a wedding present for his Marta, whom he missed terribly.

When the parcel, grubby and bruised by officialdom, eventually arrived five months later, Marta unwrapped it in great excitement, for she could tell it was a book. Royal, who'd brought it up the hill as soon as it had been delivered to his company headquarters on the waterfront, sat across the table from his wife in the large reception room, watching her with real pleasure. She was, he thought, almost lovely when she was animated. Age had served Marta well: it was as if she'd finally caught up with her face.

'Oh, how wonderful!' Marta exclaimed, as she peeled back the last layer of wrapping and revealed the beautiful old book. Then her face abruptly crumpled. 'Oh Papa,' she said in a small, pained voice before bursting into tears.

'Goodness, goodness me,' exclaimed Royal, rushing to her side. 'Darling girl, mustn't cry.' He crouched down beside her and patted her knee ineffectually.

'I'm just being silly,' said Marta, pulling herself together and wiping her tears away with her fingertips. 'I never cry. I don't have any capacity for sentimentality.'

'That's the spirit,' said Royal, standing with some difficulty. In recent years his body had become all too fond of reminding him that he wasn't as young as he used to be. 'Come on, darling girl. Let's sit together and look at your magnificent book and you can tell me all about it.' After Marta had told Merian's story, Royal, who had of course heard it many times, smiled and said, 'Just like you, m'dear.'

Marta pulled a wry face as she searched for a familiar page. 'I think you mock me a little, dear husband.'

'Perhaps,' he agreed, 'but only because you won't show me your own endeavours. But we will talk about that later. Must have been a hellish two years for the lovely Maria.'

'Well, as you can see,' said Marta, having found the plate she sought, 'it certainly doesn't show in her illustrations. This is a butterfly called *Rothschildia aurota*, which has been depicted around a Seville orange twig. That actually strikes me as a little strange.'

'How so?'

'It's a transplanted species, so why would it provide a hospitable environment for what I assume is a native butterfly.'

'Perhaps it only looks like a Seville orange and that's how it's been interpreted,' said Royal.

'What do you mean?'

'Think of the varieties of native citrus we have available here,' said Royal, making his point by lifting Marta's glass of kalmansi juice, which was sweating on the table. 'Maybe it was a native orange and when she took her pictures back to Holland it was simply interpreted as a Seville varietal and gradually over the last two hundred years that has become its truth.'

'Oh,' said Marta, 'what an interesting supposition. You may very well be right. However, what I really adore about Merian's work is her interest in metamorphism. You can see how she had captured the entire life cycle of the butterfly, in its four distinct stages. She was something of a revolutionary in this respect.'

'They're quite extraordinary, aren't they,' said Royal, turning the page and revealing a new plate. 'Metamorphism and transformation.'

'Exactly,' said Marta.

'I thought you didn't believe in transformation,' said Royal, plucking from the ether the memory of a distant conversation they'd once shared.

'I do if I can see it with my own eyes in a species capable of dramatic metaphysical change. But not in humans. Man is incapable of change. But how clever of you to remember. That was after Emma's farewell at Ulul-Nono, I think.'

Royal laughed. 'I remember everything, darling girl. That's why I drink so bloody much.'

So engaged in conversation were her sister and Royal, that Augusta, when she returned from visiting a friend in town three hours later, was able to stand unobserved in the doorway of the room and watch them for some minutes. She's happy, Augusta realised, as Marta laughed, and Royal leaned forward and gently touched her cheek. *She's truly happy.*

✳ ✳ ✳

Are you ready?' Marta asked.

'I can't think why you want to give Royal that hideous thing,' said Augusta. She was faintly horrified by the gift that Marta, after over six months of procrastination, had decided to give Royal. In truth it hadn't occurred to her to give him anything other than Gretchen's last surviving portrait. But it was such an odd, provocative thing to offer, bearing in mind their circumstances, that she'd dithered until now.

'Because I think it will amuse him,' said Marta, quite truthfully, as she briskly handed the wrapped painting to her husband one afternoon after lunch.

'You should burn it,' advised Augusta, as Royal began untying the string. 'Not only is it ugly but I'm sure it's cursed as well.'

'Beauty is in the eye of the beholder,' Marta replied calmly, as she watched her husband reveal the back of the painting. 'I think it's beautiful, if a little strange. And I hope that Royal will too.'

Augusta shuddered. 'How could you? That thing is depraved. If you wanted a nice gift, you should have bought that fantastic new Rolex watch at Carpenters'. Now that's a gift from a wife to her husband.'

Marta was unmoved. 'I think it best we let Royal judge for himself, don't you, Gustie?'

There was a moment of stunned silence after Royal turned the painting over and just before he started laughing. 'Goodness,' he said between guffaws, 'that's not what I expected at all, darling girl. It's a fantastic likeness, though. That's what you looked like the first day when you stepped of the ship at Herbertshohe … well, except your … thingies were covered, of course.'

'Thank Gott for that,' said Augusta.

'Well, I like it!' Marta stated. She bent over the painting and rubbed at the mildew that had grown back since she'd last cleaned it.

'I do too,' said Royal, moving his wife's busy hands away from the painting and picking it up. 'The brushwork is extraordinary,' he continued peering closely at it in the light. 'Who's the disgruntled baby?'

'I don't know,' replied Marta. 'I've always wondered about that. I've always assumed it was the Christ child. To me the painting is almost like a Byzantine or Renaissance icon.'

'Funnily enough,' said Royal, looking closely at the delicately painted face of the child on Marta's bare shoulder, 'I think the baby resembles Augusta.'

'Oh no,' protested Marta immediately. 'I think you're wrong about that. The baby is a definite reference to religious paintings of the fourteenth century in particular. Gretchen was very taken with those and we would go and look at them often at the Kunsthistorisches Museum.'

'And the toad,' continued Royal, paying Marta no heed, 'well, the toad looks like Bernard, don't you think?' he concluded. And now that Royal had pointed it out, the amphibian in the painting did have a distinctly Bernard-esque quality. 'Your sister seems to have had second sight. It's really jolly good. Much, much better than my daubs.' Royal leaned over and kissed Marta gently on the cheek before returning his attention to the painting. 'I love it, m'dear. It is a most generous and wonderful gift. I know how precious it must be to you.'

'Really?' said Marta. She flushed faintly pink with pleasure.

'I think we should hang it,' he said, putting the portrait down and lighting two cigarettes, one of which he handed to Marta.

'I'm so happy,' Marta said. 'I knew you'd understand it. It's fantastically good, isn't it?'

'I really don't know, but I suspect so. However, good, bad or indifferent, it's irrelevant, so long as *we* like it. Give it a clean, m'dear, and then we'll decide where to hang it. Though you know it's going to put my own efforts to shame.'

You're both mad!' declared Augusta, rolling her eyes. 'What kind of woman gives her husband a naked picture of herself?'

Royal gave Augusta a slightly old-fashioned look and laughed. 'You *are* very young, aren't you, m'dear?'

In the end the painting went in the front room on the wall facing the door, where it was unmissable by anyone who came to the bungalow. It wasn't just that it was perfectly framed for a second time by the door, but because at that distance the subject matter was lost, so all who entered, assuming it was one of Royal's kanaka paintings, were immediately compelled to walk directly to the painting to examine it more closely. The various reactions provided Royal with hours of amusement. The colony was shocked that Royal Weston would hang a pornographic painting of his wife in his front room for all to see. Augusta refused to bring her new friends to the house on Namanula Hill when Royal steadfastly ignored her entreaties to let her take it down when they had visitors, and the mission folk of every order, seeing only the work of the devil, avoided the Weston residence. All of which suited Royal and Marta very well.

A number of Royal's military friends, Colonel Pethebridge included, thought that Mrs Weston had once had a small but very pert breast, though it was a shame the artist hadn't put the other one in. All were convinced that Royal had painted it. *The old goat!* For her part Marta was faintly horrified, very embarrassed but secretly pleased. She rather liked being Royal's eccentric wife, with her trousers and short hair, and anti-social behaviour. *Let them talk!*

'I wish you would show me some of your own paintings,' Royal said, the day they hung the portrait.

'Maybe,' said Marta vaguely. 'Maybe one day.'

'I'll hold you to that,' Royal said.

'I think you should,' replied Marta.

They both stepped back as one, shoulder to shoulder, and looked at the portrait with deep satisfaction.

'It's almost queenly, like Titania in her flower glade, or any one of the countless classical goddesses associated with nature,' Royal observed.

'You don't think we've gone too far?'

Royal picked up his wife's hand and squeezed it. 'Never, darling girl.'

'Augusta's going to be so cross,' said Marta.

'Is it really the nudity or is it something else?'

'I think it reminds her how sick our sister was,' admitted Marta.

'Was she really all that mad?'

'Oh yes, completely.'

'How terribly sad.'

'Oh infinitely so,' agreed Marta, turning to her husband and smiling as the land began to shake. The bottles on the drinks trolley clinked against each other for a few moments before the guria subsided.

Twenty-two

'I don't have any stories,' Royal protested.

'*That* I'm not even going to pretend to believe,' replied Marta as she deftly topped up her husband's post-prandial brandy. She'd learned very quickly that there was a certain place, in Royal's slow quotidian stroll towards complete inebriation, where he felt sufficiently inured to really talk. It was an exploitative measure on her part, but necessary. Royal was very much a closed book and, unlike Bernard, he was a text she wanted to read. In the many years she'd known him, the conversations of any substance they'd shared could be counted on one hand. She knew close to nothing about her husband other than how he and Bernard had become friends.

'It's true, m'dear. Nothing to tell.'

'What if I trade you something for your biography.'

'Like what?' asked Royal, instantly intrigued.

'A story about myself.'

'No, no,' said Royal. 'Not nearly interesting enough.'

'Oh,' said Marta. Her dismay was palpable.

Seeing the look on her face, Royal laughed. 'I don't mean you're not interesting, it's simply because your darling sister has told me everything. She's quite the talker, isn't she?'

'I hardly think she knows everything,' said Marta. 'I was twenty when she was born.'

'Look at you,' said Royal, patting his wife's hand. 'All put out. Cheer up. You do have something you could trade me for the story of my life, though let me assure you, dear wife, that I'll definitely be getting the better end of the bargain.'

'What?'

'I would like either to ask you a question or see some of your paintings.'

Marta considered Royal's proposition for a moment. 'I agree,' she finally said, with some reluctance.

'So, what I assume you're after is something about my childhood perhaps, or those years before I washed up here in New Guinea in 1899?'

'Yes,' replied Marta. 'That's exactly it.'

'I was,' began Royal, 'lucky enough to be born into a little money, thanks mostly to my mother, who not only brought wealth to the marriage, but has proved to be a most astute business woman with varied interests. For example, on paper, she owns part of Gethsemane.'

'You're obfuscating, Royal,' said Marta. 'Tell the story. You were born in Melbourne in 1873. I know that. Any brothers or sisters?'

'Scores,' replied Royal. 'I'm Irish Catholic so there's a veritable tribe of us scattered over the globe, including one brother who farms cattle and coffee just out of Nairobi and another who's a priest in Alaska, of all places. And I have a sister who's a nun in Fiji, but she's an anomaly on the female side, as my other four sisters have proven to be quite unadventurous, though brave enough to stay in Melbourne, marry well and produce their own large families.'

'How funny, Royal, I've always thought of you as such a lone wolf.'

'No, no,' replied Royal. 'Quite the opposite, darling girl. There are Westons everywhere, because of course there's also the family that stayed on in Ireland and the tentacles they've have spread across Britain and central Europe. That's why I live here and never talk of them. It's to get away from them all.'

'Do you ever see them?'

'I met a great many of my northern relatives when I was a young man and sent to England for school, and stayed on to take my degree. They made me most welcome too. I see my sisters and oldest brother, and Mother and Father of course, most Christmases, though of course I haven't been since we married, when I go to see my own children. Costs me a fortune too – there are twenty-four nieces and nephews so far, all clamouring for treats from Uncle Royal. We're surprisingly close-knit really.' Royal paused. 'Is that enough?'

'I hardly think so,' said Marta. 'That was very meagre.'

'I can't think what else to tell you,' replied Royal. 'My father's a doctor. Retired now and happy in his garden, where he grows medicinal herbs. He leaves Mother to run the family businesses. There are numerous properties in Victoria, including a spread at Ballarat and commercial properties and land in Melbourne. As well as owning half of my company, Mother has a sizable stake in my East African brother's investments. Last time I was in Melbourne she told me that they'd recently bought land around Mount Kilimanjaro in Tanganyika and intend growing coffee.' He stopped and took a sip of his drink. 'Plantations are rather popular in my family, along with saving souls. Another of my brothers, Rupert, the quiet one, is farming cacao in Venezuela. For quite a few generations we've managed to avoid the military. I've always wondered if there wasn't something essentially craven in the Weston line.'

'I don't like the military,' Marta said vehemently. 'Everything was fine until they came along.'

'Oh, but then you've not had the best of luck with them, m'dear. It's not all that bad a vocation really,' said Royal. 'Except the warring and fighting and killing, of course. Shame it can't all be wardroom dinners and wonderful uniforms. Might have seriously considered joining if it was.'

'Ever the dilettante.'

'Oh absolutely, m'dear. Absolutely.'

'What about your schooling?'

'All of us boys were sent home to England to spend three years preparing for our exams at Colet Court, at St Paul's. After Australia it was a pretty miserable existence. My first winter there I thought I would never be warm again. But I survived, as you do.'

'I've forgotten what it's like to be cold,' Marta said. 'I really have.'

'Yes,' said Royal. 'It's odd how that happens.'

'But you stayed on in England?'

'Yes,' replied Royal. 'I took an undergraduate degree in ancient history at Magdalene, Oxford. Got a second eventually – failed to distinguish myself in any way at all. I muddled around in London for about a year after that, tried to get into the Slade to study painting but obviously wasn't up to chop. So the civil service it was. I did the interview and later, in 1894 I think, I remember it was winter anyway, they offered me a single man's posting in British Borneo. By that stage, however, I'd decided to join my brother Jupiter, who is, I think, five years older than me, and take a position with the Imperial East Africa Company in Mombasa.'

'How wonderful,' sighed Marta, who was listening intently. 'I've always longed to go to Africa.'

'Marvellous place,' agreed Royal.

'How long were you there?'

'A little over four years. Jupiter was working in an exploratory capacity for the company, making forays inland north-west of Mombasa up to Lake Victoria. This was when they were finalising the plans to build the railway from Mombasa to Kisumu. He got me a job with the company, paper shuffling in the Mombasa office, which suited me fine. I moved into his digs. The company had given him a bungalow by the water near the fort in the old town, not much of a walk from the company headquarters. And that was it, really. I might have even stayed if we hadn't fallen out.'

'What did you argue about?'

'Nothing that I can remember,' Royal said evasively, realising he had unintentionally said too much. 'It was in Mombasa, at the club, that I met Rebecca and we married in 1898 and came here to New Guinea soon after. Not much before you, in fact. I was quite new to the colony when you arrived.'

'I know,' said Marta. 'And I've always thought that was so odd because the first thing I noticed about you, and, don't laugh, I remember this very clearly, was how comfortable you appeared in New Guinea. It was as though you'd been here your entire life. I even think I was perhaps a little irked by that too.'

✳ ✳ ✳

It had been about a boy, the falling out between Royal and his brother. Well, that had been the catalyst. In truth the friction between the siblings was about Royal's hypocrisy and the way in which it rubbed against Jupiter's unequivocal quest to live his life entirely on his own, occasionally monstrous, terms.

Jupiter had discovered the boy on one of his expeditions into Masai country, through which the proposed railway would run. Because he liked to hunt for big game while out on safari, and every lion that Jupiter shot was one less to attack their cattle, he'd formed something of a bond with the semi-nomadic people, and would always stop to talk with the cattle boys out grazing their fathers' stock out on the grassy plains. As a result Jupiter sometimes arrived home from an expedition with a bag that included a live young boy, acquired in return for cattle that he would give their fathers. In the first year that Royal had lived with his brother, he'd watched three black boys walk into the house and limp out again, mere husks of their former selves. His brother, Royal had quickly concluded, was hard on his young lovers. Jupiter always did the right thing by them, though, sending them home to their people with their pockets full of trinkets.

'I like it when they squeal,' Jupiter had confided one night when the brothers had drunk too much of the cheap Cape brandy for which Jupiter had developed a taste during his time in Africa.

Who are you? Royal had thought, looking into his brother's face made ugly by lasciviousness and hard spirits. *Who are you?*

Jupiter had always possessed a cruel streak. Royal could vaguely recall an incident, when he was eight or nine. Jupiter had almost beaten a stable boy to death over a trivial matter regarding the type of bit his mare was wearing. Certainly he remembered how unsettled the house in Yarra had been in those weeks before Jupiter was put on a ship to England and sent away to school. The only lasting memories Royal had retained of his older brother were the mean little pinches he doled out when nanny wasn't looking and the time Jupiter had tried to drown him in the creek at the bottom of the garden. Everyone had been quietly relieved when Jupiter hadn't returned to Australia after school.

Unbeknown to Royal, and indeed most of the family, Mrs Weston had kept Jupiter away; she knew, as a mother of many children does, who were the bad eggs in her basket. Rather than attending Oxford or Cambridge, Jupiter, just eighteen years of age, and not even slightly wet behind the ears, was shipped off into the wilderness again, this time as a minion of the Imperial East Africa Company. Quick with his fists, a deadly shot and skilled horseman, Jupiter hadn't stayed a minion long. He befriended an old-timer who had patiently taught him everything he knew about the land and its people, and showed him the ancient ley line that traversed the country from Lake Victoria to Mombasa, which the local people had walked since the beginning of time, first as children of the land, then as shackled slaves never to return home. Wallace had died of blackwater fever while out in the field and Jupiter had left the old man's desiccated body under an acacia in the middle of the Tsavo for the lions and vultures to clean up. Nobody back at company headquarters ever questioned it. Death came quickly and without warning under Africa's skies.

Meeting his brother again as an adult, Royal had been pleased to discover him to be on the whole clever, surprisingly well read, generous and superb company, though this was tempered by the ever-present shiver of cruelty, the essence of evil that Jupiter carried so close to the surface that it bloomed like a scent from his skin, especially when he drank. He was blatant, too, about his desires and made no effort to pretend the young boys who staffed his house were anything other than catamites. Jupiter's attitude caused Royal to go into a kind of retreat from his own sexuality. It hadn't been difficult for Royal to negate this need in himself. Desire, real desire, and love, had eluded him thus far, and he had decided already, though he was barely twenty-two, that perhaps he was a confirmed bachelor, one of those men who lived an existence bereft of any kind of physical dimension. He *had* tried. There'd been liaisons both chaste and not so chaste: group encounters in the showers and darkened dormitories at school and later a few pallid fumblings with young men at Oxford. And there'd been women, too, for whom he'd felt affection – sisters and cousins of the friends he'd made while in England. In many ways the women were easier for Royal. All that was required in these times of genteel courtship were pretty words and romantic strolls in gardens. Men were much more demanding.

After he'd graduated Royal had even walked out for a while with a young lady seriously enough to ignite hopes of an engagement in the bosoms of the girl and her mama. When he'd gone to East Africa Royal had left Miss Daisy Waite of Sussex with unfulfilled expectations and a temporarily broken heart. But it had been for the best. Within weeks of arriving in Mombasa he'd received a letter from her saying she was engaged and would marry the following spring. Royal had sent a zebra skin, shot by Jupiter, and his best wishes as a wedding present.

In spite of Jupiter's sometimes shockingly flagrant behaviour, Royal was very comfortable in Kenya. It wasn't by any means an unpleasant existence. There were various communities of expatriates in Mombasa. Either by birth or empire, the Germans and the British, of course, formed the two biggest groups. The Brits congregated at the newly established Mombasa Club in the Old Town down near the harbour, next to the fort. It was there that

Royal had met Rebecca Oliver, whose father was also with the Imperial East Africa Company, though far higher up than either Royal or Jupiter. She'd debuted the season before in London and, having failed to secure a fiancé, had come out to Mombasa to escape another dreary English winter. Rebecca was a pretty wren of a girl with soft, white skin given to freckling. She was, though, perhaps a little too quick to be dissatisfied.

✳ ✳ ✳

One morning close to three years after his arrival in Mombasa, Royal was sitting in the courtyard, reading a month-old edition of *The Times*, when a young Masai boy was shown into this inner sanctum, by Abdullah, the mincing sloe-eyed Arab boy who looked after their quarters. Lowering the paper to grunt irritably at the disturbance, Royal had been instantly captivated by the Masai stripling, who was dressed from head to toe in his tribal regalia. Royal smiled wryly. Fresh from the village, he thought. You could always tell. With the paper crumpled in his lap, Royal allowed himself a moment to devour the boy inch by inch with his eyes. It was impossible not to: Jupiter's latest fancy was a magnificent specimen. And young too. The muscles on his flanks and belly, and his startling height, were newly established transformations, judging by the silk blossoms of the stretch marks on the boy's shiny black skin. Beautiful, Royal thought longingly. Utter perfection.

'Jup,' he yelled reluctantly at last. 'There a delivery for you.'

Jupiter appeared at the railing of the balcony above the courtyard on the side where his bedroom was located. He was naked. 'Oh,' he said, seeing the boy standing motionless on the stone flags below. 'I'll be right down.'

A few minutes later, nominally dressed in a flowing brocade robe, Jupiter was standing in front of the boy, looking him up and down hungrily. 'How frankly fucking delicious! Rather toothsome, don't you think, Royal? Quite the Ganymede. I paid his father a small fortune in cattle for him. Ridiculous, I know, but I had to have him.'

'Your turpitude knows no bounds, does it?' Royal observed mildly, pretending to be immersed once more in his paper. Jupiter just laughed and walked back up the stairs to his rooms with the boy silently following him. Royal, ignoring Abdullah's smirks, abandoned his paper and went for a walk a few minutes later, escaping the cries of distress and fear that floated down from the open doors of Jupiter's bedroom.

The boy was everywhere after that, a silent, painful presence in the cool shadows of the house. He haunted Royal's sleeping hours too, in that strange inexplicable way of dreams, and Royal found himself drinking heavily in the evenings to keep him away. The weeks passed, the rains finished, and the boy stayed on through into the long, hot dry.

'I don't like that new house native of Jupiter's,' said Rebecca one afternoon when they were walking together through the grounds of Jesus Fort on the way to the club for lunch. 'He scares me,' she continued melodramatically. 'Those dark staring eyes. I wouldn't like to be left alone with him. He looks dangerous. Untamed somehow. Your brother has the strangest tastes in houseboys, doesn't he?'

'Yes,' agreed Royal. 'Now your parents,' he continued, resolutely changing the subject, 'have they made a decision yet about where they'll retire?'

'As a matter of fact they have,' said Rebecca. 'Launceston in Tasmania. Papa, well Papa's agent in Tasmania, is negotiating to buy a small property there, some six miles from town. They intend becoming apple farmers. Do you know Launceston?'

'I've never been there,' he admitted. 'I'm sure it's lovely. And what will *you* do?' asked Royal, who'd realised a few weeks before that Rebecca had interpreted their friendship as courting and now had expectations of offers marital, though he'd done nothing to give her this idea. He would have to tell her soon, he knew. That he didn't want to marry her. She had another suitor, an Anglican vicar, a young widower, so it was unfair of him to give her false expectations when a perfectly acceptable alternative was readily available. He did so hope there wouldn't be a scene.

'Well,' said Rebecca. 'I'd have to go with them, of course. I can't stay in Mombasa unchaperoned.'

'I would miss you,' Royal said, seeing an open door at the end of the dark hallway and feeling an immense sense of relief.

'You don't have to, you know,' murmured Rebecca, who heard a longing and a commitment in Royal's words and voice that simply didn't exist.

'No,' he said, vaguely, pausing before a set of stone stairs so that Rebecca could organise her skirts. 'Have you perambulated enough? Are you ready for your luncheon now?'

And with that Rebecca had to be content.

Returning from the office to the bungalow for lunch one afternoon, he discovered one of Jupiter's more disreputable friends, Christo Matthews, sprawled out in a chair in the courtyard drinking brandy with his brother.

Jupiter's friends were a mixed bunch. There were those who resided in Mombasa or along the coast, where large farms were being established, respectable family men with either private business interests or involved with the company. And then there were the others, ignorant drunkards in the main, whom Jupiter had collected on his forays into the wilderness. And in Royal's opinion, Christo Matthews, the product of a Portuguese mother and an unknown father, was the worst of a bad lot. The source of his improbable English surname was something of a mystery, and the man himself was vague enough about it to suggest that it was a complete fabrication. Matthews was a short, rotund man who didn't believe in bathing, polite conversation or table manners. Jupiter had met him, and his dwarf wife, at their little farm at Tsavo, where Matthews had set up a big game hunting enterprise and bred blood horses, both of which were proving to be something of a success. Nobody on a Christo Matthews safari went home without a trophy. The Americans loved him – 'such a character' – and word on how good he was travelled fast, despite the man's utter lack of charm. One of Matthews' vilest and perennial topics of conversation was describing in graphic detail how he and his dwarf wife, a brassy blonde with a gold front tooth, made love. Now, seeing Christo sitting with Jup, Royal didn't think he could bear another lascivious story about Mrs Matthews on all fours, the dark furry purse of her cunt exposed and open, begging her husband to take her like the lascivious little animal she was.

'Christo,' acknowledged Royal without enthusiasm as he joined them. He immediately noticed the disgusting smell emanating from his brother's friend, who was having his feet washed by Abdullah.

'Royal, good to see you,' said Matthews, grimacing and letting loose a loud and odorous volley of intestinal gas. 'Jup and I were talking about organising a hunt for just a few of us up around Lake Victoria. Lion country. Need to clean it out a bit before the railway is built.'

'To be honest,' said Royal, indicating that he would like a drink and thus rescuing Abdullah from his onerous and noisome task. 'Killing wildlife has no real appeal for me. And I'm a terrible shot.'

'It's true, it's true,' said Jupiter without rancour, nodding. 'Worst I've ever seen, I think.'

Another tantara of flatulence trumpeted from Matthews' nether regions. 'Blood,' he explained with a grimace. 'I've developed a bit of a taste for the stuff but it does dreadful things to my bowels. The little woman makes me sleep with the servants when I partake.'

'I say, old man,' said Jupiter, moving his chair downwind. 'Did something die up there sometime last year? Certainly smells like it.'

'Certainly feels like it too,' Matthews said cheerfully, as he got up and trotted off to the latrine for the third time since his arrival.

'Good old Christo, eh! Always up for a laugh,' said Jupiter.

'He's a pig,' said Royal, taking his gin and tonic from Abdullah, who, noticing Matthews' absence, saw his opportunity and scuttled quickly away again.

'You're such a woman, Royal,' smirked Jupiter.

'By Christ, that's better,' said Christo, coming back into the courtyard still buttoning his flies. He sat down again gingerly. 'That's the last of it, I think.'

'I certainly hope so, old man. You're putrid,' observed Jupiter.

'My arsehole feels like a whole tribe of Bantus have had a go,' confessed Matthews.

'Extraordinary cocks on those Bantus,' said Jupiter casually. 'Last time I had one I couldn't sit for a week.'

Matthews roared with appreciative laughter. 'Now the missus, she fond of a bit of Bantu cock … '

'I'll go and check on lunch,' said Royal, hurriedly draining his gin and standing up.

'Of course he likes you, Christo. How could he not?' Royal heard Jupiter protest as he walked away.

After dinner that night they went to the club. Royal tried to cry off, but Jupiter and Christo wouldn't hear of it. The three of them threaded their way down a narrow alley and out onto the torch-lit street, which was clotted with people and animals, voices speaking a dozen or more languages, and commerce, the endless commerce that was Mombasa.

Because it was Friday night and the club put on a buffet dinner, it was crowded with regulars. The Olivers were there, playing bridge with the local Anglican vicar, William Bard, who was sweet on Rebecca. And it wasn't just necessity that drove the man of God, though with three children under five, a replacement wife – the last one had died of blackwater fever – was imperative to his survival. No, it was more than that. Rebecca's slim, frail body, pale freckled skin, rosebud mouth and surprisingly generous bottom, were a siren song that, in Bard's quiet moments when perhaps he should have been contemplating God and his glory, ignited in him most unfitting thoughts and visions of Miss Oliver. So vivid were these imaginings that Bard was sometimes forced to relieve himself, quickly and furtively, into a small towel he kept hidden in a drawer in his study.

'Can we have a break?' asked Rebecca a few moments later as she and William took the final trick and the hand. 'I feel a little faint. It's so hot. Some fresh air maybe? An ice?'

'Shall I accompany you, Miss Oliver?' Bard asked, standing.

'No, no,' Rebecca said. 'I'm fine.'

She went straight to Weston, noted Bard sourly. She didn't even bother to pretend. He'd put money on him being a sodomite, just like his deviant brother.

'You said you weren't going to come,' Rebecca said, joining Royal at the bar.

'I didn't intend to,' Royal said, 'but they made me.' He indicated his brother and Christo at the other end of the bar. 'Jupiter's hard to resist.'

'Really,' said Rebecca. 'I find it all too easy to resist your dear brother.'

'How's the vicar?' asked Royal, lighting a cigarette.

'Tedious as ever.' Rebecca pulled a face. 'He's such a boring little man. And I have no interest in his children. Imagine! Living in that dreadful little vicarage on a measly stipend. I'd rather go to Tasmania with Mummy and Daddy.'

'Oh,' Royal protested, 'Mr Bard isn't so bad. A little dry, yes, but well intentioned and a gentleman, I think.'

Rebecca wasn't convinced: the vicar was always 'accidentally' touching her bottom and breasts. 'But wouldn't you be jealous, Mr Weston?'

'No, no, not at all,' replied Royal heartily. 'All I wish for you, my dear, is happiness.'

The bridge game had folded, as a new fourth to replace Rebecca hadn't been found. It was late, and most of the families and older couples had gone home already. 'Time to go, Rebecca,' said Mrs Oliver firmly.

'Well,' said Royal, 'if you must. Goodnight then.'

He departed soon after the Olivers, leaving Christo and his brother drinking at the bar with a handful of the club's most committed dipsomaniacs, and began to walk home in the comparatively blessed cool of the East Africa night. A hundred million cold, dead stars were laid out across the universe and far out to sea, beyond the reefs, he could hear the distant thunder of the Indian Ocean. When he arrived at the house, only ten or so minutes later, Royal walked quickly through the darkness to the kitchen. He took a Dewar flask of water from the stone coolstore, got a tumbler from the cupboard and, sitting down on the concrete floor, began drinking one glass after another. The cool mineral taste of the well water was the last thing he remembered.

Royal didn't know how long he'd been asleep on the kitchen floor when he woke with a start, propped up against the wall, the glass still clutched in his hand. The house was still and dark and he desperately needed to relieve his swollen bladder. Moving as quickly as he could, Royal hobbled out into the small walled garden that led off the kitchen. He fumbled with his fly buttons, swearing in frustration at his clumsy fingers. The anticipation of release relaxed his bladder muscles just enough to allow a small amount of urine to leak out, staining the front of his trousers. Finally Royal jerked his cock out of its prison, almost crying in relief as the urine poured out of him for what seemed like hours.

Opening his eyes when the stream finally trickled to a standstill, Royal noticed the Masai boy standing in the shadows watching him. Royal beckoned and the boy came to him, warm and real in the moonlight. Unasked, he wrapped his long fingers around Royal's member, expertly peeling back the foreskin and gently stroking the exposed glans.

Royal groaned, his erection almost instantaneous. Leaning into the boy, Royal breathed in the thick meaty odour of his body. Jupiter made no effort to tame his pets and the boy's heavy musk had retained its taint of red dust and iron, the smell of a Masai blood eater. Wanting to take possession of the lips and bright pink tongue that featured so insistently in his dreams, Royal moved to kiss the boy, who jerked his head away. For some reason, which he would never understand, the rejection enraged Royal and he lashed out, hitting the boy, hard, on the side of his head.

'You little fucker,' he hissed as the boy backed away, suddenly frightened. 'I'll teach you.' The boy crumpled without a murmur of protest as Royal grabbed his arm and twisted it viciously. Royal could smell the fear, sour and thin, and he liked it. Attacking and devouring the boy's quivering mouth with his teeth and tongue, Royal shuddered as he tasted the salty, ferric taint of fresh new blood. Holding the boy by the neck, Royal first turned, then pushed him roughly up against the wall, holding him there with one hand, as the other grabbed his own bobbing member, which he thrust desperately between the boy's high, tightly muscled buttocks, pushing the head roughly against the tight puckered aperture of the anus. The pleasure he experienced as the opening suddenly blossomed, allowing his cock to slide in, turned Royal to liquid and he orgasmed immediately with a harsh cry. It was over before it had even begun.

'Go,' said Royal, after he'd pulled himself out of the boy. 'Go,' he said again, pushing him away. 'Scram.' The boy took the hint and disappeared through a small door that led from the garden out into the alley. Royal had just rearranged himself and buttoned up his trousers when a slow mocking clap came from the shadows cast by the building's overhanging balconies.

'Very pretty, don't you think, Christo,' said Jupiter, walking out into the moonlight followed by his friend.

'I especially liked it when you hit him,' said Christo. 'Nice touch.'

'Yes,' agreed Jupiter. 'That *was* good, wasn't it?'

'When did you two get home?' asked Royal.

'A few minutes before your very fine performance with my boy,' said Jupiter. 'I didn't have the heart to stop you, you did so seem to be enjoying him.'

'I'm going to bed,' said Royal, pushing between them and heading back into the house.

'You sanctimonious little shit,' Jupiter drawled at Royal's departing back.

Royal stopped and looked back. 'What did you say?' he said.

'You heard,' Jupiter replied. 'Live your lie, Royal. See how happy it makes you.'

❋ ❋ ❋

'So,' said Royal, who had actually told Marta remarkably little about his time in Africa, 'I've told you a story. Now it's your turn.' In spite of his editing it was now well past midnight.

'But the light,' said Marta. 'We wouldn't be able to see them at all. It would be a pointless exercise.'

'Who's obfuscating now? 'You can't renege on me now, darling girl. A deal's a deal. But I'm prepared to compromise. I suggest that you choose a number of the works you're prepared to let me look at and leave them on the table for me to peruse at my leisure when I rise tomorrow morning.'

Marta thought for a moment. 'Yes,' she finally said. 'That would be a most satisfactory compromise.'

And that is what happened. It was a shame that Marta missed the look on Royal's face as he went through the dozen or so illustrations she'd selected for him.

Twenty-three

Royal had bought an automobile just before the beginning of the war and had taught Marta how to drive. She took to it immediately. It was the speed, the way she could hurtle along the few perfect white roads that had been constructed on the eastern coast of New Britain, sending natives, chickens and village pigs flying for their lives.

'But I'm a good driver,' she would protest when the military police remonstrated with her. It always made them laugh and she never took a blind bit of notice.

The Westons and Augusta had quickly fallen into a routine. Most mornings Marta would drop Royal off at his offices down on Mango Street and then, after she'd retrieved Augusta from home, they would set off. If Marta was going to pick up birds for the aviary, Augusta would be left with a friend for the day. Although she missed Marie Macco dreadfully, Augusta had made many friends among the expatriate community in the year and a half she'd lived in Rabaul. Once it had become obvious that Wolfie was in no real danger in his civilian job at a solicitor's in Valparaiso, and that he still loved her, Augusta had cheered up greatly. Ebullient and chatty, Fräulein Mueller was, everyone agreed, a delight. People weren't so sure about Marta, who always seemed too busy to stop, take tea and talk. *And those clothes!* Gustie was, Marta often thought as she sped away, a fine antidote to her own anti-social behaviour.

People new to Rabaul often mistook Augusta for Royal's wife, so often did Marta decline to accompany her husband to the many social gatherings he was expected to attend. Fortunately Augusta loved such occasions, and the new dresses Royal insisted on buying her so that she always looked her best on his arm.

One of Marta and Augusta's favourite jaunts was to Herbertshohe, which had reverted to its native name of Kokopo since the occupation. It had remained a lively community, mostly because the colony's remaining Germans tended to congregate at the Trinkhalle and talk of the old days. The hotel was one of the few places on the island's east coast where German was still spoken, and they would go there for lunch whenever they were feeling homesick for the sound of their mother tongue. Sometimes Ettie joined Marta and Augusta on their journeys to the southern end of Blanche Bay and proved to be the source of many stories about the early days of the colony.

Often, after these nostalgia-steeped lunches at Kokopo, Marta would dream particularly vividly about Vienna.

One of these dreams had begun innocently enough but had transformed itself into a nightmare, from which Marta woke abruptly mid-morning in an empty house, with her heart racing wildly. It was just a nightmare, she said to herself, just a nightmare, though a particularly vivid one.

Perhaps she remembered the dream so clearly because she'd slept badly again. The winds and sea currents had started to turn in preparation for the rainy season and the humidity was staggering. It made sleep all but impossible, which caused everyone to be fractious and ill-humoured. In the last few weeks unkind words had been exchanged on many topics, mainly petty in nature, but some, like Royal's drinking, had bitten right down to the bone. For Royal *did* drink too much. *Quantify too much, m'dear.* It had taken about six weeks after their arrival in Rabaul for the sisters to realise that Royal was usually in a state of inebriation.

'I'm not really drunk,' he'd explained when Marta had first raised the subject with him. 'I just like the world to be a slightly softer place. A little gentler than it actually is.' Marta, who needed to see everything in razor- sharp focus, found it hard to understand this particular argument, but he eventually arrived at a select few excuses and justifications that did make sense to his wife. The main one was that he was very good at many things, including being an alcoholic. Well, at least it made her laugh.

The dream, the nightmare, had been about Gretchen again. It had felt like that last summer they'd all spent together on the family estate, but when Marta's dream-self had walked to the mullioned window in the tower where her sister sat in silent contemplation, and looked out across the countryside, it was blighted by winter's icy grip, with snow and ice spread across the land. It was so cold that the glass on the inside of the windows was rimed with frost. Each breath she and Gretchen took turned to vapour and it was if their words became tangible in those clouds of mist created by the warm, moist vitality of their living flesh, their wet mouths. Gretchen, blue and white, and seemingly impervious to the cold, had turned and beckoned Marta closer, so that their golden and dark heads touched. 'Look Marta, look,' she had said, gazing out across the stark white land. 'See how beautiful it is.'

Dressing quickly without washing, Marta ventured out to the cookhouse in search of coffee. With her second cup in hand – she always drank the first in a few greedy mouthfuls while standing outside the cookhouse – Marta walked through the garden to the aviary. The birds, so many housed in such close proximity, made such a tremendous din in the mornings that Brigadier General Griffiths, the third administrator since the beginning of the war, ensconced a little above them in Government House, had sent a boy with a note of complaint. Royal had replied with one suggesting that Griffiths do something anatomically impossibly with his suggestion that the Westons should throttle their bloody birds. Hostilities had escalated, with the upshot that they were no longer regular guests at Government House.

Royal, Marta had realised, was well on his way to cancelling out his credit with the new administration, and not just by marrying her. Still, it was no skin off her nose: she'd never much enjoyed going to dinners and cocktail parties with the Australians. It had made her feel disloyal when so many of her friends were facing the very real threat of losing their plantations. She hated hearing these newcomers to the colony discuss over the dinner table how much this or that plantation was worth. So the aviary had stayed and the invitations from those in power had trickled away as the war dragged on into its fifth year.

At Marta's approach the birds intensified their song and the few birds of paradise, which had indeed become remarkably tame, were waiting on their perches when she opened the aviary door. 'You little rascals,' she said as the flitted around her in a frenzy of aerial acrobatics. She sat down on the chair she had placed inside and pulled out her cigarette case. With her eyes half closed, she sat in the lambent sunlight with the birds all around her, smoking, drinking her coffee and thinking a little more about her dream.

As was usual, it had felt as if she was watching, an invisible observer. Somehow she and Gretchen had gone beyond the stone walls of the castle and into the soft, silent world of snow. Gretchen, dressed head to toe in fine white wool and pale winter furs, was ice skating on the river they always swam across in summer. She glided without effort in swooping loops from riverbank to riverbank, a soft beatific smile on her bloodless lips. Marta was almost hypnotised by the ceaseless movement of her sister on the ice. Moving slowly, she'd almost reached the riverbank when Gretchen had suddenly come to a halt in the middle of the ice. 'Marta, come,' she mouthed, her words lost in this cold, still world. Marta remembered that she had stepped out onto the ice without hesitation and had walked towards her sister as easily as if she'd been on a path in a summer garden, not a sheet of cracked, slippery blue ice. 'I knew you'd come,' Gretchen had breathed. Her words turned into snowflakes as soon as they were spoken, but Marta heard them ringing like silver bells inside her head.

'Of course,' Marta replied. 'Of course I came when you called.' As she reached out to take her sister's hand, the ice beneath Gretchen had cracked noiselessly and without a word of protest or surprise, she had suddenly fallen through the opening and vanished. By the time Marta had thrown herself down on the ice, desperately reaching out a hand to the spot where her sister had stood only a blink of an eye before, the ice crystals were already becoming a solid mass with Gretchen beneath it, her face upturned and still smiling. Marta attempted to plunge her hand, all five fingers intact, through the aperture, the same size as a grown woman's heart, which still remained in the ice. But the ice was quicker and in an instant her ring finger was gone. A single drop of ruby-red blood welled like a slow tear from the amputated stub and gracefully dropped onto the clean, cold ice, beneath which Gretchen slept.

Having refilled her coffee on the way back to the bungalow, Marta retreated to her study where she stayed happily absorbed for a good three hours, painting a bird of paradise. It was well past noon before she realised she was hungry. Royal hadn't returned for lunch, as he sometimes did, so she ate sitting in the early afternoon sun, on the front steps of the bungalow. She was still there dozing when Royal barrelled up the driveway in the auto at breakneck speed, honking the horn.

'There's news, darling girl. Great news!' he shouted, doing an extra circuit around the substantial phoenix palm that was planted on a raised bed in the middle of the driveway. 'Wonderful, wonderful news!'

'Royal, you mad man,' Marta shouted back, immensely amused by her husband's antics, though she did wonder how drunk he was.

'The war,' Royal shouted, screeching to a halt in a cloud of dust. 'The war is over. It's just been announced, Germany and her allies have surrendered.'

'Oh, thank Gott!' cried Marta. 'Thank Gott, at last it's over.'

Royal told Marta what little he knew, then hurried back down to the waterfront, where news was beginning to trickle in. Marta had declined to join him, making the excuse that she was tired, though really, it was because she had a sudden thought that now might be a good time to keep her head down. Besides there was much to think about and she wished to be alone with her thoughts. Would Augusta and Wolfie marry? Would they go back to Germany, if they did? What would happen to Gethsemane and all the other German plantations? What would the future hold for these people, some of whom she considered friends? And what did the future hold for her?

The swish-swish-swish of the coconut-frond besom, as one of the staff swept the paths around the house, was at first a backdrop to Marta's thoughts, but gradually the sound became more insistent. She walked out to the edge of the verandah and peered over the balustrade. There it was, a flash of brightly coloured cotton glimpsed through the foliage. Swish-swish-swish. The noise and its maker approached swiftly and methodically and Marta recognised the figure instantly. It was one of the house-meris' offspring, a boy of about seven.

'Api-noon lik-lik,' she cried, waving, wondering if the natives knew that the war was over and things were about to change. The child stopped sweeping, looked up and smiled. 'Api-noon Missus,' he called, before resuming the task his mother had set him for the afternoon.

Sitting down again, Marta lit a cigarette and waited for Augusta and Royal to come home.

✳ ✳ ✳

Wolfie Hoffmann returned to New Guinea in February of 1919, three months after the armistice, bringing Augusta a ring with a terribly small diamond and getting down on bended knee in the two days he spent in Rabaul before sailing for New Ireland to visit his parents and sisters. Marta was beyond delighted. Marriage would suit Augusta very well, and young Hoffmann was a nice boy, though he had no prospects now that the family plantation was definitely among those that were to be expropriated. Still, he was a lawyer, she reasoned. And where there were people and money there was always a need for lawyers. It seemed likely that they would return to Germany, which Augusta had begun to talk of with increasingly obvious longing. It hadn't been just the family she'd missed, but the city of Vienna itself: the art galleries, the theatres, the shops – goodness yes, the shops, the food and the cold too, that wet kiss of snow on a frozen cheek. And the people, the presence of humanity everywhere you looked, instead of the emptiness that was New Guinea. It had surprised Marta that her sister had missed Vienna so much. *She* hardly ever consciously thought about home at all. Except for Papa, of course – how she missed him.

Royal offered to throw the happy couple a bash at the Namanula Hill house, but the problems involved in shifting Germans around the territory, particularly if one of the Germans had been a voice of discontent throughout the war, meant that the wedding was held at the Hoffmann plantation at Namatanai. Instead, as a wedding present Royal and Marta bought the newly-weds first-class tickets all the way to the train station at Vienna. Where they would go from there was still undecided: Wolfie had Berlin connections, but Augusta was overtly agitating for them to settle in Vienna. Royal was quietly pleased that Augusta and Wolfie had elected to leave the colony. In these uncertain times, as the great land grab was about to begin, he knew it was unwise to be seen harbouring too many Germans under his roof if he wanted Gethsemane to be regarded as an Australian rather than a German property.

A week before the wedding the Westons, Augusta and a plethora of staff boarded a slow copra barge to Kavieng so that the auto, at Royal's insistence, could accompany them.

'Think of the convenience,' he'd said winningly, when Marta ventured the opinion that it was a little outrageous, even for him.

They left Rabaul shortly before midday, chugging slowly through the day and night and into another day. The barge finally docked at Bagil Wharf at Kavieng in the early part of the afternoon, and it took most of the remainder of the day to unload the wretched auto.

As she drove down Boluminski's pristine white road, an hour or so before sunset, with the wind in her hair, Marta's excitement grew palpably when, at each new bend in the road, she recognised another landmark. As she pulled up at the bungalow on dusk, the rain that had held off for most of the afternoon arrived, a sudden heavy shower as irrevocable as the end of the world, which sent her, Royal and Augusta running and laughing like children, for shelter on the verandah at Gethsemane.

'I thought the rains had finished!' Marta exclaimed three days later,

A tropical storm had lashed the northern end of New Ireland the day after their arrival and although the thunder and lightning moved quickly on, the wind and the relentless, heavy rain that flayed the bungalow remained.

'Do you think it will be all over by tomorrow?' Augusta asked.

'Sure to be,' said Royal cheerfully. 'Can't rain on the bride.'

Fortunately for Augusta, Royal proved to be right and by morning the wind had dropped and the rain had been replaced by a wash of hot, golden sun that baked the soaked earth. A few mosquitoes, opportunistically pupated by the presence of moisture, whined around the rooms of the bungalow, somnolent and easy to kill between slapping palms.

Augusta and Wolfie were married in the garden of the Hoffmann plantation by a priest from the Lutheran mission at Namatanai. It

would have been a decidedly desultory affair – the Hoffmanns' resources were meagre and the senior Hoffmanns were modest, even puritanical about their collective family displays – had it not been for Wolfie's five younger sisters, whose enthusiasm, giggles, piano playing and various wilting floral arrangements managed to temporarily lift the habitual gloom generated by Herr and Frau Hoffmann.

Herr Hoffman has let things go backwards, thought Royal, running a practised eye over the distinctly shabby bungalow. *Though who could blame him?* The drying sheds, which they'd passed while driving in, had also looked unkempt, as did the Hoffmanns and their blonde daughters in their patched and much laundered whites.

After the ceremony, Herr Hoffmann took the opportunity to collar Royal. 'I hear you are friendly with the occupation forces?' he said brusquely through a mouthful of dry fruitcake.

'Not especially,' replied Royal coolly. Hoffmann was old school German, the kind who successfully resisted being eaten alive by the tropics. He'd run very close to being interned in Rabaul during much of the war for persistent agitating, and it was only the remoteness of his plantation and the fact that he was a lone voice, that had decided the Australians against arresting him. His antipathy towards Royal during the days leading up to the wedding had been obvious and was entirely mutual. Royal was sick of the Hun blaming him personally for the war they'd started.

'My boy tells me that you live near the administrator on Namanula Hill, and that you drink with the occupation force regularly.' Hoffmann was also a teetotaller, who had made Royal put the champagne he'd bought for the celebration back in the auto. The weak, bitter home-grown coffee with which they had made the wedding toasts had been made considerably more unpalatable by the thought of all those lovely bottles of vintage Krug sitting unopened in the vehicle.

'In the early days I cultivated a friendship with Colonel Pethebridge especially,' replied Royal slowly, 'but, Herr Hoffmann, there have been a further two military administrators since then and the new man only arrived a few months ago. I barely know him.'

'Will they take our plantations?' Hoffmann asked, looking Royal straight in the eyes. His bearing took on a dignity it hadn't possessed since the early years of the occupation.

'Yes,' replied Bernard bluntly. He thought he owed Herr Hoffmann that.

'And what will happen to us?'

'I don't know,' replied Royal. 'But for what it's worth I think it's wrong that independents like you should be punished in this way. The consortiums, well, their people come and go. They have no real connection here other than commerce. But my sympathy for your plight, Herr Hoffmann, is meaningless. These decisions will be made in Europe by people who have never met the likes of Mrs Parkinson, or the Maccos or you, yourself. You have all simply become territories to be annexed and there's absolutely nothing I can say or do to change that.'

'But you, you'll be all right, won't you?' stated Herr Hoffman, his tone as bitter as the coffee.

'Yes,' replied Royal blandly. 'But you're not alone, Herr Hoffmann. So many others are in exactly the same predicament and also face uncertain futures.'

'It still doesn't make it right.'

'No,' agreed Royal. 'No, it doesn't.'

Turning from her conversation with Frau Kirchner and Marie Macco, Marta glanced across the garden, towards where her husband and Herr Hoffmann stood talking in the dappled shade of an enormous frangipani tree in full flower. She saw two men standing together, one shabby and grim, the other unreadable in his self-containment. They were turned away from each other, caught in a pause; both held their fine china Dresden cups uncomfortably. I will remember this forever, Marta thought. *I will never forget this moment.*

Twenty-four

'I'm so very angry with you Royal!' Marta exclaimed. 'You had no right.'

'There, there, m'dear. Calm down,' said Royal in his most conciliatory tone. He'd never seen his wife like this; it was exhilarating and a little frightening too. She was normally so mild and contained and here she was with bright eyes and flared nostrils, fiercely pacing the verandah, the letter that had so enraged her clutched in her hands.

'I will not calm down and you will *not* patronise me, Royal Weston. You had no business stealing my paintings and giving them to Gustie to take to Vienna. It's a violation, Royal. Nothing less and nothing more.'

'But look how it all turned out,' countered Royal. 'Surely it's not so bad? Sit down and read me the letter again.'

Marta glared at her husband, but did as she was bid and sat back down. 'You really are the most insufferable man, Royal Weston.'

Royal laughed, utterly unrepentant. 'Just read me the letter, m'dear. Leaving nothing out, mind.'

'Dear Frau Weston …' Marta began. 'Ahh, yes, here we are: "A folio of your natural history illustrations from East Neuguinea has, to our great delight, recently appeared in our offices. What pleasure this small sample of your very fine work has given us all, the wonderful life cycles and metamorphisms à la Maria Sybil Merian especially. It is, of course, of no surprise to us that your entomological work is so fine. Doktor Mueller is well known to Herr Wolff and me, from his tenure at the Naturhistorisches Museum. The letter from your father accompanying the folio intimated that you had a substantial field study of the flora and fauna of East Neuguinea and that the very fine illustrations that have found their way into our greedy hands are merely a small cross-section of an extensive survey. We at Wolff & Grunwald would very much like to peruse your collected illustrations and writings with the view to publishing sometime in the near future, if that is agreeable to you."'

'It's good news, Marta. They love your work. It has value and meaning. Can't you see that?'

'It's not the point though, is it?' she replied.

'Oh, come now. It's all right to feel pleased as well. If I hadn't done this, what would have happened to all those years of work? I think you, m'dear, would be more than happy to let the mould destroy all evidence of its existence.'

'Which illustrations did you take?' Marta asked, finally relenting a little. 'I must confess I haven't noticed anything amiss.'

Royal, pleased to be nominally forgiven, laughed and topped up Marta's coffee cup from the silver pot on the table. 'I was very careful,' he admitted. 'It was just before the wedding, after Augusta and Wolfie had decided they would go to Europe. It was Augusta who suggested that we steal them and she take them back to Vienna with her, at the very least to show your father what you'd been doing. So really it's all her fault. We did choose the works together, though. A selection of the finest works, as far as we were concerned, from all the sets. Your ornithological illustrations are very beautiful, Marta, and I was very taken with the little story you wrote about the birds of paradise and how tame they were. You have a lovely style, charming but not sentimental.'

Royal had greatly enjoyed those hours he and Augusta had spent poring over Marta's work when she was out. Augusta was a loquacious little thing, and in the course of her idle chatter she'd told him something very interesting about his wife.

'Oh, that! Those are mere jottings, daily observances, they mean nothing,' protested Marta. 'I can't believe you gave them those. What must these gentlemen think of me?'

'Rather a lot, as it happens. You're a silly goose sometimes, darling girl,' observed Royal fondly. 'Though I must say both Augusta and I were dismayed at how badly most of your early work has fared in the climate.'

'I haven't looked at those first few years work for an age. Are they beyond hope?'

'Mostly,' replied Royal.

'Time, the great editor,' Marta said, shrugging. 'It doesn't matter that they're destroyed. Most of those illustrations are simply not good enough in any case. I'm a much better painter than I was back then and I would have redone the early shell and flora works anyway, before I could allow Herren Wolff and Grunwald to see them,' she continued, unconsciously already making plans. 'How many illustrations do you think there are?'

'Augusta and I estimated, and this included all the preliminary sketches, that you had something like four thousand individual pieces of paper. Some, though, have been largely destroyed by mould and cockroaches.'

'That much?' said Marta. 'Editing it into a publishable shape is going to be a job in itself.'

'Best you make a start then.'

When Royal returned home from his offices that evening he found the front room of the house strewn with piles of paper weighted down with stones.

'Hello,' he called, as he threaded his way around twin piles of amphibians, and stepped over fishes and butterflies.

'Oh, hello Royal,' said Marta, coming into the room with another bundle of illustrations. 'I'm trying to get an idea of what I have, then I'll know what exactly I have to do.'

'Yes, yes,' agreed Royal, patting his wife on the shoulder. 'Quite right, m'dear. Organisation is everything. I'll get us a drink and you can show me your wonderful system. It looks most intriguing. A little like a paper Noah's Ark.'

'So you see, it's very simple,' said Marta, after she'd explained herself. 'And by arranging them in their species, and categorising them as ruined or acceptable, I can see at a glance where I'm lacking. Already you can see that I've done very little on this subject,' she walked to a meagre collection of papers and tapped it with her foot, 'which is snakes.'

Royal picked up a particularly lovely painting of a juvenile tree python wrapped around the branch of a jacaranda tree. The snake, its jaws unhinged, was advancing on a trio of fledglings in a nest that was wedged among the soft velvety lilac blooms. The detail on the snake in particular was extraordinary, but it was the emotion of the piece, the very real menace, the tension in the snake's pale daffodil and ivory variegated body, that made the illustration wonderful for Royal. 'I adore this,' he said, showing Marta.

'Yes,' said Marta. 'The colours work especially well together, I think. I also like this arrangement of three different examples from different species, the reptilian, the ornithological and the botanical. I think it's quite successful as a means of telling a more complete story, if very hard to know how to categorise. I only put it on the snakes and lizards pile because it's very small compared with the ornithological one over there where it also could have gone. It's something of a cheat, I must confess.'

'If I were you,' said Royal, 'I would create an entirely new pile for them.'

'Of course,' said Marta. 'You're brilliant, Royal.' She dropped to her knees in front of the marsupials and mammals stack and began to go through it.

'I'll see about dinner then, shall I?' Royal said, wandering back out onto the verandah and the drinks trolley.

'If you would,' said Marta.

Over the following days the piles began to diminish, vanishing back into Marta's study. His wife, Royal noticed, became an even more muted presence, moving around the house with a permanently distracted look on her face, her thumb endlessly caressing the end of her stump. It seemed wise to leave her to her thoughts and endeavours, so Royal took the opportunity to go to Australia to see his now grown children and visit his family, something he hadn't done since he'd married Marta three years before.

Marta barely noticed his absence. Sometimes she would look up from her solitary evening meal to where he usually sat at the end of the table and be surprised that he wasn't there watching her. Eventually, as she began to come to terms with the ramifications of an illustrated East Neuguinea natural history, and exactly what such a tome would require, Marta began to surface more regularly to gulp at the air of daily life.

Royal returned from Melbourne, his portmanteaus bursting with presents, books and art materials, just as Marta started to want to talk again. He was relieved: he'd missed his wife.

As Marta steadily progressed with the task of making new plates and clarifying her observations through the remaining months of 1920 and into the new year, it was becoming increasingly evident that she would have to seriously consider delivering them to Wolff & Grunwald in person.

'I think you *should* go,' said Royal. 'You know that. And not because of the book. You need to see your family.'

'It would be extraordinary,' Marta admitted, 'to see Mama and Papa again.'

'And your new niece too,' said Royal. Augusta had given birth to a girl, Hilde Pax Hoffmann, on the 11th of November 1919, a year, to the day, after the armistice was declared.

Marta laughed. 'Children! I don't know if I even like them.'

'Did you ever want to have children?' asked Royal.

'You know,' Marta replied. 'I don't think I ever really did. I was never very interested. Is that strange?'

'I don't know,' replied Royal. 'Men just assume that all women want to have babies.'

'But not me, as it turns out. I've often wondered in the past if there's something wrong with me.'

'And now?'

'Now I simply don't care.'

'Augusta told me something rather strange before she left,' continued Royal.

'And what was that?'

'She thinks you're her mother.'

Marta turned to her husband, her eyes wide with shock and amusement. 'Oh!' she exclaimed. 'How funny. Wherever did she come up with that?'

'So it's not true?'

'No, not at all,' replied Marta, not betraying herself for a moment. 'Augusta, as you well know, can be fanciful.'

One morning a few days after Marta had decided that she would return to Vienna sooner rather than later – well, definitely within the year – she woke suddenly, jolted out of one of her increasingly vivid dreams with the ferric taste of blood in her mouth and her badly bitten tongue throbbing in protest. She rose, and drank from the glass of water sitting on her nightstand, sluicing the tepid liquid tentatively around her mouth before walking out onto the verandah and spitting the bloody water into the garden below. It was early, just after dawn, but a thin thread of smoke already rose from the cookhouse chimney. In the distant, the waves, driven in by offshore winds, crashed over the reef, a sign that a tropical storm was on the way. Sitting in the sun on the bottom step of the bungalow with a freshly brewed cup of coffee, Marta thought about her dream.

It had definitely been Gethsemane. She'd felt herself walking out of the rainforest and into the sunlight, as she had an uncountable number of times, making her way across the dry scrubby lawn towards the bungalow where people were gathered on the verandah. As she'd got closer she'd realised that it was a family reunion. There were Mama and Papa, Gretchen and Augusta, Wolfie, Bernard and dear-heart Royal and her. Mama was sitting with Augusta and Gretchen on the divan – her dead sister remade as something far more substantial and real than she'd ever been in life. They were holding hands and talking animatedly. Gretchen, with her red-ruby lips and pink, warm skin, looked happy for perhaps the first time. Standing in the shadows of the verandah were Bernard and Wolfie, drinks in hand, gazing hungrily upon Gretchen and Augusta. Royal was sitting on the balustrade in the sun, his back to the sea, smoking a cigarette, smiling away to himself as he often did, as he listened to the conversation between Papa and the dream Marta. All was light and shadow, black and white, burned of all colour, grainy and indistinct like a photograph.

Then the scene had changed, and suddenly they were all sitting around the dining table from the Namanula Hill house, though it was still on the verandah at Gethsemane. Bernard and Wolfie were applying themselves to the dispatch of a roasted fowl, squabbling over its carcass like wild dogs. Mama, Gretchen and Augusta were still talking. And she, Papa and Royal were huddled around the end of the table nearest the foot of the stairs, opposite the Mueller women, poring over Marta's paintings. The entire table was strewn improbably with white-hot house roses, the likes of which Marta hadn't seen for almost two decades. The petals were cool and pale on the dark stained oak, seemingly unaffected by the heat.

The next moment Marta had been at the bottom of the stairs, with Royal standing in front of her. He'd said her name, clean and clear in the brightness of the New Guinea day, then reached up and cradled her face gently in his warm dry hands. But as he'd bent to kiss her, she had inexplicably drifted away, out onto Boluminski's road, where she discovered herself alone, and sitting at the wheel of Ames Miller's automobile, which was flying along the highway at breakneck speed. Her dream self took her foot off the accelerator and reached for the brake, but found none, and as the auto continued to race down the road, swaying wildly from side to side, she wrestled with the wheel, somehow knowing that if she could make the turn into Gethsemane's driveway a mile or two ahead, all would be well. And she had made that turn, managing to spin the vehicle around the twin portals of the plantation's gateway, but rather than abating, the vehicle's pace grew as it stampeded along the rudimentary road between the rows of coconut palms.

Then the dream had changed again, and the auto was screaming along the road that wound up the Namanula Hill. That's when it had happened. One moment the road was empty, the next Tomai had been there standing resolutely in the middle of the road, wearing his habitual expression of calm acceptance, and she'd run him down like a dog or a village pig. She recalled exactly the thump of soft flesh on hot metal, as man and moving machine collided. At this point in the dream she had reached instinctively once more for the brake lever, and jerked it on desperately, surprised when the auto had come to an abrupt halt and stalled. The sudden loss of velocity caused her jaw to snap shut, painfully catching one side of her tongue, splitting open the flesh in a bloom of bright red blood that flooded her mouth. She'd got out of the auto and run back to where Tomai lay on his back, as if asleep in the middle of the road, with not a mark on his beautiful obsidian body. His eyes were closed and his hands folded neatly on his chest. As she'd knelt down beside him his eyes had opened. But they hadn't been Tomai's deep, black eyes, but Royal's golden retinas into which she stared.

'You came back,' Royal had said, sitting up and smiling, seemingly unscathed.

'Yes,' she had replied. 'For you.'

'You know I love you,' he'd said, reaching for her, pulling her face to his own and licking the blood that was spilling from the corner of her mouth.

Twenty-five

＊ The cuscus (fig. 68) is a tree-dwelling herbivorous opossum-like creature the approximate size of a large house cat. The male in particular reacts aggressively when other males stray into its territory and quite often at night on Gethsemane's verandah we would hear their contretemps, which involved much hissing and snarling, in the trees that surrounded the bungalow.

Marta, *Neuguinea: Flora & Fauna*, Wolff & Grunwald, Vienna, 1923, p. 73

The expropriation of German holdings in East New Guinea took longer than anyone could have imagined. It was the waiting, the endless waiting, that ate away at those who knew they were going to be affected. Ettie Kaumann was particularly distressed, and each time Marta saw her, the worry was etched a little deeper into her friend's face so that she looked much older than her forty years. Not long before Marta was due to leave the colony she met Ettie and Phoebe Parkinson by chance at the Carpenters' store, where she was shopping without enthusiasm for some appropriate clothing for her journey.

'Marta, how lovely to see you!' exclaimed Ettie, embracing her friend. 'That's very pretty,' she said, looking at the dress Marta had been holding up speculatively. 'Are you going to buy it?'

'Oh, I don't know,' said Marta, handing the garment back to the shop assistant. 'Probably not. So what are you two doing in town?'

'We've come to pick up some photographic portraits that we've had done,' replied Ettie as the three women threaded their way through the store to the exit.

'How interesting.' Marta paused briefly to admire a shiny new auto parked in the middle of the store. 'Now *that* I would buy in a heartbeat. Anyway, photographic portraits, how intriguing.'

'There's a lady photographer, new in the territory — a Mrs Sarah Chinnery. Her husband works for the Australians in some capacity, like all the new people do, and she's set up a studio here in town. My aunt and I commissioned her to do our portraits. You must come with us. She's a charming woman. I'm sure you'd like her very much.'

'Well, if you say so, then I *must* meet this marvellous Mrs Chinnery,' Marta said, as the three women emerged into the mid-morning sun.

'Sorry to keep you waiting,' said Sarah Chinnery as she came out from behind a curtain. Marta was surprised by how young she was; she'd been expecting someone distinctly more matronly that this slim, frail woman who couldn't be much more than halfway through her third decade of life. The photographer was followed by a gentleman, crisp and starched in his whites, whom neither Ettie, Phoebe nor Marta knew. One of the newcomers, thought each of the three women silently as the gentleman left the studio.

'Now,' Mrs Chinnery said, clapping her red, inflamed hands. 'Ladies, your portraits! Yes, I'll just go fetch them.' She disappeared behind the curtain again and returned a few moments later with two large envelopes. 'These are yours, Mrs Parkinson,' she said, drawing out a heavy card folio and opening it to reveal two photographs of Phoebe sitting on a cane chair in the shadows of the verandah at Kuradui. She looked as soft, gentle and wise as she did in the flesh.

In a hundred years' time, Marta thought, anyone looking at these portraits will know who Phoebe Parkinson was, will understand that this woman was defined almost entirely by her calm and

290

serene acceptance of all that she'd faced. 'They're very beautiful,' breathed Marta. 'You're very clever, Mrs Chinnery. You have really captured Frau Parkinson's character and mien.'

The photographer smiled self-consciously. 'Your friend, Mrs Kaumann, is too kind,' she said, 'but thank you for the generous compliment.'

'I'm sorry,' said Marta, extending her hand, 'I'm Marta Weston from Namanula Hill.'

'And I,' replied the photographer, taking Marta's proffered hand and shaking it firmly, 'am Sarah Johnston Chinnery.'

She closed the two leaves of Phoebe's folio and slid it back into its envelope. 'Now Mrs Kaumann, let's have a look at you.'

'Oh,' sighed Marta as Ettie, as seen by Sarah Chinnery's camera, was revealed. 'That's just extraordinary!' she gasped, immediately drawn to the close-up image of Ettie's face and shoulders. Even without the context provided by another less successful version of the picture, Marta recognised the location immediately: the native burial ground she had first seen in 1904, and many times since.

Sarah Chinnery was clearly delighted. 'That one's my favourite too.'

The eye registered Ettie first. She looked very dignified, and yet profoundly bereft in the softness of the watery, shifting light near the rainforest-clad hills. Mrs Chinnery had chosen to slightly offset her subject in the frame, and this, Marta saw immediately, was some of the image's genius, for the observer's gaze inevitably drifted from Ettie's sad face to the slightly blurred background, from which leered three human skulls – two on left and the third on the other side of Ettie's head. The paleness of Ettie's skin and the luminosity of bone loomed out of the shadows, like ghosts from another time.

'This one,' Sarah Chinnery tapped the full-length photograph of Ettie standing in front of the wall of bones, 'I'm not so pleased with. The fault is mine – my exposure should have been longer.'

The third image was a studio portrait, and a very fine one at that, but it had none of the drama of the other close-up. This one

291

alone, however, captivated Phoebe Parkinson. 'How like Emma you are, Ettie,' she said sadly, picking it up.

'People say that more and more,' Ettie replied. The simple white dress, and hibiscus flower behind her ear had been a good choice. And her aunt was right: she *did* look like Emma. But Emma the woman, not the girl. She sighed, infected by Phoebe's sudden melancholy. 'In many ways I'm so glad that Emma didn't live to witness this.'

Phoebe smiled fondly at Ettie. Her brother Willie's daughter had always been her favourite. She was a Coe to her very core, just like Emma. And with a very good head on her shoulders, like all the Coes. 'Me too, Ettie. It would have broken her heart.'

Soon after, the women gathered their now neatly wrapped photographs, paid Mrs Chinnery and followed Marta to the Royal Weston Pacific Company offices, where she'd left the auto.

'Are you coming home for lunch?' asked Marta, poking her head around the door of Royal's office.

Royal glanced up at the clock above the door. 'Look at the time,' he said, putting down his pen. 'Right you are.'

'Frau Parkinson and Ettie are joining us.'

'Oh jolly good,' said Royal. 'I haven't had a good chinwag with Mrs P. for the longest time.'

'I knew you'd be pleased. I know how much you like her.'

'She has a humbleness that Emma never had,' said Royal.

'It's easy,' said Phoebe as they sat on the verandah after lunch drinking coffee and smoking, 'on a day like this, when the sun's shining and the sky and sea are the exact same shade of blue, and you're with friends and loved ones … well, it's easy to believe that all is well in the world, in the Pacific, on our little islands. That nothing has changed, when of course everything actually has.'

'Yes,' replied Royal. 'Bloody terrible business, this expropriation. I never thought I'd be ashamed to call myself an Australian and a British subject.'

A few weeks before, in late May of 1921, the League of Nations had passed the mandate that finally allowed the Commonwealth of Australia to begin stripping the Germans in East New Guinea of their holdings. The expansive, rich territories of the consortiums, which had been scaling down their operations since the end of the war, were the top of the expropriation list. HASAG, the Neuguineakompagnie, Hernsheim & Company and the rest were to be erased as easily as a pencil sketch. Various individual plantations deemed German had already been gazetted, including Ettie's plantation, Phoebe's beloved Kuradui, Ulul-Nono and the Hoffmann holding at Namatanai. Despite Royal having fallen out with the incumbent administration, Gethsemane had been saved, but it had been a close run thing. How close Marta would never know.

'I'm horrified,' said Marta, 'that they would take Kuradui and Kurakakaul. Neither of you is even German.'

'A fact that seems completely lost on the administration. Not even my divorcing of Fritz because of his abandonment had the slightest bearing on the outcome,' added Ettie bitterly.

'Oh Ettie,' sighed Phoebe, 'there's no point wasting breath on what's fair and right. We came here and took what we needed and now it's been taken from us.'

'But all our hard work,' protested Ettie. The biggest block of coconut on Kurakakaul was in the peak of its productive life and the world needed coconut oil for the new post-war manufacturing industries. It was like watching money, money that she'd waited two decades to see, burn fast and bright as a grass fire, leaving nothing but the pale silvery ash of their former existence. And you couldn't eat ash.

'What will you do?' asked Marta.

'We'll stay,' Ettie said. 'Get a bungalow here in town and eke out an existence.'

'We'll be fine,' said Phoebe. 'I have my work, and that will keep our bellies full and our heads dry.'

'Yes, I'd heard you'd gone back to native labour recruiting,' said Royal.

'Ridiculous!' exclaimed Ettie. 'You're sixty years old.'

'Fifty-eight,' corrected Phoebe. 'I'm fifty-eight. I was born in 1863.'

'Regardless,' continued Ettie. 'It's mad that you should be out there walking from village to village, day after day.'

'I'm assuming you're very busy, Mrs Parkinson,' said Royal.

'Yes indeed. Of course with the war many of the plantations were allowed to run down and the labour lines have been abbreviated accordingly. And now, of course, the new administration wants them up and running, and labour is very hard to come by.'

'I've noticed,' said Royal. 'I'm down to a skeleton line of Asiatics and Bukas at my Witu Island plantation and Gethsemane especially. The local kanakas at both have all disappeared back to their villages.'

'There's a certain irony,' Phoebe continued, 'in the Expropriation Board approaching *me* about resuming my recruiting work after what they've done to me and my family. How nice it would have been to say no, but sadly I have no choice. The job pays well and I do enjoy it.'

'She comes home after days away in the hills, completely exhausted,' said Ettie. 'It's a scandal.'

'Is there nothing we can do?' Marta asked Royal after Ettie and Phoebe had left.

'Not one damn thing,' Royal said, sorrowfully. He'd done some covert agitating on Phoebe's behalf early on in the piece and had been told that unless he ceased his protestation and criticism, the board would be forced to re-examine the possibilities of expropriating Gethsemane. Royal was horrified by Phoebe's treatment, but his loyalty to Marta was greater: he needed to protect Gethsemane for her. The decision didn't, however, make him feel any less of a coward.

'This will probably be the last letter I write before I leave.' Marta paused and tapped her pen against her front teeth reflectively. It was almost Christmas and in a little over a month she would be on her way, taking her manuscript home to Herren Grunwald and Wolff. It was ridiculously exciting, but nerve-wracking too. She would be an oddity now, back in Europe. She'd tried on the new dresses she'd eventually bought a few times since bringing them home. She had looked a fright and Royal hadn't helped by falling about laughing when she'd paraded for him in her new finery. *Hilarious, funny, dear man!* She wished he was coming with her: how much easier the journey, and the stresses of Vienna, would be with him at her side. However his daughter, who was only seventeen, had fallen in love and was to be married after a brief engagement, with the apparent full support of her mother and stepfather.

Although he was angry about this, there was nothing Royal felt he could do – he had, after all, been absent for most of his daughter's life – but hold his tongue and agree to give her away as she had requested. Apart from anything else he knew how much this would annoy the unimaginative clod his wife had married, the man who'd raised his son and daughter. Unfortunately the day chosen for the wedding in Melbourne, Easter of 1922, coincided with Marta's expected arrival date in Vienna, so there was no hope that he could go with her, even if she *had* asked.

Marta bent her head and continued her letter to Augusta:

I will be wending my way through the Coral Sea and up into the Indian Ocean to North Africa, then across the Mediterranean to Italy. Then home. I can barely remember it, you know. It's as if the sun here has scoured almost all but the deepest of European shadows out of my memory. What an adventure it will be, but I'm sure I will be as out of place as a scarecrow at the opera. Perhaps people will be kind and forgive my eccentricities and lack of social grace. Perhaps, though, they will expect me to be odd, having for so long been bereft of civilised company.

I'm sure you've heard already that Herr Hoffmann burned the bungalow and all the sheds on Namatanai to the ground before he left, which has not been an uncommon occurrence. Feelings about this expropriation business are running hot and fires are inevitable. It's terribly sad – so many people with no place to go. Macco and Marie, as you know, lost Ulul-Nono. The board couldn't get its claws into it fast enough. I'm sure they will make a success of their dairy farm in Sydney, as they are both such capable and cheerful characters. But Ulul-Nono has been bought by Herr Kirchner of Kavieng so Macco can breathe easy knowing that his cattle and beloved ponies are in safe hands. But how the place has changed, Gustie. I went to Kokopo the other day, and heard not a word of German spoken in the course of my business there, nor saw a single person I knew. It was very sad, I must confess.

On a much happier note, I arranged for the new lady photographer in town to take portraits of Royal and me in our natural habitat, so to speak, so that Mama and Papa could see a little of how we live. They *are* rather good I must say, some more than others. Mrs Chinnery has an eye for the unusual which I like very much, though she has confided in me that not all her clients share my appreciation.

Marta pulled out the two photographs she liked best of the eight that Sarah Chinnery had taken and developed in her fetid, chemical-soaked darkroom. After photographing Royal and Marta in front of the bungalow and in various poses individually and together in the house and garden, Mrs Chinnery had used her last plates to make a slightly more experimental frame each of Royal and Marta. Marta's, a close-up in profile, had been taken in the aviary. Dressed in her funny old hat and a man's white cotton shirt, she was gazing with uncontained pleasure at a bird of paradise perched on her outstretched finger, its wings and head a blur of motion.

The photograph of Royal was equally arresting, for Sarah had elected to include Tomai. There they were, as Sarah saw them, two men, their shoulders touching, black and white, equals in all but colour. But what Marta saw was her husband and the man who'd always been part of their life together, and the way they looked together. Although she had long since made her peace with her husband's relationship with Tomai and very rarely questioned Royal's love and loyalty to her – *and how many women can say that about their husbands?* – the photograph hurt her much more deeply than she'd ever imagined it could. And yet she was drawn to its beauty, even if it told her, without words, all that was wrong with her relationship with Royal and nothing about what was so right with it. A small part of her, a hot fire of jealousy, wanted to destroy it, but in her heart she knew this would be pointless. It was better to acknowledge the absence and keep it close so that it couldn't hurt her more than a little every day. *That* she could just bear. She laid a forefinger on the reproduction of her husband's face and whispered, 'I love you.'

✳ ✳ ✳

'Tell me something about yourself that hardly anyone knows.'

Royal laughed. 'Like what, darling girl?'

'I don't know, anything.'

'Come here,' he said. Marta did as she was requested. 'Now,' he continued, raising his left hand to the top of his head and parting his faded marmalade hair. 'Here, see, just a little to the left of the middle there … feel with your fingers … yes that's right, that's the spot.'

'Oh,' said Marta, quickly withdrawing her finger as it encountered what appeared to be a crater, surrounded by uneven bone. 'What is that?' she asked, instantly intrigued. She reinserted her fingertip in the hole in her husband's skull. It was a tight fit. 'How strange. What is it, Royal?'

'I've been trepanned,' he explained, 'years ago, to cure my homosexuality.'

'It hasn't been very successful,' observed Marta tartly, retracting her finger.

'Oh, I don't know,' replied Royal. 'It was profoundly transformative in its own way. I *did* stop feeling guilty about my predelictions after this was done. It was much bigger once, the hole. The bone has grown back over the years.'

'Does it hurt when I touch it?'

'No,' replied Royal. 'Not at all.'

'What does it feel like?'

'Like nothing at all,' replied Royal.

'Did it hurt? When it was done?'

✳ ✳ ✳

Mother had found the doctor, just as she had found the cure. He was a bland sort of chap, unmemorable really. A Jew, newly arrived in Melbourne, with certificates from the old country on his wall and, according to his shingle, a special interest in phrenology and trepanation – 'Over 100 operations successfully performed' – though few who came though the door of his rooms at the eastern end of Collins Street were looking to have holes drilled in their heads; it was all tuberculosis, whooping cough and venereal diseases.

The operation had taken place in the abandoned nursery of the family home overlooking the Yarra, on an overcast day in March. Royal had been conscious, but in a narcotic haze from the opiate his father had administered as the doctor laid out his instruments and washed his pale, long-fingered hands with carbolic soap in a bowl of warm water. With the languor of the sedative settling into his body, Royal sat in a white painted chair in the wash of light coming in through the closed window and quietly waited, distantly aware of people moving about the room, talking in blurred murmurs. His father, carrying a bowl of tepid water and a cut-throat razor, came gradually into focus. There was the snip, snip, snip of the scissors as his father trimmed the hair covering the site of the operation. Then the warmth of the water and soap, followed by the scrape of steel on skin as he gently shaved his son's head.

Although he could barely see, barely keep his eyes open, Royal's hearing had become somehow enhanced. There was the faint tearing sound of the blade against his skin, the rumble of his father's bowels as they processed a hearty breakfast, and a blowfly, bloated and self-important, buzzing languidly around the room

298

before it was abruptly silenced by his mother, who reached out and plucked it from the air. Royal could still hear the fly protesting in the cage of her hand as she carried it across the nursery; then came the rattle of the window sash opening and closing as she set it free.

'It's time,' said the doctor.

Mother stood on one side and his father on the other, their hands resting on his shoulders as the doctor approached, scalpel in hand.

'Good boy,' said his father softly, as the doctor swabbed the operation site with alcohol. 'Soon be over.'

Then came the sting of the surgical blade as the doctor neatly incised a cross into his head, followed by a dull pain as the four points of skin were peeled back – he could hear the sound of the fleshy tissue and bone being separated – to expose the skull.

'Good,' said the doctor, picking up a cloth and patting away the blood. 'Not much bleeding. We are going to start the procedure now. Are you ready, Mr Weston?'

Royal reached with some difficulty up to where his mother's hand rested on his shoulder and squeezed it. 'All be over soon, my darling,' she whispered in his ear. He wanted to say no, put a stop to this madness, but his sedative-addled tongue wouldn't form the words and his body was unreceptive to the brain's order that it stand up, shrug off the hands that held him there and walk out of this room.

'I'm starting now,' said the doctor, placing the drill bit in the middle of the expanse of exposed bone. 'There will be some pain, but I know from experience it's bearable. Of more concern will be the noise. That, too, is quite normal, it's simply an amplification in the skull.'

Then it had begun, the grinding, as the circumference of the disc of bone to be removed, was worn away by the drill. Royal had thought that it would all be over in a few minutes but it seemed to go on and on, the noise inside his head growing louder and louder. At one stage, when it became more than he could bear, he tried to struggle to his feet but his father calmly applied a pad with a dribble of chloroform on it over his mouth and nose. 'Breathe, my boy, breathe,' he said encouragingly and as Royal did as he was told he felt his will ebb away once more and the ablation continued. Then suddenly there was a crack, like a limb breaking off a tree somewhere deep in the vast garden in his mind, followed a pop, like a cork being twisted out of a bottle of champagne, and a faint hiss.

'It's done,' said the doctor with some satisfaction, laying his gore-covered instrument down on the table beside him. He picked up a clean cloth and mopped up the blood still oozing from Royal's skull. 'How do you feel, Mr Weston?'

'Nothing,' Royal mumbled, 'nothing at all.'

'Good,' replied the doctor. 'I'll apply the dressing now. It's all over, Mr Weston. Now you will get well.'

For five days and night's Royal remained sequestered in his darkened room in the family home, his father feeding him opium to keep the brain quiet, as recommended by the doctor, and tenderly changing the dressings. When Royal rose from his bed on the fifth day the flaps of skin had already knitted together and the hair was growing back. Soon all he would have to remind him of the operation was the disc of white bone, and a curious absence, a perfectly round hole in his head, that could be found only by an enquiring fingertip.

✳ ✳ ✳

'How extraordinary,' said Marta, taking the tiny piece of bone that Royal had extracted from his wallet and offered to her. 'I've of course read of the practice.' She rubbed the smooth surface of the bone, polished to a satiny smoothness by Royal's fingers over the last two decades. 'And you have this as a souvenir too.' She almost sounded jealous.

'It's kind of a talisman, or a relic,' admitted Royal. 'I don't know why I've kept it. I should really have thrown it away. What Mother did was wrong.'

'They threw away my finger,' said Marta dreamily. 'Though I suppose there was nothing really to keep.'

'Do you miss it?'

'In an odd way it feels as though it's still there.'

Twenty-six

✳ January 16 – How odd it is to spend the winter here in Bavaria. It's so different with the snow thick on the ground and all life seemingly still and slumbering. As if a great silence has fallen. I sit by the fire day after day, doing nothing except eating and sleeping and growing even bigger. I miss Papa, who has now returned to Vienna for his work, though he writes to me often. It's the transformation that amazes me, although I know it is perfectly natural and expected. Another month, they say, and then it will be over.

Marta, journal, 1890

Marta drifted slowly through the dark house on Namanula Hill, her feet encased in Chinese cotton slippers with woven straw soles that made a soft whispering noise against the wooden floors. The moon had finally risen, sending silvery light across the dark floors and white walls. Tomorrow afternoon she would be standing on board the passenger liner *Blanca Rose*, beginning a journey back to a place she could no longer think of as home. What would it be like to walk across the Volksgarten once more? To feel cold again? The ache of frozen feet and fingers, the mineral taste of snow on the air. What worried her most about going back to Vienna was the possibility that she would find herself unable to leave her family. From Klara and Augusta's letters it was clear that Egon Mueller's health was failing and it wasn't beyond the realms of possibility that she would feel compelled to stay on with her mother, in spite of Augusta, Wolfie and the children – two daughters now, another having been born in the northern autumn of 1921 – living only a few doors away.

That afternoon she'd left open the door of the aviary after visiting the birds one last time. 'Leave them,' she'd instructed the garden staff when they'd rushed to the bungalow to tell her that the birds were escaping. 'Leave them.' By dusk most of the birds had found their way out and only a few, the tame ones, remained.

Standing on the verandah Marta could clearly see, by the light of the gravid moon, the many pale bungalows that lined the neat and tidy tree-lined avenues of Rabaul. There was Mango Street down near the waterfront where the town's business centre had developed during her time in New Guinea, and Casuarina Street, back a little from the sea. Looking across the harbour, which opened up beyond the Mother and her Daughters in their perpetual volcanic sulk, and Matupi Island, the land was dark and solid against the reflective, shifting sea.

'Having trouble sleeping?' asked Royal from the shadows behind her.

Startled, Marta turned to face her husband. 'Oh Royal, I didn't see you there.'

'Are you nervous?' he asked, rising from his seat and coming to stand with her in the moonlight.

'Yes,' confessed Marta, 'and afraid and excited too. I worry about what it's going to be like.'

'That's to be expected,' observed Royal, lighting them both a cigarette. In the sudden flare of the match he looked very old. 'It's been, what, fifteen years since you left?'

'Closer to twenty,' said Marta. 'I came here in early 1904, so it's eighteen years. It's gone so fast.'

'You'll be fine,' Royal counselled. 'Don't forget, though, m'dear.'

'Forget what?'

'To come back.'

Marta laughed. 'I won't, I promise.'

Royal sighed and took her hand, the one with the missing finger, giving it a reassuring squeeze. 'You don't have to, you know. Come back. I'd understand if you didn't. It isn't much of a marriage I offer you, after all. You deserve to be loved properly and you *could* remarry if you wished.'

'I don't know if I could even bring myself to contemplate a third husband,' she replied. 'It all sounds rather exhausting.'

'But if you fell in love,' persisted Royal. 'I think you'd find that it wasn't quite the arduous undertaking you might think.'

'I rather think that ship has sailed,' Marta protested.

'You're never too old for love,' said Royal. 'Remember love, remember what it was like?'

'Yes, love,' Marta said wryly. 'I've discovered over the years that my heart isn't nearly as clever as my mind, and inclined to make irrational choices. I was once in love with you, you know, for a little while, after I found out about Bernard and Pamela Miller.'

'I did wonder,' said Royal, flicking his spent butt into the dark garden below.

So you knew?' Marta said, suddenly embarrassed.

'I think I did,' replied Royal. 'Enormously flattering for me.'

'It was impossible not to, I *liked* you so much. You've always been one of the few people in this world that I've actually liked, whose company I've always enjoyed.'

'Yes,' said Royal, smiling to himself in the dark. 'I've noticed your disinclination to form attachments. And you do ... you still like me, though, don't you? Truly?'

'Royal, you've never disappointed me. You've been a generous, kind and loving friend to me and somehow that has been enough. More than enough. Bernard, who I thought I might have loved the way a woman is supposedly meant to love a man, who awakened a physical side in me ... well, at times I despised him, and not even really because of his affair.' Marta paused. 'He was rather stupid, you know. Poor man. Mama and Papa tried to warn me before I married him, and I think really I always knew.'

'Why did you marry him?'

'I'd discovered that I had a taste for adventure and travel and it seemed such an opportunity to travel further than I'd ever imagined. But also it was a chance to be normal in society's eyes, to attain that invisibility that only a married woman enjoys. I wanted to be like everyone else, just for a little while. This love I have for solitude, it unsettles people. It either makes them nervous, or they pity me. Bernard never said anything but I know he often thought me remote and cold even before he took up with Pamela Miller.' Marta paused again. 'Maybe that's *why* he took up with her.'

'Well,' said Royal, wondering how he could put it tactfully, 'she was a less complicated woman than you, m'dear, put it that way. And from the little that Bernard told me about the relationship I think he simply fell in love.'

'I'm glad,' said Marta truthfully. 'Bernard deserved to be in love, and she did give him the child I never could. I know he asked her to leave Ames for him and she refused, and although at the time I derived a considerable amount of pleasure from this rejection, I always felt a little sad for Bernard that he couldn't claim his son.'

'So you know about that?' '

'Oh Royal!' exclaimed Marta incredulously. 'I might be going deaf but my eyes work perfectly well. The oldest boy is the very image of Bernard. I've thought about this quite deeply and have decided that, when I die, I will leave Gethsemane to Bernard's son. It won't only be the right thing to do but also my way of telling Pamela that I know and always have.'

'Good girl,' laughed Royal. 'That's the spirit.'

'Royal?' Marta turned her back on the view and looked at her husband.

'Yes, darling girl?'

'One more story?'

Royal returned to his seat in the verandah's shadows, sat down. 'One last story before you go,' he murmured. 'Anything in particular? I'm feeling generous tonight.'

'Yes,' said Marta, splashing some malt into a tumbler for herself and refreshing Royal's glass. She sat down across the table from him. 'I want you to tell me about your marriage to Rebecca. I want to know why you could touch her and not me.'

'Oh, darling girl,' said Royal sorrowfully. 'Why? Why must you do this to yourself? It serves no purpose.'

'Tell me.'

✳ ✳ ✳

With Jupiter and Christo's laughter in his ears, Royal had slunk away to his rooms and, to his shame, slept the slumber of the consummately untroubled. When he woke, he was clear about what he must do. What had happened the night before was an anomaly, but he would have to leave Mombasa. There was something profoundly contaminant about Jupiter, which he feared. He had to escape the intoxication before it enveloped him. He would do it; he would run away, prove to himself that he could be cured. After a solitary breakfast, Royal walked through the Old Town to the house that the company had taken for the Olivers, got down on one knee in the garden and proposed to a highly delighted Rebecca for entirely the wrong reason.

They were married seven weeks later in the gardens of the Mombasa Club by an obviously reluctant Vicar William Bard, who had no choice but to officiate because the Olivers were fervent and generous parishioners. Although things had been strained between the brothers since the incident with the Masai boy, Jupiter did the decent thing, left his cynicism at home for the day and stood as Royal's best man. All too soon it was over and Royal found himself husband to a woman he liked but knew he would never desire. When Bard said, 'You may kiss the bride', it occurred to him that this was the first time he had ever kissed Rebecca. It wasn't an entirely unpleasant experience. She tasted of sugared violets.

'You'll be fine,' Jupiter said, handing his brother a glass of champagne. 'Get yourself nicely drunk, turn the lights out and think of infinitely more desirable things.'

'I don't know what you're talking about,' said Royal stiffly.

'Oh, I think you do,' replied Jupiter. 'You're such a liar, Royal. But then you always were, even as a little boy.'

Royal *did* get drunk. So drunk, in fact, that he spent the first night of his honeymoon snoring on the chaise of the honeymoon suite at the Mombasa Club while his bride, in a clean, white nightdress, lay in the centre of the mosquito-net-shrouded bed, waiting to be ravished by her groom, as every risqué novel she'd read had promised her she would be.

The next morning they boarded a dhow for the south coast where they had taken a beach cottage at Diani for the duration of their honeymoon.

'How are you holding up?' asked Royal, who had miraculously escaped being too hungover, as they sailed across the river towards the mainland.

'I'm very tired,' admitted Rebecca, who hadn't slept well. The journey to Diani took most of the afternoon, and it wasn't until sunset that Royal and Rebecca arrived at their destination in a rickshaw pulled by a smiling Arab boy. That night, as she rose from the table to retire, Rebecca laid her hand gently in invitation on her husband's shoulder, but once again waited to no avail for him to join her.

'This isn't so bad, is it?' Royal said the next morning when his new wife joined him under the coconut trees in front of the cottage, where he was drinking coffee and eating newly baked bread.

Rebecca stood and looked intently at him for a long moment, trying to really see him properly, wondering if she simply wasn't desirable enough. 'Yes,' she agreed, wishing she knew how to ask him why he didn't join her in their marriage bed. She longed for him to kiss her like a new husband should, with his pale sun-blistered lips.

But Royal was right. It was actually rather beautiful out here with the breeze ruffling the coconut fronds and the Indian Ocean lapping at the pristine white sands of the beach. Apart from the servants' shack in the back garden there wasn't another cottage to be seen along the long blue and white stretch of the coast and it felt as if they were truly the only people on earth. 'It *is* lovely,' she admitted, as the Arab house servant appeared with a silver pot of freshly brewed coffee and another basket of fresh rolls.

'We should bathe later,' said Royal, yawning and stretching. 'The ocean's heavenly.'

On the fourth night Royal, having run out of acceptable procrastinations, managed to stay the right side of drunk and consummated his marriage. As Jupiter had suggested, he simply closed his eyes, thought of someone else entirely and applied himself rather efficiently to the task at hand. Afterwards, as she drifted off to sleep, with Royal snoring beside her, Rebecca hoped that she was pregnant so that they didn't have to do it again until another child was required. She'd enjoyed his dry, soft kisses, but all that poking and prodding, and the way he had suckled like a baby at her inadequate breasts, it was all so unseemly. Literature, she thought with some dismay, had got it altogether wrong.

The remaining days of their honeymoon passed peaceably enough. As she strolled arm and arm with Royal along the edge of the sea at sunset, Rebecca thought she could rather get used to all of this, even Royal climbing on top of her and pumping away for a few minutes before spilling his seed into her womb. Both prayed fervently for a conception, but God wasn't listening.

Back in Mombasa, they took a small house on the northern side of the club. Hugo Oliver's tenure with the Imperial Africa Company was coming to an end and with her parents' departure for Tasmania would vanish Rebecca's only true connection to East Africa. There was no reason to stay on in Mombasa. Certainly Royal's job offered no future and now that he was a married man it seemed appropriate for him to finally strike out on is own, and emerge from the dual shadows of the family Weston and Jupiter. Even though Jupiter was now helping to build the rail line up to Lake Victoria, Royal knew it was time to leave Mombasa and do something with the large chunk of inherited capital he had sitting in the bank on Collins Street. He would have to consult Mother; she would know.

Rebecca was delighted when Royal proposed that they should go to Melbourne and decide from there, in the collective comfort of the Weston family bosom, what they should do next.

Copra in New Guinea or cattle in Uruguay was the advice of the matriarch of the Weston family to her favourite son. 'Good money to be made in both, and I'd be prepared to double your stake.'

So Royal, without Rebecca, who'd recently discovered she was pregnant and had been packed off to stay with her parents in Launceston because Mother couldn't stand her, had set sail once again and journeyed north to German East Neuguinea to begin his research of the islands of the South Pacific that stretched between Australia and the west coast of South America.

✳ ✳ ✳

'And that's how I came to Neuguinea in 1899. Rebecca followed me out later. Obviously the trepanning had no effect on my proclivities but with the aid of drink and a lot of self-will I was able to occasionally perform my duties as a husband. I could make love to you too, m'dear, pretend that I'm not what I am.'

'So you don't find me completely repulsive?'

'No, no, darling girl. I've always considered you to be rather beautiful.'

'Then why won't you?'

'Because it's dishonest,' Royal said simply.

'Then lie to me,' Marta said. 'Just once before I go show me you love me, even if it's untrue.'

Twenty-seven

✳ When it was discovered that Jocasta was with child, she was banished by her furious family to a nunnery at the foot of the Swiss Alps. Outside the snow fell unceasingly, but Jocasta alone, of all the fallen women hidden away here, did not feel the bitter bite of winter's chill. The child growing within her kept her blood running hot and fast. She could not hibernate like the others, also held prisoner here up in the mountains, until their time came and they awoke as if from a nightmare. She must remain awake and vital so she could gather up the babe and flee, before the nuns could wrest it from her. Jocasta had no memory of how she had fallen from grace.

Sophia Constantinelli, *Moroccan Moonlight*,
Kidman & Vincent, London, 1891, p. 216

The SS *Blanca Rose* sounded 'all visitors ashore'. Royal, seeing his wife's reluctance, took her arm. 'Come on, m'dear. The time is nigh,' he said encouragingly.

'Yes,' replied Marta, squaring her shoulders. 'You're right. Time to go.'

'You'll be fine, perhaps even a triumph in the old country,' Royal teased, as they stood together at the bottom of the gangway. 'But you know, it wouldn't be the end of the world if you didn't go. Not really. I'm sure Messrs Wolff and Grunwald are more than capable of making a success of your book.'

'If it was just the book, then I probably wouldn't go,' admitted Marta. 'But it's more than that.'

'I know,' said Royal, who would be sailing in the opposite direction at the end of the month. 'Family! Both a bane and a curse.'

'Yes,' agreed Marta, laughing. 'I need to see Mama and Papa one more time. And it's not as if I'm going forever. Only a year, maybe two.'

'Good,' said Royal. 'But remember you *did* promise me that you would return.'

'I will come back,' said Marta fervently. 'I will.'

'Off you go then,' said Royal, giving her a little push. 'I'll keep the home fires burning.' And with that Marta walked up the gangway, breaking the last thread that tied her to solid land and Royal Weston.

'I love you,' Marta said as the gangway was hauled up and the crew started to cast off. But the words were lost in the inevitable noise and movement of leaving. Not that it mattered; she'd said the words the night before. 'I love you,' she said again, this time her voice nothing more than a harsh whisper.

Marta stood on deck long after all the other passengers had gone below, not leaving the rail of the *Blanca Rose* until the last smudge of East New Guinea disappeared beyond the horizon. The purser had considered saying something, but seeing the frozen look on Mrs Weston's face, he'd changed his mind and walked quickly away.

Back on dry land Royal, tall, erect and thin, with tears streaming down his face, stood in the blazing heat on the end of the main Rabaul wharf until the *Blanca Rose* had rounded Sulphur Point on the southern tip of the peninsula, and disappeared from view. Only then did he sigh, releasing all the tension that had held him upright throughout the day. 'Silly old bugger,' he mumbled to himself, pulling out a handkerchief and blowing his nose. Those there that day on the wharf swore that by the time he reached solid ground, Royal Weston had become an old man.

312

Interviewer: Of course you spent some time in New Guinea with your aunt and Royal Weston, didn't you?

Dr H. Pax Miller: After I graduated from medical school I went to live at Gethsemane [plantation] in New Guinea with my aunt and Royal Weston for three years. This was shortly after the Second World War. I worked in the native hospital in Kavieng, which led me to specialise in infectious tropical diseases. And that was where I met my husband, Tim Miller.

Int: What was your aunt like?

PM: [laughs] She was quite formidable, very tall and gaunt, not unlike me actually, in appearance. Very resolute. I wouldn't have liked to have got on the wrong side of her, but we got on very well. I liked her very much.

Int: And Royal Weston?

PM: Everyone loved Royal. He was dying by the time I went to live with them, which was very sad, but yes, a wonderful man.

[break in taping]

Int: How did you come across this story that your mother Augusta was actually Marta's child?

PM: I don't think I ever really 'came across' it as such. It was always just a persistent and, might I add unsubstantiated, family rumour. It wasn't until the exhibition [*Cannibals & Coconuts: The Art of Marta Weston*, Victoria Art Gallery, 1970] planned to coincide with the centenary of my aunt's birth, when I was asked to write a little about her from a personal viewpoint, that I did some research. Of course, as I state in the piece I wrote for the catalogue, there wasn't much to find … well, not in regard to Marta having had a child in 1890, when my mother was born, but strangely enough it was the absences that intrigued me. My aunt's extensive but not terribly revelatory papers, which, as you know, are held at the Mitchell Library in Sydney, have, I think, quite obviously been

313

edited severely by her. Quite often whole pages are torn out of her journals and later when she starts writing almost entirely in pencil, she has erased large pieces of text, though the imprint of what she'd written can still be seen. This was extremely frustrating because it leaves us with little sense of who she was as a person, as well as taking away the possibility of stumbling over a private confession. [laughs] Sadly it's not like it is in books where if one looks closely enough all will be revealed.

Int: What about your mother's birth certificate? Does that hold any clues?

PM: Well, that clearly identifies Klara Mueller as the mother, so was no help either in proving what my mother always claimed, namely that Marta Weston was her mother, not her sister.

Int: What do you think made Augusta think that Marta was her mother?

PM: My mother always said that Gretchen, that's the Mueller daughter who killed herself in 1914, I think it was, told her about Marta being pregnant and how they'd spent a winter at the family estate in Bavaria, hidden away, in order for my mother to be passed off as Klara's child. But to be honest, Gretchen was incarcerated in a mental institution from a very early age, her early twenties as far as I can tell, until her death in her mid-thirties, so it's hard to know if what she said was based on a real memory or some kind of hallucination.

No one will ever know for sure, and having a child out of wedlock was so completely against my aunt's character … She was definitely not the kind of woman who would have had an affair – she was the least frivolous person I've ever met. I've often wondered if she was raped as Sophia Constantinelli's novel suggests and it was the shame, or sense of violation, that made her deny it.

Int: The novel you mention, Moroccan Moonlight *by the Edwardian novelist Sophia Constantinelli, which was published a year after your mother was born, you think it's something of a roman au cleft?*

PM: Yes, that was a bit of a surprise, and may not mean anything. I'd been going through Marta's journals from the years in and around the date of my mother's birth, when she was working as a secretary for an English novelist with the initials S.C. Though the journals don't give away very much at all, I was intrigued by this S.C. and her brother T.G. and thought I would try and find out who she was. As it turned out, one of my colleagues from the hospital has a sister who's an English professor at Oxford so I gave her the initials and the various clues I'd gathered about the lady novelist and she and one of her graduate students very quickly worked out that my aunt had worked for the Edwardian novelist Sophia Constantinelli and that T.G. was her brother, Terence Grubb.

Int: Do you think that, like Jocasta in Moroccan Moonlight, *your aunt was raped and subsequently abandoned?*

PM: I really do.

Int: Did you never ask your aunt yourself?

PM: [laughs] My aunt wasn't the kind of woman you asked personal questions. No, I never asked, and she never told. I loved her dearly, but she was a cross old thing. To be completely honest, the only person she truly liked was Royal. They were very happy, I think. They gave each other … peace, I suppose you would call it. Their marriage may have been unconventional, but it was just the most wonderful love affair. They adored each other, they really did.

Edited extract, oral history interview, 8 October 1972
Melbourne, Australia